METHUSELAH
PROJECT
S.O.S.

A NOVEL

METHUSELAH PROJECT S.O.S.

A NOVEL

RICK BARRY

Methuselah Project S.O.S.
© 2020 by Rick Barry, www.rickcbarry.com

Published by Fithian Publications

Rick Barry is represented by Hartline Literary Agency, 123 Queenston Drive, Pittsburgh, PA 15235.

ISBN 978-1-7355886-0-5 (paperback)
ISBN 978-1-7355886-1-2 (ebook)

Fiction/Suspense

Cover design by Sarah Slattery

Printed in the United States of America

Dedicated to
Derwin, Staci, Tim, Jessica, Benji, Isaiah, and Jonny.
Thank you all for being family!

ACKNOWLEDGMENTS

I owe a debt of gratitude to many individuals who contributed to the success of this story.

Lt. Colonel David Casson, Lt. Colonel Mark Donahue, and Lt. Colonel David van Veldhuizen (Ret.) of the United States Air Force were kind enough to answer questions concerning basic procedures and life in the modern Air Force.

Linda Glaz provided valuable observations and suggestions during the developmental edit of the manuscript.

Volunteer readers went over the story to offer me objective impressions on the characters, plot, and flow of the story. I confess that I braced myself for the worst each time one of them emailed their feedback. However, rather than sending me bad news, they bolstered my morale with enthusiasm for the story. In alphabetical order, their names are Debbie Burks, Stephanie Clapp, Trina Crawford, Kimberly Joy Evers, Jim and Ruth Grosse, Lois Hudson, Diane Keating, and Melissa Troutman.

In addition to being yet another volunteer reader, my longtime friend Darren Kehrer provided a sounding board and worthwhile suggestions whenever I need to hammer out details that weren't quite fitting.

As the final version of the manuscript took shape, Amy Boeke and Emily Krajci pored over it one more time, each finding a few mistakes that had slipped past everyone else.

Designer Sarah Slattery enthusiastically applied her graphic skills to create yet another eye-catching cover.

I thank all the readers who read my first book about Roger Greene and Katherine Mueller, *The Methuselah Project: A Novel*, and encouraged me to continue the tale. Double appreciation goes to each reader who left online reviews so that others could catch their infectious enthusiasm for the story.

Most important, I thank the Lord for whatever creative skills He has given me. To Him be the glory.

CHAPTER 1

Seated in the cockpit of his F-35 Shadow, Roger Greene grew irritated at the premonition forcing its way into his thoughts. Not on the fighter's control panel, but inside his mind, a red warning light kept flashing.

But why? The day had been routine, the test flight over the Gulf of Mexico successful. No hint of trouble.

Still, the sense of foreboding clung like Velcro, as if an unseen enemy had a radar lock on him.

Concentrating on flying, Roger flicked off the Master Arm switch, halting his fighter's ability to auto-release flares or chaff. He'd completed every test of the newly installed avionics. Time for Return to Base.

Just that quickly, the nagging sensation snapped right back, stronger than ever. Was his subconscious detecting something? Or maybe he was becoming a pessimist, a guy who couldn't believe this blessed life as an Air Force pilot could last.

Per standard procedure, Roger took the avionics out of air-to-air tactical mode and put them into navigation mode. Slowing the aircraft to a more fuel-conserving three hundred knots, he banked the joystick to starboard, veering the fighter north, back to the Florida panhandle and Eglin Air Force Base.

As usual, he wished for more time in the sky. With reluctance he radioed in. "Eglin Mission, Scout 01 is ready for RTB."

"Scout 01, Eglin Mission. You are cleared direct Eglin. Contact Approach."

"Scout 01," he acknowledged.

As Roger began a smooth descent, a downward glance revealed sunlight glinting from never-ending waves rolling in from the Gulf of Mexico. But earthward wasn't the direction Roger preferred to look.

Up here, winging his way between earth below and the azure dome above, he soared in pilots' heaven. Extensive reading during his decades of confinement in Germany had instilled an appreciation for words, but which description best captured the glorious emotions of piloting a modern Air Force fighter? Elation? Exultation? Exuberance? Bliss? All of those words rolled into one still fell short.

"Thank you, God," he spoke into his oxygen mask.

Roger selected Eglin as his navigation steer point and aligned the F-35 directly with the field. Running through his descent check, he verified all switches in the cockpit were in their proper positions then switched his radio to the approach frequency.

"Eglin Approach, Scout 01 is thirty miles south VFR, with information Whiskey, request direct initial for runway 19."

The voice that radioed back was a woman's, one he didn't recognize. "Scout 01, Eglin Approach. Cleared to descend VFR, direct initial runway 19."

He chuckled. Female "airmen" was another contrast the modern Air Force offered from his Army Air Force days. Even though a female commander had already led the 53rd Wing, a woman's voice on the radio still startled him. He keyed the radio. "Scout 01, cleared direct initial 19."

That message done, he relished a few final moments of flight time. No other aircraft in sight. For this moment, the sky belonged to him alone.

Airborne freedom. Nothing compared. And to think he'd teetered on the brink of despair only a few years earlier, barely clinging to hope of ever glimpsing blue sky again. Now he not only saw it daily—he existed as an integral part of the heavens.

"Thank you, God," he repeated.

Then, there it was again—the pestering impression his days were too serene, that something in his perfect life would soon veer off course.

When he was ten miles out, the female voice radioed back, handing him off to the next controller. "Scout 01, cleared to contact tower."

"Scout 01." He adjusted his radio to the tower frequency. "Tower, Scout 01 is VFR ten miles to the southwest, direct initial for 19."

"Scout 01, Eglin Tower. Report initial runway 19."

"Scout 01." His acknowledgement may have sounded matter of fact to the controller, but Roger's own ears detected the note of depression.

If you're born to fly, what can be gloomier than landing? On the other hand, the water and the beach below looked inviting. Another advantage of balmy Florida in September. Too bad Katherine wasn't in town.

The radioed authorization "Full stop" dispelled random thought. No daydreaming while landing. Down to an altitude of 1,500 feet, Roger pulled a turn while reducing power to the pattern's airspeed.

Gear handle down. Three green lights flashed on, affirming his landing gear had lowered and locked. A final check of the cockpit showed hydraulics and fuel state normal. No warning lights.

The end of a perfect flight on a gorgeous day.

By the time Roger had touched down and taxied in, he'd forgotten his melancholy. Future days would offer more flights, all on Uncle Sam's dime. He ran through the F-35's shutdown list. Everything normal. So much for his gut's feeling of danger.

However, no sooner had Roger set his foot on the ground than the 53rd Wing's commander, Colonel William "Elvis" Jackson, appeared in his face. "Okay, Boy Scout, spill it. How did you screw up?"

Roger stared. One second under Colonel Jackson's unflinching gaze proved the Wing Commander wasn't joking.

"Sir, there was no screw-up. It was an absolutely perfect flight, from beginning to—"

"I'm not talking about the flight. I'm talking about whatever you did to get yourself called on the carpet by the Base Commander. If one of my pilots screws up, I take it personally. Now, you might be the golden-boy aviator, but this time you must've blown it. So I repeat: how did you screw up?"

Roger's mind raced. Maybe the colonel had the wrong pilot? "Sir, I don't know what to say. I'm not aware of any screw-up. I haven't been in touch with General Clark."

"Well, you're about to be nose to nose with him. I received a call from the general's assistant. He summoned you by name, and he wants your sorry-looking face in his office ASAP. As you might realize, General Clark never invites airmen over to share cookies and lemonade. I suggest you hightail it there, and whatever the problem is, you accept full blame. Got it? No blowback hits this squadron. Not one speck. Not on my watch."

"Now? What about the maintenance debrief? And the ops—?"

"The message was 'ASAP.' If the commander's fuse is burning, making him wait will increase the explosion."

"My car's in the shop—"

"Just get there!"

"Yes, sir."

Roger tucked his helmet under his arm, spun, and broke into a run under the glaring Florida sun.

By the time Roger stood before the outer office of Brigadier General Adrian Clark, the combination of humidity and jogging in his flight gear had bathed his brow with perspiration. But those weren't the only reasons to sweat. A base commander exercised more authority than a city mayor. He ruled a small kingdom. If a pilot fell out of the commander's good grace, he would find himself grounded.

Roger reached for the door handle but stopped. He took a deep breath, then wiped his brow dry.

Uncharted territory. How exactly *did* one behave in the commander's office? He turned the handle and plunged inside.

A couple of executive officers ignored him as they went about their duties, one talking on a landline telephone, another scrolling through information on a flat-screen monitor. Only the general's administrative assistant, a middle-aged brunette, looked up to acknowledge Roger.

He swallowed. "Uh, I'm Captain Roger Verde. I just got word to report to the base commander."

The woman's gaze wandered from Roger's face to his flight suit, helmet, dangling oxygen mask, and harness. All natural enough at the flight line, but not standard dress for a visit to General Clark's office.

He allowed a nervous chuckle. "Yeah, I just landed. Didn't waste time since the message said to come ASAP."

The brunette—Barb Hazelton, according to the wooden desk plaque —nodded and picked up her telephone. "Captain Verde is here to see you." A pause. "Yes, sir." She tilted her head toward the inner door. "The general will see you immediately."

"Any idea what this is about?" Roger whispered as he strode past her.

"No clue. But if you like, I can notify your next of kin."

Roger froze mid-step.

For the first time, she halfway smiled. "Standard joke, Captain. Go on in."

Hardly reassured, Roger drew himself ramrod straight. Two raps of his knuckles on the door announced his presence.

CHAPTER 2

Two months earlier ...

Devising a way to sneak a message to the outside world had taken her
months. Working up the nerve to implement the plan had taken even
longer. Would an opportunity present itself? If it did—would she be
insane to try?

Merely contemplating escape from Talent Redemption III—a clandestine intellectual slave-labor facility—increased the tremble in her fingers
as she keyboarded data.

*Breathe deeply, slowly. Don't let fear show, or they'll know you're up
to something.*

She dared a furtive glance around the room. Like her, forty or so
other detainees sat at their workstations. Clad in yellow jumpsuits and
clinking ankle chains, each prisoner hunched over computer monitors
and toiled—or pretended to toil—on their individual assignments.

Perched on his stool in the front-left corner, "Vulture" looked as he
always did—black turtleneck pulled up to his chin, shaved scalp glistening under the fluorescent lights, and the ever-present AK-47 cradled
across his legs. Had she ever seen Vulture's beady eyes blink? She didn't
recall. But at least Vulture talked. The albino guard who subbed for
Vulture—the one prisoners had nicknamed "Ice Man" due to his pallid
skin—never uttered a word. If she had her choice of guards, she would
choose Vulture over Ice Man's intense gaze and eerie silence any day.

She focused on her monitor and resumed keyboarding her findings
into the spreadsheet. Her mind, though, roamed far from her assignment.

How gullible she'd been. In her old life, she never would've believed the Heritage Organization included subterranean prisons and captive scientists—intellectual slave labor. Even if she had known, she never would've believed she herself might end up in such a—

Her eye caught movement as, down front, Dr. Baasch stood, stretched beside his desk, and scanned the Research Room.

Instantly lowering her eyes and feigning deep concentration on her computer monitor, she manipulated the 3-D image of her assigned protein's molecular surface structures left and right. No way she would give Baasch reason to suspect she was taking an unauthorized break. One punishment for such a "crime" had been enough to drive home the lesson.

Ting.

The only door to the room slid into its wall pocket. In strutted Security Chief Nikita Klimov, wearing his customary camouflage uniform. Did that gorilla seriously imagine the outfit blended with this underground labyrinth of white-walled corridors and chambers? Behind Klimov followed one of his lackeys with an automatic rifle slung over his shoulder.

Ever eager to please his superior, Vulture leapt to his feet and saluted Klimov.

Dr. Baasch frowned. "So soon, Klimov? I thought we had an hour before—"

Klimov's hand knocked away the objection. "I know what I said. Sometimes I do what I say. Sometimes I don't. When it comes to security, unpredictability is Rule Number One. Besides, I'm excited by today's opportunity. It should leave a lasting impression on your detainee colleagues."

Colleagues? As if all these prisoners were merely partners or paid employees? Klimov was so galling—and the coffee-stained grin proved he knew it.

Dr. Baasch clapped his hands. "Save your work, everyone. You'll be back shortly. Time for a short excursion."

Following the usual protocol, she shuffled forward to take her designated place in line at the exit. Looking straight ahead as required, she waited for the order to move out. Even without meeting his gaze, she felt Klimov's slimy eyes crawling over her body. In freedom, she had enjoyed turning men's heads. Here, beauty became a curse for any female prisoner.

"Standard march," Klimov ordered. "No communication in the corridor. I don't want to see so much as one smile or hand gesture. Let's go."

He swiped his key card. *Ting.* The door slid open.

Not so much as one smile? Had Klimov lost his mind? Who among these miserable prisoners had anything to smile about?

"Forward," ordered the guard who had accompanied Klimov. That man—known to prisoners as Little Big Man—exuded the typical air of an underling who craves authority. He brandished his rifle in both hands and exited first. Bringing up the rear, Vulture would likewise hold his Kalashnikov ready.

As she marched in step, ankle chains clinking, mixed emotions swirled in her mind. On one hand, she rejoiced over any distraction that slowed down research. Her days of willingly aiding the Heritage Organization were over. On the other hand, an unscheduled excursion suggested one of Klimov's "Incentive Management" sessions. A lesson in fear was the last thing she needed when courage for her scheme to contact the outside was already wilting. But if so, why lead the prisoners elsewhere when he had authority to lecture them here in the Research Room?

In line, the black, curly head of Gavrilovic in front of her remained a novelty. Ever since arriving in Talent Redemption III—such an insidious name for an underground prison—the prisoner named Victor had preceded her on every march. But Victor had disappeared three days ago without explanation. Now she followed the Serb, Gavrilovic. Had Victor hung himself? Had he somehow earned enough trust to get himself out of T.R. III? Or perhaps Victor had never been a prisoner at all? He might've been placed among them as a spy.

In another reality, she would've enjoyed a chance to chat with Gavrilovic. Not only because his background in genetics promised interesting conversation, but because the Serb was endowed with ruggedly handsome features. In freedom, he probably made the girls swoon. From time to time, Gavrilovic had made eye contact with her. Was he attracted to her, as it seemed? No matter. No point in contemplating romance. Such a distraction might undermine her determination to escape.

At the end of the corridor, Klimov halted and allowed Little Big Man to guide the column down the stairwell. Leg irons clinked, and yellow pant legs swished in unison as the column shuffled downward from Sublevel 2.

At the landing for Sublevel 3, the column continued down the stairwell.

Her heart sank with each descending step. Would it be Sublevel 4, the laboratory level? Something about the laboratories and the personnel who staffed them reminded her of Mary Shelley's *Frankenstein*. But no. Little Big Man continued downward, often turning to flash menacing glares at the prisoners.

So they were headed to Sublevel 5, the mysterious bottom level with no description she'd ever heard. Would this walk reveal the purpose of that mystery level?

As the column descended, a smell reached her nostrils. The atmosphere suggested a seashore littered with rotting fish. The moment her shoes touched the corridor's floor, goosebumps prickled her skin. Despite her training as a woman of science, she imagined a demon's wraithlike talon squeezing her intestines.

Control your fears. Don't allow vague feelings to intimidate you.

She dared raise her eyes enough to peer down the corridor. Ahead loomed double white doors. She simultaneously dreaded and wished to see whatever lay beyond. The source of Sublevel 5's fishy odor must lie behind those barriers. What scientific experiment produced such a smell? Was she about to find out?

"Halt," Little Big Man ordered meters short of the double doors. Instead of leading them onward, he turned to a side door with only a black "6" posted on it. The guard slid his keycard through the wall slot.

Ting. The door disappeared into the wall.

"Inside. Take a seat. No special order. No talking."

The room consisted of little more than plastic chairs facing a large, dark monitor. Once she and the other prisoners were seated, Klimov strutted to the front, his black military boots thumping. "My good ladies and gentlemen, although you no doubt relish your opportunity to demonstrate unwavering allegiance to the Heritage Organization with your scientific knowledge"—again Klimov's mocking grin—"it's always possible one or two of the less committed might aspire to leave our community. A foolish individual might even harbor thoughts of sabotage. Why do I say this?" Klimov strode to the side, then back to center stage, eyeing his captive audience with every step.

"Perhaps you have noticed the absence of one of your peers? This particular idiot's name was Victor Bergmann."

The breath caught in her throat. Yes, she had been plotting both escape and sabotage—and only moments earlier she'd been wondering about Victor.

"Bergmann was not as intelligent as we hoped. If he had been smarter and less rash, he would not have submitted fraudulent reports. His findings did not add up, they tell me. The only possible conclusion was that Bergmann sought to disrupt the gears in our scientific machinery. Thanks to my powers of persuasion, he conceded as much. So, how should Talent Redemption III reward such treason?"

Klimov's eyes grew wide for dramatic effect. Then, with a theatrical flourish, he directed their attention to the oversized monitor and backed away to allow an unhindered view. "Behold our response."

The overhead lights dimmed as the screen came to life. Flickering tongues of fire filled the monitor. Then, as the camera zoomed out with agonizing slowness, a rectangular portal came into view. The flames danced inside some sort of furnace. The camera continued to zoom out, revealing a metal door hanging open. Now another object entered the picture—a conveyor of metal rollers leading to the hellish inferno.

The shadowy image of Klimov announced, "The temperature inside is 593° Celsius. Hot enough to incinerate a human corpse into gray ashes."

When the camera's eye panned around to focus on the conveyor, she stopped breathing. On the rollers lay a wooden board, and secured to it lay scientist Victor Bergmann. Metal wires bit into his bare wrists and ankles as Victor fought to wrench free.

No audio accompanied the video, but she didn't need sound to understand Victor's "No, no, no!" as he writhed left and right. Sweat glistened on his forehead as the unseen cameraman zoomed for a close-up of the terror-stricken face with its fogging glasses.

Apparently, fellow prisoners had closed their eyes or averted their gaze, for Klimov barked, "All eyes on the screen!"

Gloved hands came into view. Leisurely—torturously—the hands gripped Victor's shoulders, then nudged him forward, sliding him and the board beneath him, feet first, along the conveyer's rollers, closer and closer to the crematorium's yawning mouth.

Her stomach convulsed. It tried to vomit, but there wasn't enough lunch to come up. She couldn't bear to watch—yet she must keep her eyes on the screen or risk punishment.

Overlapping gasps and sobs filled her ears. Then, while she still had time to protect her sanity, she played her sole defensive card. Eyes open, she unfocused from the hideous scene on the monitor. She willed her mind to a different place, to another time, to a childhood memory of a park with a pond and elegant white swans.

Unbidden, into her mind sprang the face of a man. Her gallant American. To distract herself, she urgently recalled as many details about him as possible—his brown hair, his twinkling blue eyes, the good-natured grin—any detail to distract her from Klimov's video.

Would Captain Greene have accepted her help had he known it would land her inside this nightmare? More to the point, would she have dared assist him had she realized the full consequences of defying the Heritage Organization?

"Enough. Turn on the lights."

The screen winked off, and Klimov reclaimed center stage. "You see, ladies and gentlemen, cooperation is your only logical course of action. What happened to Victor Bergmann will happen to anyone who chooses rebellion. Decades ago, in Germany they had a slogan—*Arbeit macht frei*. Here, productivity might not free you, but it definitely keeps you alive. Any questions?"

Klimov clamped his jaw shut and thrust his head one way, then the other.

She glanced sideways to where Gavrilovic sat. Normally stoic, even the Serb had gone pale.

"I thought not. Lead them back."

Even though she hadn't witnessed Victor's final hideous moments, her legs and hands quivered like jelly as she stood and queued with the others. How could any human commit such an atrocity?

Preoccupied by her own reaction, she literally jumped when iron fingers closed around her hand. "You're trembling, my dear. Are you cold?"

Klimov stepped closer, so close the garlic on his breath caused her to wince.

"I ..." Her thoughts refused to coalesce. "It's ... just ..."

Klimov patted her soft hand between his two calloused ones. His casual demeanor was the same as if they were a couple who had exited a film at the cinema. "Don't worry, Sophie. No need to say anything. Soon you'll be back at your warm, cozy workstation."

CHAPTER 3

In response to Roger's knock, one crisp word sounded from General Adrian Clark's office: "Enter."

Roger pushed into the room, shut the door behind him, and then shot to attention in front of a massive, polished desk where the general sat. The salute was one-hundred-percent textbook, the best in his life. "Captain Roger Verde, reporting as ordered, sir."

At first the general offered no reply. Although Roger's eyes remained glued to the wall behind the commander, peripheral vision revealed the commander leisurely turning a sheet of paper. Then another sheet.

At last the general looked up. "At ease. You're not in trouble."

Roger dropped the salute and released the breath he hadn't realized he'd been holding.

"At least, you're not in trouble from me."

Roger followed the commander's gaze to the open file on the desktop. The photo stapled to the top corner of one sheet was upside down from Roger's perspective, but the face was clearly his own. Roger's stomach tightened. No doubt his file would be abnormal, probably the most unusual one in the Air Force. But why was the commander studying it?

"The truth is, I don't know exactly why you're here, Verde. Or should I say, 'Greene'? Your original surname is a revelation to me."

Roger's heart lurched. Thanks to the CIA, "Greene" appeared nowhere in his official record. So which file was the commander reading?

"Sir, the government changed my name to Verde under the witness protection program. It's complicated."

General Clark pointed toward the window. "Maybe our visitor can shed some light."

Roger perceived a third figure in the office. His back to Roger, a tall civilian in a charcoal-gray suit stood, hands in pockets, gazing out the window.

The man turned. "Hello Roger. Long time, no see."

The tightness in Roger's stomach cinched into a full-blown knot. Jaworski. A CIA operative, and one of the few people who knew Roger's true identity.

Forcing a smile he didn't feel, Roger walked over and shook Jaworski's hand. "I had no idea what might be waiting for me here. My last guess would've been an international spy."

Jaworski's return smile was wry, but it was the biggest Roger had ever seen on that poker face. "You're melodramatic. Let's just say 'case officer.'"

General Clark stood. "Mr. Jaworski, I already knew Captain Verde—or Greene—is a unique asset to the Air Force. I'm sure Washington must have good reason for shrouding a portion of his background. So let me ask point blank—do I need to step out so you two can discuss something in confidence? I'm curious, but I understand security—"

Jaworski shook his head. "What I've got to discuss concerns you, too."

"Then let's be seated," the general said, motioning both men to his conference table and its regal leather chairs.

Once seated, Jaworski turned first to the base commander. "General, before we proceed, I must request your utmost secrecy. Circumstances compel me to discuss topics the Central Intelligence Agency wouldn't normally divulge outside the intelligence community. Nothing I disclose here today may leave this room. May I have your binding word?"

"No problem. If I didn't know how to keep my mouth shut, some other general would sit in this office."

Jaworski swung to Roger. "All right, for starters I've got to ask—what on earth are you doing here?"

Roger didn't try to stop his grin. "I'm doing as little on earth as possible." He stabbed an index finger skyward. "But up there, Eglin gives me 98,000 square miles of air space where I can fly hot fighter planes and enjoy the time of my life."

"Let me clarify. What I mean is, when the CIA pulled strings to get you into the Air Force Academy, we assumed you would be a cadet—and safely on a back burner—for at least four years. Suddenly, you're miraculously serving at an Air Force base—with the rank of captain, no less—and flying fighter planes? How is this even possible?"

Roger leaned back and crossed his arms. "I couldn't have done it without you CIA boys. Of course, I already had my pilot's license before the Academy. Whatever information you wrote up for my background check has worked miracles in helping me jump through hoops."

Jaworski's lips tightened. "That specially prepared dossier was provided solely to get you appointed to the Academy despite—" He glanced at General Clark, then back to Roger—"despite irregularities in your history."

"Yes, but you know about my 'higher education' in Germany. Once I got into the Cadet Wing, I aced every exam. Everybody kept saying, 'What are you doing here? You already know this stuff.' The faculty even suspected me of high-tech cheating. Eventually, the superintendent sat me down with three instructors and threw every final-year exam at me. I aced 'em all in record time. Boom—suddenly I was a zoomie."

General Clark interrupted. "True, Scout's rise in the ranks has been meteoric. But don't think the Air Force has lowered our standards. Despite gaps in information, his file emphasized he comes with unique training and strong backing from the Pentagon. That alone would've drawn attention to him during officer training at Maxwell."

"Scout?" Jaworski repeated with raised eyebrows.

Roger grinned. Jaworski was revealing how little he knew about the Air Force. "Scout is the radio call sign the guys gave me. Short for 'Boy Scout.'"

"Boy Scout, huh? It fits."

General Clark cut back to the point. "Based on his remarkable academic record, plus a short stint in a combat unit and incredible instinctive flying, Verde became the perfect candidate for a unique program."

Relaxing under the unexpected shower of General Clark's compliments, Roger crossed his legs. "Something tells me Mr. Jaworski didn't travel all the way from Langley just to see how well I'm fitting in. Am I right?"

The intelligence officer smoothed an invisible wrinkle in his lapel. "On target, as usual, Roger. The thing is, we need you back. Only for a temporary assignment."

"We, as in the CIA? Sorry, can't go even if I were interested. Too many irons in the fire."

"Hear me out. This concerns a certain international *organization* that you're aware of. They have quite a *heritage*." Jaworski enunciated the key words with extra emphasis. "Wouldn't you like to take a whack at them?"

Roger considered, but only for an instant. "Nope. I've had enough dealings with that particular organization. They're all yours."

"You're sure? No interest in a little payback?"

Roger shook his head. "Not a bit. You serve Uncle Sam on the ground. I'll serve him in the air. A cockpit is where I belong."

Jaworski tried a new angle. "It wouldn't be permanent. Just a short-term gig in Europe. You could see some sights."

If Roger's gut had knotted a minute earlier, the mere proposal of a jaunt to Europe doubled the knot. "Look, the last time I worked for Uncle Sam in Europe ..." Roger glanced at General Clark, who listened intently, both elbows propped on the conference table. "I expected only a year. Maybe two. You know what happened. Now I'm telling you flat out—there's no way under Heaven you can connive me into leaving Eglin and go gallivanting on a cloak-and-dagger mission for the CIA. Besides, I have classified duties here. I doubt the Air Force wants me poking around overseas without my squadron."

General Clark jumped in. "Captain Verde is correct. His responsibilities make him privy to highly sensitive information on a classified Air Force program. If he were to be captured, interrogated ..." General Clark shook his head. "Not good."

The commander's support encouraged Roger. True, he owed the CIA big time for greasing the wheels and easing him back into the military after escaping from the Methuselah Project. But he just couldn't take off the uniform with life finally going his way. "Hear that? I can't go. Uncle Sam won't let me. Have a nice trip back to Langley."

Roger stood and addressed General Clark. "Sir, with your permission, I need to go for a maintenance debrief and submit ops paperwork for the flight I just completed."

In no hurry and with great show, Jaworski withdrew a sheet of paper from his briefcase and slid it to General Clark. "The Commander-in-Chief of the United States considers this temporary assignment for 'Scout' vital to the interests of the United States. He's already signed authorization for him to assist the CIA on a covert assignment."

Roger sat back down. "The President authorized me to go to Europe? No joke?"

Jaworski eyed him. "Me, joke? You know better."

His face grave, General Clark scanned the letter, regarded Jaworski, and then slid the sheet to Roger.

Sure enough, on impressive White House letterhead, based on Roger Verde's "unique qualifications and experience," the President of the United States had personally authorized a leave of absence from Air Force duties—with pay—in order to assist the CIA with unspecified responsibilities.

General Clark's face clouded. "We have a conflict. Mr. Jaworski, a few minutes ago you requested I keep confidential any intelligence you shared. It's my turn to require the same. If you take this particular airman on a covert mission to Europe, you risk a breach of U.S. military security. You've heard of the F-35 Lightning II fighter jet?"

"Sure. I also heard the F-35 is fraught with cost overruns and under-performance. Wasn't it Senator McCain who slammed the whole program as a scandal and a tragedy?"

Somewhat stunned, Roger leaned over and handed the letter back to Jaworski.

Clark's normally stern eyes beamed with satisfaction. "Excellent, Mr. Jaworski. Then even the CIA has swallowed our deception—hook, line, and sinker. The Air Force and key insiders at Lockheed have carefully nurtured that misinformation about cost overruns."

"Misinformation?"

Despite the closed door, Clark lowered his voice. "I can't stress enough the secrecy of what I'm about to reveal. You cannot repeat this to anyone. Merely sharing certain information will require me to add your name to a database of individuals who are privy to a top-secret military project. Do you agree?"

Jaworski considered, but only for a second. "Sure, add me to your list."

"The reason the F-35 Lightning program has been so costly is that funding and development have produced not one, but *two* fighter planes. One known to the public, the other Top Secret and never mentioned. Why? Because information leaks are the Achilles heel of the military. Every time we achieve a breakthrough in technology, the Russians, the Chinese, the North Koreans, and others exert every possible effort to steal our technology. Sometimes by hacking computers. Other times by bribing or blackmailing individuals. In order to guarantee a technological edge, the Air Force has intentionally limited the abilities of the F-35 Lightning. We sell it to allies while covertly developing a second, clandestine fighter plane—the F-35 Shadow. No nation but the U.S. gets the Shadow. Even our allies can't know about it. On the outside, the Lightning and the Shadow appear nearly identical. But subtle enhancements in the wings and fuselage, plus cutting-edge avionics, place the Shadow in a class of its own."

Jaworski was visibly connecting dots. "And Greene—Verde—is involved in your hush-hush fighter?"

General Clark nodded. "Involved up to his eyeballs. Of course, the President is aware of the Shadow program. What he doesn't know is which specific pilots we've plugged in for testing and development. So far, Verde is the only man who can think and react swiftly enough to take full advantage of the constant stream of information the Shadow feeds to the pilot for maximum situational awareness. Other airmen fly the plane, but Verde—he's got golden hands on those controls."

Roger basked in the praise. His commander had just given a commendation like no other. To think he'd knocked on the door with fear and trembling.

Jaworski placed a palm on the back of his neck. Clearly, he didn't appreciate the high-level kink in his plan.

Roger almost felt sorry for the intelligence officer. "I can't take full credit for the fancy flying. Chances are, Methuselah is at least partially responsible. You know, nerve endings, thought processes, and memory functioning at peak efficiency."

General Clark's eyebrows lowered. "Methuselah?"

So, the file Jaworski had shown the general revealed his real surname, but not all of his past? Good.

Roger cleared his throat. "Methuselah was a hush-hush government project I was involved in before entering the Academy. It's been shut down but remains classified. Basically, it involved improving physical fitness."

A whopper of an understatement, but true enough, even though Methuselah had been an experiment by Nazi Germany, not the U.S. government. The less anyone knew, the better. Including the commander.

"The bottom line," Clark told Jaworski, "is that if there's one man in the entire Air Force we wouldn't appreciate the CIA sending overseas, Captain Verde is the man."

Roger's spirits soared. The guys in the squadron wouldn't believe these compliments even if he told them—which he wouldn't.

Roger pointed to the President's letter. "I paid special attention to the wording. It gives the general authorization to release me to go with you, but it doesn't flat-out order me to go. Since I have zero wish to return to Europe, nothing you say will convince me. Checkmate."

Roger stood a second time.

"There is one other little matter." Jaworski spoke casually, confidently, with the air of a card shark holding an unexpected ace. He tucked the President's letter into his briefcase, but then extracted a second sheet. "Sophie Gottschalk."

Instantly, Sophie's face popped into Roger's mind. Brave, beautiful, intelligent—but snuffed out by the Heritage Organization after she helped him escape them. "What about her? She's dead."

"Would Sophie Gottschalk have had any reason to memorize the telephone number for the CIA's information line?"

Roger sank back into his chair and considered. At the time Sophie helped him to escape the underground bunker, he didn't even know the CIA existed. But Sophie knew. "Possibly. She had a plan of action for when we reached the U.S., but she never got this far. They killed her."

"Do you have any proof she's dead?" Jaworski asked. "You weren't with her."

The commander sat at the end of the conference table, listening but obviously not comprehending the new twist. Roger would've preferred to hold this conversation outside the general's presence but replied guardedly. "You already know the story. On TV, they showed her bullet-riddled car being hauled out of a waterway."

Jaworski didn't bat an eye. "But you personally never saw a body."

Roger's mind flashed back to Germany's Frankfurt Airport. The scene on the gate-area TV remained emblazoned in his memory—the crane, water gushing out the orange Volkswagen as it dangled from a cable, the bullet holes, the smashed rear glass ...

"You never saw her dead body, because there was no body in the video. We obtained a copy of the original footage."

Roger bristled. "You know that's a painful topic. What's your point?"

"The Agency has reason to believe Miss Gottschalk is alive."

An invisible foot kicked Roger's gut. "I don't believe it."

"I've studied your entire debriefing, paying particular attention to every mention of Gottschalk. Let me ask: Did you really once tell her she'd inspired you to trade an imaginary Thunderbolt for a biplane to give her a ride in a single-engine aircraft?"

Roger cringed at the word *Thunderbolt* in front of General Clark. An antique P-47 could connect Roger to WW II. But no—Clark would assume Jaworski referred to the modern A-10 Thunderbolt.

Roger closed his eyes, remembering his prison cell in the Methuselah Bunker. He'd been sitting in the armchair with his airman's sunglasses on, passing time by mentally piloting his P-47 over the English Channel. Sophie surprised him by quietly entering the bunker and asking what he was doing. By the end of their conversation, he'd impulsively made a comment almost verbatim what Jaworski just said. In fact, the conversation had become a turning point in winning Sophie's help in escaping.

"Yes, I told her that. Funny thing is, I don't recall mentioning it during debriefing."

"You made no such remark."

Roger's heart lurched. "Then how did you—?"

"The Agency received a communication. The method of delivery was intriguing. Much more complicated than email. See what you make of this." Jaworski handed a computer printout to Roger.

> Classified. Decryption of coded message received via CIA telephone (703) 482-0623:
>
> To the American CIA: Please help! I'm one of many scientists being held prisoner by the Heritage Organization. We are forced to develop technology in a hidden facility somewhere in Eastern Europe. I don't know where. We are underground. No communication with the outside allowed under penalty of death. I'm daring to embed this hidden message onto a supervisor's USB drive in hope he will insert it into an Internet-accessible computer. If you can liberate us, we will reveal all we know about the Heritage Organization. My only proof—I'm a friend of Captain Roger Greene. He once said I inspired him to trade his imaginary Thunderbolt for a biplane and take me for my first ride in a single-engine aircraft. My name is Sophie Gottschalk.

Roger read the note a second time, and then a third. Was it true? He'd never told a soul those particular details. Surely Sophie hadn't either. So she'd survived—but was a slave of the H.O.?

"What's your conclusion?" Jaworski asked.

Roger stood to attention and addressed General Clark. "Sir, I respectfully request permission to assist the CIA on temporary reassignment."

CHAPTER 4

Roger followed as Jaworski led the way into a large room whose purpose was obviously for dining. Despite enough tables to accommodate dozens, this room in the CIA's Williamsburg, Virginia, training facility—aka "the Farm"—was now silent. A lone man sat at a table in a back corner. Jaworski headed straight toward him. Roger set down his travel bag and trailed behind.

Tilted back in his chair, the figure studied the pages of a paperback. His feet—shod with older-style black military boots—were crossed at the ankle and rested atop the table. The reader appeared thoroughly relaxed, but the broad shoulders and thick chest gave evidence this man did more in life than read.

"Howdy, Jack," the man said without looking up.

Jack? It was the first time Roger recalled hearing anything but "Jaworski" for his CIA contact.

Jaworski placed the yellow envelope he'd been carrying on the table. A flick of his fingers sent it sliding until it bumped into the black boots. "Good morning, Bert. Here's the guy I told you about. Give him a new identity and teach him as much as you can in two weeks. It's all the time we can spare."

Bert's eyes peered over the top of his book—*Genghis Khan and Our Modern World*. "Understood. But you realize I'm against this, right? There's no way I can transform a green civilian into a covert pro in two weeks."

Roger bristled. "I'm no green civilian. I'm an officer in the United States Air Force."

Bert's eyes flicked from Jaworski to Roger, then back again. He removed his boots from the table and leaned forward. "Like I was saying, your boy's wet behind the ears. Fourteen days isn't enough. I don't know your op, but if you take him into the field, he could screw up your whole team, get people killed. I don't want new stars on the Memorial Wall just because you handed me a rush job."

Roger seethed. He didn't even want to be here. Unlike the man belittling him, he had no grand admiration for cloak-and-dagger service. If it weren't for Sophie—

"He's a good man," Jaworski countered. "Quick learner. Fantastic memory. Great reflexes. You'll see."

"Great reflexes, eh?" Bert's eyes sized him up. Roger recognized the look. It was an adult version of the calculating glance a playground bully gives the new kid. Something was about to hap—

Quick as a striking cobra, Bert kicked the chair opposite him, propelling it at Roger. Instinctively, Roger countered with a kick of his own, reversing the projectile's course and adding enough lift to send it careening over the tabletop—straight back at Bert.

Bert emitted a startled gush of air as he ducked, scarcely avoiding the chair. It collided into the wall behind him before clattering to the floor. Wide-eyed, Bert muttered a curse but regarded Roger with new appreciation. "Okay, you've got reflexes. But no need to whack my head off."

Roger stepped around the table and set the chair on its feet. "I figured you wouldn't dish it out if you can't take it."

"Mighty quick figuring."

"Told you he's a good man," Jaworski repeated. "Don't sweat about transforming him into a full-fledged officer. On this op, he's primarily an observer and somewhat of an advisor. He won't be in the field alone. He doesn't need to rappel from helicopters. Just introduce him to the basics, enough to fit in without asking a million questions."

Bert unbent the metal clasp on the yellow envelope and withdrew the two sheets inside. His index finger traced back and forth down page one. "Not the kind of intel we usually receive about recruits."

"It's enough. He's not an actual recruit. Just a temporary hired hand."

Temporary hired hand? That couldn't be Jaworski's truthful assessment, considering he'd interceded with the President to get him here. Roger swallowed his pride and kept his mouth shut. Evidently, the CIA keeps secrets even from its own.

"I get no clue what this is all about?"

"Not this time, Bert."

Bert's finger stopped, and he looked at Roger. *"Du sprichts Deutsch?"*

"Ja, ich spreche Deutsch wie ein deutscher Staatsbürger."

Bert whistled. "Just like a Berliner, *mein Herr.*" He returned his gaze to the information Jaworski had provided. "Explain this next line, 'Additional degrees of ability in Spanish, Dutch, French, Norwegian, Finnish, and Russian.'"

"I've studied those languages to the point I can read and write all of them pretty well. But I lack conversation experience. Except for Russian, which I've been practicing with an airman from a Slavic background."

"Ah vy ponimayete to, chto ya govoryu, da?"

"Sure, I *ponimayu.* But understanding Russian is one thing. Properly pronouncing clusters of consonants like 'z,' 'd,' and 'r,' without vowels between them is a lot tougher."

Bert chuckled. "Ain't it the truth?" He tucked the documents back into their envelope. "Okay. You're in. We've got a group of trainees on the property. Right now, they're at the firing range. From time to time we'll have you sit in during their lessons, but the instructors will take turns coaching you one-on-one to fast-track your training."

"Thanks, Bert. I owe you one."

"You already owed me one. Don't forget Abu Dhabi. Now you'll owe me two."

Miracle of miracles, Jaworski actually chuckled. "Yeah, Abu Dhabi. Wouldn't care to repeat that trip. I'll pick him up two weeks from today." He fished car keys from a pocket.

Bert's eyebrows lifted. "No need to rush off. We've got a hot meal ready for you."

"No time. Something about this op has been niggling in the back of my mind. I need to nail down a few details ASAP. Possibly nothing, but I don't want any info leaks." He nodded goodbye to Roger. "Two weeks. See ya." Jaworski exited the same door they'd come in.

Bert stood and extended a hand to Roger. "Welcome to the Farm. Is your cell phone off?"

"Don't own one."

Bert eyed Roger's travel bag near the door. "How about a laptop? Tablet? Have yours with you?"

"I don't own those either. I'm a retro kind of guy. Devices that can track my location bug me."

"On the Farm, that pun is so old it's frayed around the edges. Do you Facebook?"

"No Facebook, no Twitter, no Instagram, no Pinterest, no Snapchat, or TikTok. No online footprint of any kind. A simple, streamlined life keeps this pilot happy."

Bert grunted. "Unusual. How about your girlfriend? I'm sure a good-lookin' Air Force jock believes in those. Did you tell her where you're headed?"

Roger shook his head. "I wanted to. Jaworski shot down the idea."

Bert twisted his head and called out. "How about it, Katherine? Did Maverick here give any clues about his destination?"

"Not a single word." A smiling Katherine Mueller appeared in a doorway that probably led to the kitchen. Dressed in a slim, beige turtleneck and jeans, she cut a figure even more striking than two months ago, when they'd soaked up sunshine at Eglin Beach Park. Her hands held an amber glass of what Roger knew would be sweet tea.

"Katherine!"

She giggled. "You should see your face."

He shot across the room and wrapped his arms around her.

"Careful, my tea."

Her giggling continued right to the moment his lips met hers. In the bliss of that kiss, Roger dispelled all thoughts of the Farm, of Bert, Jaworski, and everything else but this marvelous woman. He was just becoming conscious of the cold glass pressing into his back when Bert coughed.

"Yes, my boy, that's one way to subdue an attacker, but here at the Farm we teach faster methods."

The kiss ended in laughter.

Reluctantly, Roger released Katherine. "I had no idea you would be here. But how? I mean, when they said not to contact you—"

"One of many minor assessments," Bert said. "The CIA likes personnel who obey instructions, especially when orders conflict with personal desires."

"But she's here, at the Farm? Is that normal for employees who interpret intelligence and write reports?"

Katherine grinned and set her glass on the nearest table. "I can finally tell you. I'm no longer in the Directorate of Intelligence. The more I thought about it, the more I wanted a career that demands creativity and energy. I'm in the National Clandestine Service. You and I will be on this op together."

Roger's brain slipped a gear. "Seriously? So, we'll be training together?"

"I've already completed my training. In fact, I've been assisting here with martial arts instruction. Tonight, I fly to Europe with several of our team to do preliminary groundwork."

"Such a surprise. I don't know if I should rejoice that we'll be together or worry about you."

Bert's voice broke in. "Neither. I vote you put your hair-trigger reflexes to work and give the lady another smooch. You have a ton of training and very little sleep ahead for the next fourteen days. We start in five minutes."

Katherine smiled that pert way he adored and slid her arms around him. No sooner did their lips touch than a shrill alarm split the air.

Above the blare, Bert shouted, "Hit the deck, both of you." He ran from the room.

Roger's instincts urged him to follow, but he obeyed Bert's orders and pulled Katherine to the floor under a table, a protective arm over her back. If she was in jeopardy, this is where he should be. Besides, who knew? Maybe this was a charade to see whether he would obey Bert under stress or run outdoors the way he wanted.

The siren's earsplitting shriek rendered normal conversation impossible. Still, Katherine shouted, "What do you think is going on?"

Roger boosted his own volume. "I think it's a big prank my girlfriend invented to get me alone."

Not for the first time, Katherine regarded him with a mixture of disbelief and amusement.

No point trying to talk. All they could do was follow orders and wait while the siren blared. At last, however, the racket ceased. Even after it did, ringing continued in Roger's ears.

Katherine lifted onto one elbow. "I guess it's safe to get up."

"Do we have to?"

She gave him a mock punch to the shoulder. "Come on, Flyboy. I've never heard that siren. Didn't even know the place was wired for alarms. Something big is happening."

They stood, patting dust from their clothing, when Katherine said, "So, how did Jaworski persuade you into this jaunt across the pond? When they told me you'd accepted, I couldn't imagine any crowbar big enough to pry you out of a cockpit."

So, she didn't know about Sophie? Roger swallowed. Where to begin? Was the intel about Sophie classified?

Bert reappeared. His somber face definitely bore no "gotcha" look. No test. His body was here, walking toward them, but his mind was elsewhere. When he reached Roger and Katherine, he seemed almost to have forgotten them.

"Well?" Roger said.

Bert swallowed. "New star for the Memorial Wall. Jack's toast. He barely cleared the property before RPG's blew his car into flaming scrap metal. Not a pretty sight."

Goosebumps rose on Roger's skin. "Rocket propelled grenades— here? Who could pull that off?"

Bert shook his head. "The question is, was this a general attack on the CIA, or a pinpointed assault on Jack Jaworski as head of this new unit—whatever it is? He did mention a possible security leak. I've gotta help secure the property. Training is delayed." He hustled out.

Katherine's brows lowered. "You and I know who might pump RPG's into Jaworski's car within sight of the Farm. The Heritage Organization. I'd better check in. See you in Europe." Katherine pressed her lips to his before scurrying out the door.

Still stunned, Roger stood there, his mind reeling. Now what?

CHAPTER 5

In the following days, Bert delivered on his promise of long days and little sleep. Each morning at four thirty, Roger woke to the sensation of someone shaking his shoulder, the overhead light glaring, and Bert's cajoling voice. The first few days, Roger's lethargy sparked only mildly insulting greetings, such as "Rise and shine, slacker." Or "Hey, Sleeping Beauty, get the lead out."

The fifth morning, Roger awoke to find Bert actually slapping him on the cheeks. "C'mon, Verde. What's the matter? You guzzling Tylenol PM every night? I wonder if Jack knew how much you love your rack time?"

Roger shook his head and blinked, trying to focus. "It's not normal fatigue. I was in a military experiment. To this day it makes me sleep super deep. Working until midnight and getting up at four thirty makes it worse. I can't say anymore, but yeah, Jaworski knew."

"You don't say. Then Jack also believed you could handle the heavy-duty routine. Breakfast in five minutes."

Thus began another dizzying day packed with physical education, self-defense, and firearms training that included U.S.-manufactured weapons, NATO hardware, Russian AK-74s, variants of the Chinese QBZ-95 assault rifle with polymer housing, plus others. Evasive driving lessons took place on a special circuit of asphalt roads at the rear of the Farm.

On subsequent days, Roger skydived from airplanes in both daytime and nighttime conditions, rappelled down walls, practiced the art of escape and evasion, learned how to perform demolitions, and absorbed quick methods for improvising lethal weapons from everyday objects.

Although Bert had predicted Roger would occasionally sit in with career trainees, it happened only a couple times during the first two days.

"Too slow," Bert declared during a scant, ten-minute lunch. "I don't care what Jack said about only the basics. During these two weeks, I'm going to pound months' worth of training into you."

"Even if it kills me?" Roger mumbled as he wolfed down his ham sandwich and baked beans.

Bert ceremoniously placed his can of Dr Pepper on the table and pressed an index finger into Roger's chest. "Son, if I get to choose, I'd rather have the training kill you than the scumbags who took out Jack. You won't be a real undercover ops officer. Not by any stretch of imagination. But if you're an American going into an Agency-sanctioned overseas op, you deserve more than mere basics. Any situation can slide south in the blink of an eye."

Despite the rugged, non-stop pace, Roger found the training stimulating, even fascinating. He'd always enjoyed a challenge but, in the past, most competitions had involved sports or aircraft. Here, the intriguing world of undercover operations—"tradecraft" Bert called it—captivated him more than he'd expected. Particularly fun were the lessons in disguises and running surveillance programs. While firearms training was straightforward here's-how-to-use-it, all the tips and tricks concerning surveillance meshed into a colossal psychological game, him versus his instructors, which provided immense satisfaction whenever he outfoxed them.

Roger's life on the Farm offered no free time and zero entertainment, not even in the evening. Each night, he could barely stay conscious long enough to tug off his clothes and stumble into bed. The instructors, on the other hand, took turns, so neither Bert nor any of the others needed to maintain the insane pace they enforced for their unique trainee.

Bert offered few signs of approval. Whenever Roger demonstrated mastery of a skill, Bert typically responded with, "Okay, let's move on."

The first clue Roger was performing well came from Maria Gutierrez, a self-defense instructor. She stood talking with two other instructors during PE training when Roger caught up to—and passed—the group of career trainees during their five-mile run.

As Roger sprinted by, Gutierrez nudged the instructor beside her. "Can you believe it? I'm surprised Verde is still on his feet. Here he is, outrunning the pack."

Though he'd barely caught the comment, it injected fresh encouragement into weary muscles. Sure, the Methuselah Project had pumped his body full of extraordinary recuperative powers, but he'd never forced it through the wringer this way, stuffing his brain with volumes of raw information while forcing his body through rigorous demands. In Germany, old Doc Kossler had suspected deep sleep was key to maintaining his body's extra-quick recuperative ability. Could he damage his unique physiology if he didn't get enough shuteye?

Then came the morning when Roger snapped awake by himself. No harsh lights, no slapping. Only bright sunshine outside the window and tomblike silence. Lifting his head from the pillow, he found himself lying atop the bedspread and still wearing the olive drab tee shirt and camouflage pants from yesterday. He sat up. Even his running shoes were on his feet.

"I must've really conked out."

His eyes located the wall clock. Seven forty-three in the morning. Or was it evening? He hadn't been anywhere near a bed at seven forty-three —morning or evening—since arriving at the Farm. In the eerie silence, the slow *tick ... tick ... tick ...* of the wall clock sounded ominous.

Roger stepped to the window. Not a soul in sight.

"What's going on?"

Had he forgotten some sort of special instructions before falling onto his bunk last night? Then it hit him. Day fourteen—his last one on the Farm.

"Oh, man. I'm probably late for graduation."

Roger raced through a quick shower, and then pulled on a clean pair of camo pants. As he slipped on a fresh tee, the incessant beating of helicopter rotors grew louder, dispelling the earlier hush. Any sound of activity came as a relief, but he still wasn't wherever he should be. Why didn't Bert wake him?

Moments later, Roger burst out the dorm exit, not positive which way to go.

"There's another one!" someone shouted. "Get him!"

Roger froze. Not two hundred yards away, camo-clad men wearing black ski masks stood in a ring around a kneeling mass of individuals with their hands atop their heads—the Farm's instructors. Even Bert knelt among the pitiful-looking bunch, his hands on his head in surrender, but his eyes fastened on Roger.

Two of the captors peeled off the perimeter and broke into a dash, directly toward him.

Bert yelled, "Verde, run!"

A figure in camo rammed the butt of his rifle into Bert's head, knocking him over. The helicopter banked, swinging toward Roger. Whoever rode shotgun held a rifle, its barrel sticking out the doorway.

Bewildered, with no time to think, Roger pivoted and bolted back into the dorm. With all the building's doors and possible hiding places, two men would need time to search the premises. Right now, Roger needed every moment of delay.

He sprinted down the corridor. Should he hide? Try to find a weapon? His brief glimpse of green-clad men with ski masks conjured memories of news reports the year Russia took over Crimea. But this was Virginia, not a peninsula in the Black Sea. Who *were* those guys?

Roger ditched any notion of returning to his room. No weapons there. His pursuers would burst into the dorm any second. His only options were hide, fight, or try to give them the slip by sneaking out the opposite end of the building. But outdoors, the helicopter would spot him.

Acting on instinct, Roger yanked open a random door and ducked inside. No sooner had the latch clicked behind him than he heard boots tromping in the hallway.

"Give it up, man," an accented voice shouted. "You're cornered. Nowhere to go." Thumping and banging doors. They'd begun a room-by-room search.

Roger found himself in sleeping quarters, practically identical to his own. This room was vacant, however. No sign of recent use.

His heart sank. There went his hope some another trainee might've brought an object more tactical than his cordless razor. Hoping against hope, he glanced under the bed. Nothing but a scant layer of dust.

Muffled shouting, louder this time. "Give yourself up. The harder you make us work, the rougher it's going to go for you."

To the sound of increasingly loud banging and clomping, Roger opened the closet door. Just as expected, it was empty, with the exception of a half dozen plastic clothes hangers. He stood on tiptoe and peered into the shelf above.

Bingo. In the back corner stood an item not found in his own room— an electric iron. Roger snatched the iron, backed into the closet, and closed the door. He had maybe one crack at beating the odds, if one of them stayed in the corridor, while the other entered the room.

Outside his hiding place, the door to the room banged open. Tensed, Roger waited inside the dark closet. Peering through the narrow gap of the door, he breathed shallowly. Any second it would happen.

The accented voice shouted again, definitely close, but not inside the room. "Give it up, Roger. You know we've got—"

The shock of the pursuer saying his name hit Roger at the precise instant the closet door popped open. Wielding the iron like colossal brass knuckles, he punched it into the intruder's masked face. The man crumpled. The eyes inside the ski mask remained closed, but to Roger they'd appeared Asiatic. Was it a clue?

Stealthy as a cat, he stepped from the closet. One down, but one to go. The room's door stood open, making it the only barrier between him and the intruder still bellowing in the corridor.

"It's over, man. Come out."

Roger scanned the carpet. Where was the crumpled man's weapon? Had it flung from his fingers?

"How's that room? Report!"

What might lure Guy #2 into the doorway? Faking the voice of his partner being strangled, Roger croaked, "H-e-l-p."

Cast by corridor lights, the shadow of a pistol-bearing figure loomed onto the floor.

Now! Roger hurled himself shoulder-first against the door. Its edge crushed his opponent's forearm, pinning it against the doorframe with an audible cracking of bones.

A scream erupted as the foe's Ruger tumbled to the floor.

Roger whipped the door back open and for the second time slammed the iron into a predator's face. The man stumbled backward across the hall, where his skull rammed the wall. He slumped to the floor, out cold.

Incredible. Two knockouts. Who would've believed that would work? *Thank you, God.*

Roger dropped the iron and plucked up the Ruger. Now the odds improved, but not by much. He tucked the pistol into his belt and frisked the two men. No insignia, no wallets, no dog tags or ID of any sort.

The smart course of action might be to run for the woods, scale the perimeter fence, and escape to call for backup. But if fleeing was the smart option, it also felt cowardly. How did the first stanza of "The Airman's Creed" put it?

> *I am an American Airman.*
> *I am a Warrior.*
> *I have answered my Nation's call.*

He was a warrior. He couldn't run now. Besides, with enemy eyes in the sky, he couldn't expect to reach the fence unseen.

Into Roger's mind flashed an image of the firing range. High-caliber weapons—lots of them—locked up a quick dash from here. If only he could reach the stockpile of arms. But what about the helo hovering out there? The enemy held the high ground, the airborne position. For the first time, the airman found himself contemplating how to mount an attack on an aircraft from an earthbound position.

He raced through the building. This time he ignored the living quarters. Surely there must be a supply room, a janitor's closet, something that offered possibilities for improvised weapons.

Even as he searched, Roger couldn't imagine a jerry-rigged weapon powerful enough to fend off a helicopter. The idea seemed preposterous.

Still, his Farm training urged him to try, to consider every object, not according to its normal use, but in terms of potential impact.

He yanked open an unmarked door. Yes! A storage room. A vacuum sweeper stood against the right side. Above it, a yellow coil of heavy-duty extension cord hung from a wall hook. Along the left wall stood metal shelving loaded with spare sheets, pillowcases, packages of CFL light bulbs, kitchen cleansers, cartons of toilet paper, a spare toilet brush, cans of Glade air freshener, and plastic bottles of blue glass cleaner.

In one back corner leaned a push broom. A broom-handle javelin? Ridiculous. To take on a helo, he needed something with more wallop.

In the other corner stood a shiny metal trashcan. Roger lifted the lid. Empty. No makeshift ammo there. But what about the aluminum lid? Use it for a shield?

"What a nutty idea."

He dropped the lid in disgust.

Once again Roger squinted at the extension cord and lifted it from the hook. The cord was thick, three prongs on the end, manufactured to withstand a heavy flow of electricity. An idea leaped into his brain. Was it possible? But how could he get the cord airborne?

Roger turned and dashed back the way he'd come. Both assailants still lay unmoving where they'd fallen. Still, not a moment to spare. He snatched up the clothes iron before jogging to the dorm's rear exit. There, he swiftly knotted one end of the extension cord around the handle of the iron.

"I wouldn't give this idea one chance in a million, but it's my only shot."

He had to reach the gun locker. More enemies could show up any second. Time to go. Roger slipped the lasso of extension cord over his shoulder, shoved open the door, and broke into a full sprint. Running with an iron in his hand felt cumbersome, but no way he was letting go of his only surface-to-air weapon.

As he feared, the helo immediately rotated in a one-eighty arc directly toward him, not a hundred feet off the ground.

A loudspeaker bellowed. "Halt. Stand down."

Roger indeed halted in his tracks, but no way was he surrendering. He slid the loop of cord from his arm.

The helicopter descended, directly above and in front of him. "Drop to your knees. Put your hands on your head."

Roger grasped the electrical line about three feet from the iron. Next, almost like a cowboy winding up his lasso, he whirled the iron in faster and faster circles.

"Stand down. Drop to your—"

Roger released. The appliance and its trailing yellow tail careened skyward—not into the helicopter, but as Roger hoped, directly in front of it.

Too late, the pilot realized his danger and clawed for altitude. However, the whirling blades snagged the heavy-duty cord, snarling it around its main rotor. The iron banged and clattered all around the helo. Another instant, and the helo's Plexiglas windscreen shattered. The opposite end of the extension cord whipped every which way, twisting and writhing like a demon-possessed serpent. A half second later, the free end of the yellow cord collided with the helo's rear rotor, instantly resulting in a second tangle.

Roger jogged backward toward the building housing the firing range, unable to tear his eyes from the squealing, shuddering helo as it tilted sideways, then dropped.

The whump, whumping, whumping blades gouged into the Farm's lawn until they snapped, flinging deadly metal shards every which way. Roger dropped and buried his face in the grass.

Hallelujah, his crazy plan actually worked! But plenty of other green men were on the property. He yanked the Ruger from his belt and sprinted full speed toward the weapons locker.

A voice echoed over multiple loudspeakers. "All trainees, the drill is over! Repeat, this exercise is over! Emergency medical personnel, report to the crash site!"

Roger skidded to a halt. Exercise?

The group of kneeling "prisoners" leaped to their feet. Out of nowhere, an ambulance and fire truck sped across the manicured lawn and braked at the downed helo. No one paid Roger the least bit of attention. Wait, there was Bert, jogging toward him.

Roger shook his head. He scarcely believed it. A drill?

Bert slowed to a walk until he stood in front of Roger. He held out his hand. "Give me the gun."

Roger glanced down. He'd been so bewildered he'd forgotten about the Ruger. Somehow, he didn't want to surrender it. Another test?

Bert stepped closer. "Roger, it was all an exercise. This is your fourteenth day. We decided to plan something unique for your final evaluation. Those guys in the masks aren't terrorists. They're career trainees, the same recruits you've seen on the Farm these past two weeks."

Only then did the fact register: the huddle of prisoners had been too small. If this had been a real takeover, more trainees should've been among the prisoners. How humiliating. They'd dangled the bait, and he'd swallowed it.

Anger seethed inside him. "You idiot. You arranged this epic charade just to evaluate my reactions? I hurt people, Bert. Those two guys in the dorm are unconscious, possibly dead because of you. I destroyed expensive government property. I might've killed the men in that helo." He pointed the gun at Bert's face. "Somebody should blow your head off."

Bert nodded. "You're right. I'm an idiot. None of us dreamed the exercise would spin out of control. But if you want to blow my head off, you'll need another pistol. Yours isn't loaded. It was all play-acting."

Adrenaline ebbing, Roger realized now how light the Ruger felt in his grasp. He tossed it to Bert. "I highly suggest you never, ever, not in a million years pull a stunt like this again!"

"I made that vow the instant you released your ACME Surface-to-Air missile."

They turned to survey the wreckage. Firefighters sprayed foam onto the helicopter's remains, while EMTs bundled the occupants onto gurneys.

"Want to slug me?" Bert offered. "If you take a swing, I won't dodge or fight back."

Roger stared him in the eyes. "Somewhere in that wreck is a clothes iron. I used it to punch out your men in the dorm. Want to renew your offer after I go fetch it?"

Bert winced. "I'd prefer knuckles."

Almost on their own, Roger's fingers curled into a fist. Yeah, he knew the Bible's instructions on love, peace, and forgiveness. Yet, in this moment he didn't care. He wanted nothing more than to beat Bert to a pulp. His fist trembled, barely held in check. But then he pictured Katherine. What would she think if he lost control?

"Forget it." Roger turned away. If he looked at Bert now, he still might slug him.

"Thanks. Based on what I've just seen—"

"Just drop it. I don't want to talk about it."

Roger took several deep breaths, letting the air out slowly to regain control of his adrenaline-charged temper. "So, what's the bottom line for your evaluation? Going to say I'm mentally unstable? Too reckless for a CIA-sanctioned op?"

"You kidding? In less than twenty minutes you evaded capture, immobilized armed pursuers, and downed a hostile aircraft using little more than quick wits. If the Secret Service wanted my recommendation for the President's bodyguard, you'd be my choice, Rambo. You're definitely cleared to join that op."

CHAPTER 6

Sophie Gottschalk jerked upright in bed, her eyes practically clicking open. Her rib cage reverberated with each beat of her thumping heart. Breath came in rapid pants, as if she'd just run a footrace.

In her old existence, opening her eyes during a nightmare would've replaced any nightmare with at least the shadows of a familiar bedroom. However, here in Talent Redemption III, impenetrable blackness reigned in Women's Barrack #2. With the entire facility underground, the guards needed no light bulbs to monitor their captives by night. "Escape proof" was the guards' assessment of Talent Redemption III. The prisoners accepted their belief as fact.

Recognizing the texture of the wool blankets in her quivering grasp and hearing the faint creak of metal springs beneath her mattress, Sophie realized where she was. Still, her mind's eye replayed the nightmare against the inky backdrop of the barracks—the dancing flames, the metal conveyor rollers, the plywood sheet on which lay a frantic, struggling body. And lastly, the camera creeping in for a close-up of the face—*her* face—beaded with drops of glistening sweat and soundlessly screaming *"Nein!"* over and over. Even now, wide awake and sitting up, the vision curdled her intestines. She practically felt the intense heat igniting her prison garb.

"Sophie, what's wrong?" The whisper came from Natalia, the new Ukrainian prisoner on the neighboring bunk.

"Nothing. Only a nightmare."

A soft creak of springs preceded Natalia's touch on her shoulder. "I get them, too. I never had nightmares on the outside. Do you want to tell me your dream?"

For a split second, Sophie yearned to talk, thus purging herself of the dreamed horror of sliding alive into the crematorium. On the other hand, the rulers of Talent Redemption III reserved extreme punishment only for proven troublemakers. Even a whisper about the nightmare might suggest she'd committed an act worthy of investigation. An act such as her attempting to contact the American CIA. Instead, she said simply, "I was dying. I wanted to live."

"Good, Sophie. Keep wanting to live. If we lose our will to survive, they have won." In pitch darkness, Sophie felt Natalia's hand on her forehead. Using what must've been her sleeve, Natalia dabbed away perspiration.

"I know. But it feels so hopeless. At times I almost wish the walls would collapse and bury me. Quick death would be better than slow suffocation down here. Who knows? Death might be worth the pain if it would bog down their plans."

"Shhhh." Natalia placed her mouth close, brushing Sophie's ear. "Don't even whisper insults about them. The room might be bugged."

Sophie nearly laughed. "Of course, the rooms are bugged," she whispered back. Her words were low, probably too faint for a hidden microphone in this chamber of forty bunks and soft breathing. Still, the very fact she had dared utter them stiffened Sophie's defiance.

Patting her way in the darkness, Natalia located Sophie's hand. Using a finger, she traced letter after letter on Sophie's palm, "Be careful. Trust no one."

Natalia spoke in English, the common denominator linking all the captive scientists and guards in this international petri dish. Despite Natalia's kind intentions—a rarity in this dog-eat-dog environment— her warning smacked of naïveté. Sophie understood human nature. A drowning man might push his own brother underwater in hopes of gaining a few gulps of air. These other scientists were fellow victims; yet, one of them might betray a comrade to curry favor with the admins.

Sophie found Natalia's palm and traced back, "You, too." She patted the woman's forearm, indicating the midnight chat was over.

After Natalia departed to her own bunk, Sophie lay there, thinking. Roger Greene had been imprisoned underground, too. For years, decades even. How had he maintained sanity? How had he suppressed his anger and the urge to take at least one satisfying punch at a captor, even if it meant punishment? Was the key all those hours he'd spent reading a Bible? She'd often intended to ask for more details about his faith, but their conversations always flowed to other topics—like helping him escape. Here, she owned no Bible. Zero chance of getting one. She knew little about God. If He existed, would one despondent female scientist merit even the tiniest blip on God's divine radar? Given the 7.5 billion humans on earth, it seemed unlikely. Still, Roger's example offered hope. When he crashed in Nazi Germany, he became just one of many captured American airmen. Yet, he'd encountered God in captivity. And if the Ruler of the universe had found time to hear the prayers of a grounded fighter pilot, might not He listen to pleas from that pilot's friend?

Head on her pillow, Sophie clasped her hands together, her thumbs pressed to her lips in almost childlike fashion: *Dear God of Roger Greene and so many others. Are You real? Can You hear my thoughts? Can You see me—see all of us—in this underground prison? You're supposed to be good and caring and just. They say God is love. Please love me. Please help us. Send a miracle.*

CHAPTER 7

In the newly leased CIA location on Boulevard de la Bastille in Paris, Katherine Mueller parted the bedroom curtains of the safe house—or more technically, apartment—where she would live with several others during the course of her first overseas op. From the sixth floor, she could view the Villette Marina, the River Seine, and in the distance, across the rooftops of Paris, the Eiffel Tower.

Katherine sighed. "One of my favorite cities. If I could've chosen any destination in the world, this would be it."

As she gazed, the setting sun cast an amber glow over the city. The distant tower gleamed. Katherine felt her lips curve into a smile as she recalled the first time she had visited it.

"Something funny?" The question came from Melissa Hart, the forty-something supervisor who would occupy the second bed in this room. Item by item, Melissa unpacked her bags for the second time on this op. The hotel where the team had spent the past couple weeks had provided a place to lay their heads, but the hotel room had been incredibly cramped. Renting multiple apartments in Paris's third and fourth *arrondissements* offered the double advantage of being less conspicuous and more comfortable.

"I was just remembering a time when I went up the Eiffel Tower," Katherine said. "After I'd walked all around Platform 2 taking photos of Paris, I lined up for the elevator ride back down. When the doors opened, a load of tourists poured out. Except one girl, about college age. She was petrified. This terrified girl worked her way out of the elevator handhold by handhold, clutching any solid object for dear life. Even though she was older than me at the time, I was thinking, 'Seriously?

Like, this tower has stood here since 1889, and you think it's going to collapse now, just because you came up here?'"

Melissa chuckled as she transferred a pair of jeans from her bag to a dresser drawer. "Fear of heights. Pretty common."

Before Katherine could comment, Melissa surprised her with a follow-up remark.

"That must've been when you were fifteen, when your Uncle Kurt brought you to Paris."

Katherine released the curtain and stared at Melissa, who proceeded to unfold blouses from her suitcase and slip clothes hangers into them. "How did you know?"

Melissa permitted Katherine a languid smile as she continued emptying her bags. "It's my job to know things. Am I not a team supervisor? We're all here to crack the shell of the Heritage Organization, right? You just happen to be a former member of the same group."

Katherine bristled. "What are you saying? You don't trust me?"

"Never said that."

"Then what?"

"Then nothing—except it's irregular and potentially ill-advised to include an op participant who once served on the side of the group being monitored. I'd be slack in my duties if I didn't study your background. Imagine if the situation were reversed. You'd be a sloppy supervisor not to investigate me."

Hairs rose on the back of Katherine's neck. "You're saying I'm under investigation?"

Melissa proceeded to align toiletries on the dresser's top. "Sorry. Careless choice of words. I should've said, 'You would be a sloppy supervisor if you didn't familiarize yourself with my history.'"

"Excuse me?" Despite the apology, Katherine's insult detector crept further into the red zone. "I've worked as a writer and editor. I know how to disguise a blunt fact with velvety words. The reason for studying my background—is it because you think I might be a *traitor*?"

Melissa tilted her head back as she worked, resulting in a slightly elevated nose. "I hired into the Agency twenty-three years ago. Straight out of college. In those years, I've experienced more than I ever imagined. I've seen quiet, introvert types make split-second decisions and sacrifice their lives for their country. They're heroes, but nobody knows. I've also seen outspoken, true-blue Americans that everyone would consider patriots turn out to be sleepers for foreign powers. Sometimes we catch them. Other times, they slip between our fingers. If someday Katherine Mueller turned out to be a double agent for the Heritage Organization, it would hardly qualify as the shock of the century."

Katherine stepped around the bed to face Melissa directly. "Straight up. Do you personally believe I'm in league with the H.O.?"

Melissa paused in her chore and met Katherine's gaze. "In case the information is reassuring, I'm the one who suggested you and I share a room. Would I do volunteer to be your roommate if I believed you might slit my throat in my sleep?"

"I suppose not. Still, there's something you're not saying."

"All right then, you might as well know. I voted against adding you to this team."

Katherine blinked. No velvet glove had softened the punch to her pride. "So you didn't want to share a room for the camaraderie. You're just keeping a close eye on me."

Melissa crossed her arms. "Come on, case officers aren't supposed to give supervisors wounded-puppy looks. My recommendation reflected nothing personal. Just a precaution. This op might very well provide our first truly solid link to the Heritage Organization, which we desperately need. My vote was based on professional discretion."

"So, why am I here?"

"Because Jack Jaworski wanted you on the team. Even from the grave, Jack's decisions carry tons of weight."

"What about Roger? Is he coming against your better judgment, too?"

Katherine wasn't positive, but the timing with which Melissa averted her eyes and returned to unfolding clothing struck her as more than coincidental. She glanced at Melissa's left hand, even though she already knew her supervisor was divorced.

"Roger doesn't fall into the same category as you. He never played ball with the Heritage Organization. He was a victim—their guinea pig and longtime prisoner. Plus, he has no family in the H.O. The powers-that-be are satisfied with his loyalty to the United States and his loathing for the organization."

Katherine allowed these revelations to roll around her thoughts like so many marbles. How ironic. The one person in the CIA whose parents had been killed by the organization, the one woman with a personal reason to hate the H.O. could be regarded a risk? All because Uncle Kurt had deceived an innocent girl and tried to lead her down his own dark path. For the first time, storm clouds thickened over her decision to join the CIA. She'd never felt like Jaworski's protégé, but perhaps she had been—a calculated risk allowed into their ranks only because of Jack Jaworski's gut instincts. But now that he was dead, would her exciting new career fizzle before it got off the launch pad?

"I suppose the challenge is for me to see myself from your point of view. If you had any inkling of how much contempt my heart holds for the Heritage Organization, how much they hurt me, you'd know I could never give them one scintilla of help."

"Scintilla? Now there's a word I don't hear every day. Your writer side is showing through. I appreciate creative expressions."

If Melissa had intended the threadbare compliment to soothe ruffled feelings, she could've skipped the effort. Katherine turned back to the window and stared across the Parisian rooftops. Out there, the city hadn't changed a bit. Suddenly, though, Katherine wished she were a thousand miles away. If only Roger were here.

Behind Katherine came the sound of a long zipper, and then of Melissa tossing her empty carry-on into the corner.

"Look, Katherine, this isn't a healthy start to a crucial op. Tomorrow will be a full day. Case officers arriving by plane and train, introductions, briefings ... How about you and I reconcile by wandering up to the Bastille to grab supper and savor a bit of nightlife?"

The mention of supper elicited a low rumble in Katherine's stomach. Lunch had been skimpy, only a small ham and cheese panini on ciabatta bread with a lukewarm bottle of *eau minérale*. "You're on."

"Great. Just give me a sec to hit the restroom." Melissa plucked up her purse and sailed out the bedroom door.

Despite her supervisor's congenial offer, the conversation left Katherine unsettled. Perturbed, even. Did Melissa truly trust her enough to share a bedroom without anxiety?

Katherine's eyes swept the bedroom looking for she knew not what. The sole decorations were a print of Claude Monet's classic painting *Impression, soleil levant* framed in cheap plastic, and a pink ceramic vase of artificial flowers on the nightstand between the beds. On a whim, and not knowing why, Katherine extracted the flowers and peered inside the vase. Empty.

As she picked up her handbag, her gaze settled on Melissa's pillow. On a whim, she reached over and lifted a corner. Not actually expecting to find anything, she blinked in surprise when she did. A KA-BAR 3030 personal knife with stainless steel handle lay there, conveniently waiting any nocturnal need.

So much for trust. Katherine replaced the pillow.

CHAPTER 8

When Roger strolled out of Customs in Charles de Gaulle Airport, the Arrivals area of Terminal 2A reminded him of the last time he'd been in Europe, when he'd escaped the Heritage Organization via the Frankfurt Airport. Once again, human beings representing a cross-section of ethnic groups and languages were grinning, hugging, kissing, and assisting loved ones with their luggage. The crowd emanated energy and alertness despite the early eight o'clock hour. In other words, this babbling sample of humanity looked exactly the opposite of how Roger felt.

He blinked repeatedly as he trudged along, pulling his two-wheeled bag behind him. But blinking did nothing to wipe the gritty sensation from his eyes. Changing tactics, he maneuvered out of the throng of bodies, lifted his fake glasses with their black plastic rims, and tried massaging his weary eyes. The effort helped a bit, but not as much as a piping-hot cup of coffee would. He replaced the glasses and tugged his Nike cap lower. If the airport operated facial-recognition software, no way he'd give them clear view.

It had been a mistake letting the planners in Langley schedule him a nighttime route via Montreal on Air Canada. Maybe regular passengers rested during the night flight, but not him. With the effects of the Methuselah Project overriding his metabolism, he needed sleep—eight hours of solid slumber—to rejuvenate the cells in his body. When had he last felt truly rested? Not since entering the Farm.

At last, a Sheraton sign appeared. "The only hotel built directly into Terminal 2," they had explained at Langley.

Bag in tow, he steered toward it like a nomad toward an oasis. Weary though he was, he gave a surreptitious backward glance. Situational awareness could be as critical on the ground as in the air. No one trailing him. He rolled his bag across the threshold.

Restaurant *Les Saisons*—the designated rendezvous point—was one of two eateries inside the Sheraton, and simple to find now that he'd located the hotel. Most of the tables in *Les Saisons* were petite, big enough for only two diners to sit facing each other. Yet, in the back corner stood an unoccupied table for four. He ordered an espresso, parked his luggage behind his elbow—where no one could stick a bugging device on it—and sat down. Now all he could do was wait.

Roger had emptied his cup and was yearning for one of the Sheraton's beds when two women strolled in. The older woman he didn't recognize, but beside her—radiant as ever—glowed Katherine, with a new shade of dark brown in her hair, which was trimmed shorter than two weeks earlier. She grinned when their eyes connected, then strode toward him, the older woman following.

Roger stood and embraced Katherine. "This isn't the warm hug I'd like to give you, but it'll have to do for a public restaurant."

She giggled. "Roger that."

The two had hardly parted when the older woman offered her hand in businesslike fashion. "Hello. I'm Melissa. I've heard a lot about you."

"Was any of it good?"

"Oh, a little bit." The woman cracked a faint smile. Good. Nice to know the CIA hadn't ruined her sense of humor.

Roger faked surprise. "Only a little? Sounds like I need a new PR firm."

"You bought a new jacket," Katherine remarked.

Roger glanced down. "I hear autumn in Paris can get chilly." Like his World War II flight jacket, this one was brown leather, but with modern styling. For an instant, he considered complimenting Katherine on her new hair tint and style but caught himself. Like his Clark Kent glasses, her being here required the disguise against the slim chance members of the organization might recognize her in public.

Katherine reached for the handle of his bag. "Ready to roll?"

"More than ready. Five more minutes, and you might have caught me in Dreamland."

* * *

Despite his fatigue, Roger perked up as the trio drove away from Charles de Gaulle and headed southwest on what the signs designated Autoroute A1. Melissa sat behind the wheel of the rented Peugeot. Katherine rode shotgun, while Roger reclined in the rear, his knees canted sideways to fit.

Melissa glanced over her shoulder. "We can speak freely now. I'm the supervisor for your surveillance team. We'll take you to one of the apartments we've leased for male team members. You'll have two roommates, Ben and Gerard."

"Gerard? Sounds like the butler in a British movie."

"Gerard's family comes from France. We make use of language skills whenever possible. Ben speaks French, too, but he learned in college. As I recall, you speak French, don't you, Roger?"

"Better to say I read and write French. My last visit to Europe gave me lots of time to puzzle through grammar books for quite a few languages. But I didn't get audio practice for any of them, except German."

"Interesting," was Melissa's only comment.

Katherine held up a brown paper bag. "Hungry? We saved a croissant and cheese."

He shook his head. "No thanks. Any chance I can get a little shuteye today? It was a rough night."

"Absolutely," Melissa said, resuming control of the conversation. "We're aware of how your body goes into deep-hibernation mode as a result of the Methuselah experiment. It's vital we let you sleep."

The revelation that Melissa knew his history didn't surprise Roger. Key CIA officers needed to know at least the basics of his odd saga. Still, he wished it hadn't been necessary.

Melissa shifted lanes, maneuvering around slower vehicles before angling onto an exit marked A3. "We officially kick off the op with a joint meeting at seven o'clock tomorrow morning. You'll have plenty of time to rejuvenate, or whatever you call it."

The news washed away Roger's concerns. "Sounds blissful. In a way, I've learned how to control this need for deep sleep. But if I push too long without rack time, it can literally shut me down. One moment, I'm closing my eyes to blink. The next moment, I'm out cold. Just like inhaling chloroform."

Melissa's eyes flashed to him in the rearview mirror. "This is your first time to see France, isn't it, Roger?"

"No. Only my first time to see it up close, from the ground. I've flown over it quite a few times. Most often in a P-47. But I guess you already know."

Katherine shot a grin over her shoulder. "Oh, they know. Don't be surprised if you catch team members watching you out of the corners of their eyes."

Roger sighed. "Here we go. The new zoo attraction—a ninety-some-thing pilot who still looks like a graduate student."

Melissa spotted his expression in the mirror. "Don't worry about officers pestering you. We provided a bare bones outline to essential personnel, but everyone understands you're classified. Let me know if anyone departs from protocol."

Roger slumped in the seat and closed his eyes. "Understood. I just hate enlarging the ring of people in the know."

"Which reminds me," Melissa said. "Katherine, in the restaurant you said, 'Roger that.' From now on, no more aviation lingo in public. Chances are remote any H.O. person will accidentally overhear, but let's not open the door for slip-ups."

Roger cracked an eye in time to see Katherine nod. She turned her head toward the passenger window. Uh oh. Something wasn't right between these two. He let his eyelid drop again. "So, where's Paris? So far, no sign of it."

"It'll take over a half hour to reach our street," Katherine replied.

Despite his craving for sleep, Roger forced himself to stay awake. His brief time with Katherine at the Farm had consisted mainly of a blaring siren. At the time, she hadn't seemed aware he'd come here to help

Sophie. That fact gnawed inside him. Now he was receiving weird vibes —if that's what people nowadays called it—about her and this Agency supervisor.

He crafted a question—carefully, not trusting his sleep-deprived self to sound tactful. "Melissa, Katherine and I haven't had much chance to talk lately. I do need deep sleep, but is there any objection if she and I do supper and a stroll downtown this evening? After all, there's nothing official on the schedule until the kick-off meeting in the morning, right?"

Melissa's frown appeared in the rearview. "No one decreed you can't, but it's contrary to my instructions. I was told to get you as much sleep as possible before tomorrow's meeting. I don't think they expected you to go sight-seeing."

Roger leaned forward. "We won't make it a late night. I realize better than anyone how vital sleep is to me. If I conk out during the day, it will take off enough edge to go out this evening."

Melissa hesitated. Possibly she was one of those letter-of-the-law types who detested deviations from rules. "All right. I'll let the higher-ups know."

"Awesome."

"One word of caution—don't refer to *Star Trek* or *Star Wars* around your roommates unless you're ready for a major nerd fest. You have been warned."

"Nerd fest?" Roger repeated.

Katherine flashed her cute smile. "Nerds animatedly discussing things that don't matter in the real universe."

"That bad, huh?"

"That bad," Melissa confirmed. "In the meantime, you should sit back and try to sleep until we get there."

"Try? With me, it's either sleep, or sleep not. There is no try. Shake me awake when we get to my apartment."

*   *   *

Beneath waves of black oblivion, something shuddered. A repeating voice pierced the darkness. "Roger? Roger, wake up. *Messerschmitt*, twelve o'clock level!"

In a flash, Roger jerked upright. Once again, the wake-up phrase he and Katherine had agreed on gripped his subconscious mind and pulled him awake. He sucked in a deep breath and took his bearings.

He was lying, fully dressed, atop his bed in the apartment he shared with Ben and Gerard. Katherine leaned over him, concern in her expression.

He wiped a hand over his face. "Man, I was really out."

She squeezed his hand. "More deeply than I've ever seen you sleep. Maybe we should skip the supper and stroll so you can get a good, solid rest?"

He sat up. "What, and miss a chance to see Paris with the most beautiful woman in town? No way."

"You have me worried. That deep sleeping of yours—it's getting deeper."

He kissed her forehead. "Life has been a blur ever since I left Florida. No big deal. Give me fifteen minutes for a quick shower and change of clothes."

"Deal. I'll go see which sci-fi movie your roomies are dissecting. Pray for me!"

*   *   *

His hand holding hers, Roger and Katherine ambled along a tree-lined lane. An abundance of brown leaves crunched beneath their shoes, but quite a few green ones still clung to trees. Not for long, though. Today was already October first.

An object wafting on the late afternoon breeze caught his attention. He pointed. "A hot-air balloon. Wouldn't it be fun to float over Paris in one of those?"

Katherine's grin deepened her dimples. "Isn't a balloon a bit tame? You normally feel a need for speed."

He slipped an arm around her waist. "The important thing isn't what you do. It's who you do it with."

"Sweet talker."

When they rounded a corner, the two came upon an establishment named *Restaurant Légende*. It oozed Parisian ambiance. With its slightly darkened interior and romantic candles on each table, the place practically beckoned for Roger to enter.

"How about this one?" he suggested.

"Looks lovely."

They stepped inside and were soon seated in *Le Jardin*, a room emanating a greenhouse effect with hanging plants, colorful nature paintings, and a couple ficus trees. The room reminded him of a fairy tale he couldn't name. The table, though, was miniscule—so small their knees bumped together beneath it.

In response to Roger's request for "any popular meal," their server had brought him *escalopes de foie gras poêlées, fricassée de cèpes et pleurotes*, and *éclats d'amandes et potiron*.

Grinning at him over her haddock with light cream *"au raifort,"* Katherine asked, "Do you even know what you're eating?"

"Not exactly, but it's tasty. As long as it's not snails, I'm happy." When he looked up from his next bite, Katherine still watched him. "What?"

"I'm just savoring the moment. You, me, enjoying a romantic meal in Paris. A month ago, neither of us expected to be here."

In the amber glow of their table's two candles, Katherine looked radiant. Roger regretted not bringing the ring. But he hadn't known Katherine would be on this operation. So, the ring remained tucked away in his quarters at Eglin.

He reached for her left hand and enclosed it in his own. Gazing into her eyes, he spoke his heart. "You are incredibly beautiful, intelligent, sexy, brave, kind, thoughtful, and so much more. I'm not much, but thank you for being in my life. I don't know what I'd do without you."

He hadn't considered which emotion his words might elicit. The tears welling in Katherine's eyes caught him off guard.

"Babe, what's wrong?"

Shaking her head, she dabbed her eyes with her linen napkin.

"Katherine?" He scooted his chair around the table to place an arm around her shoulders. "What is it?"

She sniffed, and then laughed through tears. "You'll think I'm silly. I love you so much. I'm afraid of losing you." She lowered her voice. "If one of your planes ever crashed—"

With his thumb, he brushed away her tears. Whispering low, he said, "Haven't you heard? I'm the best they've got. No way I'm going to crash. But as long as we're all cozy ..." He leaned closer, meeting her waiting lips with his. Like Bogart and Bergman, they would always have Paris.

*   *   *

Later, Roger closed the taxi door in front of the building where Katherine was staying. Under a streetlight, he circled her waist with both arms. "What a great evening."

She nodded. "Almost a Cinderella kind of night. But in the morning —back to the soot and grit of reality."

He detected the shift in her mood. "Everything okay with you and Melissa? I detected tension in the car."

Her head sagged. "Things aren't turning out the way I expected."

Roger glanced around, but casually. No one was nearby. "How so?"

"After all my training, I expected a grand adventure and a career with this 'new company.' You know. Excitement. Camaraderie in a noble cause. But it turns out my supervisor doesn't trust me. In fact, she voted against bringing me along."

"Why?"

"Because of my uncle and past association with you-know-what. I'm included only because 'J' wanted me on the team."

"What about me?"

"As far as I know, they're thrilled to have you aboard. Unlike mine, your past is squeaky clean. To them, you're the ultimate patriot, here to serve his country."

A dagger of guilt plunged into his heart. "We need to talk about something. In the States, you said you were surprised I'd agreed to join this expedition. How much did 'J' tell you about recruiting me?"

She met his eyes quizzically. "Only that he planned to visit you in Florida and persuade you to come. Knowing your love for what you do, I didn't expect you to agree. Next thing I heard, you and he were on your way."

So. Jaworski hadn't told her.

"There's more to it." Once again, Roger glanced around. People strolled the avenue, but at a distance. "He didn't mention anyone named Sophie?"

She shook her head. "The only Sophie I know of is that woman who died helping you escape."

Roger stepped back to see her better under the streetlight. Clasping both of Katherine's hands in his, he said, "No, she didn't."

Confusion clouded her expression. "Didn't what? Didn't help you?"

"She never died."

"You told me she did. You said that back in 2015 you even saw her shot-up car on TV at the Frankfurt Airport."

"I believed she was dead. I had every reason to believe so. Turns out I was wrong. 'J' told me Sophie sent a coded message to 'the company.' The organization is holding her and other intellectuals as slaves in a hidden prison. As proof of her identity, she mentioned me by name."

"In other words, you didn't come here out of patriotism. You're here only because this Sophie woman is alive?"

"I had to come. If not for Sophie, I'd still be locked underground."

Katherine regarded the sidewalk, trying to process the news. "Let me get this straight. If Sophie weren't alive, would you have left Florida?"

He couldn't lie. "No. I even refused until 'J' handed me a printout of her message."

Katherine still held his hands, but her grip loosened. Only their fingertips touched. "Tell me something. You and this Sophie ... Did you ever feel romantic toward her?"

His mind flashed back to the Methuselah bunker, to the first time he saw Sophie and her movie-star good looks. To the time she trusted him enough to step forward and hug him right through the cell bars. "It wasn't like you're thinking."

"Is she pretty?"

He sighed. Not a good time to admit Sophie was drop-dead gorgeous.

"Did you and Sophie ever kiss?"

Wham. The conversation crash-landed in the rough terrain he'd wanted to avoid.

In his moment of hesitation, Katherine's fingertips slipped away.

"Hey, please understand. When the Germans were holding me prisoner, she took pity on me. That's why she sneaked me out of my cage. Now she's a prisoner for helping me escape."

"Is that how you see this op? All these people coming together, combining resources, to rescue your beautiful female scientist?"

"That's not the big picture, no. These people want to liberate a bunch of intellectuals with an axe to grind. It would provide an avalanche of information on the H.O. But my personal interest is in rescuing the person who risked her life to set me free."

A chilly breeze sprang up, sending crispy leaves swirling around them.

Katherine pulled together both sides of her unbuttoned coat. "It's getting late. I'd better get inside. I'll see you tomorrow."

She turned and entered her building.

CHAPTER 9

All around Katherine, seasoned CIA personnel twisted in their chairs, greeting one another and joking as they caught up on personal news. Seated beside her, Melissa ignored Katherine as she oohed and aahed at the wedding snapshots on her neighbor's iPhone. This gathering of intelligence personnel equaled a family reunion. Katherine would've enjoyed chatting, too, if only there were an opening for a newbie.

Down front, middle-aged Bill Baron swirled a ceramic coffee cup and gazed at the group. Possibly he was counting heads. Jaworski had once introduced Katherine to Baron back in Langley, but she hadn't realized how high he ranked in the intelligence community. Evidently quite high.

Katherine scanned faces, too. The group of fifty CIA officers consisted primarily of men, but about a fourth were women. Merely seeing this assemblage of professional female operatives lifted her sagging spirits. These women weren't the centerfold models so often depicted by Hollywood. They weren't homely either. Each woman was a bright, capable, professional who knew her business and could carry her weight as well as any man here. Katherine might be new, and her family's connection with the H.O. might cast a shadow, but these women represented something she wanted: an opportunity to exercise her full potential as an equal in a challenging environment.

Katherine's resolve hardened. No. Regardless of Melissa's lukewarm reception, Katherine wouldn't let her self-esteem crash and burn.

Crash and burn. Pilot talk. All this time, she'd been thrilled to be part of Roger's world. If he'd been slow to bring up the subject of marriage, she'd been more than sensitive to his situation. A guy who was experimented on, secluded from the world for seven decades—sure, she could understand how he might need time before committing to marriage. But this revelation about Sophie—and Roger racing to the rescue ... Had Katherine assumed too much undivided devotion from Roger? Just how many times had he kissed Sophie?

From where Katherine sat, she couldn't see every face. However, she recognized quite a few from the time Jaworski and his colleagues debriefed her on every detail she could provide about the Heritage Organization.

Two rows back and on the far right, Roger sat with Gerard and Ben. He, too, waited in quiet contemplation. He must have sensed her gaze, because he lifted his head and met her eyes.

She forced a non-committal smile.

Clink, clink, clink, clink.

Bill Baron set down his spoon and coffee mug. "All right everyone, let's get started. I know most of you very well. A few I don't. If this is our first op together, you can call me Bill Baron. Better yet, just Baron. But if you believe that's my real name, then I have several moon rocks for sale at cut-rate prices."

Laughter rippled through the group. Probably an old gag, but it served to kick off the meeting on a note of camaraderie.

"Welcome to Sword, the name we've given to our temporary substation, dedicated solely to this op. Because of certain dangers and suspicions, none of us will contact the normal substation in Paris. Nor will we be sharing information with France's General Directorate of Internal Security, nor with their DRM, nor the BRGE. The risk of compromising this effort is much too high for us to risk sharing with foreign security personnel.

"You are now officially part of 'Operation Gondor,' the umbrella name under which we will unite our talents. Why Gondor? Because in literature Gondor was the civilized world's last bastion of hope against the diabolical hordes of Mordor. We hope to exploit a minuscule chink in the armor of the Heritage Organization—a dangerous worldwide faction we're only now beginning to glimpse—and extract vital information. Ultimately, we hope to free a body of intellectuals held prisoner as slave laborers. If successful, this operation could blow the lid of secrecy right off the H.O."

A man a few rows ahead of Katherine lifted a hand. "Bill, how big is the actual threat? I mean, not long ago we shrugged off rumors about this Heritage Organization as just another wacko conspiracy theory."

"It's no theory," Baron stated. "The Heritage Organization exists. The conspiracy is real. The threat is growing year by year, not just for the United States, but around the globe. Circumstantial evidence had already been mounting when, a few years ago, good fortune smiled and dropped into our lap an American who had been held captive by the H.O. and used as a guinea pig in scientific experiments. He escaped their clutches and evaded being assassinated. You've all received an abbreviated dossier on his incredible history. He's not an intelligence officer, but for security purposes we're withholding his true name. During Operation Gondor, we will refer to him as 'Jim Johnson.' Jim, stand up."

Roger stood. All eyes locked onto him. Probably no one other than herself could spot the micro signs revealing how ill at ease the attractive airman felt. He detested enlarging the number of people privy to his incredible history. His dedication to this Sophie woman must be amazingly strong. It overruled his fear of someone selling out to a tabloid.

"Thank you for agreeing to join us in this operation, Jim."

"I'll help however I can." He sat back down.

Baron continued. "No doubt, you're all fascinated with our youthful-looking World War II veteran. I am, too. However, don't let his presence become a distraction. Do your gawking now; then get over it. Jim is here mainly because he has personally seen quite a few upper-echelon members of the H.O. in Europe. No matter how small the odds of running across those high-ranking individuals on this op, Jack Jaworski believed he's worth adding to the surveillance team. I concur."

Even after Roger sat, many eyes remained glued to him. Female eyes in particular, Katherine noticed.

Who can blame them? Roger's a hunk.

Despite their rough patch the night before, Katherine wished she'd sat beside Roger instead of next to Melissa. She could take his hand and stake her claim.

"Next, I invite Katherine Mueller to stand."

Torn from private thoughts, Katherine took her turn in the spotlight. She turned enough to let everyone see her face and offered a perfunctory nod.

"From her youth, Katherine was actively groomed for the H.O. by her own uncle, Kurt Mueller, formerly of Atlanta. His current whereabouts are unknown. Before she became aware of the group's true nature, she, too, personally met and interacted with multiple H.O. members in the southeast United States. In fact, it was largely thanks to Katherine that Jim Johnson was able to thwart the organization's efforts to assassinate him. It's a fascinating story, better than any thriller from Hollywood, but suffice it to say Katherine is now on our side. She has provided an abundance of information and will assist with surveillance."

Like a magician, Bill Baron had just whipped away her cloak. Everyone now knew a former H.O. member sat among them, soaking up every word. Necessary, she supposed, but still unpleasant to be defined by her past.

Katherine reclaimed her seat. Had the atmosphere turned chillier than when Baron introduced Roger? Or maybe she was simply paranoid?

Mustn't let Melissa's comments push her into defense mode. She needed to stay calm, businesslike. Only, remaining professional was easier thought than done while speculating about Roger and his relationship with Sophie.

Next, Bill Baron launched into an overview of the Heritage Organization—its birth as a consortium of underground SS officers in the final days of World War II, its finances using European riches squirreled away in secret depositories, plus other details, many of which she and Roger had provided. Katherine stifled a yawn. She could've moderated this portion of the meeting. With one side of her brain, she continued listening. Yet, with the other half she contemplated, re-processing mixed emotions from her talk with Roger.

Yesterday, she would have staked her life on understanding Roger Greene completely, down to the last nuance of pilot slang. Every grain of motivation. Each variation of his handsome smiles. The tiniest hint of humor. So, how could he blindside her so easily about Sophie? Despite the denials, Roger possibly harbored tender feelings for Sophie, even subconsciously. Clearly, the two shared some history. She had risked her life for him. He didn't deny that she's attractive. Most likely, she's dazzling.

Equally important, how does Sophie feel about Roger? This Sophie had risked her status in the H.O.—her very life—to whisk him out of their secret bunker and back to the USA. Was this German woman so altruistic she would jeopardize her life on sheer principle? Hard to believe. Surely, she felt at least a shred of love for the handsome *Amerikaner*? Had she expected a life alongside Roger after they reached freedom?

Against Katherine's will, into her imagination sprang an image of Roger wrapping his arms around a woman whose face she couldn't see. The vision soured Katherine's gut. Or maybe she'd nibbled too much Fol Epi cheese. How had her zest for life nosed over into such a sudden tailspin?

Tailspin. Another aviation term. Was she so hopelessly entwined in Roger Greene's life she couldn't extricate herself, even when he irritated her? She considered. Throughout her growing-up years, Uncle Kurt had carefully manipulated her decisions and emotions, cultivating a breed of happiness dependent on his approval. She'd vowed never to let such codependence happen again. However—had she slid into similar code-pendence with Roger?

A hand must have gone up behind Katherine. Baron pointed over her head. "Terri?"

A woman spoke from the rear: "I'm still trying to piece this together. You've discussed this organization's origin, their financing, and their interest in scientific experiments. I still don't understand the end game. What's their goal?"

Baron folded his arms. "Whatever the original goal, the H.O. seems to have expanded and morphed over the decades. Unforeseen advances in technology have encouraged them to reach for the stars. Let me ask the group: Based on your observations of international events, has it seemed to any of you that the world has gone crazy these last few years?"

Heads nodded all around Katherine.

"Totally bonkers."

"Inexplicable."

Baron clapped. "I'm glad you're tracking. We've seen political leaders weaken and destabilize their own nations. Religious fanatics committing mass murder. Terrorists annihilating total strangers. A worldwide pandemic where experts have disagreed with other experts and suggested outrageous courses of action. We also find evidence of covert scientific experiments. In each case, the threads lead back to the Heritage Organization.

"We believe they're manipulating banks, national economies, international politics, big business, and even religions. You name it, if it's influential, you'll find shadowy H.O. fingerprints. We have reason to believe they've infiltrated the Department of Justice, the Pentagon, and elsewhere. They're probably inside the CIA, which is why this op is off the record and why we're not coordinating with our French counterparts. This gig is far too vital to be compromised by a sleeper."

The woman in the back piped up again. "But I repeat—what is their ultimate goal?"

Katherine leaned forward. This was the exact question she had posed herself a thousand times. Uncle Kurt's typical explanation had been that the H.O. existed to construct a better society, a richer heritage for the next generation. But his nebulous answer had offered no more insight than a political slogan.

Baron sipped his coffee. "For the rank and file members on the lower levels, the attraction might be as simple as money and a sense of power, plus the satisfaction of being an insider in a worldwide secret. At the top, though, we conclude H.O. leadership is maneuvering for bigger stakes. Complete control. The rise and fall of nations. Global reengineering to suit their own ambitions for worldwide dominion—all from behind the scenes. No army needed."

A hush fell over the room. If this were true, then sure, it would be child's play for these people to neutralize even the United States by pulling invisible strings. Regardless of her citizenry's wishes, border crossings could be thrown open, the welcome mat rolled out for terrorists, water sources poisoned, Fort Knox plundered, and its gold handed over to America's enemies—and worse. Compared to the potential havoc, the 9/11 destruction of the World Trade Center amounted to little more than a pinprick.

Baron snapped his fingers to regain attention. "So far, the H.O. has been experimenting. Flexing their muscles. Quietly assassinating individuals who might pose an obstruction to their plans. Learning how to instigate public hatred to mobilize brainless mobs into doing their will. Our United States is at greater risk than I can express, but so is every nation. Don't think of the H.O. as playing a worldwide game of spy versus spy to gain a secret here, a classified blueprint there. Think of the H.O. as an elite team of puppet masters. They're pulling concealed strings to rule a planet full of pawns who don't even realize they exist."

A redheaded man pulled off his glasses. "If what you say is true, are we too late to stop them—whoever 'they' are?"

Baron shrugged. "We don't know. The toilet's been flushed, and the world as we know it is already swirling. But we're going to try. Here's how Operation Gondor starts ..."

CHAPTER 10

Seated on a cheap plastic chair with no padding, Roger leaned back, crossed his legs, and took another sip of coffee. So far, another underwhelming day of espionage from the cramped tech room on Boulevard Diderot. On the monitor, the latest visitor opened the door of their target business, Agence Jacques Grégoire Architecture, and strolled in.

"*Bonjour,*" the newcomer said to the receptionist. "*Je cherche ...*"

Roger studied the man. Medium weight. Short nose. Weak chin. Thinning brown hair. Someone else he'd never laid eyes on before. He clicked a couple buttons on the keyboard to perform a screen capture for Katherine to eyeball later, when she came on duty. A full week of scrutinizing faces, and not a single one had looked familiar. Katherine was reporting the same on her surveillance of the Grégoire residence— or so he had heard through the grapevine. If only he could talk to her. But what could he say to melt the frigid barrier between them? During the brief opportunities he'd had, it seemed he'd only increased the tension.

"Recognizing someone from your years of detention would be the longest possible long shot," Bill Baron had advised him on the first day. "The fact the Israeli Mossad has fingered Jacques Grégoire as an H.O. member doesn't mean his clients belong to the organization. But we're desperate. We've got to keep our antennae up for every possible connection."

Roger understood. He was here "just in case" he happened to recognize a face. While Ben and Gerard and other career officers performed the nitty-gritty of electronic surveillance, Roger became an afterthought, a minnow among the bigger fish. Careful not to bump electronic equipment in the cramped surveillance room, he unfolded his legs and glanced out the sixth-floor window. The Parisian sky practically called his name. What he wouldn't give for fifteen minutes in the F-35 Shadow —or any aircraft, for that matter.

"So, Jim," Ben said, as he adjusted a knob on one of the devices before him. "As long as things are slow, I was wondering if you'd like to comment on the soundness of the military strategy adopted by Rebel forces to blow up the original Death Star?"

Roger glanced at the skinny electronics expert. He wasn't joking.

"Come on, big guy," Ben continued. "I know you've seen the original trilogy. I'm not asking for information on you personally. I'm curious about your opinion as a professional fighter pilot."

"You do realize *Star Wars* is fiction, right?"

Ben lowered his eyebrows and leaned back. "Of course, I realize it's fiction. What do you think I am?"

After a week of living and operating in close quarters, Roger harbored no doubts about his geeky roomies. As Melissa had warned, Ben was half of a nerd fest waiting for a partner. And not only concerning *Star Wars*. Both Ben and Gerard needed only the slightest trigger to combust into endless "fanversation" regarding *Dr. Who*, schematic diagrams of various generations of the USS *Enterprise*, *Battlestar Galactica*, and a host of sci-fi movies Roger had never seen. If only Gerard were here to fulfill Ben's daily sci-fi fix.

Roger cleared his throat. "Well, *if* there were such a thing as the Force, and *if* there were such things as X-wing fighters, and *if* there were such things as Death Stars, then I would have to conclude the Rebel attack was fatally flawed and never would've succeeded in real life."

Ben straightened. "What do you mean, 'flawed'?"

"Picture the attack in your head. Luke's X-wing fighter flew horizontally over the surface of the Death Star, correct? He shot a futuristic payload straight ahead, also on a horizontal trajectory across the surface of the Death Star. Yet, for Luke's missile to blow the Death Star up, it had to enter a small hole, then instantly change direction by ninety degrees inside a narrow shaft and travel to a point deep inside the Death Star's core without hitting anything on the way down. It defies logic. No missile can do that. The scriptwriters bungled. The Rebel attack could not succeed with that battle plan."

Ben's eyebrows twitched. His head jerked right, then left. "But ... How can you argue with success? Everyone knows the Death Star blew up—"

Roger cut him off with a shake of his head. "End of discussion. You wanted a fighter pilot's assessment. You got it."

With a frustrated sigh, Ben turned back to his equipment. Most of the subsequent muttering was too low to catch, but interspersed words included "Vader," "high-tech payload," and "Rebel sacrifices."

Roger pressed his lips together, containing his chuckle. The exchange had provided the week's best humor, which he seriously needed. After all, he still didn't know whether Katherine was avoiding him. Sure seemed like it. Or maybe Melissa's scheduling explained why he'd barely glimpsed Katherine all week? How ironic that the first person you think of in the morning and the last person you think of at night can bring you the most joy—and the most heartbreak.

Of course, if he'd bought a cell phone as Katherine had once suggested, he could simply call her. But no. Cell phones could be pinpointed. He would stick to his guns. No tolerance for any device that could track his movements. He simply didn't trust twenty-first-century technology.

*   *   *

That evening, Katherine sat in the rear of a surveillance van packed with sensitive electronic equipment parked around the corner from the home of Jacques Grégoire himself. With her sat Adam Wainwright, her main partner on the nighttime shift keeping watch on all comings and goings at the Grégoire residence.

Adam offered her a disposable cup. "Something hot to drink?"

She hesitated. She'd already downed a coffee at the apartment to ward off sleep.

"It's your favorite," Adam tempted. "Cappuccino." His grin revealed his mischievous nature.

"You just said the magic word." She accepted the cup and took a sip. "Mmm. Gourmet quality. How did you know cappuccino is my favorite?"

"My dear coworker, need I remind you I'm a professional operative? It's my business to notice details."

She took another sip and relished the hot liquid before swallowing. "I'm not exaggerating. This is great stuff. Where did you get it?"

He chuckled. "Classified intel. All is can say is, 'Nothing but the best for my partners.'"

During the next sip, she flashed her eyes over Adam's face. Not long ago, she wouldn't have given his looks a second thought. But now, after working elbow-to-elbow with him for a week in confined quarters, she couldn't help noticing a certain attractiveness. Clean cut. Intelligent. Professional. Charm, too, as evidenced once again by the surprise cappuccino. But would she have given him even a second glance if not for the friction between Roger and herself?

"Adam, with this job, you have plenty of experience keeping secrets. And I'm not referring to gourmet coffee."

He swirled the contents of his cup. "You would be correct. Both professionally and personally. In fact, I'm quietly sitting on multiple secrets that would mortify colleagues if they suspected what I know about them. But I'm no gossip. The world would be a better place if everyone learned how to keep their mouth shut."

An encouraging reply.

"Then, could I ask you a confidential question about men? To get a man's perspective?"

"Sure. But maybe I should ask—about men in general, or a particular Air Force veteran?"

Warmth crept into her cheeks. "He and I have spent a lot of time together. Not as much as I'd like. We live miles apart. We're not engaged, but we have an understanding. Or, I believed we did. Now I wonder if he's interested in another woman."

Adam took a sip, his eyes never leaving hers. "And your question for me?"

How to express it? Conflicting emotions whirled in her head. "It's hard to put into words. Would it be possible for a man who has spent long years in captivity, isolated from all women, to eventually receive help from an attractive female without developing romantic feelings?"

Adam contemplated while taking another sip. "You want my straight-up male opinion, no sugar coating?"

His dramatic preamble caused her heart to tighten, but she nodded. "Yes. Your straight-up opinion."

"Then I'll lay my cards on the table. In my opinion, any adult man who gets locked away for as many years as he was, and without so much as a glimpse of a female, has every right to go screwy in the head. It's not normal. Women need men, and men definitely need women. Isolate a guy from women long enough, and he'll go bonkers."

"But what about when he finally does get to see a woman? And it turns out she's beautiful, and she cares enough to risk her life helping him?"

Adam tightened his lips. "I'm no psychologist, but in my male opinion, after that many decades it wouldn't matter whether she's pretty. She could be the Ugly Lady from a circus sideshow. As long as she has female anatomy, a guy in that predicament could fall for her like a ton of cinder blocks. But later, if he ever had a chance to be around lots of women again ..."

He paused, almost as if for dramatic effect.

"What?"

"Boom."

"What boom?"

"You've heard the cliché about the kid in a candy store? He might keep his hands to himself while Mommy is watching, but when she turns her back, little Billy can't keep his hands off the merchandise."

Adam's conclusion might apply to men with low morals and no self-discipline. However, his assessment didn't sound like Roger Greene.

"But what if this is a high-quality guy? Like, a dedicated patriot with firm faith in God?"

Adam drew a deep breath and slowly exhaled. With compassion in his eyes, he leaned forward and placed his hand over hers. "I've never been a church-goer, and I don't want to burst your bubble. However, in my experience men are men. Ever hear of Jim Jones and his Peoples Temple in Guyana? Or David Koresh, the wacko from Waco? Both were deeply religious. They spouted Bible verses. Yet, both of them suffered from inappropriate attraction to females. All I'm saying is that no one could blame our aviator friend if it turns out he has a life-long addiction to women. It's doubly possible he harbors feelings for this female savior."

As he pulled his hand away, Adam's fingertips traced their way across the back of her fingers. She halfway noticed yet disregarded the touch as she contemplated Roger's loyalty.

Unexpectedly, tears welled in her eyes. She turned her head and focused on the monitor showing Jacques Grégoire's front door. Sniffling, she fumbled in her purse. Didn't she have at least one tissue?

"I'm sorry. I was too blunt." Out of nowhere, he procured a crisp, white handkerchief and snapped it once to shake out the folds.

Katherine accepted the cloth and dabbed her eyes. Feminine intuition suggested Wainwright was exhibiting interest, but she ignored it. Right now, more pertinent concerns demanded thought. After all, if her hopes and dreams about Roger were truly doomed, this white linen couldn't begin to soak up the tears. Being in love with someone who loves another must be the sweetest form of torture.

CHAPTER 11

During Roger's next shift, it was his other roommate, Gerard, who kept him company instead of Ben. As both monitored every individual to enter the architectural firm of Jacques Grégoire, they passed time as best they could, making small talk during the tedious hours of observation.

"What motivated you toward this type of work?" Roger asked.

Just then a young blonde onscreen approached the reception desk under surveillance. He'd never seen the woman before. Per protocol, he clicked a couple keys to capture her image.

Gerard yawned. "A mixture of things. Partly it was movies like *Mission Impossible* and Jason Bourne flicks. Do you know what those are, or am I talking over your head?"

Roger felt ire building inside him. Not many people in the world knew his background, but he despised when those few talked down to him, just because he'd been locked away for decades. "I've seen them. Keep talking."

"Partly it was my interest in electronics. By the age of twelve, I was building computers in my parents' basement. After high school, Microsoft offered me a job. So did Apple." Gerard paused while Roger captured another image, this time of two middle-aged males standing at the reception desk. "But those kinds of jobs didn't appeal to me. I'm not a nine-to-fiver. I wanted an important job, with a privilege of being 'in the know,' so to speak. When a recruiter sat down to talk with me, I was hooked." He stifled another yawn.

"Yes, I can see you find your work highly stimulating." He faked a yawn to mirror Gerard's.

The young techie laughed. "I'm not bored. I'm tired because I stayed up late watching a movie. *Dimension* from Paramount Pictures. You would've liked it."

"Maybe. But you know how we senior citizens are. I really value my rack time."

His laid-back humor elicited a grin from Gerard. "You realize there are, like, a zillion questions I'd like to ask about your life?"

"Understandable. But even if the Feds didn't label my life Top Secret, I'd rather not discuss it. I never volunteered for the weird life that was dumped on me. If I can't go back to the past, I'll make the best of life as it is now and be a regular American, not somebody's lab rat."

"Then how about a topic not connected to your experiment? As I understand it, you're sort of religious, right? Don't you ever get mad at God for forcing you through all the garbage you've experienced?"

The light in Gerard's eyes transformed into hard glints. A hint of defiance. Perhaps even his own resentment of the Almighty?

Roger drew a deep breath as he framed a response. "Mad at God? In my long life, yeah, there were times when I was mad at God. I went from a guy who rarely thought about God, to a guy who called out to Him as a last resort, and then to a guy who was mad when God didn't answer prayers the way I wanted. But the anger disappeared when I actually sat down and read the Bible."

A twinge of guilt pricked his conscious. He might not accuse God directly, but he still got angry too easily. It was a flaw he needed to work on.

"That easy, huh?" The skepticism remained on Gerard's face.

"Nope, not so easy. I'm condensing my life for the sake of conversation. Don't think I claim to be perfect. What I'm saying is that I was on the brink of going stark raving mad. I blamed God for dealing me lousy cards. But the more I read the Bible, the more I believed in Him as Creator of the universe, the One who's weaving this vast cosmic tapestry with Himself at the center, not me. Whether I like what He does with me or not, I'm glad to be part of His family. He has my permission to do whatever He wants with me."

Gerard's eyebrows lowered. "Anything? Pretty carte blanche, don't you think?"

Roger couldn't blame the kid. After all, Roger once thought the exact same way. "I've *learned* to trust God. It's not always easy. But in the end, He always works things out for good."

Gerard stretched. "I guess religion is all right for you. Me, I'm going to stay in charge of my own destiny."

Roger couldn't resist the grin pulling at the corners of his mouth. "Your attitude is the same as mine when I was your age. Wait and see how being in charge of your destiny works in real life."

A quiet *snick* signaled a key turning in the door lock. The door swung open to reveal Baron himself stepping inside to pay a visit. Baron froze. "Careful, Gerard. Shooting your boss isn't the best career move."

Sure enough, a Glock had magically appeared in Gerard's hand, and he had the barrel trained on the doorway. He shoved the pistol into his backpack. "Sorry. Reflexes."

Baron locked the door behind him. "I approve, but next time I'll knock." He focused on Roger. "Where were you around ten o'clock last night?"

Roger's mind flashed to yesterday evening. "I took a shower then hit the sack. What's up?"

"Did you leave your apartment last evening? Enjoy some fresh Parisian air?"

The bewildering questions pulled Roger off his chair. He stood face to face with Baron. "No and no. Why do you ask?"

Baron's eyes bore into his own. Thanks to Roger's training at the Farm, he understood that Baron was watching for micro signals of lying. But why?

Gerard stood, too. "Want me to step out?"

Baron motioned him to retake his seat. "This affects the whole team."

The comment pushed Roger past baffled and into the insulted zone. "What affects the whole team? All I did was go to bed. Where's the crime?"

"But you have no witnesses?"

He laughed. "Since when does anyone need witnesses to sleep?"

"Not even Katherine?"

Roger's blood pressure mounted. "Katherine and I never sleep together. Besides, I haven't seen her in days."

For a long, drawn-out moment, Baron simply stared at him. At last, he relaxed. "I suppose you've heard the local news?"

"You suppose wrong. I haven't heard a single bit of news." A gear clicked in his brain. "Wait. Don't tell me something's happened to Katherine?"

Baron unfolded the leather cover of an electronic tablet. "Something happened, but not to Katherine. You both really don't know the president of France was murdered last evening?"

"Seriously?" Gerard blurted.

"I had no clue," Roger said. But Baron's announcement explained the animated conversation of pedestrians he'd passed on the street that morning. Spoken French flowed faster than he could comprehend. Still, he saw no connection between the assassination and Baron's questions. "Something tells me you didn't drop by to deliver a news bulletin."

Baron held up his tablet for both Roger and Gerard. "Watch." He tapped an icon.

The screen burst into a CNN Newsflash, "French President Assassinated." The first image zoomed into a futuristic-looking building, the Philarmonie de Paris, according to a male voice with a British accent. Next, the camera cut to the agitated correspondent, who recounted how the French President and his wife had attended an evening of classical music performed by the Orchestre de Paris at the famous Philarmonie concert hall.

"... and as he opened the car door for his wife, out of nowhere a bullet struck him, knocking him against the vehicle. Then, a second bullet hit, at which point he fell to the ground. Physicians at Hôpital Saint-Louis pronounced the President dead on arrival."

The newsflash proceeded to interview shocked patrons of the Philarmonie, then medical and police personnel. Lastly, the camera returned to the CNN correspondent. "So far, it's unclear whether this killing is the act of a terrorist group, or of a lone shooter with a personal vendetta.

What we can say is the French authorities will explore every possible clue to track down the killer—"

Baron ended the video.

Gerard shook his head. "That's insane."

For a long moment, Roger said nothing. The killing was tragic, but why did Baron come to discuss it? "Are you suggesting the Heritage Organization is behind the murder?"

"I'm not suggesting anything. Do you have any idea who might've done it?"

"How could I? I just now learned of it. You heard them—even the French police don't have leads."

"Correction. The newsflash was filmed late last night. At that hour, the French police did not—past tense—have any leads."

"And?"

"Since then, the French *gendarmerie* has scoured the footage of every security camera near the Philarmonie. One camera caught the assassin on video."

Once again, Baron hefted his tablet and tapped an icon. Black-and-white footage showed a long row of parked cars. Despite the late hour, streetlights dispelled enough darkness to reveal a figure approaching. As a vehicle rounded a corner, its headlights temporarily washed out the view. When the scene returned to normal, there was the man, much closer, dressed in dark clothing. He leaned over the hood of a parked vehicle and peered into the scope of a high-caliber rifle.

"The gunman holds this pose for nearly three minutes," Baron said. "Let me fast forward." He tapped the controls. When the video resumed normal speed, the sniper stood unmoved, as if frozen. An instant later, he adjusted the barrel, and then pulled the trigger. He shot a second time, paused, and finally lowered his weapon.

"Let's zoom in on the face," Baron said.

The figure in the video straightened.

"Right here." Baron froze the clip just as a passing vehicle's headlights illuminated the gunman.

Gerard started. "What the ...?"

Roger stared, speechless. Frozen onscreen was his own face. Not a face resembling his own—it was him! The same face he'd seen in mirrors millions of times. Shock prompted him to step backward, where he stumbled into his chair.

"Have anything you want to say?" Baron asked.

Say? He could scarcely *think!* "It's not possible."

Even if he'd had a twin brother—which wouldn't fit his knowledge of his own upbringing in an orphanage—a twin would be an elderly geezer by now. A random lookalike? Or maybe a killer wearing a mask like his own face?

Baron flipped shut the tablet's cover. "I have a gigantic problem. Every policeman in France now has a video capture of a face perfectly matching a member of my undercover op. French television is broadcasting it every fifteen minutes, urging citizens to be on the lookout for the killer."

"It's not me."

"It *is* your face, even if it's someone else's body. Don't believe me? Stroll down the avenue and see what happens."

Gerard stroked his chin as he voiced the gears turning in his head. "You know, there might be a scientific explanation. Suppose the Heritage Organization experimented on him with mind control. They might have programmed him to respond to a certain stimulus—"

Roger shook his head. "No way. The H.O. never performed any kind of brainwashing. They had zero intention of releasing me. After I escaped, they did their best to kill me."

"How do I know?" Baron asked. "How can even you be sure? If the organization planted commands deep inside your psyche, you wouldn't be aware of it. Another fact: the concert hall isn't more than a couple miles from your apartment."

"The guy in the video isn't me. I never sleepwalk. Besides, where would I get a rifle?"

Baron shrugged. "The organization could supply one."

On his monitor, Roger noticed an attractive, sixtyish woman standing at the information desk of the architectural firm. Capturing images of clients sank to the bottom of his concerns, but he leaned over and performed his job anyway. "Okay, boss, the executioner looks like me. I don't deny it. I can't explain it. What now?"

"Effective immediately, you're off the op."

"What?"

"I don't know what's going on, but my team needs secrecy and anonymity. Your face is a liability. Even if you are innocent—which I hope is true—we can't risk the police questioning you."

Roger pictured himself in a Parisian jail. "I've spent enough time in lockup. Nobody puts me in another cage—not ever."

Gerard's eyes flicked back and forth from Baron to Roger.

"Second, you will be escorted back to the States. I've got a makeup artist on her way right now. You can't leave this building until we give you a disguise. Even then, we might have to nail you into a wooden crate with U.S. Embassy markings to get you through security."

Roger latched onto an inspiration. "What if I wear a disguise every day? Then nobody would—"

Baron shook his head. "Too risky. Besides, maybe you are some kind of Manchurian candidate. I can't take the gamble."

Sophie's face came to mind. Roger was honor-bound to help. "I have more reason than all of you put together to stay here and finish—"

"You're off the op. Period. We're sending you home."

Roger's heart sank. Why would God bring him all this way, after so much intense training, only to send him back to the U.S.? "Anything else?"

Baron reached into his pocket and extracted an object, which he set on the table beside Roger. "This is a tamper-resistant ankle bracelet. It emits a radio signal. We can follow your movements until our people remove it in Langley."

"I'm under arrest?"

"No. But the situation requires precautions until we figure out what's going on. This op could be the most serious of my career. Even if the shooter's resemblance to you is a one-in-ten-million coincidence, I must act accordingly."

"You understand I'm allergic to tracking devices? A GPS chip embedded in my arm nearly got me killed."

Baron nodded. "I read the brief. I'm hoping you'll appreciate my position and wear this voluntarily."

Despite frustration ballooning in his chest, Roger truly could imagine himself in Baron's shoes. Wouldn't he do the same if the tables were turned? "All right. I'll wear it. But let me wait until your makeup person works her magic. It'll give me time to psych myself up for it."

Baron placed a hand on Roger's shoulder. "Thanks. And just for the record, I want to believe in you. There must be a logical explanation about the shooter, but until we—"

Out of nowhere, the tune "From the Halls of Montezuma" began playing. Baron extracted his satellite phone. The caller I.D. sparked a curse. "What could *he* want?"

During the ensuing telephone conversation, Baron ignored Roger and Gerard. His eyes closed, as if pained. "Sir, can't this wait? It's the worst possible timing."

Evidently, the matter couldn't wait. Baron listened a few seconds more. "All right, sir. The timing stinks. But if that's the bottom line, I'll go this minute."

Baron shoved the phone into his pocket. "Why couldn't someone have shot *our* president? Emergency situation. I've gotta run—literally. Gerard, you're in charge. Roger, wait here for the makeup artist. After she's worked her magic, a couple of our agents will come for you. Haven't ironed out the details, but we'll get you out of Paris safely. Understand?"

"Roger that. Will comply."

Baron patted his shoulder. "Attaboy. I'll be in touch." Baron slipped out the door.

Gerard sighed. "Weird day. I wonder what else can go wrong?"

CHAPTER 12

In a state of disbelief, Roger sank onto his plastic chair. "It makes no sense. The guy is a dead ringer for me."

Gerard shrugged. "They say that everyone on earth has a doppelgänger."

"But the timing. Right now? When I just happen to be in Paris?"

A movement on the monitor caught Roger's peripheral vision. Two men were talking in the lobby of the architectural firm. One was the owner, Jacques Grégoire himself. No need to capture his image. The second man stood with his head facing away from the camera. If Roger's assignment had seemed unglamorous before, it now seemed a lost cause. Too soon, Baron's men would be escorting him from the building. Would they let him speak with Katherine before whisking him to the airport?

Still, this job was his responsibility. Roger had been tasked with examining each face and recording images. Duty compelled him to reach for the keyboard. He'd fulfill this boring task right up to—

When the man shook Jacques Grégoire's hand, Roger's heart lurched.

"Mueller!" In his astonishment, Roger hit the wrong keys, capturing nothing. In rapid succession, his shaking fingers copied the image once, twice, three times before the target strolled out of the surveillance cam's range.

"Mueller? Katherine Mueller?" Gerard asked.

"No, her uncle. Kurt Mueller. He's one hundred percent Heritage Organization. He once tried to kill me."

Roger's mind raced. This op's first solid contact with the H.O., and it was Kurt Mueller? Could he know Katherine was in Paris? "He's getting away!"

Gerard grabbed the portable radio and fed a rapid description of Mueller to whoever was stationed on the street. But Mueller's description could match a thousand men.

"I'm going after him!" Roger blurted.

"You can't! You heard Baron. You're off the op."

"Mueller is slipping through our fingers. I've got to follow—"

Cobra-quick, Gerard's hand disappeared into his backpack and reappeared with the Glock. "You're not putting this op at risk. You will wait, just like Baron said."

"Gerard, are you nuts? Listen, that is *the* Kurt Mueller. We need to trail him."

"I like you, but don't test me. I'll use this if I have to."

Roger fought down the urge to scream—or to wring Gerard's neck. Instead, he looked at the monitor and faked excitement. "Wait, there's another one!" He pointed at the only person on the screen, a baby-faced young man with curly hair. The guy looked too young to be guilty of anything worse than stealing milk money, but he was Roger's only diversion. "Here he comes. Watch, he'll have a scar on his right cheek. Get ready to call in his description."

Gerard stepped closer.

Instantly Roger grabbed his companion's gun hand and banged it onto the tabletop with full force.

"Augh!"

The Glock flew through the air. But the younger man proved himself more than a computer nerd. Surprisingly fast, his left fist plowed into Roger's cheek, nearly twisting his head off.

"Gerard, we're on the same side!"

"Then obey orders. Maybe you really did shoot the president. This could be a trick to escape."

"No time to argue. Mueller is getting aw—"

Gerard lunged. With the agility of a bullfighter, Roger sidestepped, then increased Gerard's momentum with a well-placed kick to his posterior. The younger man's head rammed the wall. Gerard slumped to the floor. He didn't get up.

Roger snatched up his jacket but paused. Baron was right—if police or patriotic Frenchmen got a clean look at his face, he'd wind up in a Parisian jail. Gerard's backpack! Roger dumped out its contents. A pair of sunglasses! For good measure, he also grabbed the ball cap. Navy blue, the cap sported gold letters: *U.S.S. Enterprise. NCC-1701.*

"Sheesh. What a geek."

Hardly the nondescript disguise he'd hoped for, but Roger stuck it on his head anyway. A final pause. On the table where Baron had placed it sat the ankle-bracelet tracker. Roger stuffed the thing into a pocket before charging out the door.

Chapter 13

When Roger burst out the door of the building housing the surveillance post, he sprinted full speed. He'd probably just set a world record for careening down six flights of stairs in leather shoes. His one goal was to find Kurt Mueller before the man could disappear into the population of Paris. However, as Roger rounded the street corner, he collided with a middle-aged brunette, knocking a bag from her hand. Out spilled a loaf of bread and a wedge of cheese.

"Quel idiot!"

Roger paused and scooped her purchases back into the bag. *"Excusez. Excusez-moi,"* he stammered as he returned her groceries. In a rush, he blurted the first excuse his amateur French could concoct: *"Mon chien est mort."*

As he race-walked down the avenue with French epithets billowing in his wake, he chewed himself out. *My dog died.* What kind of cockamamie explanation was that?

Not important. What was crucial was to slow down. Stop looking like an escaped convict, or a French *gendarme* really would spot him. Mueller might, too, if Roger didn't act nonchalant. Across the street stood the gleaming structure bearing the name and logo of Agence Jacques Grégoire Architecture. But where was Mueller?

The street teemed with a colossal surplus of humanity. Men and women of all shapes, sizes, and ethnicities were walking, jostling for position, standing at the crosswalk, sitting at cafés, entering stores, and exiting those same businesses. In the street, others were maneuvering automobiles, motorcycles, and even bicycles through the congested Parisian traffic. People, people everywhere. But where was Mueller?

To avoid looking conspicuous, Roger backed up to an electronics store and leaned against it, arms folded, as if waiting for someone. As an afterthought, he snatched up a cast-off piece of paper, an advertisement he could pretend to read while he surveyed the crowd.

Come on, Herr Mueller, where are you?

In vain, Roger held up the advertisement and gazed over it as he searched, first in one direction, then the other. He studied each retreating male from the backside. Although many Parisians slightly resembled Mueller, he quickly discarded each one.

Another thought—Gerard's radio call had alerted the street team to Mueller's presence. Might they have picked Mueller out of the crowd and be on his six right now? And if they spotted Roger despite his thin disguise, would they interfere with him? Maybe not, if Baron hadn't yet informed the team he was off the op. But even if not, if they had seen a TV, their minds would be swirling with questions about him.

A graying woman with deep-set eyes and a long nose stopped to stare at him.

Oh great. Did she notice the resemblance between him and the shooter? But instead of screaming for the police, she glared at Roger, then at the advertisement he was holding up, and then back to Roger. With a disgusted "Humph," she shook her head and strolled away. For the first time, Roger looked directly at his paper shield and discovered it was an advertisement for brassieres.

He'd just flunked "Blending In: 101." Roger dropped the ad into a trashcan before heading down the sidewalk. Why hadn't he grabbed Gerard's radio? If nothing else, the device might've let him know whether the team was trailing Mueller.

The never-ending streams of humanity continued to flow in both directions. No sign of Mueller. Maybe a driver picked him up?

Strolling casually, but with all senses alert, Roger crossed the street. Still no trace of Mueller. Disgusted, he turned back in the direction he'd come.

Lord, what's this all about? First You bring me to France. Next, a guy who looks like me commits murder. Which in turn gets me kicked off the operation. But before they ship me away, You let me spot Mueller. Then You delay me long enough to miss Mueller?

If only Gerard hadn't slowed him down. Maybe then he would've reached the street in time to—

What the—? Dead ahead, who just stepped out the front door of Agence Jacques Grégoire bearing a briefcase but Kurt Mueller himself.

Bandit, twelve o'clock level.

Pausing only long enough to don sunglasses, Herr Mueller turned and sauntered away, barely fifty feet ahead of Roger.

Mueller had been inside the building all this time? Didn't matter. At last Roger had eyes on his rabbit.

Thank You, God!

Roger slowed his pace to widen the gap between Mueller and himself. A furtive glance around didn't reveal any CIA officers. But then again, unlike himself, they were professionals. He might not detect them even if they surrounded him. Or maybe they were tailing the wrong rabbit and didn't realize it as they tried to radio the unconscious Gerard?

Okay, as far as I know, I'm flying solo. Gotta play this carefully.

Ambling with an indifferent air, Roger reviewed the instruction in tracking a rabbit he'd received at the Farm. With a surveillance team, this would be easier.

But he didn't have luxuries. Just eyes, ears, and wits. And who knows, Mueller's dark glasses could be the kind with built-in reflectors, allowing him to observe followers with a slight twist of the head.

Roger slowed a little more and positioned himself behind a corpulent man trudging in the same direction. He allowed only one eye to peek around the human shield.

Where are you going, Mueller? Whatever you're doing, you're up to no good, just like the rest of your lousy organization.

When a white, blue, and red Peugeot emblazoned with the word *Police* crept past in bumper-to-bumper traffic, the hair on the back of Roger's neck prickled. Two officers sat inside, each scanning pedestrians.

Roger prayed they wouldn't stop him. If those cops—sometimes known as "archers" in old Parisian slang—activated their light bar or siren to challenge him, Kurt Mueller might turn to see the cause of commotion. They could warn his rabbit to bolt.

Unfortunately, according to Baron's briefing, the Paris Police Prefecture was actually a local unit of the well-trained French National Police, and had been so since the time of Napoleon I. The Peugeot might seem small by western standards, but its occupants were no Keystone Cops. They would be highly trained lawmen, seeking a male of Roger's description.

He exhaled a calming breath and sauntered as nonchalantly as possible. To truly blend in, he ought to have a mobile phone to stare at like so many street zombies. Even a nonfunctioning smart phone could serve as a prop.

When at last the police car crawled past, Roger relaxed. The experience echoed memories of a historical novel he'd once read. In the book, a Hoosier airman named Yoder had escaped Nazi pursuers and attempted to mix with the populace of Paris. Now, here was Roger Greene, a former World War II airman, attempting to escape notice in Paris decades later. Occasionally, truth really did imitate fiction.

But there—Mueller opened the door of a gray Mercedes.

Roger halted. If Mueller drove away, there would be no catching him. If Roger sprinted to memorize the license plate, there was no guarantee the CIA could relocate the car, let alone the driver. Worse, Mueller might spot him.

He glanced around, hoping to spot a CIA colleague. Not one in sight.

Hotwire a car? He had no tools. Busting a window in broad daylight would certainly invite arrest.

God, please help me to—

Roger cut short his petition to the Almighty at the sight rolling down the avenue—an auto marked "Taxi Parisien."

Thank You, Lord!

Trying not to appear conspicuous, Roger stepped into the street and beckoned to the taxi. When the vehicle stopped, he jumped into the rear and ordered the driver to follow the gray car.

"Suivez cette voiture grise."

The man laughed then asked in French if Roger were a policeman.

Roger carried no badge. He couldn't masquerade as a cop. As Mueller's car pulled away, he blurted that the man owed him money. It seemed plausible. But so much for his Boy Scout reputation.

The driver swallowed it. He put the taxi in gear.

Roger extracted his wallet. Did he have enough Euros to stay on Mueller's tail? For the first time, he regretted his own refusal to carry credit cards or a mobile phone. His phobia of being tracked in this modern world would be his downfall.

CHAPTER 14

As the last rays of the setting sun slanted through the window, Katherine perched on the edge of one of the plastic seats in "Sword," the makeshift substation. Facing her sat Baron and Melissa Hart.

"So that's our situation," Baron summarized. "I showed him video footage of the shooter and offered him benefit of the doubt. The moment my back was turned, he slammed Gerard into the wall and bolted out the door. Pretty damning reaction."

"A clear admission of guilt," Melissa said.

Katherine sat stunned. Baron's assessment sounded logical, but totally inconsistent with the Roger Greene she knew. "How's Gerard?"

"Bruises galore, plus head trauma. Conscious but confused. We fabricated a tale about him getting into a brawl with a drunk for the hospital."

Melissa placed a sympathetic hand on Katherine's forearm. "You know your boyfriend better than anyone else. Can you think of any reason why he would assassinate the French president? Or where he might flee?"

"No idea at all."

"Think carefully," Baron suggested. "Even a passing comment might provide a clue. A dream? Maybe a grudge?"

Katherine dug through her memory, but in vain. Ordering French toast at an IHOP restaurant was the closest French connection she could pull from memory. "There's nothing. He might be a fighter pilot, but as an individual he's never violent. Sure, he gets frustrated when he doesn't understand something modern, but he's never hurt anyone."

"What about guns? Does he own many?"

"None. With his military training, he knows how to shoot, but airplanes are his passion. He carries nothing more dangerous than a Swiss army knife."

"And you have no idea where in France he might go if he wanted to hide?" Baron asked.

"Zilch. He's never been in France before. To the best of my knowledge, he doesn't know a soul. Just the op members he met after arriving here."

With a sigh, Baron leaned back. "Among us three, I'm dropping the fake name. From what Jaworski told me, Roger didn't want to come to Europe. He balked at the idea despite the President's direct intervention. So, why would he agree, but then murder the head of state?"

Katherine's eyes bore into Baron's. "Wait. You're telling me the President of the United States personally ordered Roger to assist with this op?"

"Not verbally, but by letter. Jack saw to it."

This chunk of information thudded into Katherine's hurting heart.

"He never mentioned it. Maybe I didn't let him. He and I hit a bit of friction."

"I noticed," Melissa said. "But it wasn't my business."

Baron tilted backward and gazed toward the ceiling. "Off hours allowed him unobserved freedom of movement. I wonder if any outsiders contacted him? Blackmail is one possibility."

Katherine shook her head. "You'd have better luck blackmailing a choirboy."

Melissa crossed her arms. "If only men really were so transparent. I don't mean to burst your bubble, but every human on the planet is capable of hiding a skeleton in his closet. Even Baron here."

Baron tapped a cigarette from a pack of Camels. "Guilty. I'm hiding enough skeletons to stock a graveyard."

Melissa raised an eyebrow. "I thought you swore off smoking?"

He lit the tip. "I carry one pack for emergencies. Today's fouled-up situation qualifies as an emergency of epic proportions."

"Fouled-up? Tame vocabulary for the Baron I know."

"I'm exercising restraint." He took a long drag. "Hang it all, here I am, heading up the juiciest op of my career, when suddenly a civilian advisor goes rogue and murders a foreign head of state. I can't tip off French authorities without exposing our op to every newspaper and late-night talk show in the world. But if the police do spot Roger—which is highly likely since they're scouring the country for his face—they'll lock him up and squeeze him for every drop of information. He could blow everything—our presence in France, our one chance of penetrating the Heritage Organization, plus U.S.-French relations for the foreseeable future. The CIA will be a laughingstock, and the H.O. will button down security tighter than ever."

Melissa reached for Baron's Camels and helped herself to one. "You left out the part about the U.S. President demanding our heads on a silver platter." She held up a cigarette, which Baron lit with his own glowing tip.

"What will you do?" Katherine asked.

Baron blew a plume of smoke at the ceiling. "The only thing I can do. For now, we'll freeze all activity on Operation Gondor. We must locate and silence our rogue."

An icy chill shivered down Katherine's spine. "Silence him? Don't you mean capture him?"

Baron stood. "We'll recapture him if it can be done safely. I'd love to conduct my own interrogation. But I'm not playing games. If we can't reacquire him, we silence him. The success of this op is far more important than one traitor's life."

Katherine didn't argue. One contrary word might bounce her from the op. Baron could banish her anyway, considering her relationship with Roger. Yet, maybe she could help Roger in other ways? "We should hunt for clues in his apartment."

"Happening even as we speak."

"The surveillance post, too? I know it's a long shot, but worth checking. "

"It's our next stop. Wanted to speak with you first. Let's go."

*   *   *

As Baron unlocked the door to the cramped surveillance post, Katherine noticed Melissa hanging back, allowing Katherine to enter before her. No politeness here. Her supervisor was keeping this former H.O. member in sight.

Baron voiced the standard procedure: "Look for any clue. The tiniest detail."

When the door swung open, the word that sprang to Katherine's mind was *shambles*. The floor was littered with coffee cups, an over-turned chair, an ink pen, a wireless computer mouse, the sifted contents of Gerard's now-empty backpack, and a handheld radio ... On the two desks, electronic surveillance equipment still glowed. A monitor showed the now-deserted lobby of Agence Jacques Grégoire Architecture.

Katherine pointed. "There's a Glock under the desk."

Baron crouched and retrieved the weapon. "Gerard's. Interesting that Roger didn't take it."

"Maybe he didn't notice it," Melissa speculated.

An alternate reason sprang to Katherine's mind. "I'd guess he left it on purpose. If Gerard pulled a gun, Roger noticed. He didn't want it."

Baron stood. "Check out the wall."

The spot where Gerard's head had collided was visibly dented.

Melissa ran her fingertips across the depression. "Ouch."

Layer upon layer of confusion descended onto Katherine. She couldn't deny the chaotic scene, but it didn't fit the character of Roger Greene. Except when fighting assassins, she'd never known him to hurt anyone. "This is a wild idea, but is there a chance we're looking at this all wrong? What if Gerard is the problem?"

"If so, why would Roger flee after winning the fight?"

"Good point." She turned in a circle. "Roger, Roger. What on earth have you been up to? If only he carried a cell phone. We could use it to triangulate his position. But he won't have anything to do with them."

Baron's head shot upright, a new light in his eyes. He glanced left, then right, scanned the floor, even dropped to hands and knees and peered beneath the desks.

"What?" Melissa asked.

"The ankle bracelet. It's missing. Roger agreed to snap it on before leaving. But why would a fleeing murderer take the one object that would allow us to track him?"

The truth exploded in Katherine's mind. "He wants us to follow him. Something unexpected happened. He had no time to write a message."

"If so, Gerard would naturally try to stop him," Melissa said. "But it's all conjecture."

Katherine snatched the wireless mouse and dropped into the chair at the computer. "Let's pull up the most recent screenshots."

After clicking the mouse several times, Katherine gasped at the face on the monitor. Seeing the proverbial ghost couldn't make her jerk backward faster. Her very own uncle.

"Who is he?" Melissa asked.

Baron whistled. "Katherine's uncle, the slippery Kurt Mueller himself. An assassin who's totally loyal to the Heritage Organization."

Recovering from her shock, Katherine zoomed in on the image. "He's dyed his hair from gray to black, but it's Uncle Kurt." She clicked further and discovered two more screen captures. "I don't know what happened to the French president, but these photos explain why Roger would stop at nothing to get out of this room. I say he isn't running from us. He's tracking Uncle Kurt and needs our help."

CHAPTER 15

At the head of Sophie's column of prisoners, the guard nicknamed "Vulture" swiped his electronic key through the door lock.

Ting. The portal to the gymnasium slid open.

"Inside," Vulture ordered the prisoners. "March."

Once the entire group stood inside the gymnasium, Vulture recited the same instructions he repeated every week: "Nobody sits. You are valuable to us only as long as you are healthy. You can be healthy only if you receive sufficient exercise. Therefore, you will spend the next hour walking counterclockwise around the perimeter of the Exercise Room. Walk."

Her ankle chains clinking, Sophie stepped forward and took the lead position. Although basketball hoops hung at each end, Sophie had never heard of them ever being used for actual games. Neither did the floor include markings for a basketball court. The room was simply a large box with two hoops and the ubiquitous white walls, white ceiling, and white tile floor found throughout Talent Redemption III. Basketballs were nowhere to be found, and prisoners didn't dare request them. Even if they wanted to play, ankle chains made it impossible.

Unlike the prisoners who quietly cursed or muttered during the weekly ritual, Sophie relished exercise day. If permitted, she would've gladly jogged the circuit. Her heart, lungs, and muscles all craved physical exertion. However, in the two-plus years she'd been in T.R. III, the only time guards had removed her chains was for the weekly shower and change of clothing.

Natalia shuffled forward, puffing to match Sophie's quick pace. "Are you training for the Olympics? You always walk so fast."

"I used to lead an active life. I miss my workouts."

"What's the point?" Natalia glanced backward, causing Sophie to do likewise. A widening gap separated them from the bulk of prisoners. Natalia's voice dropped to a whisper. "You're not gearing up for an escape, are you?"

The mere suggestion of a covert plan caused Sophie's heart to flutter. She forced herself to keep her eyes forward, with no change of expression. "Don't talk crazy. We can't escape."

"Then how do you stay so ..." Natalia searched for an adjective. "So positive? So motivated?"

"I told you. I enjoy physical activity. Why should I become flabby just because I'm here?" As a quick afterthought, Sophie whispered, "If you're hoping to escape, you're hoping for the impossible."

"But shouldn't we—"

"Shhh. Don't even think it. If you ever concoct a scheme to get out of here, don't tell me. Such ideas can end only in pain. Or death. Or both."

"I only—"

Sophie shot her a stern glance. "Don't. I plan to keep my head down, obey orders, and stay alive as long as I can. Understand?"

Sophie disliked speaking so brusquely to this young woman in the same plight as herself. But Sophie lived in survival mode. One fact her H.O. schooling taught was that things are not always what they seem. Better to portray herself as a pessimist lest someone suspect the truth.

Natalia opened her mouth briefly but shut it again. She actually smiled. In this high-tech dungeon, any smile from a prisoner was a rarity, but even among rarities this smile was unique. "You're right. Escaping is impossible."

Arms swinging, the two stepped along in silence.

"I can't maintain this pace," Natalia finally said. "I'm slowing down."

By the time Sophie turned the next corner, she could glimpse Natalia with a new conversation partner—Dr. Pavel Kuznetsov, the Russian endocrinologist. Since they both understood Russian, no doubt they were conversing in that tongue. Here and there, other prisoners walked side by side and spoke. Most shuffled along in their own thoughts.

Sophie considered their conversations. Sincere or not, Natalia's demeanor often suggested naiveté. Naïve people could be dangerous.

Perhaps she was becoming paranoid, but Sophie resolved to stay extra guarded in all conversations.

CHAPTER 16

By the time Herr Mueller's car turned into a warehouse district on the outskirts of Paris, evening darkness had settled, dispelled only here and there by streetlights and the headlights of an occasional truck rumbling past. Time to stop.

"*Arrêtez ici,*" Roger instructed his driver.

Proceeding on foot would be a gamble. But he had no choice. A taxi would attract attention.

Roger peeled off the requested Euros, and then added extra for goodwill. "*Merci beaucoup.*"

"*Bonne chance,*" the taxi driver said with a grin. In English he repeated, "Good luck."

After the taxi swung in a U-turn and drove back the way they'd come, Roger glanced upward. Due to the scarcity of streetlights, the stars glittered extra brightly.

Lord, I need Your help. Please, guide me to Mueller.

Eyes and ears alert, he set forward at a quick pace. Crickets helped mask the sound of his footfalls. So did random clunks and hums from the midnight shifts of a few warehouses.

Roger skirted the illuminated circles under streetlights.

"Walk as children of light," the Bible instructed. But for tonight, darkness was his ally.

Ahead, a chain-link gate clanked its way open, and a truck rolled out. Just in time, Roger ducked behind a sign.

At the end of the rutted street, Roger turned right, the same direction Mueller had gone. By squinting, he could discern an international road sign meaning "Dead end."

Excellent. A dead-end road guaranteed Herr Mueller hadn't simply driven through this warehouse district to evade followers. He was here —somewhere.

The "where" soon became clear. On the right, uninterrupted fencing and the backside of a warehouse ruled out any turns in that direction. To the left, however, stood one final, foreboding structure. The brightest illumination lit up the solitary gate and its guardhouse. Smaller lights feebly revealed four letters painted onto the building: "A. J. G. A." Agence Jacques Grégoire Architecture. What was Mueller's connection?

Roger had no intention of approaching the well-illuminated gate. He flitted across the street to a more obscure section of fencing. He paused, watching and listening for any sign his presence was detected.

Silence.

A check of the barbed wire at the fence's top revealed no ceramic insulators. Good. He wouldn't get fried.

After a final glance around, Roger began scaling the chain-link. Praise God, the links weren't the small, tight variety. He could insert the toes of his shoes, but nothing more, so he relied mainly on the strength in his arms to pull himself up. At the top, he gingerly worked his way over the triple strands of barbed wire. Still no alarm. He dropped nimbly to the ground inside.

Doing his best imitation of a phantom, Roger drifted toward the warehouse. No windows to peek through. He spotted a door and headed toward it. Yet, even as his hand closed over the doorknob, its tarnished feel suggested no one used this entry. Sure enough, locked. Just as well, since doors were no doubt wired to a security system.

Roger eased his way left along the building to the corner. No entry or windows here, either. As he continued advancing, he wondered whether he should stop. Maybe find his way back to Baron? Report that he'd followed Kurt Mueller to this location and then turned tail and scurried home?

"I am an American Airman.
I am a warrior.
I have answered my nation's call...."

No way was he going to chicken out. Mueller was here for a reason. What was it?

When Roger reached the rear corner of the building, he could hear his own heart thudding as he leaned forward for a quick peek. A few lights revealed a parking lot. Half a dozen large trucks were parked with their noses toward the rear fence line. Another truck waited on a loading dock, where the overhead door stood open. Here and there outside the overhead door, barrels and wooden crates were piled on wooden pallets.

The river of light flowing from the overhead door ruled out the idea of simply walking over for a peek. He'd be spotted. However, the pallets loaded with cargo cast long shadows—decent hiding places for a closer look.

Just as Roger geared himself to step around the corner, a man exited the loading dock. Roger ducked backward, leaving only one eye to keep watch. The man sauntered to the cab of the truck in the loading area, opened the door, removed a clipboard, and then walked back into the building.

Once again, the coast was clear. Roger hustled forward with quick, silent steps, into the shadow cast by a pallet loaded with metal drums. When he reached the drums, he paused to listen. No shouts or whistles. Just the faint hum of machinery emanating from indoors. What kind of machinery would an architectural firm need?

Crouching behind the drums, Roger could make out something stenciled on the side of each: "T.R.III." The abbreviation meant nothing to him, but a movie line popped into his mind. "Soylent Green is people."

Despite the tension, Roger couldn't help grinning to himself. The Heritage Organization was weird. So were the die-hard Nazis who gave birth to it. But he hoped they weren't so bizarre as the Charlton Heston film where humans became tasty wafers in the food chain.

From his concealment, Roger was still at a poor angle to see inside the overhead doorway. He needed to move closer. Peering around a metal drum, he spotted the ideal vantage point. About thirty feet in front of him, a rectangular skid bearing a wooden crate about three feet high and six feet long stood, half in darkness, half in the light streaming from the building. Roger race-walked to it. Once his hands touched the rough-sawn boards of the crate, he exhaled the breath he hadn't realized he'd been holding. The crate bore the same stenciled abbreviation: "T.R. III."

Cautious as a burglar, he peeped around the side of the crate. A glimpse of the building's interior came into view: Electrical equipment. Tall units painted olive drab. The face of each unit bore a multitude of dials, switches, buttons, and red-and-green winking lights. The place resembled a factory more than a warehouse.

The only way to gain a direct look inside would require stepping— alone and unarmed—from the shadows and into the bright glare.

Foolhardy.

Where were Baron and his team? Roger closed a hand over the lump in his leather jacket's pocket. The ankle bracelet lay there. Why hadn't they traced the signal? Or maybe they were surrounding him right now and were simply in stealth mode, like himself?

An inspiration sprang to Roger's mind. This elongated crate. If he could squeeze inside it, he could safely observe between the slats on the front end, where the crate jutted into the light. No more dangerous peek-a-boo.

Roger straightened enough to study the crate's top. Instead of being one solid lid, the top consisted of parallel slats nailed down. He tried an experimental tug on one. The slat flexed but remained nailed in place. Same with the next board. And the third. Roger might have succeeded in wrenching them loose with his bare hands, but only at the risk of loud creaks or cracking wood. Instead, he pulled out his precision-crafted Swiss Army Champ knife. He chose the thicker of the two stainless steel blades and inserted it under the first wooden slat. Working gingerly, he pried loose the near end. Once he'd created a gap, he switched to the flathead screwdriver tool and succeed in working the slat loose. Encouraged, he repeated this trick on neighboring slats. However, when he lifted them and felt inside, his heart sank. Instead of a piece of machinery leaving airspace large enough for his body, the crate was packed tight with industrial-strength plastic bags.

He poked the nearest bag. Pellets? Capsules?

Noticing a dumpster alongside the building, Roger adjusted his plan. He lifted out a bag. Then another, and another. When he'd removed enough to wriggle into the crate, he ferried each bag to the dumpster, where he quietly deposited them. That done, he climbed into the crate and pulled the slats back down above him. Success. Now, even the most conscientious security guard couldn't spot him.

Not bad. Even Jaworski wouldn't have conjured up this trick.

Sure enough, once he'd slithered to the front end of the crate, Roger could see through the slits, directly into the overhead doorway.

Despite the decrepit and sleepy appearance from the road, the place hummed with glistening machinery. A forklift intermittently crisscrossed his line of sight as the dark-haired driver hoisted skids bearing boxes and transported them elsewhere. Other workmen in navy blue coveralls walked back and forth, tending the machines.

Two other men strolled into his line of sight. The first was a middle-aged man in casual business attire. The second figure was none other than Mueller, who glanced at his wristwatch as his companion gesticulated and evidently continued some sort of explanation.

Roger kicked himself for not keeping an Agency-issued bug in his pocket. With caution, he might have succeeded in sticking one onto Mueller's gray Mercedes.

Mueller was saying something while pointing out the open door. However, they stood too far away for Roger to make out the words, or even to determine which language they spoke.

The sound of a vehicle grew louder, and light flashed across the rear of the building. A panel van swung through the lot, then halted near the loading dock.

A latecomer to the party?

Mueller grinned and clasped his hands together, as if in triumph.

The van's driver—also in blue coveralls—stepped out and trudged into the building, where he joined Mueller and the other man. All three seemed immensely pleased about something. Mueller grinned as he pointed to his wristwatch.

Roger shifted in the cramped space. He'd seen enough. Time to beat a strategic retreat and report to Baron. If there was one person in the world Roger didn't want to see him, Kurt Mueller was the man.

But wait. The driver opened the rear of his panel van, and Mueller observed as the forklift approached, then deposited a crate into the vehicle. Next, Mueller's companion pointed directly to where Roger lay hidden.

Watching as the sturdy little vehicle made a beeline toward him, Roger cocked his head. *No. Don't tell me ...*

Sure enough—the twin forks slid beneath the crate containing Roger. It lifted his crate, and then rolled back to the panel van, where it deposited both crate and Roger inside.

All right, not cool, but don't panic. I can't jump ship in front of witnesses. Especially not Mueller. They'd be on my six in no time, probably with guns.

Turning around in his confined space wasn't easy, but Roger managed it. Now he could peer out the back of the van.

As soon as the coast is clear, I'll sneak out of here and—

Once more, the forklift hove into view with more cargo. Horrified, Roger watched as the driver eased another crate atop his own. Right onto the boards he had worked so hard to loosen.

Definitely. Not. Good.

Roger's last vision before the rear doors of the van banged shut was of Mueller shaking hands with his comrade. Then, utter darkness.

Seconds later, Roger's hiding place jostled as the vehicle shifted into motion.

No doubt about it. Jaworski never would have hidden in this particular spot.

CHAPTER 17

In the rear seat of Melissa's rented Peugeot, Katherine clung to the seat Baron occupied in front of her. Despite Melissa's high-speed maneuvers in and out of traffic on Highway D306, Katherine's position in the rear gave her time to reflect. These two still seemed convinced Roger was some sort of deranged killer. Yet, if they'd known him deep down, they'd realize Roger couldn't commit cold-blooded murder. No way he could betray his country. Sure, circumstantial evidence looked incriminating, but to her those photos of Uncle Kurt explained a lot.

Katherine's thoughts flashed back, remembering countless dates with Roger. She recalled the way he'd pulled a candle and matches from his pocket to provide romantic ambiance at Chico's Mexican restaurant. The loving tenderness when he gazed into her eyes. The night they'd sat, arm in arm, silently enjoying each other under a glorious full moon. Even though she knew Roger was sexually attracted to her, he'd remained a perfect gentleman. His kisses were passionate, but his touches never strayed into immorality. He simply wasn't the psycho they feared he was.

Katherine's heart ached at the realization of her own guiltiness. In her own private trial, she'd convicted Roger of caring too much for Sophie. The idea of him kissing another woman had sparked the green-eyed demon. So what if he'd kissed Sophie? He didn't know Katherine back then. Besides, hadn't she kissed other guys in her life? She wouldn't want her past dates locked underground, but that didn't mean she loved them. She'd allowed jealousy to hoist an icy barrier between herself and the one man she'd truly loved.

Seeing a gap in traffic, Melissa accelerated. She swerved around yet another slower moving auto. A sign reading Savigny-le-Temple flashed past.

Baron ignored blaring car horns as he spoke into his handheld radio. "Talk to me, Ben. What's the signal doing?"

Ben's voice crackled over the receiver. "The target has changed directions. Definitely headed back from the suburbs. I make his current location as northbound, Route N7."

Baron regarded Melissa. "Route N7. Can you get to it?"

She glanced at the Navigator mounted to the dashboard. "Easier said than done. From here, I'll either have to continue on D306 southeast to Melun to stay on fast roads, or else turn off the main route and navigate west using smaller roads—if that's even possible."

Not wanting to distract her, Baron keyed his radio. "Ben, plot our options. What's the best way for us to reach N7 from southbound D306?"

A pause, then Ben's voice returned. "Tough call. The distance will be shorter if you exit onto a smaller street and work your way west. What I can't calculate is the time factor due to local traffic and traffic lights."

"Give us the short route."

While Ben's voice fed directions to Melissa, Katherine studied the map on her iPhone. "Baron, Route N7 heads toward downtown Paris."

"It does, if we stay on it. Trouble is, there are plenty of east-west crossroads. He could change directions at the drop of a hat." He cursed. "If we'd known he would head that way, we could've intercepted him instead of driving all the way to the south side."

With her thumb and index finger, Katherine enlarged the map to view local details. "I don't get it. For the direction he's going, Route A6 would've been a quicker way to head north. It's practically parallel to N7, but wider and faster."

Then she saw it, the complex located dead ahead of Roger's current position.

"Orly Airport! It makes sense to travel north on N7 if you're headed to the airport."

Melissa muttered something. Following Ben's instructions, she'd run into thick traffic. They might as well be trailing a herd of elephants. The traffic light flashed red.

"No, no, no," Baron growled. "Ben, isn't there a better way?"

"Negative. Not from your current location."

Katherine considered. If Roger was, indeed, shadowing Uncle Kurt, he might be in a taxi. Or maybe he'd hot-wired a car—which he wouldn't do except in emergency. But what if he wasn't pursuing her uncle? What if the H.O. had spotted Roger and either beat him unconscious or shot him? Their trio could be tracking a corpse. But no. Uncle Kurt conducted business with meticulous attention to detail. If Roger were incapacitated, her uncle would've discovered the tracking device and destroyed it. The fact it still functioned suggested Roger was alive and wanted them to follow.

Ben's voice returned. "Heads up: The target has now left the main highway and is moving along a service drive outside of Orly Airport. Correction. The signal has now entered the territory of Orly Airport, but not through a main entrance."

Melissa gunned her way through the red light. Horns blasted, tires screeched, but at least they were through.

"I don't like it," Katherine said. "If Kurt Mueller is sneaking into Orly, he might be planning to exit the country."

"Possibly," Baron replied. "But I have to keep in mind Roger might be the person fleeing. He knows how to steal an aircraft. Don't forget, an assassin with his face murdered the French president. Taking the tracking device doesn't exonerate him."

"But ..." Katherine didn't finish her sentence. How could she explain her deep trust in Roger?

On the other hand, even she couldn't suggest a logical explanation for a shooter who looked like Roger's twin. Was it possible the H.O. brainwashed her boyfriend?

Once again, Melissa slammed on the brake as a traffic signal changed to red. This time, cross traffic remained heavy, with no gaps. "Why are all these people on the road? They should be home in bed."

Katherine voiced her conclusion. "Today's Friday. Everyone is out enjoying their weekend."

At last, the light turned green. Melissa punched the gas pedal. The tires squealed as they sped forward.

"Talk to me, Ben," Baron said. "What's happening?"

"The target is stationary on the rear of Orly Airport. Absolutely no movement. Wait—the signal is moving again. Slowly, slowly ... Oh man, you're not gonna like this."

Baron bolted upright in his seat, slamming the dashboard with his palm. "Don't tell me what I'm not going to like. Give me details."

Even over the radio, the sound of Ben taking a deep breath foreshadowed an answer none of them would enjoy.

Chapter 18

Trapped inside his wooden hiding place, Roger found no option except to wait in absolute darkness and accept developments as they happened. Despite the crash course in spy craft he'd received at the Farm, on-the-ground intelligence work would never be his forte. He'd much rather meet an enemy in the air than guess his way through cloak-and-dagger techniques.

Over the muffled sounds of the panel van, another noise caught Roger's attention—the roar of powerful engines increasing in volume, and then fading away.

The third airplane within several minutes meant an airport. Charles de Gaulle? Too far north. But a big city like Paris could support smaller airports for budget airlines and cargo.

Was the situation really out of control? His faith in God didn't permit him to believe it.

Lord, You see me even in darkness. I don't know whether I'm trapped in this crate because I messed up, or because You're doing something special. But please keep me alive. Don't let me do anything stupid. Please help Katherine, Baron, and the others to latch onto my signal—no matter where I end up.

The prayer completed, he decided to take stock. What useful items was he carrying? Front right jeans pocket—a metal ring holding the key to his Mustang convertible back home, a key to the apartment in Paris, plus his Swiss army knife. Right rear pocket—his wallet. It contained Euros, his driver's license, and a photo of Katherine, but nothing else. He'd emptied it before flying to Europe. Left rear pocket—a folded handkerchief. No tactical advantage there.

Roger concluded his inventory by patting the jacket pocket containing the ankle bracelet. But then he recalled stuffing Gerard's sunglasses into the jacket's inner breast pocket, which he rarely used. Anything else in there?

He removed the sunglasses and felt again. He extracted two items: one was a forgotten pack of chewing gum. The light fragrance of Juicy Fruit reached his nostrils. The other object felt like an ink pen.

Odd. He didn't normally carry pens.

Then he recalled—Flashy Al's Truck Stop, the brand-new service plaza where he'd stopped to buy a Coke after leaving the Farm. To promote their grand opening, Flashy Al's had given away free promos. At the cash register, Roger had accepted the gift of an ink pen. But wait, those weren't regular pens.

With his thumb, he clicked the button on top. Instantly the tip emanated steady white light, illuminating Roger's hand, the inside of the crate, and the plastic bags beneath him, which he now saw were orange.

"Flashy Al, bless your heart, wherever you are."

Possessing light provided a sense of control. Into his mind sprang a Bible verse. Christ had said, "I am the light of the world. Whoever follows me will not walk in darkness."

Did God work even in tiny ways, prompting Roger to accept an ink pen? Or was the pen sheer coincidence? Roger would ponder theology later. Right now, he wanted a closer look at this cargo.

Using his knife, he cut a three-inch slit into one of the bags. He inserted an index finger and fished out samples: blue-green pellets. At an inch long, surely they were too large to be medication.

He switched his knife from the blade to the file and scraped the surface of a pellet into powder. The odor struck him as vaguely fishy, like an aquarium.

The artificial thunder of another jet grew in intensity and then roared overhead, even louder than before. The van slowed, rounded a corner, proceeded at a slower speed, turned again then halted.

Roger clicked off his ink-pen light. If anyone peeked into the van's rear, a light glowing inside the crate would spell disaster.

A moment later, the vehicle rumbled forward in low gear then stopped again. The engine cut off.

What now?

The rear doors of the van swung open with double creaks. Soon Roger felt his miniature prison lifted once again by a forklift. The sound of another aircraft whooshed overhead and faded into the distance.

No. Don't tell me they're shipping this thing by air!

Despite Roger's mental protests, the slits in the crate revealed his portable prison being repositioned into what looked like the interior of a small cargo plane.

Cool night air filtered between the slats, but perspiration broke out on Roger's forehead.

God, this would be a fantastic time to work a miracle.

Mueller's voice, speaking German: "We're behind schedule. Strap everything down."

No voice replied, but someone must have reacted. Mueller blurted, "You know I don't understand sign language. Just follow instructions. If you have an urgent message, write it down so I can understand."

Sign language?

Wordlessly, someone began clunking around the cargo bay, apparently securing the freight with ratchet straps.

Roger's mind raced. Was there any trick he was overlooking? Perhaps a clever espionage method of extracting himself from this situation? He arched his back, performing a cramped pushup as he applied upward force to the slats he had loosened earlier. No go. The combination of the skid load on top plus the cargo straps guaranteed he wasn't getting out.

Mueller's voice sounded again. "Finished? Good."

Baron, this would be a great chance to capture Mueller.

But no cavalry charged in. Not so much as a verbal, "Where do you guys think you're going?"

Instead, the cargo bay door thumped shut.

Roger shook his head in disbelief when the aircraft reverberated from engines roaring to life. This was too weird to be happening.

God, when I said I'd rather meet the enemy from inside an airplane, this isn't what I meant.

Increased vibration indicated the aircraft was taxiing.

Uh, Scotty? I suggest you beam me out of here.

Maybe someday that memory would give Ben and Gerard a belly laugh. Assuming he escaped to tell the story. Poor Gerard. He crashed into the wall pretty hard.

The irony of the situation filtered into his thoughts. Baron had wanted to smuggle Roger out of Paris by airplane before anyone spotted his face. Now, here he was, getting smuggled out of Paris by airplane—an organization plane.

The aircraft braked, too abruptly in Roger's opinion, causing him to frown at the unseen pilot's skill.

Then came a sensation Roger knew perfectly. The aircraft moved again, swinging ninety degrees before coming to another complete stop. Even without seeing, he realized the airplane now sat at the beginning of a runway.

The engines revved louder. Inertia nudged him backward inside the crate as the aircraft increased speed. The vibration of wheels on runway vanished, and Roger's inner gyro felt the increased angle as the aircraft nosed skyward. In which direction? Too bad his key ring carried no compass.

With an effort, Roger flipped onto his back in the constricted space. Another unpleasant reality pressed into his mind: Although he didn't feel the need this minute, sooner or later nature would call.

No. He refused to think about it.

His next thought sobered him even more: Katherine. During this op, she'd been close geographically, but emotionally distant. No matter how hard he'd tried to formulate an explanation for his need to help Sophie, he'd never mustered the perfect words. Katherine could still interpret his actions as long-lasting affection for another woman. He sighed.

If anything permanent did happen to him, he sure would've liked a chance to set things straight.

CHAPTER 19

When a digital chime signaled the end of lunchtime, Sophie Gottschalk was still chewing. However, she dutifully stood and marched her tray to the return window, where she placed it on the plastic conveyor. First again. Excellent. Quick adherence to rules was becoming one more brick in her façade of submission. At all costs, no one must suspect her duplicity.

She strode to the exit door and stood, head angled toward the white vinyl floor, in what she hoped was the perfect picture of compliance.

How many weeks had passed since she'd embedded her covert message and its self-erasing program onto Baasch's flash drive? Six? Hard to say. Inside T.R. III, days were nearly as identical as the vanilla walls, ceilings, and floors.

Sure, the captors' faces would change as Dr. Baasch, the guards, and administrators rotated out for weekends or other downtime. Even Klimov—despite his pleasure in lording over "detainees"—regularly vanished for excursions to the outside world. In contrast, prisoners' days offered little variety.

Dr. Naresh Chakrala—the only prisoner here from India—approached and took a place beside her. What was he doing? Prisoners normally lined up single file to exit rooms. She'd never spoken with Dr. Chakrala, but Sophie knew him by reputation. As far as she could tell, Chakrala was a model prisoner. He replied respectfully to all staff in T.R. III and kept his eyes down during marches.

Dr. Chakrala feigned stretching his back as he leaned closer and whispered, "We must accept finite disappointment, but never lose infinite hope."

He kept his eyes averted.

"It's a quotation from the American, Martin Luther King, Jr." Chakrala stepped away, taking the position behind her.

Sophie reviewed the phrase in her mind. *We must accept finite disappointment, but never lose infinite hope.* The simple strength and eloquence of those words buoyed her drooping spirits. She'd needed such words. Each day she managed to dredge up inner strength to endure until bedtime. But, lately, her supply had been running dry, like a pump sucking air when the water level dropped. Chakrala's offering had dumped a bucket of life-sustaining hope into her needy reservoir.

Sophie half-turned, as if to see whether all the prisoners were now in line. "Thank you," she whispered, the way a ventriloquist speaks, without moving her lips.

Ting.

The door in front of her slid open. Sophie caught her breath. There stood the pitted face of Klimov, who tilted his head and grinned upon sight of the first prisoner in line.

"Why, Sophie. First to finish, and eager to return to work. I should've guessed."

Every syllable from Klimov's mouth puffed the mingled odors of garlic and cigarettes into her face. Sophie fought the urge to step backward. She loathed the security chief, but dared not insult him, not even with an instinctive reaction.

Klimov's grin disappeared as he eyed her frame. "You've lost weight. Eat more. I enjoy furniture with more upholstery." He placed his fingertips on her shoulder and ran them down to her hips.

Sophie struggled not to shiver at his touch.

He chuckled, puffing more fetid breath into her face. "Step into the corridor, please."

Klimov's order would've caught Sophie by surprise anytime. His use of "please" doubled the shock. Did he mean just her or the whole column queuing behind her?

Seeing her hesitate, Klimov stepped backward. He brusquely pointed, first to Sophie, then to the corridor floor beside him. "You. Here. Chakrala, you too. Step out."

She stepped out of the Refectory, confused but relieved Klimov hadn't planned to take her anywhere alone.

The doctor from India obeyed.

Klimov called to Vulture, the guard who stood inside the Refectory at the end of the queue. "I'm borrowing these two. A big mess in the lab needs cleaning up."

"Yes, sir," Vulture replied.

Klimov pointed. "That way."

Sophie marched. Not since the day of her arrival had she been in the corridor without a whole queue of prisoners. When she and Chakrala reached the stairwell at the end of the corridor, Klimov said, "To the bottom. Sublevel 5."

What? He'd told Vulture they were going to the laboratory, Sublevel 4. However, she dared not question the volatile Russian.

When they reached the lowest level of T.R. III, Klimov ordered a halt outside the unmarked double doors.

"I didn't want the rest of that rabble knowing where I'm taking you. Normally detainees are not allowed beyond these doors, but there's a special need. I chose you two because you're quick to obey. Also, I believe you can keep your mouths shut. You will clean up a mess. Afterward, I will take you back to your workstations. Understood?"

"Understood," Chakrala said.

Sophie nodded, but sincerely wished the security chief had trusted someone else.

"Then we can proceed." Klimov swiped his key card through the reader, then stepped back as the double doors swung outward.

In this section of corridor, the humidity instantly increased. The same peculiar smell as before permeated the place, a moist odor like a cross between that of a medical clinic and an aquarium. Even the visual appearance of Sublevel 5 changed. Instead of milk-white tiles, the floor became ordinary concrete, glistening with sealant.

Klimov stopped outside another set of double doors. He again swiped his key card, then stepped aside to motion Sophie and Dr. Chakrala forward when the doors opened.

Sophie stepped over the threshold and found herself in an enormous chamber, the longest she'd seen in T.R. III. Row upon row of upright Plexiglas tubes the size of old-fashioned telephone booths stretched as far as the eye could see. The nearer tubes were dark and empty, but farther down other tubes shimmered with yellowish liquid. Lab-coated workers bearing electronic tablets gave the newcomers a cursory glance as they examined digital readouts on the tubes and jotted notes.

From behind, Klimov leaned forward, inserting his head between hers and Chakrala's. "No matter what you see, you didn't see it. Loose lips will cost more than you want to pay."

A middle-aged man wearing wire-rim glasses approached. "These must be the maintenance volunteers."

Klimov laughed. "You have a flare for euphemisms, Dr. Richter. Yes, give them your orders. I guarantee they'll do a quality job."

The scientist named Richter pointed to an unmarked door. "That's the custodial closet. Each of you, fetch a mop and a bucket."

Again leading the way, Sophie opened the door. Like maintenance closets worldwide, this one contained a slightly organized assortment of cleansers, paper towels, replacement light fixtures, rags, and tools hanging on the walls—brooms, dust pans, mops, squeegees ... Ordinary. Nothing scary.

Sophie selected a mop and one of two janitorial buckets, the rolling type with a built-in wringer. Dr. Chakrala imitated her example.

"This way," Richter said. He set off at a brisk pace.

Sophie followed, but clumsily, since one wheel on her bucket refused to swivel properly and needed constant forcing. When she finally raised her eyes from the recalcitrant bucket, she gasped. Here, the tubes contained more than yellow liquid. Child-sized bodies floated in the fluid. Some male. Others female. Goosebumps rose on her neck and arms.

Klimov pressed the small of her back. "Follow the good doctor, my dear. Keep telling yourself it's only a dream." He laughed.

Sophie plucked up her courage and forced the rebellious bucket forward. The stubborn wheel personified her own apprehension about penetrating deeper into this watery morgue.

The farther the group walked, the larger the tubes and the bodies inside them became. Now the specimens appeared about thirteen or fourteen years old, visible only from the waist up since the lower halves of the larger tubes weren't transparent. Who were all these children? How had they died? And why were the scientists of T.R. III preserving their corpses?

As Sophie walked past a tube bearing a male with curling, blond hair, the floating figure jerked a hand toward her.

Startled, Sophie shrieked, stumbled, and tripped over her mop. She scrambled to her feet but backed away from the tube. "That thing's alive!"

Dr. Richter joined Klimov in laughing. "Of course, he's alive," Richter said. "It's why we're even here."

Klimov wiped away tears of laughter, an image Sophie had never expected from the security chief.

Richter stepped closer to the tube. "You will observe twitching and other movement, just like fetuses in the womb. Nothing to be alarmed about. This way."

He led the trio to an aisle where one tube stood dark and empty. Wickedly sharp cracks marred the Plexiglas. Around it, an enormous puddle of fluid emitted an odor reminiscent of urine mixed with bleach. Red splatters added a macabre, horror-movie effect.

Klimov whistled. "You reported 'a bit of a muddle.' Looks like your team experienced some excitement?"

Richter nodded. "One of the newer R-generation units. We've been attempting to define the DNA sequencing. Instead of correcting the speech impediment, we apparently instigated mental aberration. That's the theory. When he saw a duplicate of his face in the amnio chamber, he went berserk. Seized a fire ax and began hacking. He lopped off Hoffman's head, too, before we could disable him."

Klimov regarded Richter with a light akin to admiration. "You 'disabled' him, eh? I wouldn't have expected your scientific staff to handle that kind of emergency."

"It's not the first time we've experienced mental instability in a subject. We're going to miss Hoffman, though. He was an efficient assistant."

Sophie's mind reeled. *Amnio chamber?* Amniotic fluid? Instead of a morgue, this place was a human cloning center.

"Welcome to the Brewery," Klimov said to her and Dr. Chakrala. "Or the Hatchery. Or the Wizard's Cauldron. The official name is Incubation Department, but everybody seems to invent their own nickname."

"You're growing them from test tubes?" Dr. Chakrala blurted. "Incredible. Nowhere in the world has any cloning project approached this degree of success."

Sophie cringed. No one had granted Chakrala permission to speak. However, under the circumstances, Klimov didn't bat an eye. Richter basked in the praise.

"You've glimpsed only the tip of our biological iceberg. Our more recent graduates truly encourage us."

Now that the shock was past, Sophie, too, regarded the row of amnio chambers with wonder. "So amazing. I'd heard rumors the Chinese were experimenting with human cloning, but never did I expect any research team to achieve what you have here."

Richter scoffed. "The Chinese! We're aware of the Chinese efforts. In fact, our people have fed them disinformation to keep them following dead ends." He swept a grand hand toward the room. "Here is where the breakthroughs are happening."

Klimov grunted. "I'll be more impressed when you can teach them to talk. Until then, they remind me of robots created out of flesh and bone."

"In time, we will conquer the speech impediment. But for now, I need all this amniosyn mopped up. One hundred fifty liters of it. Slippery stuff, so watch your step."

"Amniosyn?" Sophie echoed as she pushed her mop into the puddle.

"Synthetic amniotic fluid. An in-house abbreviation. There's a sink against the wall. Dump the amniosyn there. Afterward, wipe down the affected floor with clean water. I'll bring you disinfectant. We require a contaminate-free environment."

"They'll do a proper job," Klimov promised.

After Richter walked away, Klimov crossed his arms and leaned against the nearest "amnio chamber." Sophie had never seen the beast so relaxed.

Contrary to his typical gruffness, Klimov said, "Interesting place, isn't it? They don't pay me enough to understand everything in here, but sometimes at night I stroll through and check out the latest crop."

As if inspired, Klimov straightened, then looked right and left. "Say, you two want to see something funny? With these larger specimens, you can spark funny reactions. Watch."

Under orders, Sophie and Dr. Chakrala had no choice but to cease mopping and give the security chief full attention.

Klimov rapped on the tube with his knuckles. "Hey, you in there. You awake?"

The male body inside didn't respond. It simply floated upright, facing the opposite direction.

Klimov tried again. He drew his pistol and tapped the tube with its grip. "Come on, you naked idiot. Wake up. Give a reaction."

A chill ran down her back. Although the science intrigued her, the moral and ethical ramifications appalled and frightened her. She didn't want this gun-toting gorilla tinkering with biology far beyond his primitive brain.

"Please, leave it alone."

Klimov ignored her. He rapped his pistol harder against the Plexiglas. "Hear me in there? Give us a show."

The figure in the tank convulsed, as if snapping awake. The head swiveled toward Klimov, although its now-open eyes remained confused, unfocused.

Sophie gasped. The mop slipped from her fingers.

Klimov chuckled. "What's the matter? Did our swimmer give you a wink? I couldn't blame him if he did."

Words fled. All Sophie could do was stare at the face of the being floating before her—a face like a youthful version of her American friend, Roger Greene.

Dr. Richter reappeared beside her. Her peripheral vision noted his return, but she couldn't tear her eyes from the face in the tube, which had closed its eyes again.

"He will soon be ready for harvest. He's the next generation. Soon he'll undergo an advanced program of education and training. Number 49 in that series is our best work yet."

"Even though Number 49 can't talk," Klimov deadpanned.

Irritation fluttered over Richter's face. "You always repeat the same thing. Cloning a human is more complicated than you'll ever know." Then, to Sophie and Chakrala, he said, "We learn from our mistakes. Perhaps you have seen Number 49 in the corridors? It's the same face."

"I don't believe so," Dr. Chakrala replied.

Sophie shook her head. She definitely would've noticed this face. At some point, the team from the Methuselah Project must have forwarded cell samples from Roger Greene to this lab.

"I believe Number 49 is away on assignment. But he'll be back soon. As scientists, you would be amazed."

Chakrala's face glowed. "So fascinating."

Sophie sensed the need to agree. Mustn't let them see how appalled she felt. "Groundbreaking. What discoveries you must have made."

Richter beamed. "The most significant breakthroughs have come in the past couple years." He looked at Klimov. "You know, with Hoffman dead, I'm going to need a new assistant. Possibly two."

CHAPTER 20

When the cargo plane carrying him touched down, Roger jerked awake. He blinked in the darkness and rubbed his eyes. How long had he been out?

Less than four hours. He'd stake his life on it. So how far from Paris could a small cargo carrier fly in roughly four hours?

He envisioned a map of Europe and mentally penciled a large circle around Paris. Westward wasn't likely, since that would plop them in the Atlantic Ocean. South, to Africa? Possible. Yet, his gut feeling was that North Africa wouldn't rate on the H.O.'s list of priorities. Northerly routes might position them in Iceland, Norway, or Sweden. On the other hand, heading east from Paris presented numerous possibilities, from Finland in the north to Turkey in the south. The Middle East? Probably too far.

He rubbed his eyes. Normally the effects of the Methuselah Project on his body demanded at least six hours of shuteye for him to function at decent efficiency. Eight hours were ideal. But for today, the three or four he'd grabbed during this unplanned flight would have to suffice.

When the cargo bay door opened, voices speaking accented English reached Roger's ears.

"We expected you hours ago."

"Not our fault. There was a breakdown at the manufacturing plant."

"Richter will be glad to see this lot. He's practically crying for it."

"Congratulations on the Paris job. Your boy did well."

"What? No Bordeaux wine?" A laugh. "We'd better refuel and send you back to get some!"

Roger listened intently, hoping for clues of his whereabouts. Everyone spoke English, although with accents ranging from British to Slavic. So where on earth was he?

Once again, the crate containing him jiggled, then lifted from the deck of the cargo bay. Someone was easing it out with a forklift. Roger peered between the slats. Although darkness reigned, a bright moon plus artificial lights revealed this was no commercial airport. Indeed, trees—some sort of evergreens—hemmed the solitary runway.

When the forklift swung a one-eighty-degree turn, Roger caught his breath. Despite the meager lighting, a nearby hillock definitely ended in a vertical cutaway. Jutting from it was the tail of an aircraft. In the darkness beyond, the silhouette of an identical hill showed against the night sky.

Russia?

As part of his Air Force training, Roger had seen photographs of Soviet-era aircraft hangars disguised to look like natural hills. Grass and bushes grew from soil that had been bulldozed atop concrete hangars. Although the tactic hadn't fooled Aerial Intelligence, camouflaged hangars did render the presence of aircraft much less obvious, especially in isolated areas. And in theory, the cushioning afforded by such earthworks provided the hangars an extra measure of protection from bombardment.

"Standard procedure?" a voice asked.

"Yes, the usual. Unless you really do discover French wine. In which case we will celebrate first, and distribute cargo later."

Roger continued peering out the gaps of his wooden prison as the forklift carried him toward the nearer camouflaged hangar. Few bulbs illuminated the interior. Good. The less light, the better. The minute no one was watching, he would bolt out of here and make a beeline for the woods. He'd already seen plenty to report to Baron.

But now the forklift rounded the corner into the hanger, and Roger's blood froze. The feeble light inside revealed what looked to be an American F-35 Lightning II.

No way.

His mind scrambled to comprehend. Sure, the U.S. sold F-35s to other countries, but strictly to friendly NATO allies. From what he'd seen and heard, all these clowns were in league with the Heritage Organization. So how did a shadowy coalition get their mitts on pricey American hardware?

In one glimpse, Roger's sense of duty shifted. In France, Baron had been on the verge of shipping him stateside, which wouldn't help anyone. This unexpected trip as a stowaway wasn't helping Sophie, wherever she was. However, as an American airman, he was staring at proof that American military equipment was falling into dangerous hands.

Questions raced through his mind. *Do I even have the right to run away? Shouldn't I reconnoiter, find out what's going on?* For the second time within twenty-four hours, lines from the "Airman's Creed" flowed through his thoughts:

I am an American Airman.
Guardian of Freedom and Justice,
My Nation's Sword and Shield,
Its Sentry and Avenger.
I defend my Country with my Life.

Roger sucked a deep breath and slowly exhaled it. He couldn't leave. Not yet. As a U.S. airman, he'd expected to defend his nation from a cockpit. But aircraft or no, he'd vowed to protect his country. Even—the thought sent chills through him—if it resulted in getting captured and locked inside another H.O. cage.

His mind flashed back to the underground bunker in Germany, where they'd confined him for decades. He'd nearly gone insane. Only by God's grace did he escape with his mind intact. Despite his Air Force and CIA training, the possibility of getting caught and imprisoned a second time caused his hands to tremble.

Get a grip. These are the cards you were dealt.

As the forklift rolled him deeper into the hangar, Roger took a long, appraising look at the F-35. Although an untrained eye could never detect the differences, subtle nuances in the control surfaces verified this was definitely an F-35 Lighting II, not the secret F-35 Shadow. So the H.O. had gotten hold of American hardware—but not the best.

Roger's options remained few. Still, he did have one or two tactics he could employ, if only he could muster the guts.

The driver halted and lowered his load in a small room. However, instead of removing the second pallet of cargo atop Roger's, he backed away and drove off. Roger remained trapped.

Unwilling to leave anything to chance, he pulled his Swiss army knife from his pocket and selected the flathead screwdriver.

I've got to get out of here—now.

However, the forklift returned and deposited more freight alongside Roger's crate before its motor cut off. Multiple pairs of footsteps approached. A voice spoke in Russian, "*Ostorozhno. Dveri zakryvayutsya. Sleduyushaya stantsiya—'Ad.'*"

His comrades guffawed.

Thanks to his Russian lessons with Captain Shevchenko back at Eglin Air Force Base, Roger translated the phrase: "Caution. The doors are closing. Next stop—Hell." It sounded like a twisted version of a train conductor's announcement.

A door did, indeed, clunk shut. When Roger sensed himself descending, the truth slammed home. This freight wasn't going to be stored in the hangar. It was descending to somewhere subterranean.

Roger's hands curled into fists. After being held prisoner for decades inside a bunker-laboratory beneath the estate of Otto Kossler in Germany, the very word *underground* gave him goose bumps. Now, sliding downward into the earth made his stomach queasy. He'd never admitted the new phobia, not even to himself. But his skin broke into pinpricks of perspiration.

Stop it! You're a fighter pilot. It's just a building with dirt on top.

At last, the elevator thumped to a halt. The men riding down with him sauntered away, their Russian jokes and conversation receding with them.

Was he alone?

Not yet. A humming sound approached. An electrically powered lift was removing freight from the elevator. When at last the pallet resting atop his own crate was lifted and shuttled away, Roger rejoiced. He hadn't drunk so much as a drop of water in the past ten or so hours. Worse, he hadn't visited a restroom for the same period.

Come on, come on.

However, the solitary driver took his time as he hoisted and rearranged loads. Twice he ferried away cargo to another location, but each time he returned too quickly for Roger to escape.

Finish up then scram out of here!

Lastly, Roger's own crate raised from the elevator floor, then hummed down a corridor. Relief swept through Roger when his crate settled to the floor and the forklift glided away.

Roger listened, straining to catch even the faintest noise above the beating of his own heart. Was the driver gone?

After he had waited and listened about three minutes, Roger pushed up the ends of the wooden slats he had loosened earlier. Silent as a cat, he eased out of his prison, and then replaced the slats. At a glance, the crate appeared intact.

Not all the overhead lights were on, yet this place was definitely bulging with supplies. Industrial-strength steel shelving stockpiled material in a wide variety of containers.

Roger prowled to the end of the aisle, then down the next one. He repeated this process until, several aisles later, a most welcome sight came into view: a door with the silhouette of a male figure on it. Hallelujah!

This probably wasn't the first time somebody thanked God for a restroom, but it was Roger's first.

When he pushed inside, he found a combination restroom-locker room. After making sure he was alone, he blissfully used the last stall. Even when flushing, Roger depressed the handle only slightly in order to refresh the water unobtrusively. After rinsing his hands at a sink, he twisted his head and gulped cool water.

Next, the locker area attracted his attention. Both in Paris and in the hangar above, the rank and file H.O. workers wore navy-blue coveralls. Might there be a spare pair?

The first lockers he opened were empty. Past those, however, sat a large canvas hamper mounted on wheels. Eureka! It was filled halfway with laundered and folded coveralls.

Roger picked out a pair his size and doffed his leather jacket. The instant he started unbuttoning his shirt, the door behind him creaked open.

Roger whirled. Facing him was a man dressed in these same navy-blue coveralls—but with a face identical to his own. Judging by the expression, the newcomer was just as astonished to see Roger's face.

Without a word, the other man squinted, as if sizing up the situation. He cocked his head and made several gestures with his hands. When Roger didn't respond, the man's eyebrows lowered. He repeated the sign language with obvious impatience.

Roger couldn't sign. He bluffed by shaking his head.

The light of suspicion flashed across the other man's face. He might not be capable of speech, but he was thinking—and quickly. He eased backward a step. His eyes strayed to the exit.

When the double turned to escape, Roger blurted, "No, you don't." He body-slammed the man from behind, ramming him into a sink.

Roger's foe grunted, then twisted like a cobra and attacked faster than anticipated. The man aimed a fist at Roger's face, missed, but then landed a solid punch to Roger's stomach.

Roger changed tactics, now assuming the stance of a boxer. He had shadowboxed before. But this time the shadow had come to life—and was returning rock-hard blows like a pro.

The two circled in silence, each offering jabs and feints as they probed one another's skill and reactions.

"What's the matter?" Roger taunted. "Cat got your tongue?"

His mirror image didn't utter a word, but confusion clouded his expression.

The pair continued circling, each hunting for weakness. Then, while the double was facing away from the shower area, Roger looked over the man's shoulder and blurted. "Now, Joe—hit him!"

Almost to Roger's surprise, his opponent fell for the oldest trick in the book. Just as the man twisted to see the non-existent Joe, Roger smashed a right fist to his opponent's floating rib. His left caught the man under the chin with an uppercut that literally lifted him from the floor. The double stumbled backward.

With a *whomp* like a watermelon slamming onto concrete, the double's head struck the floor. He lay there, eyes closed and unmoving.

Roger placed a hand over his throbbing midsection. "You actually fell for that? You might be handsome, but you're too naive."

Even now, thanks to the amazing recuperative powers granted by the Methuselah Project, the ache in Roger's stomach eased then disappeared. He pressed a finger against the man's neck. Blood still pulsed in the carotid artery.

So, was this the shooter from Paris? Why did he look like Roger's twin? If his face was cosmetically altered, the plastic surgeon achieved an incredible likeness. But why?

Now a moral dilemma presented itself. If this were a Hollywood thriller, the hero might give the double's head a sharp twist to snap his neck. Killing the man would silence him. Yet, even though Roger had no qualms about killing in self-defense, the fight was over. Killing an unconscious man would be murder, not self-defense. Roger wasn't a perfect Christian, but he knew the Ten Commandments. "Thou shalt not kill."

He couldn't do it.

However, this turn of events presented possibilities for exploring. This guy was a normal part of the underground landscape here. Roger removed his double's clothing, then exchanged it for his own, including his brown leather jacket. That done, he pulled out his pocketknife and the tracking bracelet. He'd feared tracking technology long enough. If he wanted Baron to find him, he needed to embrace the gizmo.

To be on the safe side, he gagged his unconscious double and hogtied his hands to his ankles behind him. Lastly, he hid the body beneath a layer of coveralls in the hamper.

*   *   *

When Roger ventured from the warehouse and into the corridor, his instincts for self-preservation urged him back to the elevator. He'd already seen plenty to tell the CIA. Also, he wanted a closer look at the F-35. Perhaps he could find a clue to who possessed it before the H.O. got their paws on it?

Instead, he turned the opposite direction. With his counterpart bound, gagged, and concealed, he now had a prime opportunity to infiltrate this place. The fact it was constructed below ground didn't guarantee this was the underground prison Sophie mentioned. Yet, if there was even one chance, he must learn what he could.

However, no sooner had he ventured through a pair of double doors than a familiar German accent rang out. "Ah, there you are."

Descending a stairwell was none other than Kurt Mueller, the man who had tried to murder him in Indianapolis.

Roger tensed, ready for fight or flight. But Mueller's hands bore no weapons. In fact, the man's demeanor suggested simple weariness.

"I've been searching for you. All done in the warehouse?"

Forcing himself to relax, Roger nodded. If the fake Roger couldn't speak, then he wouldn't either.

"Excellent. I'm exhausted, but I wanted a few words with you before I sleep. I'll accompany you to your quarters."

Roger nodded again. He had no inkling where "his quarters" might be, but evidently Mueller did. He fell into step as they mounted the steps together.

"You performed admirably in Paris. Good, clean shots from a discreet distance. Even though a stray security camera captured your image, you executed your mission efficiently." He laughed. "Executed. I don't usually pun."

Roger nodded even though he felt like slugging Mueller.

"Anyway, I applaud you again. As planned, our H.O. man has been sworn in as president of France. Thanks to you, another piece of master strategy has fallen into place."

As they walked, Roger memorized the route. Surely, other exits besides the freight elevator existed. But in case of emergency, he needed to know the way back to the warehouse.

Mueller led the way to an elevator and punched the button. Inside, Roger casually studied the elevator panel. Five levels, starting with 1 at the top and descending to Sublevel 5, the bottommost. They stood on Sublevel 4, and Mueller pressed the button marked 1.

Roger filed away each tidbit of information.

"Next, we have another assignment for you. This time right here in Ukraine."

Ukraine, eh? Sophie's secret communiqué to the CIA stated she was somewhere in Eastern Europe. Could this really be the same place? Such a coincidence struck him as too amazing for hope. Yet, he had prayed for God's intervention. Wasn't God powerful enough to transport Roger here, even though he hadn't known the way?

"I won't burden you with the political ramifications. Suffice it to say the president of Ukraine, too, has become expendable. He's stubborn, an obstacle to the new global order. We need him removed."

The elevator halted at "Sublevel 1." They stepped into a vanilla-colored corridor.

"Of course, you can't use the same rifle as in France. Instead of the German PSG1, I've decided to equip you with an SKS-45 semiautomatic carbine. The Soviets took it out of frontline service decades ago. These days, it is generally a ceremonial rifle. Yet, with a new scope, you'll find it more than adequate for the mission. First, though, we will position provocateurs. They will incite confusion with a grassroots call to reunify Ukraine and Russia. We will manipulate the masses. Once we have laid the groundwork, your bullet will facilitate the transition."

Mueller halted at a door marked 49, where he placed a hand on Roger's shoulder. "So, once again you will nudge the world a step closer to unified control, bringing harmony where there is now chaos. Rest for now. Monday you shall practice with the SKS-45."

Roger gave a confident nod, hoping he correctly imitated his mute double. Would anything else be expected? A salute?

Mueller frowned. "Well, are you going to enter?"

Roger looked at door 49. He almost extended his hand for the doorknob but caught himself. There wasn't one. Instead, an electronic slot on the wall awaited a keycard. He faked a yawn while searching the pockets of his double's coveralls. Bingo. A plastic card with a magnetic strip. He swiped it through the slot.

Ting. Door 49 slid open.

"Sleep, Number 49. You are more fatigued than I realized."

Roger stepped inside. When the door shut behind him, he sighed with relief. "Thank You, Lord, for getting me this far."

Chapter 21

In the Incubation Department, his assigned tablet in hand, Dr. Naresh Chakrala paused beside Sophie. "A nice development for us, isn't it? Definitely a step up the ladder from where we were."

Only two days into their new work assignment, and he was grinning like a Cheshire cat?

Sophie lowered her voice. "I like the improved food, the private quarters, and the chance to learn about their breakthroughs in cloning. But I'd be lying if I said this place doesn't give me the creeps."

"Some would call it coincidence we were brought here on the very day Dr. Richter lost his assistant. Positive karma, I say."

He turned to go, but Sophie was curious.

"Were you in the H.O. for long before they brought you here?"

Chakrala's dark eyes flashed with anger. "I have never been a member of their organization. A colleague of mine at Previon Pharmaceuticals—it's a biotech company in India—he's a member. He received permission to recruit me. By the time I declined, I had learned too much. Three men jumped me on the street, threw me into a car, and gave me an injection. I woke up in an airplane on the way here."

With that, Dr. Chakrala—still wearing ankle chains despite new duties—tapped the electronic tablet and clinked away on whatever task Richter had given.

Sophie watched him go. Was Chakrala Hindu or Buddhist? Now that she thought about it, she wasn't positive she knew the difference.

There's no karma. There's a God who created the universe. And even though people ignore Him or use His name as a curse, He cares. He helped Roger. Perhaps He will help me.

Sophie returned to the amnio chamber she'd been tasked with monitoring. Electrolytes in the fluid registered normal. So did the protein and carbohydrate levels. But the lipids and phospholipids? She frowned. Percentages lingered at the lower end of the scale. She entered a note on her tablet so Richter or one of his associates could investigate. Not that she wanted to aid the Heritage Organization. But no doubt they were observing her and Chakrala during this probation as "detainee assistants."

The main downside of these new duties was the personal escort she got before and after work. She hoped today's post-shift escort would be Vulture or any of the normal guards. Too often, Klimov accompanied her. How long could she evade his crude advances without angering him?

Intriguing though Richter's discoveries were, Sophie remained a woman first, scientist second. As a woman, she now stepped backward and pondered the amnio chamber and its pint-sized occupant. This wasn't normal. Babies were meant to develop inside a loving mother's womb. A fetus deserved a comforting, protective amniotic sac to grow in, not a rigid Plexiglas container. Why, nearly a hundred years ago a psychologist—what was his name? Harlow?—had demonstrated how rhesus monkeys given a wire monkey mother instead of a normal one became emotionally disturbed. Who could guarantee these shiny tubes weren't inculcating emotional deficiencies? Maybe it explained why Richter's clones couldn't speak.

Her mind returned to the row of chambers bearing "Roger lookalikes," as she thought of them. When had samples of his cells been brought here? Why clone him? She wanted to go and stare but didn't dare.

She mentally repeated her mantra. *Just do the job. Survive.*

Neither Richter nor Klimov seemed aware of her connection with the Methuselah Project. No wonder. With so many prisoners in T.R. III, which of the limited staff had time to study the particulars of each prisoner's file? To them, she was just another organization scientist who had foolishly gone astray and required being "reassigned" to Talent Redemption III.

The fetus's heart monitor caught her eye. According to the digital readout, this one's heart was pumping more slowly than normal. Sophie had never been pregnant, but her maternal instincts kicked in.

Poor thing. She was struggling. But why?

"Easily eighty percent of our subjects don't survive to maturity," Richter had said. "Part of our goal is to learn why so many self-terminate."

Of course, another of his goals was to discover why not a single clone could speak.

The tiny pink body drifted in its watery world. Eyes closed and one dinky thumb in its mouth, this unborn female looked so innocent, so frail. If she lived, what future task would the H.O. assign her? Suicide bomber?

Revulsion twisted Sophie's stomach. Although she dared not express it, everything she learned added fuel to her hatred for this insidious organization. She had despised "Talent Redemption III" for its inhumane treatment of adult intelligentsia. Now she despised it all the more for its clinical disregard of human dignity. If she couldn't escape, she'd fight back. Not today, maybe not tomorrow, but eventually, she'd plunge a dagger into the heart of the Heritage Organization.

Might this new assignment reveal a way of escape? So much time had passed since she planted her coded message on Baasch's USB drive. Time to face reality—the Americans weren't coming. Maybe Baasch never inserted it into a computer with Internet access. Even more likely, her homemade program could've failed to launch. Even if it did, the CIA might have updated its telephone number since the day she memorized it. Or maybe this underground facility was simply too well hidden for the Americans? After all, even a high-tech reconnaissance satellite couldn't peer below ground.

Don't yield to despair. What did Chakrala say? "We must accept finite disappointment, but never lose infinite hope."

God had helped Roger Greene through worse than she was enduring. God would help her, too. She felt sure. Only how? More importantly, when?

CHAPTER 22

Security Chief Nikita Klimov was in love. Sitting with legs crossed on the bed in his quarters, he lovingly caressed the pixelated camouflage stock of his new AK-12 assault rifle. He slid his fingers across the top, along the Picatinny rail, which enabled quick and easy installation of day and night sights. Another Picatinny rail on the underside provided mounts for any tactical accessory he might wish—vertical grip, flashlight, laser ...

Klimov recalled his instant enchantment the day the Kalashnikov Concern unveiled an AK-12 at Moscow's "Army-2017" Military-Technical Forum. With every reply the Kalashnikov reps gave to his questions, the stronger grew his lust for this upgrade from the AK-47. Yes, he'd known he must possess an AK-12. Now—courtesy of his superiors in the organization—this one belonged to him.

"Three modes," he repeated aloud. "Single shot, two-round bursts, and fully automatic." He hefted the weapon vertically and pressed his lips to its barrel. Just as tenderly, he wiped any moisture from the spot with his camo shirtsleeve.

"Such a sexy weapon should have love-inspired name." What moniker would suit his latest acquisition?

He considered naming it "Sophie" in honor of the German detainee who had caught his eye. Someday, he would have her in his quarters. Whatever Nikita Klimov wanted, Nikita Klimov got. Sophie Gottschalk would be his for the plucking whenever he tired of the game. Lately, though, she had become skinnier, bonier. Even worse, "Sophie the Scientist" had not smiled and ingratiated herself the way others had done. No, Sophie's name wasn't worthy of such a fine killing machine as the AK-12.

His mind drifted back to the North Caucasus, to his days in the 10th Spetsnaz Brigade headquartered in Molkino. One weekend he had met a sensuous blonde in the bar. What was her name? Hard to recall, since Stolichnaya vodka had flowed freely. And why not? He'd been a soldier of the Russian Federation and deserving of proper entertainment.

Details of the evening remained foggy, but wow, she'd been a beauty. Cunning, too. He still admired her spunk in disappearing with his wallet before dawn's early light. Of course, she'd given him no choice but to track her down and break her arm. Nobody made a fool of Nikita Klimov.

Marusya? That was her name!

He hefted the AK-12 again. "No doubt, you and I will enjoy many adventures, my hot little Marusya."

Klimov yearned to break it down, to touch and wipe each component to perfection. But what was the point? He'd cleaned the rifle just yesterday but still hadn't fired it. T.R. III—the place was as challenging as a kindergarten. Not like his days in Chechnya, where he and his boys had fought hard, drank harder, and reveled in the soldierly life. Ah, the glory days!

Klimov cradled the weapon across his lap. "My Marusya. At times I wish I were back in the army. Even 'volunteering' in Donetsk or Lugansk. You and I could teach those amateurs how to spill blood."

A knock on the door interrupted Klimov's reverie.

"Who is it?" he barked.

"General Wolf," came the muffled reply.

Resentment evaporated. Klimov leaped from the bed and activated the door. When it slid into the wall, there indeed stood General Wolf, the organization boss who had finagled this assignment for him.

Klimov saluted.

General Wolf returned a perfunctory salute. "May I come in?"

"Of course." Klimov hurried to remove his half-finished bottle of Nevskoe Imperial Lager from the table. With a rag, he wiped away the glistening ring it left.

"Something to drink, General Wolf?"

Wolf stood, glancing around. First, he studied the mounted display of pistols adorning one wall. Even though the organization had provided many of them, Klimov basked in the tacit praise of Wolf's admiring nod.

Next, the general pointed at the AK-12 atop the rumpled bedclothes. "I see you've received the latest toy. I trust you find it satisfactory?"

"More than satisfactory. It's a remarkable piece of equipment."

Wolf stepped closer to a group photograph mounted over Klimov's bed. "I recognize several of your past comrades. Mikhailov. Nikolaev. Dmitriyev. Why, is that Vanya Voronin winking from the back row? I've never seen Voronin caught on film."

Klimov removed the photo from the wall for Wolf to inspect it more closely. "It's Voronin, all right. He hated cameras. Ducked his head whenever one of the boys pointed one. But he was in rare mood. We had just blasted a stronghold of Chechen rebels into dust."

For the first time since entering, General Wolf allowed himself to grin. "The joy of victory. Only fighting men understand." He handed the photograph back, then pulled one of the two chairs from the miniature table. "Let's talk."

Klimov yanked out the opposite chair and sat. "I hope there are no problems?"

"Possibly no problems, but challenges continue to arise. Ever since an American guinea pig escaped Laboratory 1, we've been extinguishing one brush fire after another. It's a messy, tedious chore. But you're probably not familiar with Laboratory 1?"

Klimov tilted back in his chair. "Not specifically. It was home to the organization's earliest experiments. Somebody escaped."

"The whole affair has become quite the fiasco. Which brings me to this visit. Ever since the American subject escaped, we have been forced to reorganize entire departments."

Klimov searched his memory. "But didn't the escaper commit suicide? Seems I vaguely recall—"

With a shake of his head, Wolf cut off Klimov's words. "That's what was reported at the time. We had grave doubts then, and now we know it was a subterfuge. Ever since, the intelligence communities of the United States, England—even upstart little Israel—have been diligently searching, inquiring, probing, trying to locate an entity that can only be the Heritage Organization."

Klimov narrowed his eyes at the general. When Wolf had granted him the title of Security Chief in T.R. III, he'd promised the worldwide tentacles of the Heritage Organization were achieving nothing less than spectacular success—and invisibly to the world's existing governments. "I don't like it."

"Neither do the Directors. Twice they've met to assess the damage and determine our best responses."

"And?"

"Inconclusive. Greene is alive. We are convinced of it. However, where and what he's doing is uncertain. In addition, there is a female who broke from our ranks. Evidently Greene seduced her into assisting him."

"Greene?" Klimov repeated.

"Roger Greene was the American's actual name. We don't know what alias he operates under."

"How does all this involve me?"

"It might not affect you directly. But the Council has instructed each of us sub-directors to visit every organization facility. We're underscoring the dangers. We must heighten our vigilance and leave nothing to chance. For example, I assume curious wanderers occasionally explore the forest?" Wolf pointed a finger upward, toward the surface.

"It happens. My people observe them, making sure they do nothing suspicious. Typically, they explore the complex at Duga-3, or the deserted buildings in Pripyat, then hike back out of the Exclusion Zone."

"Glad to hear it," the general said. "But from this point forward, we assume nothing about interlopers' intentions. With the exception of official tourist buses, visitors must be neutralized."

"Neutralized—how?"

The corners of General Wolf's lips curled upward. "You're creative. I leave it you. But if a curiosity seeker happens to have an accident—say, falls down an empty elevator shaft in Pripyat and breaks his neck—it would be a pity. But accidents happen."

The general lifted Klimov's new weapon from the bed and admired its craftsmanship. "On the other hand, if you ever spot intruders who seem to be prowling in search of this facility, consider yourself assigned to target practice." He tossed the AK-12 to Klimov. "Just dispose of corpses in a way they won't be found."

The security chief felt the smirk growing on his face. Now Wolf was speaking his language. "Thank you, sir. By coincidence, I'd been thinking this job is too quiet lately. This twist opens new possibilities for entertainment."

Wolf laughed. "I knew you would grasp the situation, Nikita. If meddlers disturb your territory, happy hunting."

Klimov's heart swelled to the bursting point. For the first time ever, General Wolf had addressed him by his first name.

"Before I leave, let me verify you're not going soft." Wolf placed his right elbow on the table, his hand open.

Pleased at the challenge, Klimov placed his own elbow on the table and gripped Wolf's hand. The general's palm felt tough, almost like dry leather fitted over steel.

"One, two ... go!"

Klimov urged all his might into his forearm. Last year, he'd lasted sixty seconds before the general bested him.

Both hands trembled as each man grunted and dug deep for energy. Some moments, Wolf gained a couple of centimeters. Then Klimov pushed him back. By the time three minutes had passed, Klimov felt beads of perspiration dotting his brow. Every muscle from his wrist to his shoulder screamed for relief.

With a shout and an unexpected burst of vigor, Wolf pressed the attack. Klimov's arm ground backward until the back of his hand touched the tabletop.

"Excellent," Wolf declared. "You held out much longer than last time."

Klimov massaged his aching arm. "Perhaps next time I'll win."

Wolf chuckled. "I admire a man who works toward goals." He stood and stepped to the door.

A final thought popped into Klimov's mind. "When you get back to Kiev, give my greetings to Jaeger."

Wolf paused. His lips pressed together. With a poker face he said, "Unfortunately, Jaeger is no longer with us. He suffered a coronary attack. Totally unexpected."

The mental picture of Jaeger's inert body in a coffin deflated Klimov's jubilant mood. More than once, he and Jaeger had enjoyed a round of Friday night bars and Ukrainian women. "Sorry to hear it. Jaeger was a worthy comrade."

Wolf's eyes remained on his own. "Yes. A shame."

CHAPTER 23

Roger paced inside the private quarters of "Number 49." What now? The bed and its plump pillow attempted to seduce him, but he dared not lie down. After the scant hours of shuteye aboard the airplane, he might conk out for longer than he could afford. His thinking already felt fuzzy, as if he had cotton stuffed into his cranium.

He shook his head. Must concentrate.

Today was Saturday, very early. Above ground, the October sun probably hadn't cleared the horizon. He was far from help, with no hope of contacting friendly forces. Possibly, this was the same underground complex where Sophie was imprisoned. But maybe not.

In his favor was the fact "Number 49" was a normal part of this organization community. Theoretically, Roger could poke around without arousing suspicion. But for how long? Most likely, Kurt Mueller would sleep for hours. Yet, three levels below, an android, or clone, or whoever he was lay bound, gagged, and covered with uniforms in a canvas laundry hamper. How long would he remain safely unconscious?

In the U.S., Saturdays were free days for many employees. A chance to sleep in. If the same were true here, this pre-dawn hour might be an ideal time to reconnoiter.

Roger stopped pacing and ransacked the efficiency apartment. He opened every drawer, every cupboard and closet. Not one weapon to be found. In fact, this Number 49 evidently lived a Spartan existence. Roger found no music, no reading material, and no indication of interests or hobbies. Not so much as a single decoration.

The guy might look like him, but he sure didn't think like him. Didn't he have a personality?

Now Roger liked his predicament even less. Fact: if he stayed here, he would be discovered and captured. Yet, leaving the compartment unarmed might speed up capture. For defense, he possessed only his fists —and his wits.

Wait. Not true. He raised his eyes to the ceiling. *Dear God, this isn't the first time I've been underground and in a pickle. You've helped me before. Please help again.*

Whether he was ready or not, this predicament required action. Roger stepped into the corridor. Deserted. Only the whisper of air circulating through overhead vents disturbed the silence.

He already knew a myriad of living quarters lined the corridor the way he'd come. Roger turned in the opposite direction. Time to explore.

When he reached the end of the passageway, the final door bore the numeral 100. From there, the corridor made a ninety-degree turn to the right. Succeeding doors bore English words instead of numbers: "Polyclinic," "Director," "Assistant Director." "Administrative Office."

Roger swiped his key card at the Administrative Office door. Instead of a green light and a *ting*, nothing happened. Roger swiped again. No response. Apparently, his lookalike didn't rate carte blanche clearance.

Would anyone notice his unsuccessful attempts? The notion prompted his heart to beat faster, especially since the neighboring door read, "Security Chief." Roger hurried past. Whoever the security chief might be, this wasn't the ideal moment for introductions.

By the time Roger finished navigating all of Level 1, he realized this place wasn't the complicated maze he'd imagined. This level was shaped like a digital figure 8—an enormous rectangle bisected with a cross passage in the middle. In opposite corners of the rectangle, two stairwells descended into the bowels of the place. But the stairwells were redundant, possibly a safety feature, since elevator doors stood at the center of the cross-passage.

Outside the elevator, Roger swiped his keycard through the slot. Obediently, the twin doors began sliding apart. He tensed. In Indianapolis, elevator doors had once opened to reveal an organization hit man, who shot him from point-blank range. The memory of the slug punching into his shoulder prompted a wince. But this elevator stood empty. He entered and mashed the Sublevel 2 button.

Prowling the belly of the beast.

Incredible that he hadn't run into anyone. Thank God, these people enjoyed Saturday morning sack time.

He glanced up and spotted a security camera in the elevator's corner. Did a live person monitor the cameras 24/7? If so, he had to trust no one would think it strange to see Number 49 roaming at this early hour. Otherwise, Roger's excursion could end swiftly. He struck a casual stance until the doors reopened.

On Sublevel 2, some doors bore no identification whatsoever. But then he found a series of doors set farther apart. Signs designated them Barracks 1, Barracks 2, Barracks 3, and Barracks 4. Barracks for whom —prisoners, or organization workers? He bypassed them. Next came a solitary door marked "Refectory."

What was a refectory? On a whim, he swiped his keycard.

When the door tinged open, Roger at last found people—lots of them. In what appeared to be a cafeteria were long rows of tables where yellow-clad men and women ate from trays. A few regarded him with curiosity. Most busied themselves with their meal and conversation. Beneath the tables, shiny chains connected each prisoner's two ankles, for prisoners they clearly were.

Roger scanned the tables in search of Sophie. He didn't spot her and was about to step back into the corridor when a voice rang out.

"Forty-nine!"

A husky man with a rifle slung over his shoulder navigated his way across the cafeteria. Roger felt instant dislike for the man. Not because of his shaved pate or the downward-curved nose resembling a vulture's beak. It was the man's eyes—they suggested a vital slice of humanity was missing.

"I didn't hear you're back. Get in last night?"

Was the man expecting sign language? Roger nodded and rubbed his bleary eyes. No need to fake the fatigue.

"Way to go on that French hit. Nothing succeeds like success, eh? But if it's breakfast you expected, you got your times zones mixed up. Another twenty minutes until your shift."

Roger wanted to nod understanding and bow out the door, but his unknown companion placed an arm around his shoulders and drew him inside. "Come on. I'll grab you a coffee."

With no way to decline, Roger permitted the man to guide him to a private table.

"Sit."

As the other man headed toward the kitchen, Roger maintained a detached air while studying each yellow-clad female. No, even if they'd cut her hair, Sophie definitely wasn't here. But he'd seen four compartments designated as barracks. Were there more prisoners than these?

Perched on a stool in a back corner sat an expressionless albino man. Across his legs rested a rifle, pegging him as a second guard. The albino noticed Roger's gaze and offered a sloppy salute. Roger returned the gesture.

All too soon, Roger's amiable host returned with two coffees. He placed one in front of Roger. "Black, no milk, no sugar."

With unfeigned appreciation, Roger tilted the cup to his lips. He was flying on insufficient rest. A caffeinated turbocharge was never more welcome. The aroma smelled superb, and the flavor matched. At last, he'd found one thing about this lousy organization he could appreciate.

"So, did they give you a couple days off after the French job?"

Roger licked his lips and nodded.

"Too bad I'm on duty. We could've driven down to Kiev for fun. Any special plans today?"

Roger's coffee cup halted. How could he reply?

"Didn't bring your pen and pocket notebook? Too bad. And no interpreter. Exposito is off to Chernigov to visit his woman."

How far could Roger push the charade? He smiled slightly and tipped his free hand with an expression of resignation.

"Say, that was half a smile. Something new out of you. So you're still learning things?"

Roger kicked himself for the blunder. Evidently his lookalike didn't express humor. As best he could, he recovered with a shrug, followed by another swig of coffee. How could he extricate himself?

Vulture Beak wiped his mouth with his sleeve. "Say, did I tell you about the time they sent Kladivo and me into Prague? What a trip." With that introduction—and occasional glances toward the prisoners— the man lowered his voice and launched into a detailed saga worthy of a Robert Ludlum novel. Roger occasionally nodded or raised his eyebrows to pretend admiration. But how could he escape? If Sophie were in this facility, he needed to find out ASAP. If not, he needed to hightail it out and report back to Baron.

At last, a digital tone sounded, interrupting Vulture Beak.

"So soon? I'll have to finish the story next time. You won't believe what happened to the Czech cop. Catch you later!" With a fraternal clap on Roger's shoulder, Vulture Beak strode to the door, where prisoners were lining up. The taciturn albino took his position at the rear of the column.

Roger replayed his companion's parting phrase: "Catch you later." Hopefully, the prediction wouldn't come true.

"Forward."

Within sixty seconds, Roger sat alone in this "Refectory"—such an odd word for a dining hall. Clunks, clanks and an occasional voice from the kitchen were the only indications of life. Time to scram.

Even before Roger reached the exit, two middle-aged women entered, but barely glanced at him as they picked up trays and silverware. In the corridor, other men and women—evidently staff—streamed past on their way to breakfast.

When Roger reached the elevator, its doors stood open. He stepped inside just before they slid shut. Sweet relief.

But where to go? The next level down was Sublevel 3. Somehow, it felt too close to Level 2 and its swarm of hungry staff members. Sublevel 4? He could return to the warehouse and attempt his escape up the freight elevator. No doubt, armed guards would be protecting the hangar and that F-35, but unless he found a weapon, he'd have to brave them with only guts and his fists.

Most worrisome of all—his duplicate might have regained conscious-ness. Awake, the real Number 49 might eventually work loose from his bonds. Or somebody might discover him struggling in the laundry hamper. Then, as people used to say in the 1940s, "the jig was up."

Roger's hand hovered over the elevator buttons. What should he do? A vision popped into his mind. The Polyclinic. Chemicals. Medica-tions. Would his key card access the clinic? Knowing the staff was busy with breakfast emboldened him. Roger pressed the "1" button.

Minutes later, when the Polyclinic door slid open, Roger whispered an exultant, "Yes!" Better yet, darkness reigned inside. From his hip pocket came the trusty penlight from Flashy Al's Truck Stop.

Like clinics everywhere, this one featured rooms with examining tables, scales, and anatomical charts—even a dentist chair. Roger ignored those accouterments as he scanned the cabinets of tongue depressors, cotton swabs, and bandages. Worthless. Weren't there any scalpels? Medicines?

Then—a door marked Pharmacy. It even sported an old-fashioned doorknob. Inside, Roger's pen illuminated shelf after shelf of plastic bottles, vials, tablets, capsules, syrups, and miniature cartons. He'd assumed the inventory would be organized alphabetically, but not so. Maybe they were organized by brand names, or generic names, or by a system unknown outside the pharmaceutical community. Further confusing matters, countless containers bore Cyrillic labels, which usually meant nothing even when Roger sounded out the Russian letters. Precious minutes were ticking past. Any minute, clinic staff might enter.

At last, his search located one of the anesthetics he'd learned about at the Farm: "Isoflurane – Liquid for inhalation." At 250 milliliters, the brown plastic bottle contained slightly more than one cup. He tucked it into a pocket of his coveralls and hoped no one would notice the bulge.

Roger had just turned toward the door leading from the Pharmacy to the outer clinic when light appeared beneath the door. Footsteps ap-proached.

He was trapped.

Panicked, Roger flitted behind a freestanding shelving unit and flicked off his penlight. He stood there, heart pounding, expecting the door to burst open. If anyone discovered him, he'd have to slug his way out. No way he could fake entering by accident.

A minute passed. Then two. Roger crept back to the door, his breathing shallow and senses alert. No sound, not even conversation.

Agonizingly slowly, he twisted the knob and cracked the door a hair. Catty-corner across the hallway, light glowed in an office.

The sound of a file drawer sliding shut. Then female humming.

Roger frowned. He wouldn't hesitate to punch a man, but his upbringing wouldn't let him sock a woman unless she outright attacked him.

Soft clicking indicated the mystery woman was keyboarding. Just great. With his luck, she might be a wannabe novelist, pecking out a medical mystery. What to do?

A buzz.

"Zimmermann," her voice answered. In response to the caller, the Zimmerman woman offered brief replies in German. From his decades in Germany, Roger understood her explanation of updating medical records of "detainees." She ended by saying, "I'll be there in ten minutes."

A few more moments of keyboarding. Then the squeak of a chair.

Roger eased the Pharmacy door shut, positioning himself behind it in case she entered. He needn't have worried. The glow beneath the door went dark, followed by the sound of the outer door sliding open then shutting again.

For good measure, Roger waited thirty seconds before exiting. As he headed for the outer door, however, he noticed the still-glowing screen of Zimmerman's computer. Could he shoot an email to the outside world?

Against his better judgment, Roger plopped onto the seat and scrutinized the monitor. Amazingly, every word was in English. Probably the universal language among an international staff. The operating system was unlike anything he'd encountered on PCs or Macs. The Heritage

Organization probably developed its own. No web browser. No Internet connection whatsoever.

Roger stood to leave, but then a menu caught his eye: "Medical Histories." He sat back down. There she was. "Gottschalk, Sophie." He skimmed and learned this detainee had received treatment for a broken arm and fractured ribs upon arrival. Since then, she'd been declared healthy and fit for duty. A space marked "Date of Death" remained empty. Date of transfer out—also blank. So Sophie really was here!

Thank You, God.

Roger closed Sophie's medical record. In a flash, he was out the door.

As he feared, when Roger arrived back at the laundry hamper on Sublevel 4, the genuine Number 49 was thrashing and yanking his bonds so violently the wheeled hamper jiggled and bounced. The pile of coveralls boiled as his duplicate fought to work loose.

When Roger lifted the top uniforms, the most malicious expression he'd ever seen glared up. On a face that seemed a carbon copy of his own, the raw malevolence took Roger aback. Did he look so ugly when he lost his temper? No way he'd want Katherine to see his face so enraged.

"Well, buddy, you might not smile, but you've got anger down to a science. Here, I brought you a gift."

From his pocket, Roger withdrew the Isoflurane. He dribbled the clear, colorless liquid liberally over the leg of some coveralls.

"Good night, sleep tight." Roger clamped the musty-smelling cloth over his duplicate's nose.

The bound figure twisted away from the saturated fabric. However, Roger had the advantage of free hands, plus higher ground. The anesthetic didn't take effect immediately as Roger expected, but it worked its magic. His double's efforts became weaker then stopped altogether as the man dropped into unconsciousness.

Roger rolled the hamper back into place. What time was it? No clock in sight, but he'd wasted more time on this imposter than he'd intended. Sophie was here somewhere. Before he could escape to contact Baron and his operatives, he wanted to reconnoiter Sublevel 5. Maybe Sophie worked down there?

Chapter 24

From the catwalk above the row of amnio chambers, Dr. Richter manned the controls, lowering a transparent, six-liter container into the amniosyn liquid of the adult-sized tube beneath him.

Watching from the floor with Dr. Chakrala and a dozen visiting H.O. researchers, Sophie realized she was holding her breath. She exhaled, but still breathed shallowly, as if that would assist the miniature transplant to succeed.

"Delicately," Richter intoned to himself.

This first time witnessing the actual procedure of transferring an embryo conceived in a test tube into a full-sized incubation chamber gripped Sophie's attention. So many factors had to be perfect—identical temperatures in the small container and the larger tube, plus consistency of the amniosyn fluids, were only the beginning of multiple standards dictated by Richter.

Satisfied with the transfer, Richter smiled down at his audience and rubbed his hands together. "And that, my dear colleagues, is how we do it."

"Dr. Richter," said Evans, a scientist from Talent Redemption I, wherever that was. "Don't you find it difficult serving as both Senior Administrator and Senior Researcher?"

"It's a challenge. I've learned to delegate the bulk of my administrative duties to focus on Project Duplication."

A visitor with a Spanish accent said, "From the time you first began your experiments with cloning, how long did it take to develop this procedure?"

Richter kept his gaze on the task at hand. "My early years focused on somatic cell nuclear transfer. I needed to expand the foundation of knowledge I had learned in university, and also to investigate burning questions no laboratory was asking. I don't include that initial period in my time scale of producing genetically identical individuals. In fact, monozygotic twins ..."

Sophie mentally chuckled at her supervisor. Waxing eloquent, as usual, when striving to impress.

After working in the Incubation Department a short time, Sophie already knew Richter had toiled twenty-three years to reach this level of achievement—which remained imperfect and fraught with failures. But Richter never groped for words in front of an audience. He could orate about himself for hours. However, she didn't doubt the man's genius. He and his team were achieving what no other lab had accomplished— creating functional, educable humanoids. At first, he'd depended on female wombs, but now the scientist had bypassed even the age-old requirement for birth. Richter was truly producing humans from bottles.

Despite ethical objections, Sophie couldn't squelch her grudging respect for Richter's intellect. She might cringe as a woman, yet her scientific nature yearned to know more.

Did she still wish to escape?

Stupid question. Of course, she wanted out of prison. Still, if she must labor in captivity, she couldn't imagine a more fascinating place to grow in knowledge.

Still droning on about methodology, Richter extracted the glass container that had borne the baby—for in her own mind Sophie insisted on thinking of them as babies—before securing the lid of the amnio chamber. He met her gaze. "How are the readings?"

Startled, Sophie examined the digital readout on the chamber's panel. "Heart rate normal. Brain activity appears usual, with no sign of distress. Transplant procedure apparently successful."

"Transplant procedure—*successful*," Richter emphasized.

Touchy in front of colleagues, wasn't he? Richter wouldn't criticize her margin of doubt in front of the visitors, but he might rebuke her later.

Instead of descending from the metal catwalk, Richter sat Japanese *seiza*-style, kneeling with toes pointed behind him. Gazing down on his audience, he continued his recitation on the history of Project Duplication.

Sophie reflected. Richter was a biological mastermind but worked underground, where he achieved the most incredible discoveries in obscurity—all for the sake of the Heritage Organization. Now, though, she glimpsed a new facet of him. He remained a human who craved admiration among his H.O. peers.

Someone's stomach growled. The scientists chuckled.

Sophie sympathized. With the transplant complete, she realized hunger was gnawing her own stomach as well.

Richter glanced at his wristwatch. "Forgive me. I can ramble for hours on my favorite topics. Thank you again for graciously consenting to begin our symposium before breakfast. But if we don't take a break, we'll miss breakfast entirely. Let's halt and reassemble in one hour."

A smattering of applause erupted. Richter stood and bowed. A satisfied smile stuck to his face.

Richter descended the metal steps and led the group to the exit. As they walked, the visitors bombarded him with questions. The only other detainee, Dr. Chakrala, followed closely, hanging onto each question and answer. Sophie brought up the rear. After all, her white lab coat provided only an appearance of camaraderie. Below the knees, her yellow pant legs and ankle chains provided testimony of her true status.

The American—was his name Evans?—fell into step beside her. "I notice you're a detainee, yet an active assistant on Dr. Richter's team. May I ask your name?"

"Sophie."

"I'm curious. Our policy at Talent Redemption I is to not permit detainees in the laboratory. Neither does T.R. II, if I'm not mistaken. How did you and Chakrala merit such distinction?"

She hesitated. Richter would go ballistic if she revealed one of his clones had beheaded an assistant. "Dr. Richter needed an assistant or two. We were already in T.R. III, and we each have degrees in cell and developmental biology, so he offered us duties. Pending satisfactory performance, of course."

"Oh, certainly. Every level of the H.O. hinges on satisfactory ... performance."

Puzzled, she turned to see Evans's face. His lips curved into a congenial smile—just before his eyes dropped to admire her body. He made no pretense of tact as he slowed a step, long enough to perform a thorough study of her figure.

Sophie's stomach tightened. Evans embodied Hans Heinkel all over again. Had the supply of honorable men in this world run dry?

Unbidden, the image of Captain Roger Greene materialized in her mind—the day she helped him escape, the last moment in Frankfurt when she'd dropped him at a taxi and he'd said, "You won't take any unnecessary chances?" Now there was an upright man. Chivalrous. Freeing Roger had been like poking a stick into the H.O.'s eye. Even though she was still paying for rebellion, she'd done the moral thing. Given a chance, she'd do it all over—except this time she would bash Hans over the head harder and tie better knots, so he couldn't wriggle loose and sound the alarm.

When the group paused at the elevator, Sophie crossed her arms and ignored Evans. His view obstructed, Evans drifted away.

As the elevator doors parted, Richter said, "Hungriest go first. The rest of us will grab the next train."

Sophie exhaled with relief when Evans squeezed in with the first group.

"As I was saying," Richter continued, "our most successful graduates have been trained and farmed out to various H.O. sections for specialized assignments. However, we retain a few here in T.R. III. Number 27 surprised us by turning out as an albino with extreme sensitivity to sunlight. We learned from our mistakes, but he has become useful as a guard. You'll meet him later."

What? The albino—"Ice Man" to the prisoners—had often guarded her section in Dr. Baasch's work area. His taciturn stares had made her skin crawl, but she'd never guessed he was a product of bioengineering. But now the reason behind his silence became clear. It wasn't that Ice

Man preferred silence. He simply couldn't talk. Like all of Richter's duplications, Ice Man must be mute.

The glowing numeral over the elevator indicated Sublevel 2. The first group would be entering the Refectory. Sophie made a note to sit as far as possible from Evans and his shameless eyes.

"Dr. Richter, I note you refer to your creations by number. Don't you give them names? After all, they are human."

"Names not only suggest personality but would tempt my staff into emotional rapport with the clones. The organization doesn't wish it. We cultivate them to exhibit minimal emotion so they can perform assignments unhindered by sentiment. The clones understand we engineered them for the betterment of society, so they never question being called by number."

"Interesting," said the scientist who had asked.

Ghoulish was the word that sprang to Sophie's mind. The Heritage Organization was fabricating humans, but they filtered out emotions and morality.

When the elevator door reopened, Sophie's heart lurched. Standing inside, in living color, was Roger Greene.

"Number 49!" Richter blurted. "Totally unexpected, but delightful timing. Gentlemen, this is the prize clone I was planning to introduce later. But, 49, what are you doing here?"

Sophie's mind raced. The resemblance was uncanny! Richter was definitely cloning cells from Roger Greene. But how many Rogers were there? And did they inherit the real Roger's resistance to aging and physical trauma?

After what seemed a split second of indecision in the clone, Richter answered his own question. "Ah, your monthly checkup! How diligent of you."

The elevator doors began sliding together, but Richter caught one, forcing them to reopen. "You see how far we've come, gentlemen? Even though your visit distracted me from my calendar, Number 49 has a keen mind, plus initiative. He's come for his routine checkup without any summons from me."

"Remarkable."

"We have so much to learn."

Still holding the door, Richter motioned everyone inside. "My apologies, Number 49—no time for a checkup this minute. You caught us on the way to breakfast. You may join us, or else relax in your quarters. Your choice."

Sophie stepped forward with the others, each person shuffling and positioning according to worldwide elevator protocol. Despite herself, she couldn't resist studying the clone's face. Such an incredible likeness.

Then—Number 49 spotted her. Contrary to the cursory glances he'd given the males, the clone blinked, almost as if startled. He glanced away. Although she'd never seen this clone before, surely he'd seen other females in T.R. III? There—he eyed her again, and with more than passing curiosity. His eerie resemblance to the real Roger sparked an icy shiver up her spine.

If only he were the real Roger. She might as well wish for the moon.

At the Refectory entrance, a backward glance revealed the clone sticking with the group of scientists. Some studied him in awe but didn't address him. She studied him, too. His appearance, even his mannerisms —the resemblance to the real Roger was more than uncanny. Unnerving was the word.

When Sophie picked up a plastic meal tray, her hands literally trembled. She let out a slow breath as she willed her hands not to tremble. Why did the clone have to join them? This felt surreal. Nearly supernatural.

At the dining tables, rather than sitting near Richter as she expected, Number 49 placed his tray beside hers. What irony of fate was torturing her? Beneath the table, Sophie wiped her perspiring palms on her lab coat. One of Richter's creations had axed a staff member to death. Could this one come unhinged?

Doing her best to ignore the being beside her, Sophie devoted full attention to the breakfast of pierogies, Ukrainian sausage, eggs, and cream—better fare than she'd ever received while working under Dr. Baasch.

Between mouthfuls, Richter and his colleagues bantered about biology. Even Chakrala, catty-corner across the table, dared inject occasional biology-based puns, adding laughter and sporadic clapping to the meal. Sophie and the clone chewed in silence.

When she was halfway through breakfast, she risked a sideways glance. Nothing wrong with the clone's appetite. Already devouring his last sausage. He reached to the dispenser in front of Sophie and removed a napkin.

Well, if Number 49 was on the verge of going berserk, he would do so with good manners.

However, instead of using the napkin or even setting it on the table, the clone placed it on the empty chair beside him. Then he withdrew an object from a pocket and focused attention on the napkin. What the devil was this creature doing? Whatever it was, she comforted herself knowing the disposable paper was an unlikely weapon.

Another second, then the clone folded the napkin and did the most inexplicable thing: he placed it atop her thigh and gave it two firm pats. Done, he stood, carried his tray to the return window, then strode out of the Refectory.

Bewildered, Sophie placed a hand over the napkin. It was soft. Evidently nothing tucked inside.

No one paid her the least attention as Richter regaled his audience with his account of another breakthrough.

Nonchalantly, Sophie sipped coffee with her left hand. With her right, she unfolded the napkin. Shock and confusion caught her in mid-swallow. Sophie erupted into spontaneous, uncontrollable coughing.

Richter stopped his story. "Are we experiencing a medical emergency?"

All eyes now watched her. She shook her head and cleared her throat. "I swallowed the wrong way."

"Well, raise your hand if you need mouth-to-mouth resuscitation. One of our guests might welcome the opportunity."

The visitors cackled. Richter had scored a point. When he resumed his story, Sophie stole a longer glance at the napkin in her palm. Inked onto it was a message: "Sophie, I'm no clone. I'm Roger. I'll be back with help!"

CHAPTER 25

As nimbly as possible without looking suspicious, Roger descended one of the stairwells, into the bowels of this underground complex. Other exits to the surface must exist, but so far, the only one he knew was the freight elevator that had lowered him to the warehouse. Now sure that Sophie was here, it was time to kick the tires, light the fires, and fly out of this H.O. dungeon. Once in the clear, he could contact Baron.

He pulled open the warehouse door and froze. Inside, the real Number 49 was groggily gesturing in sign language to a half-dozen rifle-toting goons dressed in camouflage. He shut the door.

Oh great. They found him.

Even before this development, he'd expected getting past security on the surface to be ticklish. Now it might prove impossible.

The next moment, the air rent with an ear-shattering screech. An alarm!

Roger dared not linger in the corridor. He turned and bolted back to the stairwell. But where to go? Those guys with rifles blocked his only exit.

The alarm cut off, replaced by a voice: "Attention. Security breach. We have a Code 10 situation. This is no drill. Secure all exits. Secure all detainees. Be on the alert for an intruder wearing our own organization-issue blue …"

Into Roger's mind sprang one of the axioms drilled into him at the Farm: *In a crisis, act fast. Do the unexpected.*

On impulse, Roger hit the stairs leading downward—Sublevel 5. Going down instead of up might be the stupidest mistake of his life. They might corner him. Yet, instinct told him this would be the unexpected direction. Security would race toward the surface to block exits. He needed time to think.

When Roger burst into the huge chamber on the bottom level, the sight froze him in his tracks. Before him extended a nightmare of human bodies floating upright in liquid-filled tubes.

What the devil? Pickled people? Into his mind sprang memories of high school biology and frogs floating in formaldehyde with its repulsive stench. Was the H.O. dissecting humans?

Regardless of the bizarre tubes and their contents, no immediate threats confronted him. No sign of life. He proceeded further. Row upon row of Plexiglas tubes gurgled with figures ranging from infants to adults. Contrary to his first impression of deceased humans, closer inspection revealed occasional twitches, reflexes proving these beings were alive.

Of course—clones!

Pieces of information fell into place, like the tumblers of a lock, partially solving several riddles, including the shooter in Paris.

He stopped at a row of tubes containing males sporting curly, blond hair. His mind snapped back to White River State Park in Indianapolis. Kurt Mueller had sent two blond assassins after him. Roger had assumed the men were twins. But they weren't. The gunmen must have been clones, predecessors of the creatures growing in these very pods.

Ten more rows of tubes brought Roger face to face with three youthful replicas of himself. His own tissue samples must have been delivered to this lab for experimentation. The realization made his skin crawl.

In this row, a fourth and fifth tube were filled with fluid, but were empty of bodies. Had the clones already been harvested?

Once again, a voice sounded over the PA system. "Lockdown is complete. Levels 1, 2, and 3 report all clear. All available security units, proceed to Sublevels 4 and 5 for a systematic sweep."

Holy cow, H.O. security worked like lightning. Any second, they'd be swarming like locusts.

Once again, the Farm's emergency advice echoed in his brain: *Act fast. Do the unexpected.*

No way he was going to cower in a closet until they found him. One glance at the catwalks hanging overhead provided swift inspiration. Roger kicked off his shoes, then ripped off the H.O. clothing. Since the PA had described him, the disguise was now useless. Down to boxer briefs, he stuffed his clothing behind an array of electronic equipment.

Sure hope this works, or I'm going to be the most embarrassed prisoner these guys have ever captured.

His heart hammering triple time, Roger darted up the steps to the catwalk. There, he raised the lid of an empty tube in the lineup of Roger Greene duplicates. Maneuvering from the catwalk into the tube proved awkward, but within seconds his body was settling into warm liquid. He had barely managed to pull the lid down when, through the refracted light of the tubes before him, camo-clad bodies with rifles burst into the room.

Mentally urging himself to remain calm, Roger breathed in and out deeply, purposely hyperventilating to capture every possible molecule of oxygen. As the security detail drew closer, he sucked in a final breath and held it. Relaxing to imitate the neighboring bodies, he submerged and closed his eyes. Fortunately, the tubes were solid from the waist down. They'd never see one "clone" sporting underwear.

How crazy. Playing Hide and Seek among my own duplicates.

Through the liquid muffled shouts reverberated, voices of officers issuing orders to their underlings. At first, Roger struggled to understand the distorted words coming through the liquid. Then he realized the words weren't English. They were Russian.

He cracked one eye. The pursuers had divided. They systematically investigated each aisle. Smart strategy. This way, they effectively prevented an evader from hiding in one row then slipping into another after they passed.

Roger willed every muscle to relax. Unlike the clones, his body wasn't attached to the capsule via high-tech umbilical cord. Another difference was that the clones looked younger, smoother, without the muscular definition of his physique. Richter would spot the imposter. But would these guys? They were grunts, commandos trained to understand weapons, not futuristic biology.

How long could he hold his breath? As far back as his teen years, he and the guys on the Plainfield High football team used to challenge each other, seeing who could hold their breath the longest. Even then, as quarterback, he could stay underwater for nearly two minutes. Now, thanks to the Methuselah Project and his own running regime, his lungs could stretch a deep breath to last three or four minutes. But he must remain calm.

There. Even through closed eyelids, he sensed a shadow walking past his tube. Although his lungs ached for air, he willed himself to remain motionless. One wrong impulse, and these guys would haul him out like an oversized catfish.

At last, when his lungs neared bursting, he cracked an eye. In the direction he was facing, searchers had moved on, leaving none nearby. But what about behind him?

Didn't matter. No point escaping detection if he drowned.

With minimal motion, Roger eased himself to the surface, where he repeatedly breathed deeply before allowing himself to sink once again.

Success. No shouts.

Once more he dared crack a peek. The security detail was filing out. Most of them anyway. A couple were talking to a man in a white lab coat. Through the distortion of the tube in front of him, Richter, the scientist who had been bragging to his peers over the meal, gesticulated in what appeared to be near hysterics.

Evidently, Roger's impromptu scheme was working. By hiding in plain sight, he'd avoided detection and bought precious minutes of freedom. Still, the entire complex was on lockdown. If he didn't come up with a plan, a more thorough search would discover him.

By the next time Roger broke the surface for air, all of the grunts in camouflage had disappeared, leaving only Richter. Evidently concerned for his lab after the mass invasion, Richter scurried around, observing gizmos, gadgets, and readings.

Wait. Not all the green men were gone. One leaned through the doorway and called to Richter before sealing the door again. They posted a sentry? Valuable intel.

When Richter turned his back and leaned over a computer console, Roger pushed the lid off his tube. Thank goodness it hadn't locked into place. With many a sideways glance at Richter, he gingerly pulled himself up, back to the catwalk. Crouched and dripping in his skivvies, he felt horribly exposed.

Yeah, in more ways than one.

Gambling that Richter was sufficiently distracted, Roger padded down the catwalk steps. He hustled toward the spot where he'd stashed his clothing. A running glance toward Richter—

Thunk! The plastic trashcan his toes had struck flipped over and spun away, clunking and depositing a trail of wastepaper down the aisle.

Roger stooped but kept an eye on the scientist.

Richter stood alert, peering left and right. "Is someone there?"

No time to conceal the trashcan or the clutter. Roger reached into the gap behind the electronics cabinet and felt around for his clothing. By the time he located them, Richter was approaching and much too close for comfort.

I bet Superman never had to fight crime without his tights.

"I said, is anyone there?"

With no ideal hiding place, Roger tried squeezing behind a console. Woefully inadequate, this location left him visible from his bare chest up.

Dear God, a little help, please?

"Dr. Eberhardt? I thought you had remained upstairs with our guests. But if you're checking on the—"

Richter halted, gazing at the floor, then up to the catwalk. He'd spotted the trail of watery drops, which would lead him straight to—

The scientist straightened. The heels of his shoes clicking on the floor, he rounded the corner, where he stood regarding the overturned waste can and scattered trash. The man froze, then stepped backward. Clearly spooked, he turned and hustled toward the door.

Do the unexpected.

Dropping his clothes, Roger slid from his confinement and sprinted barefoot toward Richter. Just before he reached him, the scientist whirled. Horror broke over Richter's face as he saw what must have looked like one of his dripping clones, escaped from his tube and charging to attack. He opened his mouth to scream.

Roger's fist connected with Richter's jaw. Amazingly, the man's fight-or-flight instincts kicked in. He bounced back with fists flailing. Two more punches from Roger, and the scientist slumped to the floor, kayoed for the count.

Roger dragged the man's body to a spot where he wouldn't be seen if the sentry reentered. Hands trembling, he stripped Richter of his clothes and donned them—including the lab coat and glasses.

Retrieving the clothing he'd worn earlier, Roger used them to bind and gag the scientist. Dragging the inert body across the floor to a storage closet took mere seconds. There, he lashed Richter to a vertical pipe.

"Sorry, pal. Can't leave you running loose."

Closing the door on his unconscious captive, Roger probed the cavernous room. Might there be an alternate exit? His search discovered restrooms, maintenance facilities, emergency generators, and storage shelves. But no exit other than the one guarded by the sentry.

Didn't these people believe in safety codes? What if a fire broke out?

Of course, this place was built by a clandestine organization. Why should they heed government standards?

No other option, then. If he wanted out, only one door led the way. He strode toward the exit. But what to do when he got there?

I hate this. I'm no CIA spook. Give me a fighter plane and a clear target any day.

He paused at the door. Should he burst through with fists flying? Insanity. He needed a clever, quiet tactic.

Swiping Richter's electronic card through the slot, Roger activated the door.

Ting.

In his best effort at imitating Richter's German accent he called, "Please, come here. I have found something and need your opinion." Immediately he turned away. No reason to let this grunt see his very non-Richter face.

When the sentry appeared beside him, Roger pointed toward the rear of the room. "There."

"Where? I don't see any—"

The instant the automatic door slid shut behind them, Roger karate kicked the man's knee. Seizing the rifle even as the sentry collapsed, Roger flipped the weapon and rammed the stock onto the man's skull.

Out like the proverbial light. Not very sporting, but they wouldn't have been fair with him either.

For the second time in minutes, Roger dragged an unconscious body to the storage room.

"Thanks, buddy," he said, adjusting the belt of the newly acquired security camo pants around his waist. "The way I see it, a white-coated scientist will stand out like a charging elephant. But there are tons of you green guys running helter skelter. Who has time to check every face?"

The next time Roger swiped an electronic key, his uniform and posture matched those of a confident H.O. security guard. He held his rifle ready. However, stillness reigned in the corridor.

Good. The farther I can go without pulling this trigger, the better.

Senses alert, he padded down the corridor. But how could he escape both the underground prison and the manhunt?

I'm flying over uncharted, hostile territory with no radar. I don't have a prayer.

He paused. Actually, a prayer was the only thing he did have.

Dear Lord, you're my one Hope. Show me what to do.

CHAPTER 26

Strutting through the woods of the Exclusion Zone around Chernobyl, Nikita Klimov seethed. During all his months as security chief of T.R. III, no weakness or threat had escaped his attention. He'd beefed up nighttime patrols of the forest. He'd requisitioned night-vision goggles. He'd installed hidden, high-tech monitors with infrared capabilities. That any outsider could approach undetected was inconceivable.

But somewhere, one or more of his men had bungled and permitted an intruder to penetrate not only the vicinity above ground, but T.R. III itself. Not for the first time in his life, someone else's gaffe made Klimov look incompetent. And it had happened precisely when a delegation of H.O. scientists was visiting.

The moment Klimov spotted a rotting tree stump, his army boot delivered a savage kick, exploding the dead wood into a hail of pulpy bits. Somebody would pay.

He paused, peering at the blue sky through the thinning veil of golden leaves overhead. Wait. The timing of it all ... Could one of those visiting brains be involved? He would interrogate each one. Then a worse thought surfaced—was it possible one of his own security men had assisted an outsider? A big enough bribe might tempt one of them.

Klimov curled his fingers into a fist, then punched a dead branch off the tree trunk beside him.

He would personally murder the cretin making him look foolish. If this intruder had inside help, Klimov would feed the culprit to the crematorium.

He continued along the barely discernible trail connecting each of the aboveground guard posts. Until today, the strategy of hiding T.R. III beneath Chernobyl's "dangerous" Exclusion Zone had fulfilled the goal of keeping away all but the lost and the reckless. But evidently, tales of lethal radiation had fallen short of keeping out at least one interloper.

When—not if—this fake Number 49 was captured, Klimov would interrogate the man until he begged for death. That meant Klimov must bottle his anger for now. It would do no good to murder the slob before he was squeezed for details of his mission.

Klimov turned the new AK-12 in his hands and switched it from full automatic mode to two-round bursts. In his current state of mind, he was likely to cut the imposter in two with full auto. That would be satisfying, but stupid for his career.

He twisted his head to the left and keyed the mic attached to his epaulet.

"Glava-1 to all surface units. Be alert for absolutely anything out of the ordinary, on the ground or in the air. Footprints, sounds, airborne drones—anything. If so much as a crow looks suspicious, shoot it down and bring it to me."

Of course, it was possible the intruder had escaped detection and still hid inside T.R. III. He keyed the shoulder mic again.

"SurTech-4, talk to me. What does the footage from those internal cams reveal?"

The voice of SurTech-4, the duty officer in charge of electronic surveillance, crackled back. "We're still sorting evidence. Much video footage to review. Preliminary examination shows nothing unusual, with one exception: After checking back in from his mission this morning, Number 49 seems to have engaged in prolonged foot traffic throughout the facility. Alone. It's definitely his face, and computer records verify repeated use of his personal key card."

That clone. Richter's Wonder child. Could Number 49's brain be unraveling, just like the clone who beheaded Hoffman?

He keyed the mic again. "Zaschita-10, come in."

A pause. "Zaschita-10."

"Question: This entire search was launched on the say-so of Number 49, who claimed he was attacked. Is it possible there has been no breach at all?"

A pause. "Clarify."

Klimov fought down his urge to unleash a string of white-hot obscenities. "I mean, we initiated Code 10 based solely on a story recited by Number 49. Conjecture: If Number 49 were suffering from mental stress on the heels of his recent mission, could he have become delusional? Maybe concocted a fictional attack in his mind?"

Klimov released the mic. If that's what happened, he'd punch the clone's nose to the back of his skull.

Zaschita-10's voice: "We have Number 49 in the Infirmary right now. His body is covered with bruises that are consistent with hand-to-hand combat. He heard your question. His hands are flying to deny it. Also, even though injuries can be self-inflicted, our people don't believe he could have tied himself up in the manner he was found."

So much for the screwball-clone theory. Perturbed though Klimov would be if this whole Code 10 had been sparked by an unbalanced clone, at least that scenario would've placed full blame on Richter, not himself.

The radio receiver crackled again. Zaschita-10's voice continued: "Also, be advised we discovered a handkerchief soaked in blood. It was hidden in the trashcan of the same room where Number 49 was found. Number 49 has no open wounds, and no T.R. III personnel have reported injuries. Possibly Number 49 gave his assailant a bloody nose or other injury."

A bloody handkerchief? Was it clue?

Klimov keyed his mic. "Understood. Get one of those laboratory people to examine the blood specimen. If there's anything useful about it, I want to know. And locate Richter! Find out if this intruder could be one of his creations. We need to know what we're dealing with."

"*Tak tochno,*" Zaschita-10 agreed.

"Find Mueller, too. If Number 49 showed the least bit of unusual behavior during yesterday's mission, I want to know about it."

"*Tak tochno.*"

Mueller. Most likely snoozing in his quarters after the late-night flight. The man might not be involved, but right now Klimov wanted blood, and his dislike for Mueller gurgled to the surface. Sure, Mueller had been an effective termination agent—in his day. But Mueller was old. His cockiness was based on ancient glories. When was the last time the German had completed a termination? Why, Mueller wouldn't even be in Europe if he hadn't bungled ...

Klimov halted beside a tall pine. He probed his memory, trying to piece together half-forgotten details from Mueller's file. Off in the distance, the derelict Soviet antenna system the West had dubbed "the Woodpecker" stood silently pointing to the sky. The Duga-3 array remained a ridiculously expensive leftover of Soviet times. In a sense, the metal monstrosity and Mueller resembled each other. One antique now stood silent, whereas the other still had an active mouth—too active when Mueller dared criticize Klimov's security protocols.

However, Mueller had once botched an assignment in the United States. As a result, H.O. leadership had yanked him out. What was that job?

The case files of workers and detainees in T.R. III were too numerous for the security chief to memorize. Still, there had been oddities in Mueller's file. Something about an old experiment at Laboratory 1. A key extermination had gone wrong. As a result, the H.O. had transferred Mueller the Jeweler out of North America. Even when Klimov had read the material, the file struck him as vague, as if someone high up had sanitized details to spare Mueller embarrassment.

But perhaps Mueller's protector placed too much confidence in the German. What if Mueller himself was a double agent? He and Number 49 had returned from Paris this morning. Suddenly T.R. III was on lockdown. Coincidence?

Klimov reversed course and charged back the way he'd come. As hoped, the jaunt in fresh forest air had crystalized his thoughts. No need to inspect every outpost. Gut instincts told him the answer he sought was below ground. Richter, Mueller, or one of those visiting science brains held the key to this mystery.

As he double-timed through the woods, another strategy occurred to him. A security protocol he himself had created, but never expected to implement. He keyed the mic. "Glava-1, all units. General Order 50. Repeat, General Order 50 is now in effect. No exceptions!"

CHAPTER 27

Aboard the CIA's unofficial Learjet 35, Katherine opened sleepy eyes just as Baron twisted in his seat and called to the pilot.

"Not to sound childish, but are we there yet?"

The pilot half-turned his head. "Getting close. Just entered Ukrainian airspace."

Brow furrowed, Baron added an afterthought. "Flying under radio silence and with no transponder ... Any chance of the Ukrainian Air Force shooting us down?"

The pilot shrugged. "I think we'll be okay. I should be able to zip in, set you down in Shestovytsia, and hightail it out before the Ukrainian Air Force can scramble anything to check us."

Baron lifted an approving thumb before turning back to Katherine, Melissa, Wainwright, and the two men she didn't know, only that they were crack marksmen. Even now, one of them was cleaning yet another pistol—one of several since they'd taken off from Charles de Gaulle Airport. She'd never seen one exactly like it, but the pistol looked to be a Sig Sauer. Sig pistols were attractive—proud-looking guns. The mismatched assortment of firearms attested to the fact this mission was an impromptu affair thrown together on short notice.

"Shestovytsia?" Melissa echoed. "Sounds like a bogus name invented by Marvel Studios for an Avengers movie."

Wainwright squinted sideways. "The Avengers? Gerard and Ben are rubbing off on you."

Baron clapped his hands, summoning the attention of everyone but the pilot. "All right, people, time for a quick mission brief. This will be short, since we don't have much intel. I hate it, but we're going in practically blind."

The officer with the Sig stuffed the weapon into a backpack at his feet.

"Okay, to recap: The radio signal on our quarry went silent inside the Chernobyl Exclusion Zone. Silence might mean the transmitter has been destroyed, which would make our job of locating 'Jim Johnson' impossible. However, there's a chance the signal is only muffled. We know the H.O. maintains at least one underground facility. Possibly more. If they operate an underground complex here, Johnson could be inside it. That would silence the signal. But if he comes back out wearing the transmitter, we'll get our chance to pinpoint his location."

"So, what is Shestovytsia?" Melissa asked.

"The Chernobyl Zone has no airport. Besides, I'm not about to reveal our presence by conducting aerial reconnaissance. We're going to touch down fifteen clicks southeast of Chernigov. There's an old airport called Shestovytsia. The Ukrainians closed it in 2002, but the asphalt runways are serviceable. Once on the ground, we'll jump out and rendezvous with our people from Kiev. The pilot will hightail out of Ukrainian air space before anyone realizes we're here."

Melissa nodded with her typical, contemplative expression.

"Why all the cloak-and-dagger?" asked Officer Gun Cleaner. "Why not call in help from the Ukrainian government?"

When a pained expression crossed Baron's face, Wainwright spared him the trouble of answering. "I spent four years in the Kiev office. Corruption runs rampant in Eastern Europe. Kiev's got it. Even if we knew for sure no H.O. people are embedded in their government— which isn't likely—we need to keep a lid on this little escapade."

This non-essential chatter was eating Katherine's nerves. "What's the plan once we hit the ground?"

Baron leaned back and crossed his legs. "Sketchy at best. We'll proceed to a deserted location on the edge of Chernobyl's Exclusion Zone and then wait. If the signal reappears, we'll double-time in that direction."

The other sharpshooter broke his silence. "Why not enter the Zone and reconnoiter while waiting? We might stumble across something even without the signal."

Baron spread his arms toward their small group. "Look. Six of us. Not enough manpower. The Exclusion Zone is a thousand square miles, created and guarded by the Ukrainian army to keep the public away from radioactivity. If the H.O. really does operate here, they'd spot us bumbling around long before we stumbled onto them."

"And what if we do catch up with 'Jim Johnson'?" said Officer Gun Cleaner.

"Priority Number One," Baron said, "is to capture our fugitive—hopefully alive—and extract. Wounded, if he won't come peaceably. Dead, if he resists. If we don't bring him back, a whole lot of—" Baron glanced at Katherine. "A gigantic truckload of manure is going to dump on my head. Langley has already gotten a whiff of trouble. They're breathing down my neck for details."

Wainwright placed a hand on Katherine's knee. With a tender voice, he said, "Katherine, I know you have mixed emotions about your former boyfriend—"

Once again, Wainwright's approach grated. Earlier, clouded emotions had prevented her from seeing her colleague's *modus operandi*. Now, though, she detected a pattern. Each time Wainwright mentioned Roger, he included a negative slant. At the same time, his words and actions portrayed himself as the one who truly cared. As one interested in establishing intimacy.

Katherine pulled Wainwright's hand off her leg. "I never said 'former' boyfriend. I've only been perturbed. And confused."

Wainwright sat straighter. "What I'm trying to say is, your mixed emotions might compromise your involvement in this op. If we find our man, and if he won't come peaceably ... Well, maybe it's better if you fly back to Paris with the pilot."

Melissa's gaze locked on her. "I was thinking the same. You and I got off to a rocky start, but I've learned to appreciate you. I don't want you hurt. I also don't want personal feelings to jeopardize the mission."

Baron's turn. "How about it, Mueller? Can you maintain sufficient emotional detachment to proceed? No one will think badly if you back out. I would respect your decision."

Katherine sucked in a breath to answer, but Baron added a P.S.

"By emotional detachment, I mean readiness to shoot the fugitive if the situation requires."

Shoot Roger? Regardless of the friction between them, the mental image of herself pumping bullets into Roger appalled her. "Ro—" She caught herself. "The man you know as Jim Johnson would never do anything illegal or immoral. We won't—"

Baron raised a hand to halt her. "Mueller, we don't know why our target still has the transmitter. For all I know, this could be a trap. But the available information leads me to suspect something in his brain has gone haywire. I repeat: If the situation demands it, are you prepared to respond with lethal force?"

All eyes rested on her. Only the steady roar of the Lear jet's engines filled the silence.

Drawing on her former life as a freelance editor, Katherine spotted her escape—Baron's specific wording. "I'm a professional, the same as any of you. If our target's behavior requires it, then absolutely—I will shoot to kill."

Baron's eyebrows lifted. He exchanged glances with Melissa, who likewise expressed surprise, then shrugged.

"Attagirl," Wainwright said, with an uninvited pat to her knee.

Resentment flared in Katherine's chest. "Mr. Wainwright, your approach may work with some females, but for the record, I do not appreciate men touching me without an invitation. In the future, please refrain from placing your hands on my arms, my legs, or any other part of my body."

Caught in the unexpected crossfire of multiple eyes, Wainwright leaned back then shrugged and smirked. "Yeah, sure. I didn't mean nothing."

Baron returned to the topic. "Mueller, you can stay with us. I appreciate your professionalism. However, due to your past affiliations, I must insist you remain in sight of at least one of us at all times."

"I'll keep her in sight," Melissa volunteered. "We've become buds. Besides, restroom considerations make me the logical partner."

Katherine grunted acquiescence. Better Melissa than Wainwright. What she refrained from expressing was her rock-solid belief Roger could do nothing requiring lethal action from any of them.

Her stomach detected a change in altitude.

"Now descending toward Shestovytsia. And … surprise! The Ukrainian Air Force is radioing for me to identify myself. They're scrambling a reception committee faster than I expected. Buckle up, everybody. This is gonna be one hot landing."

CHAPTER 28

As the freight elevator approached Surface Level, perspiration beaded Roger's brow. He dabbed away the moisture with a sleeve. Incredible he'd made it this far. He couldn't afford to look jittery.

Trouble was, "jittery" described him perfectly just now. Poker had never been his game. His bluffing skills left much to be desired.

The elevator clunked to a stop. The doors parted, and there he stood, gazing into this hangar built into a hill. Directly opposite him, the overhead door stood open, revealing bright sunshine.

Here, the crisp breeze caressing his face bore the chilliness of October. Despite the danger, relief at being out of the subterranean complex swept through him. It was as if an invisible hand had been squeezing his chest, but now evaporated.

With the aid of a calming breath, he strode out, aiming toward the hangar's wide-open exit. A glance to the right confirmed what he'd expected: No fewer than four men in green camo stood guard around the F-35. Not only did they grip rifles, but they wore heavy-duty body armor. No pilfering that bird.

Okay, scrap the dream of escaping by air. Plan B: get outside—preferably without gunfire—and vanish into the forest ASAP.

As Roger strode toward freedom, he fished out his sunglasses. The less he looked like his double, the better.

"*Stoi!*" a voice ordered in Russian. "Halt!" Two green-clad men angled to intercept him.

So much for Plan B.

Like the purloined gear Roger wore, these men's uniforms bore no insignia. How did these guys determine rank, anyway?

The bigger of the two shot him a rapid-fire question in Russian. Although Roger had studied the language, his ears weren't quick enough to understand. All he caught were the words "alone" and "Order 50."

A fact struck him. Except for himself, every H.O. man in sight had a comrade within arm's reach. A buddy system. By operating alone, Roger attracted attention.

The pair planted themselves in front of Roger. The taller one fired more high-speed questions, each one ramping in volume and anger.

Roger caught only "why" and "where." No way his amateur Russky could wriggle him out of this predicament. Instead, he confidently held up his index finger in the universal "Just a moment" sign. Roger pulled his hand back as if to extract something from a chest pocket but quickly curled his fingers into a fist and punched Comrade Fast Talker in his Adam's apple.

Like a wooden board, the man fell straight backward and lay there, coughing and wheezing.

Roger tried to grab the rifle off his shoulder, but Opponent #2 proved quicker. With surprising speed, the man clamped his hands on the weapon and wrenched it from Roger.

Weaponless, Roger delivered a swift kick of his army boot to his opponent's unarmored knee.

With an agonized bellow, the man fell to the oil-stained concrete.

Shouts erupted.

Roger vaulted his two adversaries and dashed toward the exit.

An ear-shattering alarm split the air. The overhead door started grinding downward.

Roger poured on a burst of speed. Lower, lower slid the hangar door.

Roger threw wild glances left and right. No walk-in doors. Maybe one existed, but for the moment, this opening offered his one escape.

Behind him, a rifle barked. Suddenly, bullet holes stitched a line into the descending door.

With the exit to freedom now less than knee-high and bullets flying, Roger dove and rolled.

He was out—but wait! The heavyweight door crunched down onto the heel of Roger's right boot. Unlike domestic garage doors, this one didn't auto-respond to resistance. Instead, it clamped down with inexorable pressure, pinning his foot to the concrete.

More shouting issued from the gap under the door.

Roger ignored the voices. Bracing the sole of his free foot against the massive door, he pulled the right boot with all his might. The boot popped free, letting the door clunk into place. He scrambled to his feet only to find two more security men nearly on top of him.

Summoning his most authentic Russian accent, Roger pointed toward the hangar. "They're shooting—we need help!" Without waiting, Roger pushed between the open-mouthed men and dashed across a narrow runway painted camo-style in greens and browns. Beyond, a thick stand of evergreens offered protection.

In his wake flowed the Russian word "*Stoi!*" plus what must have been a barrage of Slavic curses.

Roger's boots were already pounding up a low embankment of sand and sparse brown grass when the sound of gunfire rent the air. Much as he wanted to run straight to the cover of those trees, bullets flew faster than feet. A straight course offered a predictable target.

Roger spun this way and that, using the same broken-field running he'd used to out-maneuver tacklers in Plainfield High football. Amazed by his own success, he was plunging between pine trees when searing pain erupted in his right side. The combination of shock and the bullet's impact sent him sprawling among gnarled roots and a mat of copper-colored pine needles.

Flat on the ground and breathing hard, Roger placed his hand over the aching spot. When he pulled it away, fresh blood glistened on his fingers.

Which vital organs are on the right side? Colon. Kidney. Liver. Right lung. Gall bladder. He had no idea what color fluid from a liver or gall bladder might be, but blood was the only liquid he saw.

Apparently, the bullet had struck the extreme outside edge of his back, then exited just inches away, in the front. But judging from the pain, the round must have nicked a rib bone along the way.

Roger's mind raced. He was free—but not for long. Thanks to the Methuselah Project, the wound should heal fast, but he needed a place to hide.

No way I'm letting them lock me up!

Clamping his right palm over both entrance and exit holes, Roger stood and gritted his teeth against the pain as he loped deeper into the forest. He was no longer sprinting, but neither was he wearing bulky body armor. He still had a chance.

CHAPTER 29

Katherine perched on the edge of the inflatable boat the group had used to cross the Dnieper River. Slipping through Regional Landshaftny Park without being seen on the east side of the Dnieper had been easy, even interesting due to glimpses of wildlife. But quietly sitting and waiting on the edge of Zakaznyk Zoological Reserve, a district poisoned by Chernobyl's nuclear radiation? No matter how many times she willed the tension out of her muscles, it kept creeping back.

Was Roger truly here? Or was this a wild goose chase? Never the patient type, she wanted to do something—anything—instead of simply waiting for the elusive radio signal.

Thirty feet away, the two expert marksmen—whose names turned out to be Henderson and Powell—hunkered behind tree trunks as they stood guard. Each occasionally peered through compact binoculars. Like her, Melissa sat on the opposite side of the black inflatable.

Conserving energy with eyes closed, Wainwright sat beside Baron on a fallen log that appeared ancient yet didn't rot. A side effect of Chernobyl radiation?

Of the group, only Baron remained active. Satellite phone in hand, he typed, swiped, squinted, and occasionally nodded as he sifted information and busied himself with whatever CIA bosses do in such moments.

Confound this waiting! Katherine was no more helpful here than she would've been in Paris. Maybe she should pray? She'd neglected her prayer life ever since the quarrel with Roger.

Katherine didn't shut her eyes. The situation required vigilance. Yet, her thoughts stretched toward Heaven. *Lord, forgive me. I've been living as if You don't even exist. I know better, but I've been relying on my own strength. No amount of positive thinking can replace You. Please help me—help all of us—to do what's best. Please protect Roger from any—*

Without warning, Baron stood. "Bingo. The signal just went live. Our boy is on the move."

Katherine concluded with a quick *Amen* before clustering with the others.

Holding his satellite phone in front of him, Baron pointed into the woods. "That direction. Single file. Voices low. Firearms down. If we spot local citizenry, we avoid contact. If contact becomes unavoidable, we're American birdwatchers, come to view the fascinating birdlife in the Exclusion Zone."

Wainwright frowned. "Birdwatchers? You do realize entry into the Zone is by permit only? Without permits, your cover story falls apart."

Baron shrugged. "Act confident, or act ignorant. Both tactics work miracles. Let's go."

When Melissa stepped into line behind her, Katherine understood: Melissa was keeping both eyes on this former H.O. cadet.

CHAPTER 30

Hungry to spill blood, Security Chief Klimov swiped his key card into the Administrative Office. Whatever reason they summoned him had better be good.

When the door slid open, a babbling horde met Klimov's gaze. Mixed among a detail of his own security men and others was Kurt Mueller, who was waving his arms and ranting at first one man, then another. Along with the scientists who typically worked on Sublevel 5 was Dr. Richter—T.R. III's Administrator. For some odd reason, Richter stood there clad in nothing but boxer shorts and a sleeveless undershirt. Like Mueller, Richter gesticulated and ranted with indignation, but the hubbub swallowed his words. And there was Dubovik, the sentry who had been stationed outside the Incubation Department. Like Richter, Dubovik sported only his underwear and socks. Was everyone going insane?

The babbling mass ignited Klimov's powder keg. "Everybody—shut up!"

All eyes turned to him. The closer personnel stepped backward at sight of him. Klimov guessed he resembled a demon from hell. He felt like one. A single wrong word, and his rock-hard knuckles would consign the offender to that fiery pit.

How to untangle this mess? Klimov jammed a finger at his nearly naked sentry. "Dubovik, why are you out of uniform? And absent from your post?"

"Dr. Richter summoned me into the laboratory. The moment I entered, he knocked me unconscious. When I woke up, my hands and feet were tied. This is all I was wearing."

"I did no such thing," Richter retorted. "I was alone in the laboratory when Number 49 attacked me without his own clothing. I fought, but he knocked me out. When I came to, most of my clothes were gone, and I was tied up, too!"

Number 49—who was fully clothed—began rapid-fire signing with both hands.

"Says he didn't do it," someone interpreted. "Claims he was nowhere near Sublevel 5. We can substantiate. He was with us in the clinic."

Renewed pandemonium broke out.

"Silence!" Klimov bellowed. He brandished his AK-12. "It's my responsibility to maintain security for this complex, both above and below. I need information, not idiotic arguing. I warn you all, I'm ready to split the skull of the next person who speaks without permission."

"But—" began Kurt Mueller.

Hoisting the rifle butt over his head, Klimov took two menacing steps toward the German.

Lifting both hands, Mueller shrank into silent submission.

With a *ting*, the door slid open. In hustled one of Richter's lab technicians, who glanced around in bewilderment. Spotting Richter, he hurried forward and offered him a computer printout. "Sir, you'll want to see this. It's the analysis of that blood sample."

In utter silence, Richter studied the printout. "Incredible. This blood —it's type O negative, universal donor." In shock, he locked eyes with Klimov. "But the coagulation factors ... The adenosine triphosphate ... The aldosterone ... Although there are signs of degradation, every component is off the chart. I've never seen such readings."

Klimov closed his eyes, summing reserves of patience. "Help me, people. You're supposed to be brilliant. How do we explain the riddle of a replica of Number 49 running around the laboratory, knocking people unconscious and stealing their clothing?"

Like a scolded schoolboy, Kurt Mueller raised one hand and waited.

"Talk," Klimov barked.

Mueller dared step closer. "There's only one explanation. The Methuselah Project. We are not dealing with a berserk clone. The intruder must be Roger Greene—the escaped American who was the test subject for the H.O.'s very first biological experiment. The project enhanced his physiology. It provided his body with amazing recuperative powers."

Richter clapped his hands together. "Of course! It fits. If only I hadn't been so focused on my own experiments, I would've realized—."

Klimov waved a hand to silence everyone. He stared into Mueller's eyes. "Are you telling me you know our spy? He's some sort of super soldier?"

"Not superhuman. But a unique individual with inconceivable physiology. The organization was trying to unlock the secrets inside his body when he escaped our people in Germany."

Klimov squinted. "How do you know so much about this Greene? You're no scientist."

The German's face radiated defiance. "In the United States, I received a dossier on Greene. The High Council assigned me to eliminate him. He got away. Shortly afterward, it was reported that he'd committed suicide, but I always suspected a cover-up."

So. Here was the story. If Mueller had properly executed his target, this run-amok American wouldn't be here, wreaking havoc with Klimov's reputation.

Richter, too, stepped closer. "But why would the American be here? How did he find T.R. III?"

"Why?" Mueller echoed. "Does it matter why? After being held captive by our people, Greene might want revenge. Because I tried to kill him, he might have a vendetta against me."

"I have an idea." Dr. Baasch pushed through the crowd of bodies. "Could he be connected with the detainee, Sophie Gottschalk? She once worked on the Methuselah Project."

In Klimov's brain, a light clicked on. Sophie—the pretty detainee who'd resisted his charms. "Gottschalk must be the key. You've seen Hollywood movies. American men fancy themselves heroes, the cowboys who gallop to rescue the woman in danger!"

"Don't underestimate Greene," Mueller warned. "The man is resourceful. Before coming to this office, I checked the supplies we flew in from Paris. One crate shows signs of tampering. I believe Greene smuggled himself here inside it."

Klimov pinned Mueller with a cold stare. By attempting to demonstrate clever detective skills, the German had confessed a gigantic blunder—unwittingly helping an outsider to penetrate the very core of T.R. III. And he'd said it in front of witnesses. Mueller had just provided the scapegoat Klimov needed.

Articulating his thoughts with an icy chill calculated to let everyone catch his meaning, Klimov said, "Herr Mueller, if you are correct, let us take comfort in the knowledge this intruder did *not* previously know the location of T.R. III, and that he did *not* penetrate my carefully created security perimeter on his own, and that he brought *no* other colleagues with him. Instead, one of our more geriatric members provided this intruder with personal escort service, transporting him all the way from Paris to Sublevel 4 of this top-secret installation."

"Now see here—"

"No!" Klimov blasted back. "This entire facility is at risk because of your ineptitude. The High Council ordered this American terminated? Very well. Me and my team will complete the assignment you botched."

Klimov swiped open the door. "Security detail, follow me. Dubovik, find a uniform! And Mueller—you might want to consider suicide before I submit my report to the Council. Death by your own hand will be far more pleasant than the conveyer to the crematorium."

CHAPTER 31

Incensed, Kurt Mueller watched the security chief and his gang jostle out the doorway. For the first time, he yearned to snuff a fellow member of the Heritage Organization.

It was bad enough Klimov's every breath reeked of garlic. Now he was planning to hang a security breach around Mueller's neck. Greene had cost him his daughter and his post in America. Now, because of Klimov, Greene may have cost his very life.

Unless ...

Dr. Richter and his lab associates also filed out, leaving Mueller and Number 49. The secretaries on administrative staff avoided Mueller's eyes as they returned to their individual tasks.

Since neither Mueller nor Number 49 operated under T.R. III's security department, they were now free to do as they pleased. The clone studied him in a curious, detached manner. The being looked one hundred percent like a normal man; yet he wasn't. Who could imagine what thought processes passed through this artificial creature's gray matter?

Mueller stiffened his backbone. "Let's step into the corridor."

Once outside Administration, he said, "Number 49, as you just heard, this installation has been infiltrated by a hostile intruder, the very man from whose cells you were created. The very man who beat you up. Evidently, he despises you. How does that make you feel?"

The clone's eyes glinted like polished granite.

"Exactly. Me too. At the moment, our beloved security chief mistakenly believes you and I are at fault for the intruder's presence. But we can rectify the situation. Are you ready for an unscheduled mission?"

Jaw set, Number 49 offered a single nod.

Once again, Mueller was struck by the artificial being's uncanny resemblance to the real Roger Greene. Because of the likeness, part of Mueller loathed the face. Yet, the clone was his last ally. "I'm ready, too. Go change into field gear. I will do the same, and I will check out two rifles. We rendezvous here in fifteen minutes."

Ever obedient, the clone offered his customary nod before double-timing down the corridor.

"So malleable. Like wet clay. What couldn't I accomplish with an army of artificial men!"

*   *   *

Fifteen minutes later, Mueller returned and found Number 49 silently waiting. "Take this rifle. It's the same one you used in Paris. If we're lucky, one of us will score on this Roger Greene, thus salvaging your honor and mine."

As the clone accepted the weapon, Mueller wondered for an instant whether he truly needed his unspeaking ally. Defeating Greene solo would rebut Klimov's insinuation he was obsolete. Then again, Klimov's "General Order 50" remained in effect: No T.R. III personnel were to operate individually above ground. Until Klimov rescinded the command, working alone might earn a swift bullet.

Mueller activated the door to the Security office and led the clone inside.

The brunette behind the desk looked up in surprise.

"I need a personal radio, plus ear bud."

"We have none left. With such a massive search in progress—"

"None in all of T.R. III?"

"There might be a few down in the warehouse. But there's no one I can send. If you'd like to go check personally—"

Mueller shook his head. Time was wasting, and Greene was outside, on the move. "Never mind. Be advised Number 49 and I are joining the search effort. We will proceed under radio silence."

Doubt registered in the brunette's eyes. "Shall I inform Glava-1?"

"Not necessary. Based on my personal security authorization, 39554."

Looking less than pleased, the brunette typed the notation into her computerized blotter. "Entered as ordered, sir."

Of course, Klimov would've forbidden any exterior activity by Mueller. Yet, with a little luck, Mueller's experience at tracking and eliminating human prey might deliver the American into his hand before Klimov realized what happened.

"Situation status?" Mueller asked.

"Inconclusive, sir. Preliminary evidence indicated the intruder was wounded and moving away in a northwesterly direction. However, just moments ago one of the motion-detector cams to the east recorded an image. According to the report, a male figure flitted past it, walking westward."

"Westward?" Mueller pondered. It made no sense. If Greene had been wounded and headed northwest from this location, then how could he suddenly appear east of here—but still headed west? Such a course would bring him straight back ...

Of course. The hangars. Greene must think he can achieve surprise by circling back, shooting the guards, and escaping by air while Klimov's crew is beating the bushes. Clever.

Imposing on the secretary's personal space, Mueller stepped behind her desk. "Quick. Pull up an aerial map. Show me the position of the motion-detector cam."

The secretary opened a map on her monitor. With a nicely manicured fingernail, she pointed to a spot. "Here, sir."

"I see." Inwardly, Mueller rejoiced. The lake just east of the old power plant would force anyone walking west on foot to dip south, circumnavigating the lake. This information simplified his task of plotting an intercept course. "Is Klimov heading to intercept?"

"Negative. He believes it's a stray backpacker, but has dispatched a couple men to check."

"We'll check, too," Mueller snapped.

In his mind's eye, he could already picture the cunning Greene, quickly healed from the morning's wound and circling back while

Klimov and the bulk of his men wasted energy in a *fruchtloses Unterfangen*, what Americans called a "wild-goose chase." But the wily Greene wouldn't outfox Kurt Mueller.

"Let's go," he ordered the clone.

*   *   *

When Mueller and Number 49 stepped out the surface door of Emergency Exit 3, he held out his compass. "This way. Quick march. I want to reach Greene before Klimov's men." Mentally, he reviewed and approved his decision to travel lightly, without armor, carrying only rifles and spare ammunition.

"Geriatric, am I? I'm in better physical condition than that imbecile realizes."

However, even as Mueller muttered the words, he recalled his one weakness—his heart condition. He'd never reported the cardiac arrest to the organization. A low-ranking clerk might have stamped his file as unfit and put him out to pasture.

Even as he marched, he grinned at his own shrewdness. A lesser H.O. member might timidly submit to every regulation, but not Kurt Mueller.

However, dashing off without his daily meds ... It was bad enough he'd flown to Paris and neglected to take along his pillbox. But when the messenger from Klimov startled him from a sound sleep—

Well, forgetting to take the pills wasn't due to age, just distractions.

How long had he gone without his Warfarin, beta-blockers, antianginals, and blood-pressure meds? Three days? No, today made the fourth day. Of course, he might not actually need them. "A prudent precaution" the physician had advised. No matter. He would pace himself. Not do anything overly strenuous. His blood pressure and pulse would stay at comfortable levels.

After all, Number 49 was beside him. The clone possessed a young, athletic body. Let him bear the stress on this expedition. Wouldn't it be sweet revenge if an organization clone cultivated from the American's own cells became the instrument of his death?

As he and the clone marched eastward through evacuated territory, Mueller appreciated another characteristic of Number 49—his muteness. He never interrupted Mueller's thoughts with stray comments. The clone listened, understood, and obeyed. Fortunately, even though none of the clones spoke, there was nothing wrong with their auditory nerves. At this stage of life, Mueller had no wish to dabble in sign language for the sake of these creatures. The important thing was Number 49 understood and carried out orders.

At first, Mueller didn't worry about the noise of their footfalls as they crunched through dead leaves or thumped across crumbling asphalt roads. However, as they drew closer to the intercept point, he grew more cautious.

"From here on, let's be extra vigilant," he told the clone. "Make no unnecessary noise. Avoid stepping on dry sticks. We're approaching a broad, grassy area where there will be few trees. It will allow an unob-structed view to spot anyone approaching from the east."

Soon enough, they emerged from a stand of fir trees and stood on the edge of a vast field, probably a Soviet collective farm in the years before Reactor 4 exploded. At this stage of autumn, only brown grass and scattered shrubs decorated the terrain.

"Down. Into the shadow of the firs," Mueller whispered. He pulled a pair of folding binoculars from his pocket. "We'll wait here for the quarry."

Surprising Mueller, Number 49 pulled out a monocular and per-formed his own scans. Excellent initiative.

With the eye of a hunter, Mueller studied not only the field, but also the serene flock of crows. A rabbit hopped along, paused, hopped again. "No humans out there. I believe we have a perfect ambush point."

The clone touched his shoulder. Using basic motions that weren't actual sign language, he pointed first to Mueller, then to the ground beneath Mueller's boots. Next, he indicated himself before pointing forward and toward the left.

Mueller nodded. Number 49's idea showed tactical understanding. "Superb idea. If you crawl out there and hunker down, we can command a wider field of fire. If ever in doubt, look to me. I'll point the way for you."

Number 49 pocketed the monocular, then slithered forward with fluid motions that suggested a giant salamander more than a man. Mueller had never seen any man move in such an odd variant of the sniper low crawl. Had the clone invented the maneuver, or did someone teach it to him?

Before long, the clone had positioned himself far forward and to the left, behind a bush that still retained scattered leaves.

In the shade of an overhanging fir bough, Mueller sat on his haunches and waited. Not for long, however. He was meticulously scanning the opposite side when his binoculars caught movement, a darker green against the lifeless tans and browns of the field. A figure wearing camouflage.

But wait. Mueller sharpened the focus. The man wasn't alone. Behind him plodded five companions, all wearing similar apparel and caps.

Six men in camo. No body armor.

Mueller squinted, but couldn't sharpen the image. On this unseasonably warm October day, sunshine created heat shimmers over the field.

Definitely not Klimov's men. Not Ukrainian Army, either. Must be outsiders. But not curiosity seekers. They look too organized.

There. The two in front definitely carried firearms, although in a low-profile manner.

Mueller muttered a German curse.

The group continued trekking his way, but with stealth. Their heads turned left and right, watchful. Hard to be sure, but it seemed they weren't talking.

What is going on here?

This new wrinkle confounded him. His whole purpose for squatting under this pine was to kill or capture the meddlesome Greene. Yet, the motion-detector cam hadn't caught Greene's image at all. It must have been one of these newcomers. As much as his vendetta longed to withdraw and hunt for Greene, loyalty to the organization didn't permit Mueller to ignore this new threat.

Surely these were allies of Greene's. Even if not, the order of the day was to eliminate anyone suspicious.

Perhaps fate had blessed him. Even if he couldn't snuff Greene, a bullet in each of these trespassers whom Klimov dismissed as one stray backpacker might exonerate his name.

In the distance, Number 49 had spotted the newcomers and now trained his monocular on Mueller for guidance.

Using his fingers, Mueller silently conveyed the numeral six. A slash across his throat confirmed the command: Eliminate all six.

With a slight nod, Number 49 eased into a kneeling position. It would allow him to shoot over the shrub concealing him.

Mueller observed with approval. The clone performed in textbook fashion, just as Mueller had taught. The clone pointed his left knee and foot toward the targets. Next, he wrapped his left arm once around the rifle's carrying strap to use the "hasty sling"—a method of creating isometric pressure to increase steadiness.

Excellent.

Then, with his left elbow resting just over his left knee—not directly on top to avoid slipping—Number 49 pulled the stock of his weapon into his shoulder. Perfect form. Kneeling instead of sitting to lift a bit higher, the best position when the target is too far for a standing shot.

Mueller couldn't have been prouder if this mute pupil had been his own son.

Crack!

Number 49's round found its mark. The first of the six targets jerked to the ground.

Crack!

CHAPTER 32

Sitting in the darkness of the dry well that had become his hiding place, Roger focused his groggy brain on one concern: *Why am I not healing?*

He pulled out his one piece of equipment that was proving indispensable: the ink pen from Flashy Al's Truck Stop. When he clicked the tip, the burst of brilliance in this gloomy hole forced him to squint.

Gingerly, he examined the bullet wound. It looked better than when it was fresh, but it definitely wasn't healing as quickly as expected. Why not? He clicked the light off.

When Roger had discovered a collapsed cottage and descended its old, hand-dug well and found the bottom dry, he'd permitted himself the luxury of a couple hours of sleep. Based on past experience, he'd assumed his Methuselah-enhanced physiology would swing into high gear and repair the worst tissue damage before he woke. Yet, here he was, and the spot no longer bled, but it remained ugly red and stung with each movement. What was wrong?

The short stint of sleep had taken off the edge, but his body craved more. The regular need for super-deep slumber was the one drawback of the Methuselah Project. Maybe if he sat still and just rested awhile?

When his head nodded forward, Roger jerked it up again. He'd nearly dozed off. Mustn't sleep. He had to think. What might interfere with the healing process?

The first notion to creep into his mind was his very lack of rest. During training at the Farm, and now these past twenty-four hours, he'd forced himself to exist with scant amounts of shuteye. Could he have abused the Methuselah effect by overruling sleep too often?

His next thought concerned the bullet that pierced him. Was it special? Maybe treated with a toxin, the way aborigines dipped arrow-heads in poison? Nah. Aimed properly, a bullet needed no poison to kill.

A third possibility jolted his mind to alertness: Radiation?

Even if he hadn't any other clue to his whereabouts, the fleeting glimpses of the one-hundred-fifty-meter-tall radar array once known as "the Woodpecker" would've pegged his location as the evacuated Chernobyl region of the former Soviet Union. Diabolically clever, hiding an H.O. installation beneath a district that remained off limits to the public due to radiation poisoning.

Could radiation be affecting his cells, dampening their ability to recuperate? If so, would the effect be permanent?

These past decades, all he'd wanted was to be a normal man, not an H.O. guinea pig. For the first time, the prospect of losing his miraculous healing ability sent a shiver down his spine. Especially now, while on the run from a pack of goons with guns. Suddenly, losing the Methuselah effect seemed a very real possibility.

I need a mirror.

In the darkness, Roger probed his face with his fingers. Thanks to the Methuselah process, his body hadn't aged more than a matter of months since 1944. His muscles, too, had retained mass and flexibility, working at peak efficiency. His fingers detected no wrinkles, but that was no guarantee wrinkles weren't beginning.

He was over ninety years old. If the Methuselah effect wore off, would he decay into a wrinkled old corpse? He could die in this hole, with no strength to climb out. Katherine would never know.

Katherine. The very thought of her sent a pleasant wave through his heart. He tilted his head backward, resting it against the well's brick wall as he imagined her lovely face ...

"Aha. Here's where you're hiding." With a tinkle of playful laughter, Katherine settled beside him and wrapped one arm around his, inter-twining their fingers. "I've missed you!"

"Oh, Babe, I've missed you, too. But I don't understand. Where did you—?"

"Shhh. No questions. The world is brimming with questions, and never enough answers." She snuggled closer, resting her head on his shoulder. *"Let's forget about problems. This is our moment. Only you and me."*

"Suits me fine." He kissed the top of her head, the same way he once had under a full moon. *"Do you have any idea how much I love you?"*

Once again, Katherine's light-hearted giggle echoed in the well. *"Oh, you've given me a clue or two."*

"This feels like magic, having you with me, no matter where I am."

"Only God is with you everywhere. Even in the valley of the shadow of death. Or a dusty, dry well. But no matter where you go, I hope you take me in your heart."

"Babe, you're definitely in my heart."

She shifted position, moving to sit on his lap so she could wrap both arms around his neck. Instead of the kiss he expected, she leaned close to his ear. *"I have to tell you something. Be careful out here. If anything happens to you, I'll be devastated. Losing you would leave a gigantic black hole in my life. Nothing and nobody could ever fill such a big hole."*

He pulled her closer, rejoicing in the light pressure of her body against his. Simply holding her filled his heart with joy and made the world fade away ...

Fade away? If the effects of the Methuselah Project fizzled, he himself might fade away. *"Katherine, I have to tell you something, too."*

"Shhh. Just let me hold you. Love doesn't depend on words. Sometimes, simply being together is enough."

"But it's important. I'm wounded. Maybe aging. I think the Methuselah thing wore off."

"I believe in you, Flyboy. If there's any way back to me, you'll find it. Roger that?"

"Yes, but—"

Roger jerked upright. His upper body had been sliding sideways. He caught himself and straightened. But when he reached for Katherine, his hand met empty air. He sat, blinking in darkness.

Just a dream!

Or some sort of Methuselah Project hallucination. Yet, Katherine had seemed so real. For a moment, he replayed the fantasy in his mind, relishing the vivid memory of her weight on his lap, of the lilac scent of her perfume.

Part of him longed to succumb to slumber. Maybe the dream would return. But no. If his body really were losing its youth and vigor, he had to get moving. Fully healed or not, he needed out of this pit while he possessed enough strength to climb.

Roger braced his back against one wall of the well and his feet against the opposite side. He'd shimmied his way upward about five feet, when the sound of voices echoed down from above. Russian voices.

Roger snapped fully alert. He slid back down. Of course, they must investigate the tumbledown cottage. Would they think to investigate the well? If they carried high-beam flashlights, he was doomed.

Stiff as a statue, Roger stood with his spine against the wall.

Two voices became louder. A gravelly bass voice shouted unintelligible, echoing words from above. Coarse laughter followed.

The next moment, something weighty thudded into the dirt at Roger's feet and shattered. Then another impact.

Into Roger's mind sprang the image of the abandoned hovel above. Its roof of corrugated gray asbestos had collapsed, along with a wall of bricks.

As chunks of debris pelted down, Roger shielded his head with his forearms. Not for the first time, he wished he'd grabbed a Kevlar vest before his mad dash to freedom. Bulletproof plates would've protected his skull.

God, shield me!

The cascade of broken bricks halted. Roger struggled not to cough despite the gritty dust he was inhaling.

A rifle report echoed down the well, followed by two more. Men up there cackled as if enjoying great sport.

Roger stood frozen. So, no flashlights?

After five full minutes of silent breathing through his nose, he dared to lower his arms. Had they moved on? Unsure, he remained in place about a quarter of an hour, eyes gazing upward and ears cocked for the slightest sound of life.

Go for it.

Once again bracing his feet and spine against opposite sides of his hiding place, he inched his way upward. The ache from the bullet wound reminded him to proceed gingerly.

After a seeming eternity, he arrived at the top and stretched his neck to peer above the rim. There stood the ancient dwelling. Birds flitted among the bare tree branches. A couple pecked the ground. No humans.

With a groan, he pulled himself out. Massaging his arms provided meager relief for the bruises imposed by falling bricks. Until recently, a bruise would've healed in minutes. Today—who could guess?

Now that the initial getaway had succeeded and he'd rested his eyes, Roger dredged up the escape-and-evasion techniques he'd learned, both in the Air Force and at the Farm.

"Don't look like anything," Bert had advised. "Create no silhouette that differs from your surroundings. Blend with the patterns of nature. When possible, use burlap, cloth, or twine to create a homemade ghillie suit incorporating scraps of foliage from the area."

Roger had no burlap, twine, or camo makeup, but he spotted a depression in the ground. Scraping the spot with his fingers, he raked up a mix of damp earth and decaying leaves, which he rubbed over his hands until his skin tone disappeared.

Perfect.

Another handful of soil soon coated his face and neck.

A glance at his clothing elicited a quiet grunt. No good. However well the pixelated greens of his pilfered uniform might blend with the forest in summer, they now stood out as unnaturally brighter than the browns, grays, and yellows of the forest in October. He scooped more moist dirt and ground it into his clothing. Crawling into the crumbling cottage, he didn't find a fireplace as he had hoped. However, the remains of a wood stove provided black soot, which further muted the greens he wore.

"Your speed should match your environment," was another axiom of evasion. "Don't let your speed attract attention or disturb the wildlife."

Roger considered. He'd traveled from the east. The searchers who were just here must have come from the same direction. Whether they'd picked up signs of his passing or not, he didn't dare continue westward. He might run smack into them.

He lifted his eyes to the clear sky overhead. *Which way, Lord?*

Unfortunately, he'd never studied the geography of Eastern Europe. Although he vaguely knew Ukraine lay east of Poland, he had no recollection of Chernobyl's exact location inside Ukraine, nor which direction might point him toward Kiev, where the U.S. would have its embassy.

No sound, except the breeze in the treetops and an occasional bird chirp.

For now, he decided to head northeast. That direction led away from the underground prison, but also away from the men searching for him.

Cautious to avoid crackling leaves and brittle twigs, he drifted through the forest at a quarter of his normal pace.

Sneak back to the hangar? Swipe an airplane?

Ridiculous. Such plots might work in Hollywood movies, but his enemies were no imbeciles. Even if those aircraft were fueled—which he doubted—the sentries guarding them would be on maximum alert. Nope, slow and easy was the best bet. If nothing else, the longer he could remain free and above ground, the more time he gave Baron and his team to pick up his radio signal.

Sure hope they're tracking me.

At one point, the sound of a motorized vehicle reached his ears. Barely in time, he dove to the ground. Head flat against the earth, he cracked an eye and watched through the grass as an olive-drab truck idled its way along a track that evidently lay perpendicular to his path. Because of the vehicle's snail pace, its occupants must be scanning the woods on either side.

After the truck passed, he remained pressed to the ground another full minute. Evidently just one vehicle. He rose, approached the road, studied both directions, then took an extra-long step to avoid planting his boot into the dirt shoulder as he crossed it. On the far side, he once again merged with nature.

At this pace, he was making little progress. Still, he was free—and alive.

After what he guessed must be a mile, he swerved more directly north. The compass heading didn't concern him. Right now, the main goal was not to be anywhere near the H.O.

Occasionally Roger chanced upon other roads, or abandoned homes, and a vacated store. These he avoided. Although the natural temptation was to shelter in manmade structures, nothing would invite investigation so quickly as buildings. Safer to blend with the wide outdoors.

At one point, an unpaved two-track lane crossed his path. Keeping to his new custom, he paused behind a tree to watch and listen before crossing.

It occurred to him the bullet wound finally ached less. He lifted the camo shirt and examined the spot. Sure enough, the wound had closed. Yet, it remained clearly visible. A week ago, nothing but a pink spot would've remained by this time.

Once more, his fingertips touched his face. The caked layer of dry mud made it impossible to guess whether age lines were forming. Might his body be aging from the inside out? Assuming he could successfully evade the H.O. goons hunting him—which was a king-sized assumption —how might Katherine react if he degenerated into a wispy-headed senior citizen with wrinkles and shaky hands? No one could expect a beautiful girl in her twenties to feel romance for an old codger in his nineties.

If he really did lose the life-stretching effects of Methuselah, would his memory decay with dementia? Would he even recognize Katherine? Or would he suffer the worse fate of remembering her perfectly—and still loving her—but never again wrapping his arms around her, never again relishing the touch of her lips on his?

Moisture welled in his eyes. Had he already kissed his girlfriend for the final time, and not even realized it?

Roger's mind shot back to his quarters at Eglin Air Force Base and the velvety, heart-shaped box he'd left in his dresser drawer—the engagement ring he'd purchased at that jewelry store in Destin.

Thank God he didn't know Katherine would be at the Farm when he arrived. If he'd known, he would've taken the ring. What a mess if he'd proposed, but then degenerated into an old fogey less than a month later.

For the first time, he viewed the rough patch he and Katherine had experienced as a possible blessing in disguise. If he really did disintegrate into old age, maybe God let those misunderstandings happen to create emotional distance, lessen her pain?

A faint purring penetrated Roger's thoughts. It sounded manmade, but much quieter than a vehicle. More like the light hum of an electrical transformer.

Peering left and right revealed nothing. Gazing into the branches overhead proved useless. The hum continued, paused, and resumed.

Bracing himself with both palms against the tree he had chosen as a shield from the road, Roger eased his upper body around it for an unobstructed view.

Bingo.

Mounted ten feet off the ground on the opposite side of his tree trunk was a well-disguised video camera. Its housing resembled the cracked gray bark of the tree supporting it. Although the cam was performing a slow pan, evidently giving its operator a 180° view of this forest road, when motionless the protrusion would resemble a broken tree branch.

If he hadn't paused to check his injury, he would've waltzed across this road in full view of H.O. security.

Thank You, Lord.

Now he must be doubly vigilant, for both human and electronic surveillance. Yet, trees surrounded him. Had he already walked within range of other cams?

Roger eased away, quieter than a sparrow in case the device included a microphone.

Eventually, he reached a bend in the road where he could cross out of sight of the camera. However, the new threat of camouflaged surveillance equipment hindered his progress even more than before. Was there any way to slow down pursuers if they tracked him this far?

The sight of an abandoned house attracted his attention. No, he wouldn't hide there, but maybe he could find something useful? After a furtive glance around, he slipped inside. Except for a wooden chair with a broken leg, all furniture was gone. With the home's door ajar and windows vandalized, the floor of every room crunched with shattered glass and dry leaves.

In the kitchen, Roger rummaged each door and cupboard. The scant remaining items proved he wasn't the first scavenger. A rusty bottle opener. A bent fork. A half-empty box of wooden matches. Would they still work? He struck one. It ignited.

Might not be useful, but he kept the matches, just in case.

The last item in the drawer was an ancient spool of fishing line. Thinking the slender line might be helpful to fabricate a ghillie suit, he dropped the spool into his pocket.

Finding nothing else, Roger turned to leave the kitchen. The sole of his boot wobbled over something hard. Brushing away the leaves, he uncovered a grimy knife with a wooden handle. The blade bore countless nicks and scratches, as if the previous owner had sharpened it on rocks.

He didn't need a second knife. His Swiss army knife provided a better blade. Yet, the combination of the aged blade plus fishing line sparked an inspiration.

Whoa. That just might work.

CHAPTER 33

Scouring the woods with his men in a drawn-out line abreast of each other, Klimov scowled. Where could the accursed American be? The man had been wounded. Klimov had seen the blood. Yet, the footprints and blood drops had dwindled the farther the man fled. Now, no signs at all were to be found.

This American was bewitched. Or he'd grown wings. Never in Klimov's memory had frustration and anger churned his gut like today.

Mueller. This fiasco was all his fault. Klimov hoped the High Council really did authorize him to eliminate Mueller. It would be a pleasure to strap that old goat onto the conveyer. But revenge must wait. Right now, the pressing need was to stop Greene from escaping the Zone.

Klimov keyed the mic on his left epaulet. "Glava-1 to Dispatch. Contact whichever Ukrainian army commander is currently overseeing the Zone's perimeter. Tell him I have a ..." He paused. What to call this American? "Tell him we have a foreign spy trying to escape Ukraine on foot through the Zone. If his men apprehend this enemy of the state, he will be richly rewarded."

"Understood."

Klimov spat. He had no respect for the Ukrainian generals who enforced the quarantine around Chernobyl. Back in the day, hadn't their predecessors colluded with black marketers to salvage every television, radio, and skillet, right down to the aluminum window frames in Chernobyl and Pripyat? By law, nothing was to be removed. Yet, greed had motivated vermin to steal everything, and then to sell it to unsuspecting countrymen in open-air markets.

He spat again. Greed—the Achilles' heel of humans. No doubt, Russian commanders would likewise yield to temptation if a nuclear explosion had radiated Kursk, or Omsk, or Saratov. But since the tragedy hadn't occurred in mother Russia, it was easy to revile the Ukrainian military for corruption.

Klimov keyed his mic again. "Dispatch, inform the Ukrainian guards to cancel all tour buses until the intruder is captured. We don't need civilians poking around."

"Already done. Glava-2 gave the order as soon as the search began."

"Very good. Glava-1, out."

Excellent. Voronin was proving himself worthy of last month's promotion to Security Lieutenant. This American mongrel might be shrewd, but in the end, Klimov, Voronin, and their men would corner the intruder.

Just as quickly, doubt re-rooted itself in Klimov's confidence. Trouble was, the security department for T.R. III wasn't geared for a massive, aboveground manhunt. His boys weren't trained for this.

Emerging from the woods into a clearing, he and his men approached yet another, run-down hut that had been some family's home before the 1986 disaster.

Disaster? Klimov grunted. If only the idiots knew. The event historians would forever consider "a flawed reactor design and inadequately trained personnel" had never been connected to a shadowy, worldwide league known as the Heritage Organization. Jaws worldwide would have dropped if the simpletons realized the worst nuclear "accident" in history had been engineered on purpose. The simple truth was the H.O. needed a clever hiding place for its third Talent Redemption facility. What genius to arrange a site with a wide off-limits ring, a perimeter even guarded by Ukraine's military!

Repeating the procedure that he and his men had developed earlier, Klimov and his men surrounded the former dwelling with weapons at the ready. The windows had all been smashed, and the door stood half open. As Klimov approached, something rustled the crisp leaves inside.

Finally, the American was cornered. Klimov allowed a gloating tone as he called, "Come out, Greene. Good try, but we have you surrounded."

More rustling.

"Greene, come out, with hands up."

Was the American armed, possibly waiting to ambush him?

"Last chance, or I shoot."

Silence.

Klimov raised Marusya and blasted several rapid rounds through the gaping doorway.

A high-pitched scream like the wail of a terrified girl erupted from the house. In the same instant, a blur of brown fur hurtled out the doorway, tiny paws barely touching the earth as a fox darted for safety.

After an astonished moment, Klimov's men burst into laughter. The security chief joined them. A chance to fire Marusya and the comical result uncorked his pent-up tension.

"All right, men, it was good practice. But let's get back to business. Sokolov, check the house. Make sure the American isn't lying in there, dead of a bullet wound. The rest of you, fan out. Look for signs."

The men hadn't spread far before one shouted, "Sir, a cloth stained with blood!"

Every searcher turned toward the excited man, who reached down.

For a split second, Klimov's voice caught in his throat. "Polyakov, wait!"

The man snatched up the cloth, but tied to it was a taut string.

A swish and a blur resulted in a howl from Polyakov. From nowhere, a crude, featherless arrow had embedded itself in the man's unprotected thigh.

Every searcher froze, as if caught in a minefield. Klimov strode forward and grabbed the cloth from the grimacing Polyakov.

Klimov held up the red-stained fabric. "Heavy-duty fishing line. Watch." He followed the line to a spot on the forest floor where several whittled sticks protruded from the ground. Parallel to the ground, a homemade bow was affixed to the sticks. Mueller had warned the American was devious. Here was evidence.

"Congratulations, gentlemen. You have just witnessed an excellent example of a booby trap. Specifically, the bow trap." Klimov turned to the wounded man. "Polyakov, pull that thing out."

"It won't come out. The tip must be whittled like a fishhook."

A worthy adversary, this American. Klimov strode back to Polyakov and snapped off the shaft, leaving several centimeters jutting from his leg.

Polyakov yelped.

"Don't be such a woman. There's the road. Hobble back to T.R. III. Report to the clinic."

With a rueful glance at his superior, the wounded man turned and limped away.

"The rest of you, here are the lessons we just gleaned: First, we're headed the right direction. Second, our quarry is no fool. Third, don't touch anything unusual. Let's go."

As the men re-formed their line and proceeded through the woods, Klimov suddenly realized his anger had vanished. Not his anger toward Mueller; he would deal with the German imbecile later. But his anger toward the American had transformed into something else. Respect.

He had always appreciated an opponent with guts and brains.

Of course, they would still track down Greene and make him pay. But the American was making the hunt stimulating. For the first time since accepting the post at T.R. III, Klimov got to hunt a true adversary. He felt like a soldier again.

He would have to thank that cursed American—right before ending his miserable life.

CHAPTER 34

"I don't like this. Too exposed. Every eye and ear on full alert." Bill Baron's tracking app had led the CIA group out of the woods and into a huge field. Katherine scanned the panorama—an expanse of dead grass dotted with an occasional shrub. Of more interest to her, in the distance at the ten o'clock position stood a massive structure looking like a gigantic section of fencing constructed of interconnected pipes. The "Woodpecker" Baron had called it, a curious antenna leftover from the USSR. Hopefully, nobody was perched up there with a telescope.

Wainwright grunted. "Not a speck of cover."

Henderson trudged at the point. Next came the second marksman, Powell, then Baron with his tracking app. Following them were Wainwright, Katherine, and Melissa as rearguard. Like the others, Katherine preferred the visual obscurity of the woods, but this was their route.

A distant *Crack!*

Henderson crumpled. A splotch of crimson blossomed on the front of his camo shirt. The man's eyes registered shock. A gurgle issued from his throat.

Powell dove for the ground even as another shot rang out.

The bullet meant for Powell struck Baron's right forearm. The arm jerked, flinging his satellite phone into the grass.

"Down!" Wainwright shouted. But he was too slow for his own warning. A third bullet hammered into his chest. Wainwright tumbled into the dead grass.

Katherine was already diving when Melissa tackled her from behind.

With an expression of shock, Wainwright looked at Katherine. "Sorry."

Even as Wainwright's eyes closed, a fourth shot sounded. This one found no mark. The survivors lay flat on their stomachs amid thigh-deep grasses.

While Powell tried to draw a bead on the shooter's position, Melissa crawled to Wainwright. "He's dead."

Katherine forced herself to look away, lest she vomit. Wainwright had been brash, flirtatious, sometimes charming, and sometimes annoying. But he deserved a more meaningful death than this.

She had to focus. Do the next right thing.

Since they still had Powell for defense, Katherine inched forward to where Baron lay sprawled, applying direct pressure to his forearm. She undid the button on the hem of the sleeve. "Let's see how bad it is." Despite Baron's wince, she slid the sleeve up. As soon as the pressure was off, a rivulet of blood issued from the wound. She pressed his right hand over the spot.

"I can't feel my fingers," Baron said through gritted teeth.

"I bet it fractured the bone." Faking more confidence than she felt, Katherine added, "Could've been a lot worse. Melissa, give me your KA-BAR."

Melissa extended the KA-BAR 3030 personal knife Katherine had spotted under her pillow in Paris. "How did you know I carry a KA-BAR?"

"I'm an intelligence agent. It's my job to know things."

Powell popped his head up, then back down. Another rifle report sounded.

"We need to stop the blood flow. Plus make a sling." Thinking creatively, Katherine lifted her own camo shirt and sliced off the bottom half of her cotton undershirt. Melissa's razor-sharp blade glided through the fabric as if it weren't there. In seconds, she had a swatch of material. Part of this she folded into a wad, which she had Baron hold over the wound while she tied it in place.

Meanwhile, Powell continued to scuttle back and forth, raising his head in various locations for quick peeks before ducking back down. Each glimpse earned a rifle shot.

"I spotted him. One man, about a hundred yards out. He was hunched over and moving closer."

Baron's eyebrows lowered. "Only one? Can you take him out?"

"Sure gonna try. He's quick on the trigger."

Melissa pulled Henderson's rifle from his lifeless fingers. "Let's change tactics. The sniper might believe you're the only one who's armed. I'll creep off to the right. On your 'Go,' I'll start blasting. Maybe I can distract him long enough for you to get him in your sights."

Powell nodded. "Let's do it." He slithered to the left, where he assumed a fresh position.

Katherine overheard the exchange but continued fashioning a sling for Baron. She could pull her sidearm from its holster, offer more covering fire for Powell. But no. She had to trust her team. Her top priority must be to prep Baron for action. Trouble was, she'd fashioned only one sling in her entire life, while standing up, during a no-stress first aid course. "Never thought I'd have to do this while hugging the ground under flying bullets."

"Now!" shouted Powell.

Melissa's rifle began popping.

By the time Katherine finished the awkward maneuver of tying the sling at an appropriate length around Baron's neck while flat, she still hadn't heard a single shot from Powell. Was he ...?

There he was, in the kneeling position, peering through his scope and scanning back and forth.

Katherine dared pop her head up for a glance of her own. Nothing. Empty grass, with a stand of evergreens on a rise of ground beyond.

Powell waved an arm to catch Melissa's attention. "Cease fire." He scooted into a new position in case the sniper's crosshairs were targeting the airspace he'd just vacated. "I've lost sight of him." He lifted for a peek.

Crack! The report sounded close.

"Unh."

From Katherine's perspective, she couldn't see the point of impact, but Powell was breathing hard. He swung his rifle to the left—

Crack!

Powell jerked as his body absorbed a second bullet. Still, the man struggled to raise his weapon.

*   *   *

Through his field glasses, Kurt Mueller observed Number 49 with father-like pride. Within seconds, the clone had definitely slain at least two of the trespassers. Another bullet had wounded or killed a third.

"Textbook perfect. The element of surprise."

Indeed, watching his prize pupil in action reminded Mueller of his own youth. Back then, he could run like the wind, leap obstacles, and shoot simultaneously. Although Mueller being a mentor wasn't as exciting as the hunt, a vicarious thrill swept through him. Number 49 was implementing all the lessons Mueller had drilled into him.

"Excellent. He's got them pinned down and terrified."

Number 49 pulled out his monocular and looked to Mueller.

The German returned a thumbs up, followed by hand signals to indicate two definite kills. He ended by gesturing a sweeping curve toward the group—sneaking around their flank and pressing the attack from closer quarters.

The clone nodded, pocketed the monocular, and moved forward. One of the trespassers seemed particularly intent on getting his skull blown open. Number 49 obliged by firing every time a head showed itself.

Mueller chortled. "Marvelous. Too bad we can't film this."

Of course, he hadn't forgotten his vendetta against Greene. But running into these armed meddlers was a stroke of luck. Wiping out six intruders that Klimov had written off as one probable hiker would countermand whatever rubbish the Russian might report. Besides, at the rate Number 49 was mowing them down, this shouldn't take long. Could Fate be so kind as to deliver Kurt Mueller a double victory, both this group and Greene? Klimov would be livid, but two triumphs in one day would enshrine the name of Kurt Mueller in the annals of Heritage Organization history.

The German refocused the binoculars. Number 49 had dropped to all fours and nearly disappeared from sight. However, a slight swaying of tall grass revealed his location. Performing that fast crawl of his, no doubt.

All this time, Mueller had been observing while sitting on his haunches, his own rifle cradled across his legs. However, his leg muscles began cramping. He stood and leaned his rifle against a bough of the nearest pine. When he raised the field glasses again, Number 49 had disappeared.

Then, as if ejected from the ground by a spring, Number 49 leaped from the deep grass and ran, shooting, straight toward the huddled intruders.

"Excellent!" the German cried when another trespasser slumped. "Finish them off!"

*   *   *

Powell's body shuddered under the onslaught of bullets. His rifle dropped. Miraculously, Powell didn't fall.

Now quite close, the sniper halted and regarded the group with malice. As if basking in victory, he tilted up the brim of his cap.

Katherine gasped at the sight of her boyfriend's face. Her brain refused to accept it. *Impossible!*

A click sounded behind Katherine. Another click. Melissa shouted, "I'm out of ammo. Shoot him!"

The assailant leisurely targeted the defenseless Powell at point-blank range.

Katherine found her voice. "Roger, no! You're shooting fellow Americans!"

"Shoot him!" Melissa hissed.

Was he drugged? Hypnotized? "Roger, it's me, Katherine."

The shooter paused. His rifle pointed at Powell, but he squinted at her with curiosity.

"It's me! And Baron. And Melissa. We've come to rescue you."

The shooter maintained eye contact with Katherine, but pulled his trigger. Powell collapsed.

"Mueller, do something!" Melissa's useless rifle hurtled overhead toward their attacker. The man sidestepped, but now stared at Melissa, as if she'd said something very odd.

Katherine raised her pistol. "Forgive me." She pumped two rounds into his midriff.

Shock registered in the shooter's eyes. He looked from Katherine to his own stomach. He dropped his rifle and sank to his knees.

Having witnessed Roger's incredibly fast healing ability in the past, she almost expected him to take a couple breaths and leap back to his feet. He didn't. His fading gaze meandered from Katherine, to the body of Powell, to Wainwright, to Baron, to Melissa. As if remembering something, he half turned and stared toward the distant pines, the spot where somebody with binoculars must be watching.

Surely Roger would stand back up? His amazing, death-defying metabolism couldn't be stopped by two slugs—could it?

Melissa snatched up Powell's rifle. "All right, you—talk. Why did you flee Paris? Why did you double-cross us?"

His only response was to cover his bleeding stomach with his hands. When he coughed, up came spatters of blood.

"Don't you dare die," Melissa commanded. "You owe us answers."

Astonishment and disbelief knotted inside Katherine. She felt twin trails of tears on her cheeks even as her victim closed his eyes, coughed again, then crumpled. With or without Melissa's permission, he was breathing his last—and Katherine had been the executioner.

"No!" She rushed forward.

Melissa shot out a hand of warning. "It could be a trick."

Katherine paid no heed. She knelt beside her lifeless boyfriend. After all their conversations, after countless smiles and kisses, how could he die like this—a murdering machine, fulfilling the whims of the Heritage Organization? How did they brainwash him?

Baron's voice penetrated her sobbing. "Mueller, this is not your boyfriend. You're weeping over a lookalike."

"A lookalike?" Katherine performed a more clinical, unemotional inspection. She'd hugged Roger more times than she could count. If anyone could detect a difference—

"The likeness is eerie," she said, studying him with a more objective eye. "But you're right. The real Roger has a mole behind his left ear. This man doesn't. The eyebrows are different, too. Longer, thinner."

His right arm in the sling Katherine had rigged, Baron crouched beside her. In his left hand, he held his satphone. "Also, this imposter isn't wearing the ankle bracelet. The radio signal is still west of us. And moving."

Melissa remained the incarnation of straight-faced business. "We've got three dead, one wounded, and our presence has been compromised. This might be a suitable time for a strategic retreat."

Baron studied his satphone. "A withdrawal might be in order. Only problem is, I'm no quitter. Satellite imagery shows plenty of trees will provide cover once we get past this field. What do you say, Mueller?"

He was actually asking her opinion? "I'm no quitter either. You're in a lot of pain, but if you can handle the discomfort, I'd like to push forward. We still have weapons, and there's more ammunition in the backpacks."

He tightened his lips. "Gutsy answer, especially from a first-timer. Then again, you want to find our man."

Melissa stood, performing a visual sweep. "So, we continue?"

A pain-tinged determination appeared on Baron's face. "Let's proceed. You two will have to wear the backpacks."

Melissa unfastened the pack from Henderson's body and adjusted the straps for her more slender physique. "You don't believe in playing it safe, do you?"

"If I believed in playing it safe, I never would've left my previous job."

The statement piqued Katherine's curiosity. "Which was what?"

"I was an auditor for the IRS. I still make trouble for people. This way is more fun." He studied his tracker. "That way."

CHAPTER 35

From his vantage point under a pine, Kurt Mueller literally dropped his field glasses. Incredibly, his star pupil had failed—and gotten himself killed.

Why had Number 49 stood there, hesitating, with victory within reach?

"The *Dummkopf!* I taught him better. We show no mercy."

Even more bewildering, one of the intruders was a woman in a ponytail. After shooting Number 49, she had rushed forward and hugged him.

Recovering somewhat from shock, he retrieved the field glasses. The organization needed answers—quickly. He fine-tuned the focus by half a hair, adjusting the faces into high definition.

The first two faces meant nothing. But then—

"Katarina!" Mueller clutched his chest as his heart launched into a rapid staccato.

What was happening? First the American Roger Greene had penetrated their clandestine facility. Suddenly Mueller's own renegade niece appeared with a band of intruders. Very possibly, more intruders were converging on T.R. III from other directions. The American military? Special Forces—it was the only answer that made sense.

No time for revenge. The secrecy of the entire organization teetered on the edge of a razor. With Klimov and most of his men out scouring the forest for Greene, the installation was left much too vulnerable. If the American military forced its way into T.R. III and confiscated the computers, the result would be disastrous.

Never in his bleakest nightmares had Kurt Mueller imagined the Heritage Organization so exposed. If only he had a radio!

He snatched up his rifle and broke into a run.

CHAPTER 36

Picking his way through the forest, Roger considered his homemade bow. The object was crude. Except for where he'd whittled the tips to make notches for the fishing-line, a thin layer of bark clung to the stave. Without a drawknife, or at least a hatchet, his rough job would have to suffice. Of course, the wood was green. A true bow should be dried for weeks, then shaped. But would he even be alive in several weeks?

There went his chance to impress the editors at *Field & Stream*.

Of course, without arrows even a professionally manufactured bow would be useless. Still, fashioning a weapon had provided a feeling of proactive defiance. The effort had also helped him to stay awake and focused.

Ahead, an intriguing sight came into view. An ancient, weed-filled cemetery. The monuments were a mishmash of weatherworn stone slabs and crosses. The crosses must represent Orthodox believers, since they sported the traditional crosspiece for Christ's arms, plus a smaller crosspiece cocked on an angle. Fencing enclosed quite a few gravesites, the rusting iron still dotted with occasional flecks of pastel blue paint. In this ancient site, fair-sized trees competed with headstones for the same territory. Rotted logs littered the ground, even atop broken markers.

Like something out of Dr. Zhivago. *Must've been a village in bygone days.*

Now, only the dead remained—which would include him, if he didn't keep walking. So far, he'd spotted three video cameras, but saw none here. Apparently, no human had disturbed these Slavic bones for ages. He trudged forward, navigating straight through the graveyard.

Eerie silence hung like heavy cloak. Creepy. Not so much as a crow in sight.

Get a grip. You've got a bunch of trigger-happy men on your six, and you let a bunch of old bones give you the shivers?

He stepped onto a grave.

Instantly, Roger's boots broke through the ground, sinking him up to the knees. The coffin beneath must have rotted. Something brittle snapped beneath his weight.

"Whoa!"

In a flash, he imagined ghostly claws clutching at his ankles, pulling him deeper. With a surge of adrenaline, Roger kicked and pulled in an effort to free his legs. A moment later, he was charging pell-mell through the cemetery. Not until he was clear of graves did he stop to collect his thoughts.

Despite himself, he laughed and wiped sweat from his brow. Villagers must not have planted bodies very deep in olden days.

"Big chicken. Take away your fighter plane, and you're no good."

But now he faced a dilemma. In his panic, he'd left a trail so obvious a kindergartner could follow it. Should he go back and—?"

Soft whirring overhead. Not twenty feet away, a disguised video cam pointed directly at him.

Roger broke into a run, dashing directly under the cam, which could pan only left and right. Three hundred feet beyond, like a jackrabbit, he altered direction, then changed direction again three or four minutes later. No time for blending with nature. Survival depended on getting far from the place where they'd spotted him. Eventually, he changed course a final time and slowed his pace, minimizing the signs of his passing. Direction wasn't crucial, as long as he didn't veer back toward the H.O.

What a knucklehead. Those few seconds of schoolgirl panic might've cost him his freedom—or his life.

An ache emanated from his bullet wound. It hadn't bothered him as long as he stepped gingerly. He placed a palm over the pain.

Where on earth was Baron and his CIA technology?

Of course, Chernobyl, Ukraine, was many miles from Paris. In fact, considering the startling way Roger had plunged into this mess, Baron might not have even noticed the ankle bracelet was missing.

Roger swallowed. Or rather, tried to swallow. His mouth couldn't quite muster enough saliva. How much blood had he lost?

For the first time, thirst pressed into his thoughts. His concentration had been so focused on dangers that he'd disregarded basic needs.

Where might he find water?

In October, he wouldn't find wild berries. His escape-and-evasion courses had taught him how to tap birches for watery sap, but time-consuming techniques serve best when one is merely lost. Being hunted, he couldn't afford the time. He'd have to ignore his thirst.

At this point, he was treading lightly, but not so lightly an experienced tracker couldn't detect his tracks. He needed to slow down his pursuers. Confuse them. Another evasion trick came to mind. "The Large Tree." When he spotted an ancient oak, he passed it, heading into an area dominated by pines. Here he stopped, then carefully walked backward, stepping only in his own footfalls.

When he once again stood beside the large oak, he slid his homemade bow over his shoulder on its fishing-line string. Next, he placed both hands against the tree trunk before taking an extra-long step left, around the tree.

Don't disturb the lichen on the bark. Don't scuff the moss on the ground.

The Large Tree trick would be useless if he left telltale signs. He recalled the words of his instructors: "Under ideal conditions with this tactic, you'd be wearing felt shoe covers to soften and mask the outline of your footprints."

Yeah, right. Other than training school, how often does the average guy carry around felt shoe covers?

On the far side of the oak, Roger glanced backward and awarded himself an A+ for the maneuver. Resuming his cautious pace, he continued at ninety degrees from his previous course.

Might not slow 'em down long, but every delay helps me out.

Occasionally, he discovered edges of the forest, places where woods ended at clearings or meadows. Off in the distance, the roofs of what looked like apartment buildings rose fifteen or sixteen stories over the treetops. Whether they revealed the city of Chernobyl or another town, he couldn't guess. Since they were in the radioactive region, they would be deserted.

Tall buildings guarantee plenty of nooks and crannies. Hiding places?

The man-made structures tempted, but he shook his head. The H.O. must have the place under surveillance, just waiting for him to bumble into their clutches.

He turned away and continued his silent trek. For October, though, the day had turned unseasonably warm. Above these trees and their thinning leaves, the azure sky was providing non-stop sunshine.

What I'd give for an airplane.

He plodded on. At last he discovered a welcome sight. A stream of cool water crossed his way. Roger paused. Drink from a stream in the radiated Chernobyl region?

He shrugged. Without water, his body would dehydrate. Besides, the steady current hinted this water flowed from somewhere else. He knelt and lifted handful after handful of cool, refreshing liquid to his mouth.

On the bright side, if I end up glowing in the dark, I won't need my pen from Flashy Al's.

The chuckle bolstered his morale.

Too bad the little waterway wasn't wider and deeper. If it were, he could lash a couple logs together and float downstream.

But what lay downstream? Without knowing local geography, downstream might lead him straight back to the organization's open arms.

He stepped into the stream, then splashed water to remove his footprints from the damp sand. Done, he waded upstream, searching for a point where he could climb out without disturbing the ground.

Those trackers had better be good. He wasn't going to make this easy.

Leaving the waterway behind, Roger pushed onward, staying as alert as his weary brain allowed. Physically, his pace was relaxed. Mentally, the science of evasion with every sense on high alert taxed his nerves and was birthing a headache.

Wait. A headache?

He hadn't experienced a single headache since 1943, when Doctor von Blomberg subjected his body to the gamut of procedures to alter his physiology. In all those decades, Roger hadn't popped a single aspirin. Head pain offered further evidence his physiology was changing.

Roger shot a plea to God: *Lord, please help me survive. At least long enough to see Katherine. And please free Sophie. She sacrificed everything for my sake.*

His prayer completed, Roger looked down barely in time to avoid stepping on a corroded object peeking from the leaves.

Whoa! He shot a hand to the nearest tree trunk to steady himself.

With a sigh of relief, he stooped for a closer look—a rusty cylinder with a pointed nose and metal fins. A mortar? An old bazooka shell? Definitely unexploded ordnance. Probably from World War II. Nazi forces once overran this territory.

A verse from Psalm 119 came to mind: "Thy word is a lamp unto my feet." The Scripture didn't fit the situation perfectly, but he still whispered thanks to the Almighty for not letting him trample an unexploded shell. News reports occasionally told of newly unearthed bombs exploding, killing the innocents who found them.

He straightened, intending to bypass the relic.

Hold on. Might there be a way to recycle this thing?

Using fingertips, Roger brushed away leaves, twigs, and brittle pine needles. Despite superficial rust, the casing appeared intact. The thing really might be live. Holding his breath, he picked up the shell with more tenderness than he would've used for a sleeping baby.

How could he use it against his pursuers? Lash it to a spear? Too heavy. Construct a tiny catapult? No time, no tools, and his brain felt too groggy. Besides, catapults don't fire themselves. An operator has to work it.

His mind drifted back to the booby trap he'd set near the hut. The fishing line. Quite a bit remained on the spool. Could he rig a trip wire?

The longer he remained stationary, the more intensely the yearning to sleep pressed into his brain. So, he paced while deliberating. As he walked, he studied the surrounding trees and the angles of their branches, the rocks strewn about, rotted logs, even miscellaneous chunks of fallen bark ... Now that his mind tackled a specific problem, the challenge perked him up like a double espresso brewed with Robusta beans.

After ten or twelve laps around the unexploded projectile, the beginnings of a plan took shape. Roger scanned the branches overhead.

It just might work.

Out of his pocket came the pen from Flashy Al's Truck Stop. From another pocket he pulled the spool of fishing line. He studied again the branch he'd selected. Did he have enough line?

A simple granny knot secured the line to the pen's pocket clip. In the history of the world, had anyone ever used a ballpoint pen to jerry-rig a booby trap with an old-fashioned bomb? "Learn to see beyond an object's normal function," Bert had counseled at the Farm. "Exercise creativity. Overcome functional fixedness."

Here goes nothing.

Throwing the pen like a knife, Roger sent it twirling upward. However, he hadn't paid out enough fishing line. Several feet short of his target branch, the string jerked taut, causing the pen to recoil back to the ground. On his next try, the pen looped over the wrong branch, a mere twig that looked too flimsy to support the bomb's weight. He pulled it back down.

On his third try, the ballpoint finally sailed over his intended branch. Next, he paid out more line, allowing the pen to descend back to him.

Hurry. This is taking too long.

Despite his need for speed Roger continued to work, but with attentive ears and many a glance around. Leaving the pen tied to one end, he passed the spool of fishing line beneath a gnarled root exposed at the tree's base. The root would serve as an eyehook. Next he unwound the line and stretched it horizontally just inches above the ground to a spot near another oak.

Faster than he'd hoped, the spool unwound to its last few feet. Roger pulled the line, simultaneously hoisting the ballpoint tied to its opposite end up to the spot where he hoped to suspend the old-time bomb.

When he ran out of slack, Roger whittled a short stake, which would serve as a partial anchor. To complete the anchor, he retrieved a rock he'd spotted among the exposed roots of a fallen tree. Alone, the short stake pressed into the earth would never support the full weight of his bomb. Neither would the heaviness of the rock resting on the line. But the combination of the two should hold the bomb dangling high over-head—unless a pursuer's toe snagged the heavy-duty line.

At least, that was the plan. Roger cut off the last few feet of fishing line and stuffed it into a shirt pocket. Probably pointless, but waste not, want not.

Of course, there was every possibility moisture had breached the casing and neutralized the shell. It was also possible he'd shaken his pursuers, which mean they'd never come near his tripwire. That would be the best imaginable outcome. Yet, sixth sense warned him that they were following. Maybe not closely, but they were back there, some-where, and not likely to give up the hunt. If so, his trap might slow them down.

Within two more minutes, he'd lowered the flashlight pen, cut it loose, wrapped that end of the line around the tail fins of the shell, and then gingerly hauled the projectile up to the branch. At the last step, though, his efforts seemed thwarted. Against the steady pull of the bomb's weight, both the anchoring stake and rock proved insufficient. When his fingers eased off, the shell's weight pulled the tripwire free.

Roger searched the ground and spotted a sizeable rock, half buried. By stretching one leg, he reached the rock with his boot. His toe scraped away the dirt, loosened the rock, then wriggled it free. The combined weight of both rocks, plus the stake in the earth, secured the tripwire. Gradually, Roger released his grip. The shell dangled exactly as hoped.

He backed away. This time he would leave no decoy other than his own footprints.

With each backward step, he kept the bomb in sight. The old fishing line had lain untouched for years. There were no guarantees it could withstand the strain without snapping.

At what seemed a discreet distance, Roger turned and continued walking away. Before long, though, he paused. On the side of a tree, two slender limbs, both long dead and dry, seemed straight enough to fashion into arrows. He snapped them off, ending up with two sticks roughly twenty-five inches long. Out came the pocketknife. He whittled a notch for the bowstring into one end of each stick. Two arrows made a meager arsenal. He would need more. Especially since he couldn't expect these crazy sticks to fly straight. But might there be some way to maximize each arrow's firepower?

That last word lodged in Roger's brain. *Firepower?*

He squatted and scooped a pile of brittle leaves. Using the last of his fishing line, he lashed a bundle of leaves to the end of each stick. When finished, his creations resembled ridiculously overgrown matches.

Good enough for now.

Primitive arrows in hand, he set off. Had his attempt at a booby trap been a waste of time? The shell might be nothing but dead weight.

Even so, if those H.O. guys picked up his trail and hit the tripwire, they just might get the snot scared out of them when it dropped. The experience might teach them to slow them down and search for booby traps.

Which was the very goal he hoped to achieve.

CHAPTER 37

In her prisoner's quarters, with ankle chains clinking, Sophie Gottschalk paced and prayed aloud. "Dear God in Heaven, please help Roger. Don't let them catch him."

The very thought of her American friend coming so far—even to the incredible point of discovering and penetrating Talent Redemption III—struck cold fear to her heart. She couldn't be the cause of his death. Better for her to remain a prisoner than for the organization to sink their claws into Roger a second time.

Yet, if Roger had received her communiqué from the CIA, then surely the U.S. government hadn't sent him here solo? Wouldn't their military be standing by?

Sophie snatched the pillow off her bunk and clutched it to her chest. "Being stuck in here is maddening. What's happening out there?"

After Roger had slipped her his napkin and its handwritten note, her heart had soared. At last, someone in the outside world knew where she was!

Before long, though, that ear-blasting alarm had sounded. Judging by the panic among the T.R. III personnel, the alarm must have been their first. Then followed the intruder announcement, complete with a description of Roger.

Now, here she was, confined to quarters ever since "Ice Man" had yanked her from the visiting scientists and shoved her in here.

After the initial excitement of feet pounding up and down the corridor and muffled shouting, a silence had descended. The barely perceptible whisper of fresh air from the ceiling register had been the only sound for at least an hour.

"It sounds like they evacuated the entire complex, except for me."

A memory shot into her mind, halting her pacing. The "Brussels incident." She'd never heard precise details, but even in the H.O. people were human and shared information. In this case, she didn't doubt the story's source—her former boss at the Methuselah Project, Dr. Hans Heinkel. Nothing had fed Hans's self-aggrandizement so effectively as sharing details intended to impress others.

She tried to recall Hans's brief account. It had involved an upscale Brussels restaurant that provided a front for H.O. operations. What had he called it, Chez Robert? But somehow the Belgian State Security Service got wind of nefarious happenings. Hans had gloated, "Before the Belgian authorities raided it, our mole in the Administrator-General's office sent a warning. Not only did our people have time to sterilize all information concerning the Heritage Organization, but they exploded the building just as the secret police were raiding it. The best part? Everyone blamed the explosion on terrorists. Another attack by radical Islam. Brilliant!"

In so telling, Hans Heinkel had unwittingly struck a lethal blow to Sophie's esteem for the H.O. A worldwide association existing for the betterment of mankind had blown up a restaurant to conceal their clandestine activities? And they timed the detonation to slaughter innocent diners and investigators?

How ironic. An organization devotee like Hans had become the tool that pried off the lid and showed her what disgusting deeds their "beloved" H.O. could do. Confining Captain Greene underground for decades had been bad enough. Only her dedication to science had enabled her to stomach it. But after Hans's sickening revelation, all she needed was enough boldness to flee. Of course, she couldn't leave Roger behind.

Helping him escape was the one noble act I've ever done. Now he's in danger because I sent a message. She hurled the pillow at the wall.

Before this moment, the distasteful account from Brussels had simply revealed the rottenness of the H.O.'s core. Now, with T.R. III under lockdown and the possibility of the U.S. positioning Special Forces, the report gained new significance.

"What a fool I was, sending a communiqué. If this place comes under attack, the organization will slaughter us to keep us silent."

If only there were a way to help Roger. A diversion to distract the security team hunting him. But how? Locked in her quarters, she was harmless as a parakeet in a cage.

Again, the incessant whisper of air through the overhead duct pressed into her consciousness. Was God sending an inspiration?

This room hadn't been constructed for prisoners. They had modified staff quarters for Dr. Chakrala and herself. Might the air duct be a weakness she could exploit? The chain connecting her ankles was too short for Sophie to step onto the bed. She sat on it, then swung her legs up. From there, she stood and peered at the overhead grille.

Still too far to scrutinize inside the metal vent, Sophie hopped down long enough to retrieve the wooden chair from her tiny table. Standing it atop the bunk, she clambered up for a closer inspection.

Her face now centimeters from the grille, Sophie peered inside, squinting against the stream of air blowing into her eyes.

"A flashlight would help."

But she had none. Nor a meter stick, nor any other thin object to gauge the size of the ductwork. At last, though, her eyes adjusted enough to reach a conclusion: "Too small. Only a baby could crawl through there."

So much for the overworked plot device employed in cheap novels and Hollywood movies. Real-life air passages simply weren't large enough for adults to sneak through.

"Probably just as well," she told herself as she returned the chair to the floor. "With my luck, I'd be crawling through ductwork above the gymnasium, only to have it break loose and send me plunging to my death."

Sophie was in the process of hopping to the floor when—

Ting. The door slid open. There stood Ice Man, his rifle slung over his shoulder.

The albino guard typically sported a face void of emotion. Now, though, he cocked his head suspiciously as he stepped inside and allowed the door to slide shut behind him. His gaze traveled from Sophie to the bed—where the imprints of the chair's four feet were clearly visible—to the chair, and then to the ceiling register.

Unsure of the albino clone's actual intelligence, Sophie said, "Hello. I was just exercising. Stretching. I've been cooped up ever since the alarm."

Ice Man said nothing. Of course not, he was mute. However, his eyes narrowed.

She feigned light-heartedness. "Have you come to escort me to lunch? I'm famished."

Unblinking, he continued staring. But not merely into her eyes.

With no other option, Sophie stood facing Ice Man as his inspection traveled southward. Klimov's lustful ogling had been torturous enough. The taciturn eyes now prowling her figure caused an involuntary tremble. Maggots crawling in her underwear would be less disgusting than these inhuman eyes.

Ice Man skulked closer. He unslung the rifle and placed the barrel's tip against the inside of her left foot. He pressed it sideways, forcing her to edge her foot outward until the ankle chain went taut. He stepped back and studied the effect.

She trembled again. Could he be measuring the distance the chain allowed her legs to spread?

When Ice Man looked into her face, the frost in his eyes had melted, replaced by the heat of lust.

Then Sophie knew.

The clone gestured something with his hands.

"I-I'm sorry. I don't understand sign language."

No longer signing, the clone resorted to basic pantomiming. He jabbed a finger toward Sophie, then to the bunk. He repeated the motion for emphasis.

"You're telling me to sit down?"

He nodded. After leaning his rifle in the corner, he removed his camo military cap and deposited it beside the rifle. It was the first time Sophie had seen his pallid, hairless scalp and the deep furrows of his brow. He unbuttoned his camouflage shirt.

Heart pounding, Sophie eased down onto the wooden chair.

For the first time in her memory, Ice Man's face contorted with anger. He shook his head and jabbed a finger repeatedly at Sophie, and then to the bunk. He attempted to communicate something with his mouth but managed only a croak.

Despite her tightening gut, Sophie attempted to sound unruffled. "Oh. You want me to sit over there? I didn't quite understand."

She shifted to the bunk, assuming a mask of docility while her mind raced. No hero would burst in to save her. This was just her—and Ice Man.

He discarded the outer shirt onto his cap. The sleeveless undershirt rivaled his skin for whiteness. In one swift motion, he pulled it off and flung it over his shoulder.

To Sophie's mind, Ice Man's scrawny torso with its visible ribs suggested a grotesquely overgrown beetle larva. The thought of this abominable clone straddling her body ignited full-fledged terror.

Even if I scream, no one will hear.

Sophie clasped her hands to keep them from shaking. The emotions rushing through her were dark, horrible, sickening. If she couldn't somehow save herself—

Studying her, Ice Man hoisted a foot and pulled the lace of his boot. Then, oddly, he paused, as if coming to a decision. The albino clone reached into his pocket and withdrew a shiny ring bearing a single key. He tossed it onto Sophie's lap, then indicated the ankle chains. It was the first time any H.O. guard had entrusted her to remove the restraint personally. If only she could get hold of his electronic door key, she might escape to the safety of the corridor.

By the time Sophie had removed the leg restraints, Ice Man had kicked off both boots and was removing his socks. Clearly, sunshine had never graced those grub-like feet. The epidermis appeared slightly translucent, revealing the veins beneath.

Her eyes collided with his. Sophie could no longer disguise her terror. She sat frozen, holding the leg chain, her breaths coming in staccato gasps.

Ice Man grinned. Not a cheerful grin. His lips parted in a plastic leer that made the clone appear less human while advertising lustful intentions. He unbuckled his belt.

Dear God, no. No!

As Ice Man unzipped the fly of his cargo trousers, Sophie seized her chance. Grabbing the seat of the wooden chair, she charged Ice Man and rammed the chair's feet into his bare chest.

Caught off guard with his hands down, Ice Man staggered backward, stopped only when his spine slammed the wall of her cramped quarters.

Sophie abandoned the chair and sprang for the rifle—but not quick enough. With an inhuman squawk, the albino shoved the chair back even harder, knocking Sophie onto the bunk. Enraged, he lunged onto her, intentionally banging his bald skull into her face.

Pain radiated in Sophie's consciousness. Flecks swirled before her eyes. Not thinking, just reacting, she groped the bed cover with her hands, scrabbling for any solid object. Something cold, metallic, met her fingers. The leg restraint. She snatched it. Gripping both cuffs as handles, Sophie whipped the chain's length around Ice Man's throat, jerking it as tight as she could.

His whole head crimson with fury, Ice Man snatched the chain constricting his windpipe and wrenched it from Sophie's grasp. Over his shoulder it flew.

His face now so near she could smell his sour breath in her nostrils, Sophie couldn't distinguish the lust in his eyes from the steely glint of murder.

When the clone clutched her throat, Sophie reacted with her sole remaining weapon—fingernails. Aiming for his eyes, she raked Ice Man's face, gouging as deeply as possible.

Bellowing like an injured elephant, he recoiled, both palms clapped over his face.

Sophie's fear transformed to wrath. Flat on her back, she drew both knees to her chest, and then slammed the soles of both shoes into Ice Man's chest with all the power her legs could deliver. If her human battering ram cracked ribs, so much the better.

"Oof."

Air spewed from the clone's lungs as his body careened backward. With a nauseating thump, the rear of his hairless skull smacked the edge of the table. Just that fast, Ice Man collapsed onto the floor.

Panting hard, Sophie leapt from the bed and snatched the rifle from the corner. She aimed its muzzle at the clone but needn't have bothered. He lay face down. Not so much as a twitch. Was he unconscious, or something more permanent?

"You deserve whatever you got. You might be a fake human, but you're genuine scum!"

Detesting the need, Sophie slid two fingers into the clone's hip pocket and retrieved his electronic key card. A quick swipe beside the door rewarded her with the musical *Ting* she herself had never created. The door slid wide, revealing a wonderfully vacant corridor.

However, with the surge of adrenaline ebbing, Sophie's more calculating mind took control. She'd never get far running around in yellow detainee garb. Manhunt or no, someone in security must be manning the internal cams.

The door slid shut. She needed a disguise and a plan.

Sophie regarded Ice Man's inert form. No matter how repugnant, his uniform presented the only garb to deflect scrutiny. Hardly believing she was doing it, she grasped both hems of his cargo trousers and tugged until she'd extricated them from the ghostly legs.

Even as her prayer of thanks winged its way toward Heaven, Sophie reflected on how she'd never given God much thought until meeting Captain Greene. He'd come to faith in captivity and eventually learned to "pray without ceasing," as he'd called it, regularly shooting the Almighty a phrase or two without the formality of lowering his head or closing his eyes.

Thank goodness Roger had shared a little about his faith. How could she survive this H.O. madhouse without belief in something bigger than herself?

Sophie doffed her yellow prison garb and donned Ice Man's outer clothing, including the boots, which were a size too large. The trouser legs were overlong and bunched around her ankles, so she folded them inward and upward to fake a proper fit. The sleeveless undershirt remained on the floor. She couldn't stomach the thought of any cloth that had hugged Ice Man's body cuddling her own physique.

Sophie's thoughts raced. Running free with a semi-automatic rifle she'd never been trained to use, she might inflict a trivial blow to Talent Redemption III. But to truly wreak carnage and help Roger escape, she needed a real diversion. A big one!

To complete her disguise, she tucked her ponytail under Ice Man's camo cap, pulling the bill down to obscure her features. Knowing the location of every security cam, she could glance down as she passed them.

"Time for reinforcements." She picked up the rifle and started toward the door.

A vice-like grip clamped around her ankle, nearly toppling her. Ice Man! He lifted his clawed face and bellowed as his second hand grappled for a higher hold on her calf.

More furious than afraid, Sophie hoisted the rifle with both hands and cracked its butt onto Ice Man's head with every syllable: "I ... am ... sick ... of ... you!"

On the final blow, the clone's grip released. He appeared unconscious yet again. Sophie considered chaining the troublesome creature but decided not to waste the time. She just wanted to get away from him. Besides, even if she hadn't given him a concussion, she had his electronic pass. Once she exited, the jailer would become the jailed.

Ting.

Into the corridor she stepped—alone. And with a loaded weapon over her shoulder. For the sake of appearance, she mimicked the casual, confident gait of a security guard as she sauntered along to the next door, Dr. Chakrala's.

Ting.

When she entered, her colleague from India was reclining on his bunk. In languid leisure, he turned his head. When he did, the flurry of blinks before he bolted upright sparked a laugh from Sophie.

"Get up. We're leaving."

Chakrala's mouth opened and shut several times before he found his voice. "Sophie, why are you in that uniform? And armed?"

"I got promoted. Come on. We're getting out."

An announcement about invading aliens from the planet Neptune couldn't have plastered a more bewildered expression on Chakrala. "Out? You and me? I don't understand."

Sophie fought down the impatience welling inside her. After all, wouldn't she have reacted the same way if Chakrala had burst into her quarters in uniform?

"Listen, T.R. III is experiencing a disaster. A foreign agent from the outside world infiltrated the complex. Not until he was sneaking out did Klimov's people realize a spy had been here. Now the entire security department is above ground searching for him. This is our chance to escape."

Of course, Sophie was speculating on details. But after Roger's note and the subsequent alarms, she figured her guesses must hit close to the truth.

Chakrala sat glued to his bunk. "Escape? But it's impossible."

"The impossible is only that which hasn't yet been done. Today, we make the impossible happen. And we're taking all the detainees." She grabbed his arm and hauled him to his feet.

"With only one rifle? We can't. They'll shoot us like rats. Or catch us and roll us into Klimov's crematorium. No. I'm staying here."

Sophie couldn't believe her colleague's defeatism. This opportunity was pure gold, but it wouldn't last forever. She stepped to the door.

"I'm not wasting time. If you believe the magnanimous, humanitarian H.O. is going to permit any military force to storm these corridors and capture all their dirty secrets, you can keep your fantasies. Me, I'm leaving. And I'll take along every detainee gutsy enough to carry a weapon. The Armory door isn't marked, but I know where it is."

She swiped her key card through its slot. *Ting.* Still no one in the passageway. She turned to Chakrala. "Any last words for your wife?"

Just as the door started to shut, Chakrala blurted, "Wait!"

Sophie shot a hand to the door.

"All right, I'll come. I don't know if it's smart, but if you believe there's a chance, I'll risk it."

"Now you're talking sense. Pretend you're my prisoner. Look submissive."

Down the corridor she marched him.

"Not to the elevator," Sophie whispered. "The security cam will be too close for me to hide my identity."

So Chakrala shuffled to the end of the deserted corridor, to the nearest stairwell, and started upward.

When they reached Barracks #1 on Level 2, Sophie accessed the door. She and Chakrala hustled inside, where they sparked astonished reactions from her former bunkmates.

"Sophie!"

"What the devil?"

"And Dr. Chakrala?"

"What's happening?"

Natalia, the young Russian who had pledged confidentiality to Sophie threaded her way through the mass of women. "Sophie, why the masquerade?"

In reply, Sophie aimed her rifle at the security cam up in the corner. The noise from her blast ricocheted off concrete walls as hot lead obliterated it.

Not wanting to waste time, Sophie leaped atop a bunk. "Everybody, listen. How many of you have heard of Sobibor, the extermination camp the Nazis built in Poland?"

Scattered hands went up.

"During World War II, in Sobibor, hundreds of Jews from Poland, France, Germany, Czechoslovakia, and other parts of Europe performed the most successful mass escape of the war. They accomplished it by arming themselves and rushing the fences at the same time. Today, we have an opportunity to do something similar. While Klimov and his men are out searching for their intruder, we prisoners can raid the Armory. As soon as we all have weapons, we can get out of T.R. III once and for all. Are you with me?"

Here and there, women prisoners raised fists and shouted agreement.

"Yes!"

"*Ja!*"

"Allons!"

However, other detainees remained confused, or incredulous. She would have to supply details.

Sophie handed Ice Man's key for the leg restraints to Dr. Chakrala. "Work fast. Get everyone out of their chains."

Natalia touched Sophie's forearm. "But there are so many of us. Do the other barracks have weapons?"

"Not yet. We're starting right here. All of us will raid the Armory together."

With a speed and determination Natalia had never before demonstrated, she punched Sophie in the face before snatching away the rifle. "No one is going anywhere. I'm no stupid detainee. I'm eyes and ears for the Heritage Organization." From the pocket of her yellow prisoner pants she produced an electronic door pass. "Well, what do you know? Natalia Petrovna has single-handedly stopped a mass escape. My reward will be handsome."

On his knees to unlock ankle chains, Dr. Chakrala tackled Natalia's legs. She managed to release a single shot at him before tumbling to the barracks floor. The instant she hit, outraged women pounced, kicking and punching as they vented wrath for the H.O. onto the spy who had lived among them.

Sophie stepped in. "Stop. We need her alive."

Two women seized Natalia's arms and hauled her to her feet. Someone handed Sophie's rifle back, but she was more concerned for Dr. Chakrala.

"Are you all right?" Even as she asked, her eyes searched for blood, but she saw none.

Chakrala rose from the floor. He trembled like a leaf in a windstorm. "She nearly killed me."

"But you're alive. You're a hero thanks to quick thinking."

A fleeting glimpse of appreciation graced his visage. But this hero remained too shocked to complete his job. One of the other women snatched the key and continued unlocking the leg chains.

Sophie faced Natalia. Only Sophie's need for information kept the rifle butt from smashing the spy's teeth.

Despite the welts on her face, Natalia maintained her new air of contempt. "You'll never succeed. You can't defy the Heritage Organization."

Sophie cut to the point: "Who are the other spies among the prisoners?"

"I have no reason to tell you."

With a fury that frightened even herself, Sophie jammed the rifle's muzzle into Natalia's navel. "Listen, you little fool. Unless you talk fast, you're going to die right here. Five. Four. Three. Two …"

"All right, I'll tell you. There's one other informant among the males. Barracks #4. A Frenchman going by the name of Dr. Corbin Chastain."

"Tie her up. Gag her," Sophie ordered.

*   *   *

In Barracks #2, the amazed women quickly joined the revolt when Sophie's mob stormed into their quarters. So did the male prisoners in their two barracks. However, curses and punches ensued when the men learned "Dr. Chastain" was an organization snoop.

"To the Armory!" Sophie shouted when the last man's chain fell off.

No need for pretense remained as a yellow throng two hundred strong surged down the stairwell, with Sophie in the lead. When they reached Sublevel 5, instead of turning toward the Incubation Chamber, she led her troop in the opposite direction.

"This is the Amory." She swiped the electronic card. Instead of winking green, a red LED flashed. Sophie tried again. Same result.

"What's wrong?" someone wailed.

"They're onto us," another cried.

Sophie wasn't sure whether security had deactivated Ice Man's card, or whether the clone simply didn't have high enough clearance. One thing she did know was that only God could make a door thick enough to stop her now.

She raised the rifle. "Stand clear."

"Wait." A male detainee she knew only by face squeezed through the throng. He held up another electronic pass. "We took this from Chastain."

Ting. The door slid open, revealing a massive cache of systematically organized rifles, pistols, ammunition, and even heavy-duty armaments. Clearly, the organization had stashed much more than it needed to guard captive intellectuals.

An ear-piercing alarm ripped the air.

Sophie waved the yellow tide inside. "Arm yourselves. Today, Talent Redemption III goes out of business!"

CHAPTER 38

With his tracker app guiding the way, Baron led Katherine and Melissa deeper into Chernobyl's radioactive Exclusion Zone. At his suggestion, the three walked with wide gaps between themselves in case another shooter appeared. No point in offering an easy-to-hit cluster of bodies. However, as satellite imagery had foretold, once they cleared the field where their comrades had fallen, they encountered plentiful trees, which offered visual protection.

As the three trekked in silence, the gears inside Katherine's analytical mind were clicking. Her degree from University of Georgia may have been in English, but she prided herself on keeping abreast of scientific breakthroughs. That, plus her knowledge of the H.O. and experiments like the Methuselah Project, repeatedly pointed to the same conclusion.

The organization is creating clones.

Roger had mentioned how Dr. Kossler, and later younger scientists, had periodically collected samples of his epidermis, blood, and hair clippings. Roger's assumption had been they were simply examining the cells for clues in their quest to reconstruct the Methuselah process. However, this new evidence proved the H.O. had rerouted some of those sample tissues to assist in experimenting with a different branch of biology.

The sense of isolation provided by tree trunks emboldened Katherine to whisper a question to Baron. "If we do find the real Roger, what's your game plan?"

Baron half-turned his head to say in a low voice, "Impossible to say based on current intel. Depends on whether he's alone, or with others.

And if with others, whether he's with them voluntarily, or under guard. First, we locate. Then, we observe."

Baron halted and looked Katherine full in the face. "By observe, I mean without revealing our presence unless I make the call. Each of us must keep our emotions in check."

She didn't need her boss to spell out his worries. "Of course."

"Down," Melissa hissed.

Responding as trained, Katherine dropped without knowing why. Despite the layer of decaying leaves, the trio went prone with no more rustling than a field mouse might make.

After easing her pistol from its holster, Katherine twisted her head to glimpse Melissa. Baron would be doing the same.

Gesturing, Melissa indicated two possible hostiles, followed by an index finger pointing toward the ten o'clock direction.

Within seconds, voices reached Katherine's ears. Whatever language the men spoke struck her as Slavic, but they were distant enough she might not have understood even if they'd been speaking English.

Such perfect timing …

Had she not asked Baron a question, the three of them would've been walking, a motion that catches attention amid stationary trees. Because of her, they'd been standing still at the exact second Melissa spotted these others' movement. A mind-blowing coincidence? She didn't believe so. Surely this must be another "God thing," as Roger called them. Her faith in the Almighty inched up another notch.

As she knew Roger would've done, she thought, *Thank you, Lord.*

Baron allowed the armed men to pass without contact. Stealth at all costs. After a discreet minute, he stood. "Proceed with caution. Minimal talking."

*   *   *

Bathed in cold sweat, and feeling light-headed, Kurt Mueller writhed in sparse grass and sand as he waited for the agony in his chest to pass. Catching his breath was a struggle. The ache radiated from the center of his chest, as if a ghostly hand had reached inside his ribcage and squeezed his heart with increasing pressure. Because it was the second time in life he'd experienced the symptoms, he recognized cardiac arrest.

"Not now. Must report ..."

Mueller's sole concern was to warn his beloved Organization of impending danger. But the extreme need had triggered extreme misery—he'd run farther and faster than he had in years, all without medication in his system.

Lapsing into native German, Mueller muttered curses for missing his medicines for four days straight. He cursed Klimov and his men, who had taken all the portable radios and left him disconnected. Next he cursed his niece Katarina for abandoning him and the H.O. after all he had done to raise her. And he cursed the armed intruders with whom Katarina had obviously conspired against the organization. But in the depths of his physical and emotional anguish, Mueller saved his most blasphemous invectives for the American.

Captain Roger Greene. Mueller would've spat, if only the thought didn't worsen the nausea churning his stomach.

The execrable American and his escape from the laboratory in Germany had started an avalanche of events—the loss of Katarina, the destruction of his house in Atlanta, and the stain to his reputation among associates. Now the damnable American might cost him his life, plus the security of the entire organization.

That filthy Greene. If Mueller survived this heart attack, he would slaughter Greene and chop him into pieces for the crows.

The fist constricting his heart crushed harder, increasing the torture and squeezing until the angina overflowed from his chest into his shoulders, arms, and neck.

The pain. So much worse than last time.

No longer able to suppress nausea, Mueller's stomach heaved. Hot vomit gurgled up his throat and exploded from his mouth with such force that acrid droplets of bile mingled with dirt blasted back into his face.

He fought to rise, to crawl to a spot free of the reek filling his nostrils. A second spasm gushed from his esophagus. Hot liquid splashed his fingers, rendering them slick and stinking. Hands slipping, he collapsed face down into his own stinking fluids. All he could do was lie there, clutching his heart.

Greene. With all his being, he wished the American dead.

Despite the murderous desire, Kurt Mueller sensed his own mortality now more than ever. Like an old-fashioned slide show, he glimpsed alternating scenes from his too-brief life: The alcoholic father who had beat welts into his young body. Cousin Dieter, who had recruited him and his brother Frank into the Heritage Organization. His rise in wealth and influence as a member of the worldwide consortium. The day he pulled the trigger on Frank and Ruth to stop them from betraying the H.O. And of course, the day he received the urgent H.O. communiqué in Botswana, ordering him back to the U.S. because of an escaped test-subject named Roger Greene.

All of those events ultimately funneled the once-indomitable Kurt Mueller to this revolting moment of wallowing in his own vomitus. For the first time since his father's last beating, stinging tears welled in Kurt Mueller's eyes. Losing control, he lowered his face into the wet soil and sobbed even as another wave of agony compressed his chest.

"Please. Not this way," he gasped, not to God nor to the Devil, but to any unknown cosmic force that might take pity.

"It isn't fair. Please. Let me sink a bullet into Greene's head before I die."

CHAPTER 39

Trekking through the woods with his men, Security Chief Klimov reveled in his growing satisfaction. Twice he'd lost the American's trail, but Greene had unwittingly stumbled into range of motion-activated cams Klimov himself had requisitioned. Of course, his people monitoring the cams in T.R. III had immediately radioed Greene's coordinates. A few higher-ups in the H.O. had questioned the expense of Klimov's security measures, but now they would see how expedient his foresight had been.

But wait. Greene's trail vanished. "Halt."

Klimov sat on his haunches, scrutinizing the ground before him. This American was proving his shrewdness, but no human could move through forestland without leaving signs of his passing.

There. In one spot, desiccated leaves that should have lain curled had been crushed flat and broken. A step beyond them were more flattened leaves.

Klimov stood. "This way. We're getting closer. No way this troublemaker is getting out of the Exclusion Zone."

"How I want to catch this American dog," muttered his aide, Dubovik.

Klimov grunted. "I want to do more than catch him. I want to spit on his rotting bones. Don't worry. We'll get him."

Another fifty meters, and signs of Greene's presence suddenly became plentiful. Confusingly so. Patterns of crushed leaves continued forward, but also to the left and to the right, crisscrossing each other for no obvious reason. A cheap attempt to bewilder trackers?

"Stand!" Klimov ordered. "The target has walked in circles all around this vicinity. He might be trying to disguise another change in direction. Fan out left and right. If you find an article of clothing or any man-made object, do not touch it. Stop and give me a shout."

Once his men were in position, Klimov gave the order. "Forward."

Irritated though he was concerning the problems this American created, he couldn't deny the thrill of the hunt. Of course, today's exercise couldn't compare to his glory days in Azerbaijan. But men like him reveled in action. Overseeing security at T.R. III provided perks, but the job had become mind-numbing. Monotonous.

Perhaps I should thank this American before blowing his head off?

Klimov chuckled. His men would love it. Nothing like mixing humor with a well-earned execution. In their eyes, Klimov's stature would rise quite a few notches.

But the overlapping tracks now became ridiculous in abundance. Perhaps the American was searching for something? If so, what? This corner of the forest offered nothing in the way of food—

On his left, Dubovik exclaimed, *"Blin!"*

Klimov's peripheral vision caught a blur of motion, a falling object. With battlefield instincts, he bellowed "Drop!" even as he dove for the shelter of an oak.

An instant later, an explosion shattered the peace.

For a long moment, the security chief sprawled there, dazed from the concussion. Through ringing ears, unintelligible shouts pressed into his consciousness.

A bomb? Where did the devious pig collect the makings for an explosive? From the lab at T.R. III? Impossible. Perhaps the bomb had been concealed here in advance, in case he needed it? It would explain the crisscrossing footprints.

Neither conjecture satisfied him. But now his men were crowding around, helping him to his feet. "Sir, are you all right?"

Blinking, Klimov spat out dirt and bits of bark. "American mongrel. He's going to pay."

"Dubovik is dead," someone reported.

"Kravets, too."

Still dazed, but not wanting to admit it, Klimov steadied himself and accepted his AK-12 from someone else's hands. He marched to the point of impact and surveyed the scene, including the motionless bodies of two men.

Dubovik. The fool must have snagged a tripwire.

With Klimov's years of experience, he automatically detected such tricks. But he'd never trained his guards at T.R. III in such matters. Who could've foreseen they would need it?

The men's faces reflected a range of emotions. Shock. Dismay. Pity for fallen comrades. But also, indignation and rage.

"Men, this American intruder thinks he's clever. He probably expects his little trick to fill you with fear. Are we going to let him escape?"

"No!" they chorused.

"Who wants to see that dog's blood?"

Grim voices responded in the affirmative as the men brandished their rifles.

"Then back to the hunt. If you spot him, feel free to put a bullet in his legs or arms. But save the kill for me."

Once more, the men lined up left and right of Klimov then proceeded forward. Past Greene's boobytrap, the footprints became easier to follow. The American must be hurrying.

The fool. He's rushing to the end of the forest. Once he steps into the clear, we'll spot him all the quicker.

Klimov keyed the mic clipped to his left epaulet. "Glava-1 to Glava-3."

"Glava-3," came the reply.

"Your location?"

"Sector 23. All quiet."

Sokolov and his detachment were practically due north. Perfect. Klimov keyed the mic again. "Proceed south with your men. My squad is pursuing the target in your direction from Sector 26. We can box him between us."

"Tak tochno."

Klimov added a final instruction. "Do not terminate the target. You may wound or capture, but do not terminate."

"Understood."

"All units, acknowledge this message and converge on said coordinates."

One after another, Klimov's lieutenants radioed their acknowledgement.

Eyes on the forest floor in case of more American devilry, Klimov allowed himself the pleasure of a grin. Greene had led them on a jolly chase, but the chase was nearing conclusion.

*   *   *

Vigilant for both humans and disguised video cams, Roger had been walking north when he heard an explosion in the distance behind him.

His bomb. But did the fishing line snap, or had someone—

Unintelligible shouts revealed someone had indeed stumbled into his tripwire. Whoever was tracking him must really know his stuff. But if his hunters were close enough to hear, they were too close period.

Time to hustle!

A headwind had developed from the northerly direction he was walking, providing welcome relief from the perspiration prickling his face. This H.O. gear was too thick for such an unseasonably warm afternoon.

With every step, the force of the air flowing past him increased. Either the wind was growing stronger, or he was running out of—

There was the answer. Ahead, the increasing brightness between tree trunks signaled he was approaching the edge of the forest.

Uh, Lord, this isn't the best time to take away my protective cover.

Another hundred feet, and there he stood at the end of his woods. Ahead lay an expanse of what must've once been cultivated farmland. In fact, on the far side of the field stood barns and other agricultural buildings. No sign of life.

But once I step out of these trees, I'll be a clear target if snipers are watching.

Watching. The word raised more questions. Although he'd learned tons about this twenty-first century since escaping Germany, much modern technology remained hazy in his understanding. However, low-orbit satellites could definitely observe weather patterns or spot military threats. Was the H.O. capable of overriding a spy satellite's programming to search for a threat such as him?

Roger shrugged. No way to know. But he wasn't going to let a high-tech "maybe" saddle him with new fears. The H.O. was mighty powerful, yet it wasn't the Almighty.

He stepped into the open, where the full wind from the field rippled and tugged at his clothing.

Behind him, the hunters' shouts grew closer. Perhaps his bomb had enraged his enemies and sped them up instead of slowing them down? No time like the present to try his crazy plan with the arrows.

Roger dropped to one knee. He felt a pocket. Then another.

Don't tell me I lost the matches?

But no—in the last pocket he located the box of wooden matches from the hut. He turned his back to the wind and held the matchbox close to his stomach. He struck one. It lit immediately. Held beneath the leaves he'd bundled to one of his homemade arrows, the tiny flame took hold. Once the fire took root in the kindling, he fitted the shaft to bow and aimed for the tree line far to his right. Not behaving at all like a genuine arrow, the wooden projectile corkscrewed through the air, leaving a trail of smoke and flaming leaf bits. However, once the missile landed, orange flames soon sprang from the bed of brittle leaves.

Encouraged, Roger extricated another wooden match and struck it. Nothing. He struck it again. Not even a spark. He threw down the dud and dug out another, aware of the approach of irate voices.

The next match not only didn't light, the whole head crumbled off.

"You've gotta be kidding."

The next match finally rewarded Roger with the flame he wanted. But as he held the match under the leaves bunched to his arrow, the wind puffed it out. Only a few matches remained.

Roger literally looked skyward. "God, please help."

One quick scrape over the igniter strip, and the next match flared. Using his body and a cupped hand to shield the flicker, he held it to the bundle of leaves tied around his arrow. It lit!

Roger fitted the notch into his bowstring. His flaming arrow sped toward the tree line on his left side. This time the flames must've eaten through the line holding the bundle. In mid-trajectory, the flaming clump detached and fluttered to earth while the shaft continued on course.

However, Roger was relieved to see smoke, then tongues of flames, growing from the spot where the clump landed. Good enough.

As he'd hoped, fanned by the steady wind, the first crackling fire was already leaping higher, spitting smoke and flames as it hungrily gobbled the limitless supply of dry leaves, twigs, and pine needles carpeting the forest floor. Better yet, flaming fireflies were taking flight, igniting dead leaves still clinging to the branches of oaks, which in turn produced more airborne sparks.

Using his last couple matches, Roger scraped together pyramids of brittle leaves at his feet and ignited them. Even quicker than hoped, the wind fanned and spread the growing blazes into the direction he'd come —straight toward his pursuers.

He stood back and admired his handiwork. "This trick should make them blazing mad."

Who knew, maybe the burning forest would attract the attention of someone in the outside world. But could Roger trust even a fire department not to have ties with the H.O.?

"Well, boys, you're the ones who started shooting. Don't blame me if I fight fire with fire." Roger turned and started across the field at a jog.

*   *   *

Nikita Klimov's men were halting.

"*Blin*, I smell smoke!"

"What's burning?"

Klimov glanced around. Wood smoke reached his nostrils, too. The whole squad was stopped, sniffing and exchanging perplexed glances.

Who would need a wood fire? Not a soul lived in this vicinity. Surely the American couldn't be so stupid as to stop and roast a squirrel?

Klimov pointed. "Forward. He can't be far ahead."

Soon, though, the light, woodsy aroma of firewood thickened, transforming into acrid, blinding billows that stung eyes and irritated lungs.

"The forest is burning!"

Klimov cursed. Doesn't this American ever run out of tricks? "Run toward the fire. Maybe we can hold our breath and leap over the flames."

However, Klimov—hacking and half-blinded by lung-searing smoke —soon realized his order was futile. Perhaps they could have raced through a line of burning grass on a plain, but here? Pine trees were bursting into flames like giant torches. The nonstop wind was fanning the conflagration straight toward them.

His dismayed men shouted, panicking and urging him to turn back.

Greene. His death would be as grisly as Klimov could contrive. After Greene, he'd take care of Sophie Gottschalk. If Mueller was correct and she was the magnet that lured Greene to T.R. III, she must pay.

"Run around it. Save yourselves!"

Chapter 40

As Roger approached the far side of the field, he sank to a sitting position in the thigh-high grass to scout out his situation. Behind him, his handiwork still yielded thick billows of dark smoke. Normally, of course, he would never start a forest fire. However, as long as he was running for his life in the Heritage Organization's backyard, normal rules of engagement were out the window.

Especially if they insist on using me for target practice.

Ahead, though ... That was the perplexing direction. A half dozen weatherworn brick and wooden buildings suggested the remains of an agricultural complex. What did they call them in Soviet days? Collective farms? Across the white bricks of one structure, faded ruddy letters proclaimed in Russian, "50 Years of the USSR!"

Yeah, well, sooner or later every Party must end.

Like other buildings in this Chernobyl region, the place appeared not only deserted, but disintegrating under the gradual decay of time. Moss-covered roofs with missing sections. Broken windows. Since the farm was so visible, no doubt looters had long since stolen any objects worth taking.

Roger looked backward. Smoke and flames wouldn't deter his pursuers forever. Even now, trackers might be circling, outflanking the fire.

He rose and strode forward through the dense grass. He wouldn't waste time entering buildings. He would merely slip between them in his quest to put distance between himself and his pursuers.

Although Roger kept his senses on high alert, the scene remained tranquil. No faces appeared in the gaping doorways. No rifles poked out the shattered remains of windows. Under other circumstances, his adventurous nature might want to explore. Not today.

Approaching the nearest building, Roger refined his speculation from agriculture to dairy operations. Not that this place resembled the farms he'd grown up seeing in Indiana, but it was his best guess, judging from the fences and shapes of the dilapidated buildings.

Not important. Just keep your eyes peeled and ears open.

From nearby, a clunk sounded. Roger hurried to the wall of the first building and froze, listening.

Another clunk, and a bump. No pattern to the sounds. Probably just the wind toying with a loose shutter.

He prowled along the wall of white bricks. At a window he paused and peered between the shards of dirty glass. As expected, there wasn't much to see. Gaps in the wooden roof allowed beams of sunlight to stab between the trusses. Near the far wall were stacked slabs of prefab concrete material. Broken chunks of the same material plus broken bottles littered the floor. Down each side of the floor ran two shallow channels, which would've funneled off urine from a barn full of cows.

But it was a ghost farm.

As he crept past the window, Roger wondered what had become of the cows. Had the radiated beef been transported to markets and sold to unsuspecting citizens?

Quit thinking so much. Just survive.

Roger smiled when he spotted a tilted, one-door structure of unpainted boards. A Soviet privy. Its door hung crookedly by a rusted hinge and bumped back and forth with each gust of wind. The source of the noises. Nothing to sweat about there.

But the moment Roger stepped past the outhouse, he found himself face to face with a man in camouflage taking a drag of cigarette. Almost comically, the man's eyes shot wide. With a startled grunt, he hustled to unsling his rifle.

Roger slugged the H.O. man's face.

The enemy toppled but maintained his wits. He rolled away, scrambled to his knees, and this time managed to get the weapon off his shoulder.

Roger leaped onto the man. No way he wanted a rifle shot alerting the whole countryside. Alternating between punches and old-fashioned wrestling, he managed to shove his antagonist's gun out of reach.

In a desperate effort to summon help, the man sucked in a deep breath for a shout.

Roger's fist to the man's midriff expelled the wind from his lungs. But still the man fought, attempting to lock his hands around Roger's throat. Amazed at his enemy's ability to absorb hits, Roger continued punching and dodging until—at last—a final clout knocked the man to the ground, unconscious.

On his knees, Roger panted for breath. "Hollywood makes it look so easy."

Assured the H.O. man truly was in dreamland, Roger dragged him around the outhouse to be out of sight from the road and the other buildings. Adrenaline still pumping, he needed no knife to rip his adversary's shirt into strips. With these, he bound the man's hands and ankles. A gag provided the final touch.

Plugged into a portable radio attached to the man's belt, an ear bud crackled with the faint sound of static. Too quiet for Roger to comprehend, a Russian-speaking voice said something.

He picked up the ear bud in time to hear an answering voice say the Russian word "Understood."

"You won't be needing this anymore." Roger unsnapped the radio from the man's belt and unclipped the mic from his epaulet. These he added to his own gear, just as the H.O. man had worn them. "I won't understand everything. Still, a little eavesdropping won't hurt."

But what to do with this unconscious guy? He couldn't leave him here in plain sight.

The privy? With a heave, Roger lifted the dead weight and lugged him inside, where he settled the man onto the moldering seat. A rusty latch clung to the door, so Roger fastened the hook, blocking the man from casual inspection.

Roger chuckled. *I guess an outhouse is the Number 1 place to hide a body.*

From the grass, Roger retrieved his opponent's weapon, an AK-47 with a 30-round polymer mag.

Finally. This should even the odds a little.

Bent over to reduce his profile, Roger hustled forward on his northerly course. But every instinct warned that, where there was one H.O. security man, others might be lurking. Sure enough, no sooner did he reach the road running past the defunct farm than he spotted camouflaged men hiking down it from the east, directly toward his position.

A glance westward revealed a black panel van and more men closing in on foot. Not good.

Despite his H.O. gear, both squads must've guessed who he was, for they shouted and broke into a run. Roger darted across the road. Fast footwork had saved him before. Maybe he could outrun—

Seven or eight H.O. men emerged from the tree line ahead of him.

"Amerikanets!" one yelled.

A shot rang out.

Roger turned and bolted in the only direction left to him—south, the way he'd come. Maybe he could lose them in the burning forest?

Past the outhouse his feet pounded, past the brick cow barn. Meanwhile, the cracking of gunfire in his wake lent speed to his feet. As he'd done earlier, he zigzagged to make himself a more difficult target. He could sprint faster without the AK-47, but no way would he jettison it now.

CHAPTER 41

"How many are with you?" Klimov asked into his shoulder mic.

A crackle of static preceded the radioed reply. "Five of us. Dirty and sweaty, but ready for revenge. Your orders?"

Klimov glanced at the four ash-covered faces waiting on him. Dirty, sweaty, and ready for revenge was a perfect description. He keyed the mic. "You have only five, not six?"

"We're missing Mikhailov. Not sure whether he deserted, or if the fire swallowed him."

"If Mikhailov deserted, he'll soon wish the fire got him. Take your men north into the field. We'll do the same and link up. With Sokolov's group closing from Sector 23, we'll trap the target between us."

"*Tak tochno.*"

Leading the way with Marusya, Klimov strode north into the tall grass. Never in his life had Klimov been so ready to sacrifice a man's blood to the gods of war.

"Sir, since we have the target surrounded, is the plan definitely to capture him?"

Klimov merely clenched his teeth. No doubt, the High Council would praise him for capturing Greene alive. Lock up the American and continue whatever hush-hush experiment they were doing when the subject escaped. But no reward from the H.O. would match the sweetness of snuffing out this troublemaker. High Council or no, within the hour, Roger Greene would be rat food.

Sporadic radio chatter from other units confirmed Klimov's picture: the American mongrel might be loose for the moment, but he was trapped inside a shrinking box.

In the distance to the left, Klimov spotted the rest of his squad. "Let's pick up the pace, reconnect."

In that same moment, the radio came alive with excited, overlapping voices.

"Eyes on target."

"He's running north!"

"No, he reversed course. Now headed south."

"All units, be aware the target is armed. He's got a rifle."

Klimov cursed. Where the devil did this American get supplies? That morning, every eyewitness reported him fleeing empty-handed. Suddenly the man is rigging bombs and brandishing a rifle. What next, a tank?

From the direction of the abandoned farm came the distinctive sound of AK-47s firing.

"Glava-1," came a radioed voice. "Target now moving in your direction."

Sure enough. In the distance, a lone figure sprinted as if rabid wolves were on his tail.

"There he is," growled one of his squad.

At last, the universe had dealt Klimov a winning hand of cards. "Let's get him, boys."

Klimov and his squad broke into a full run. At the same time, he keyed his mic. "All units, cease fire. Close in, but do not terminate the target."

*   *   *

Roger halted in indecision. Ahead, H.O. security men hustled toward him from the burning forest. North, east, west, he was outflanked, outnumbered, outgunned. Attempting a shootout in this open field would be suicide.

Surrender? Into his mind flashed a picture of himself on his knees with uplifted hands. But these guys were H.O. Even if they didn't kill him, they'd lock him in a cage, just like their bosses had done for seventy years.

A cage—Roger's worst nightmare. The memory of his old cell beneath Dr. Kossler's estate made his knees weak.

No way. He wouldn't let the H.O. cage him again. He'd rather die.

*   *   *

Nikita Klimov uttered a whoop of victory. Ahead, the trapped American stood still. Greene thought he'd been so clever. Maybe now he would realize his wits were no match for Nikita Klimov.

The security chief couldn't resist gloating. "Watch, boys! Any moment, this American will drop his weapon and beg for mercy. I bet he's wetting his pants right now."

Yet, even as the men howled with laughter, the American proved Klimov wrong again. Instead of surrendering, he turned tail and bolted toward the nearest barn.

Klimov keyed the mic. "Somebody shoot his legs! Don't let him take cover!"

Too late. Even as the unique sound of AK-47s erupted, Greene reached his goal. From this distance, Klimov could only watch in frustration as the barn door shut behind Greene.

"Slow to a walk," he ordered. "Conserve energy. That dog isn't going anywhere." Into the mic he added, "Glava-1 to all units: Can anyone identify the target's weapon?"

"*Avtomat Kalashnikova.* Looked like one of ours. No shots fired since we made visual contact. He could have a full mag."

Klimov spat. Greene must've jumped one of his men to pinch the Kalashnikov. Well, whichever fool it was deserved death for falling victim to an unarmed man. "All units, circle and contain. If he makes a run for it, shoot for his legs, not to kill."

A burst of gunfire from the barn, and two H.O. men crumpled. A moment later, another shot sounded. A security man on the opposite side of the barn spun and collapsed.

Fury swelled in Klimov's chest. He clamped on the mic. "I said circle and contain! Do not approach. The target carries a weapon identical to yours. If your bullets can reach him, then his can strike you. Use your brains!"

Idiots. True, he had never trained them for such a scenario, but didn't they have common sense?

When Klimov and his squad reached a prudent distance, he ordered, "Hold up. Spread out right and left. Complete the ring."

Excellent. Unless this magical American could sprout wings, he had no way to escape.

Klimov keyed his mic. "Glava-1 here. Do we have a vehicle nearby? I need a bullhorn."

"Right away," crackled a reply.

Moments later, a man came running with the bullhorn. A shot from the cow barn window didn't drop the runner, but it succeeded in enlarging his arc around the barn.

Klimov shook his head. His men might not be professional mercenaries, but until today he'd given them more credit for intelligence.

The security chief accepted the horn from the puffing runner. Facing the barn, he said in English, "Roger Greene, my name is Nikita Klimov. I am security chief of the installation you recently visited. In case you have not noticed, we have you surrounded. Give up peacefully, and I promise you will live."

From nearby, a squad member whispered, "I thought you decided to soak the intruder?"

"Of course, I'm going to soak him. But I can't let him know."

The barn remained silent.

"He's thinking about it."

Klimov put the bullhorn to his mouth and changed tactics. "Mr. Greene, as a professional military man, I admire you. You have demonstrated intelligence, excellent physical agility, and perseverance. I wish all my men were as skillful as you. I'd like to shake your hand, man to man. I promise you your life. If you're interested, I might even have a lucrative position for a man of your abilities."

Long moments dragged past. Still no response. The men were exchanging glances, regarding their boss with expectation.

Klimov spat. Curse this American. Even while trapped and outnum-bered, he was succeeding in making him, Klimov, look like an impotent mouse before the men. He keyed the bullhorn and feigned a sympathetic tone. "Come on, Mr. Greene. This standoff is getting you nowhere. I've already promised your life, plus the possibility of a great-paying job. I've ordered my men not to shoot. Lay down your weapon. Let me shake your hand. We'll talk."

Still no reaction.

Rage bubbled inside Klimov like hot bile. Stalemate was not accept-able. Especially not with his men watching.

"Greene, be reasonable. We're all hot and tired. You and I—we're cut from the same cloth. Men of action. There's more to unite us than divide us. Come out and talk."

A minute ticked past. Then another.

Studying the dilapidated barn, Klimov noted the doors and the windows. He calculated options for rushing the American. Problem was, there's no safe way to rush a determined soldier bearing an AK-47. Greene had already given Klimov too many casualties to explain to the High Council. No more men must die—except Greene himself.

The wooden roof! Holes gaped here and there. Klimov tried not to smile at the plan developing in his mind. He keyed his radio's mic. "Sokolov, you're on the north side of the building, correct?"

CHAPTER 42

As soon as every prisoner held a weapon, Sophie Gottschalk shouted, "Let's go!"

Back up the stairwell the mass of yellow-clad bodies surged. By the time they reached Level 2, the hairs on the back of her neck were prickling. A premonition?

Something's wrong. This is too easy.

Sure enough, when her throng flowed from the stairs into the corridor of Level 1, they rounded a corner, only to be confronted by half a dozen security men in helmets and full body armor, crouched shoulder to shoulder and pointing rifles straight at them.

"Halt! Drop your weapons."

Armed, outraged, and on the verge of freedom, Sophie's followers weren't about to let six persecutors bully them. All around her, bursts of machine-gun fire and small arms reverberated in the close confines of the corridor. When the man beside Sophie took a hit and crumpled, she dove to the floor to present a smaller target.

Despite their protective gear, the H.O. guards never stood a chance against such a concentrated barrage. Almost instantly, all six were down, eliciting cheers from the escapers. Sophie climbed to her feet.

"They can't stop us now," someone yelled.

"Let's get out of here."

Among the prisoners, several lay dead. Freedom was coming at a cost. Sophie grieved even as the crowd boiled forward.

A lot more of us would be dead if Klimov and his men weren't out chasing Roger.

Then again, without the diversion Roger was creating, this escape attempt would be impossible. But where was Roger now? Had Klimov caught him?

Ever practical, Sophie considered how the computers in Talent Redemption III must contain a wealth of damaging information about the H.O. However, this was no time for time-consuming downloads. Especially since none of them knew Klimov's location. If she didn't stick with her crowd—

"The Administrative Office," a voice yelled over the blaring alarm. "Kill them all!"

"The Security Office, too, whoever is left in there."

"No!" Sophie shouted. Although she harbored no love for the captors, neither did she wish to spark a gangster-style bloodbath. "Don't waste time on vengeance. Stick together and rush for the exit before Klimov and his crew come back."

"The surface—it's this way!"

Sophie herself had no clue how to exit T.R. III. She'd been drugged into oblivion when they transported her. But in previous conversations, certain prisoners mentioned coming down "the main steps" in handcuffs and ankle chains. The escapees now depended on those memories.

The mob surged around a corner.

"The exit!"

Dead ahead, four security men in body armor stood before closed doors bearing a simple blue arrow shape pointed upward. Without warning, the H.O. men opened fire.

Prisoners screamed and fell. Others returned fire.

Once again, the outnumbered security detail proved no match for the concentrated onslaught. Three died within moments. The fourth dropped behind the armored body of a comrade, using it as a shield to continue the firefight.

Sophie became aware of vicious stinging from her left leg.

"Oh." Amidst all the confusion, she hadn't realized a bullet had grazed her thigh. A bloody trickle spread down her pant leg.

A crimson splotch blossomed on the arm of the last security guard. With his other hand, he seemed to be shouting into a microphone.

Between the exit and the would-be escapees, a barrier of metal bars descended from the ceiling and locked into position.

"There's another one behind us!"

Sure enough, an identical barrier already prevented the prisoners from retreating the way they'd come. Someone with a cunning mind had designed this installation.

"He's getting away!"

Operated from a remote location, the exit door had slid open, allowing its last living protector to slither backward to safety. The door slid shut again.

The alarm cut off. Silence descended over this killing zone. Yet, even now, someone must be …

There—a camera mounted in the corner of the corridor. Amazingly, it appeared unscathed despite the multitude of bullet holes pockmarking the door and walls beneath it.

Sophie pointed at the cam. "They're watching us. Someone who's a good aim, shoot out that camera."

Kuklis, a heavyset Czech, rushed to the bars with a machine gun. His initial rounds struck wide of the camera, proving him less than "a good aim," but eventually the spray of lead found its mark, shattering the electronic spy.

"We're trapped," wailed Laetitia, the petite Frenchwoman who had sometimes commiserated with Sophie during mealtimes. "Sophie, this was your idea. What do we do?"

"Yes, what?"

All eyes on her, Sophie asked herself the same question. She'd never anticipated such a predicament.

"Did anyone bring something bigger, stronger, from the Armory?"

A man in the rear—the handsome Serb, Gavrilovic—pressed forward with an olive-drab tube. "I grabbed this bazooka. Plus two bombs, or whatever you call them in English."

Incredulous, Sophie stared at the man. "You were holding a bazooka during this whole gun battle and never thought to fire it? You could've ended the fight with one shot."

Gavrilovic remained impassive. "I'm no soldier. I specialize in life, not death. I don't even know the proper way to fire this thing."

If it had been any other man, Sophie might have given him a verbal lashing. Somehow, though, she couldn't muster anger toward Gavrilovic. Even now, the man handed her the bazooka, then knelt to examine her leg wound. Without another word, he pulled off his shirt and ripped loose one sleeve, which he bound around her bleeding thigh. His gesture touched in more ways than one. Something inside her stirred. But the situation left no time for tenderness.

"Okay, people, you're intellectuals. Who can figure out how to fire this thing before Klimov comes back and catches us penned up like sheep?"

Several men huddled to study the object. From snatches of discussion Sophie caught, they seemed to be drawing impressions from old war movies. Her heart sank when one actually mentioned *Saving Private Ryan*. In truth, Sophie doubted the weapon was an old-fashioned bazooka. But it was definitely some sort of shoulder-fired missile.

"The rest of you, tend the wounded," Sophie suggested. "This, uh, might take a minute."

At last, one man whose name she didn't know balanced the weapon on his shoulder. "Okay, I've never done this before, but we will try." The uncertainty in his voice was anything but assuring.

Sophie swallowed. "Everyone back up as far as you can go. Those who know how to pray, please do. Or this might be the shortest escape in history."

Bazooka Man descended to one knee—probably to duplicate something he'd seen from Hollywood—and pointed the weapon toward the bars obstructing their exit.

Boom!

A cloud of smoke, dust, and solid chunks mushroomed back toward them.

Prisoners rushed forward, congratulating the shooter with "Yes!" and "Good job." However, when the billows cleared, the metal bars remained solid as ever. Only the door beyond the bars had been destroyed, offering an even more tantalizing vision of the freedom they couldn't reach.

Sophie darted forward. "The bars! You were supposed to blast the bars."

"I did aim at the bars. But bars, they are not so easy to hit. The bomb flew between them. I have one last try."

"Wait." It was Gavriloc. "Although I am only a geneticist, I understand probability and statistics. If you aim at the bars, you have a greater probability of missing than hitting."

"What choice do I have? The bars are what keep us trapped."

Gavriloc trotted forward and patted the white wall to the left of the bars. "Maybe aim here? If you can blast a cavity in the wall at this point, then we can bypass the bars."

Dozens of voices broke into heated debate.

"That's insane."

"No, it sounds logical."

Valuable seconds were ticking past. Impatience built inside Sophie like steam in a kettle. Decision by committee. This could take all day.

She leaned down and whispered to Bazooka Man, who still knelt on one knee. "We can't wait. Just do it. Aim for the wall beside the bars, just like he said."

He nodded, then sighted on his objective while the mob behind him argued the pros and cons.

A whoosh and a boom halted all discussion. Another shockwave laden with dust and smoke billowed over them.

Instantly, Sophie and everyone else were coughing on the airborne grit invading throats and lungs.

"I will check," Gavrilovic shouted. With his elbow covering his mouth and nose, he disappeared into the haze. A moment later, he reappeared, grinning through a face caked with white dust. "It worked! We can squeeze around the bars."

Still coughing, the detainees surged forward.

The breach in the wall wasn't nearly so deep as Sophie had pictured. However, the force of the exploding concrete had also bent the nearest bar away from the blast. The resulting gap proved wide enough for one human body at a time. She squeezed around the bars using the cavity in the wall.

"Watch your feet," she cautioned. "Don't turn an ankle on this rubble. Not with freedom so close."

"No one should go outside yet," Bazooka Man advised. "They'll be waiting for us. We must rush them in full force."

As more of their number gathered on the exit side of the bars, volunteers hauled the deceased security men out of the way.

While the last few prisoners were squeezing through, all eyes trained on Sophie. She struggled not to flinch. The role of military leader didn't sit comfortably, but this collection of intellectuals clearly viewed her as their inspiration.

I wonder if this is how Joan of Arc felt?

Realizing Ice Man's camo shirt put her at risk of friendly fire in the coming shootout, she unbuttoned it and dropped it on the floor. Her white cotton undershirt became her battledress.

"Well, Sophie?"

She swallowed, attempting to muster non-existent courage. Time to fake it until she made it. "My friends, the way to freedom is up those steps. But the organization won't give up without a fight. Are you ready for battle?"

A cacophony of male and female voices yelled, "Yes!" and "Freedom!" and "We fight for our lives!"

Sophie stepped to the shattered exit and brandished her AK-47. "Then let's get out of this rat cellar—now!"

Pushing past her, Bazooka Man and other men charged up the steps, yelling battle cries in more languages than she could distinguish. From the top of the stairwell came the sound of automatic weapons.

Fear gripped Sophie's stomach with eagle-like talons, but the yearning for liberty overruled her dread. "Freedom!" She pounded up the steps. Switching to her native German, she repeated the cry. *"Freiheit!"*

CHAPTER 43

Inside the shadowy barn, the October air remained chillier than outdoors, but Roger felt perspiration beading his brow. Surrounded by this large force of well-armed organization men, he couldn't survive long. Had his good luck finally run out?

Wait, why was he thinking about luck? Wasn't God on his side? He glanced to the patches of pure sky showing through the decrepit roof.

You are noticing all of this, right, Lord?

No reply thundered from the heavens. No flurry of rescuing angels. Instead, Roger recalled something from a radio sermon he'd once heard while driving his Mustang across Eglin Air Force Base: "Sometimes, God glorifies Himself by healing us, by prolonging our lives. Other times, God allows His children to die, safely bringing their immortal souls to their eternal home with Him."

So, was it time for this pilot to wing his way to Heaven? Careful to stick to the shadows, he peered through shattered panes of grimy glass. Seeing no one advancing, he hustled to the opposite side. What was Klimov scheming?

Through his pilfered radio and ear bud came Klimov's voice, speaking Russian: "Sokolov, you're on the north side of the building, correct?"

"The north side," another voice radioed back.

"Find a ladder or other means of getting a man onto the roof. But silently. I'll distract the American with empty talk. Once your man has eyes on the target, he is to shoot to wound. Not to kill. Understand? I claim the final bullet."

"*Tak tochno.* The men beside me are already lining up to volunteer."

"Proceed at your discretion."

Only a student of the Russian language, Roger struggled to catch words at the speed Klimov was speaking. However, he grasped enough to realize a sniper would soon be targeting him through a hole in the roof.

He glanced up. Both sides of the rotting roof had holes big enough to shoot through. He took a moment to reorient himself. Which way was north? There—that three-foot-wide opening near the ridge. If he were a sniper, that's the perch he would shoot from.

Klimov's voice sounded through the ear bud: "Glava-1 to all units. You just heard what is about to happen. Pay no attention to the barn roof. Give the target no visual clue of a shooter on the roof."

Too funny, Bozo. You already spilled the beans.

At least now he didn't need to sweat about someone crawling under a windowsill and lobbing in grenades. But the clock was ticking. Was there truly no way out of this situation?

From the field, Klimov resumed talking through his handheld bullhorn. "Mr. Greene, I hope you are considering my offer. As you can imagine, I have access to a much more powerful arsenal than mere rifles. If I truly desired to kill you, I could bring in RPG's or other high-power hardware. However, as you see, I'm patient. No need for either of us to shed more blood."

Roger ignored him. After all, Klimov had already revealed his intention of distracting the American with "empty talk."

Never try to bluff when the opponent has seen your cards.

Outside, Klimov continued his light-hearted banter. "Mr. Greene, I'm getting a little hungry. I have not eaten lunch. Are you hungry? Maybe I should telephone Pizza Hut?"

Roger chuckled. Did Klimov seriously believe he wouldn't recognize a stall tactic?

"Unless, of course, you are a fan of hamburgers. You know, they have a very fine McDonald's on Kyrponosa Street in Chernigov. I could drive you there. Just you and me. It would be fascinating to enjoy a Big Mac, potato fries, and cola while discussing world affairs with such an extraordinary American." Using this time to best advantage, Roger circled the pile of abandoned construction material heaped on one side of the barn. Up close, much of the pile consisted of rectangular concrete slabs containing parallel hollow pipes. Maybe to lighten the weight of the slab while strengthening it, like rebar? But there were also smaller squares of concrete, along with ordinary bricks. Many bricks were broken, which explained why they'd been rejected.

A crackle on the radio preceded a new message. Sokolov's voice: "We have a man on the roof. Proceeding as ordered."

Thanks for the status report.

Roger peered into every nook and cranny of the pile. He didn't know what he was searching for. Just something—any handy object—that might've been trashed or forgotten.

Klimov's voice sound over the bullhorn again: "Mr. Greene, I'm getting hungry." More stalling for his man on the roof.

Blah, blah, blah. "The American" isn't one bit distracted.

Occasional bits of dust filtered down from the ceiling, revealing the sniper's progress. A sloth could creep faster. At this rate, he wouldn't reach the hole for a couple minutes. Plenty of time for some deception of his own.

Roger removed his camo shirt. Using broken bricks and rubble, he created a three-dimensional man-sized figure reclining on the floor. After draping the shirt over the figure's body and arms, he added his hat for a final touch. Inside the barn, his subterfuge wouldn't fool a preschooler. But to a sniper peering into shadows from bright sunshine, the ploy might deceive him a couple seconds. And a couple seconds is all Roger needed.

Meanwhile, he stood in the center of the barn and performed a three-hundred-sixty-degree scan of the interior. Was he overlooking any advantageous detail? Brick walls. Shattered windows. Rotting wooden roof. Chunks of concrete. Plus, the concrete floor, with a deep channel on each side to drain off cow urine. And, of course, the AK-47, which was the only thing keeping the enemy at bay.

These surroundings offered literally nothing he could weaponize.

Lord, I'm in a serious fix. If this is how You plan to end my days, so be it. But if I'm missing something crucial—

Klimov spoke again: "Mr. Greene, you surprise me. My impression was that Americans are loud and boisterous. Yet, you remain silent. I hope my conversation is not so boring you have gone to sleep?"

Roger took position behind the pile of cast-off construction debris. His AK-47 held ready, he waited for the sniper.

"You know what, Mr. Greene?" said Klimov.

Didn't that guy ever shut up? Klimov's attempts at diversion were pathetic. But hey, it was free entertainment.

"They tell me you are acquainted with someone in our care. Her name is Sophie Gottschalk. Would you like for me to arrange a conversation with her? I have the authority to make it happen, with no obligation on your part."

Roger bristled. Someone with more brains than Klimov had put two and two together. Instead of helping Sophie, had his coming endangered her?

For a split second, he was tempted to approach the window. Last time he looked, Klimov was maintaining a prudent distance. But what if Roger increased the rifle's angle of trajectory? Could an angle of, say, fifty degrees stretch the reach of his bullets enough to nail the security chief? If he could take out the leader, maybe his followers would forget about Sophie?

Dust drifted down from above, wafting through the shaft of sunlight entering the very hole he'd predicted the sniper would choose.

Sure enough, silhouetted against blue sky the dark muzzle of a rifle appeared. It pointed at the decoy.

Roger trained his own AK-47 on a wooden plank just short of the hole and fired.

The sniper's rifle tumbled through and clattered to the concrete floor. At the same moment, a trail of descending dust particles tracked the path of the sniper's body sliding down the roof. Whether dead or wounded, he was no longer a threat.

Roger keyed the mic on his confiscated radio. "Security Chief Klimov, this is Roger Greene. Although I've enjoyed what you call 'empty talk,' let me give you advice. The next time you radio for Sokolov or anyone else to shoot an enemy, please be sure the enemy isn't listening to your conversation."

He released the mic. The goal wasn't to get chatty. If he could enrage Klimov, funnel his wrath directly at Roger alone, perhaps the man would forget Sophie. That was as far as Roger could plan under the circumstances.

*　*　*

Out in the field, rage curled Klimov's hands into rock-like fists. The demon had stolen one of their radios! Greene had leisurely listened while Klimov blathered like an imbecile. Now every radio-bearing member of the security department knew it.

"This American—he can read our minds," someone blurted.

"Now he has a second rifle, plus another full mag," another griped.

Was he merely making an observation, or was he condemning Klimov's tactics? The security chief glared at the man.

The radio crackled. "Klimov, if you're still ordering lunch, get me chicken nuggets with a caramel macchiato. If they don't have macchiato in Ukraine, I'll settle for a chocolate milkshake. No whipped cream, please."

His cheeks and ears afire, Klimov imagined the crimson shade the men regarding him must see. High Council or no High Council, it was time to pry the snail from his shell.

"Maintain positions," Klimov snapped. Walking a wide arc around the cow barn, Klimov stalked up to Sokolov on the opposite side.

Alarm flickered in Sokolov's eyes. "Sir, I had no way of knowing—"

Klimov brushed away the excuse. "Your support vehicle. What kind of firepower do you carry?"

"Mostly standard issue. AK-47s and spare magazines. Plus grenades. One GM-94—"

That last item sparked Klimov's interest. "You brought a GM-94? Which kinds of payloads?" Klimov hadn't expected the pump-action grenade launcher. This might be fun.

"We carry high-explosives. Also frag canisters, plus a few incendiaries."

Incendiaries? And the GM-94 could plaster a target from well over three hundred meters. This day, revenge would be sweeter than honey. "Get it. Incendiaries, too."

"*Tak tochno.*" Sokolov broke into a run. He wasn't gone long. When he returned, he handed over the grenade launcher. "We had three incendiary cartridges in the service van. I loaded all three."

As Klimov trudged back with his new toy, he felt every man's eyes on him. No doubt, Greene was observing, too.

Klimov keyed the mic. "Roger Greene, the device you see in my hands is a grenade launcher. Its operation is simple, yet highly effective. This is your last chance to exit and surrender. What is your reply?"

A pause, and then a radioed, "Go fish!"

The American's answer made no sense. However, he recognized Greene's insolence.

"In the forest you played with matches. You must enjoy fire, Mr. Greene. Allow me to provide all the fire your heart can desire."

Klimov peered through the launcher's fixed-iron sights. Aiming for the exposed wooden boards of the roof, he squeezed the trigger.

Although the cartridge struck lower than the spot Klimov selected, it nevertheless struck weather-worn wood above the brick wall, just under the barn's peak. Like dry kindling, the aged lumber erupted into a crackling inferno.

The men burst into cheers.

Klimov pumped the second cartridge into place. This time, he aimed slightly higher before triggering the GM-94.

With a loud *sploosh*, flames exploded in the exact location Klimov wished.

He lowered the grenade launcher. One cartridge remained, but he wouldn't need it. Thanks to the dryness of the sun-bleached wood, orange and yellow tongues blazed in the wind, spreading along the length of the barn's roof. Soon enough, the whole raging mess would collapse into the barn.

Into his mic, Klimov said, "All units, stand by. If the target exits, shoot for his legs. If he remains inside—then our job is done."

No sooner had he released the transmit button than a woman's voice broke over the radio: "Security Central to Glava-1. Emergency situation in T.R. III!"

Chapter 44

Inside the barn, when Roger had seen Klimov raise the grenade launcher, he dove behind the pile of concrete slabs and covered his ears. But instead of the expected grenade blast, crackling flames exploded onto the wall and roof.

Incendiaries!

Hungry tongues of fire and smoke boiled into the barn through gaps in the aged planks. One glance confirmed what Roger already knew: The entire roof system was constructed of wood—very old, very dry wood.

Death by fire? Please, God, no.

Frantic, Roger glanced this way and that. If he ran outdoors, they'd shoot him. If he stayed here, the blazing roof would eventually cave in, roasting him alive.

If only there were a basement, or a storage cellar. He could use it like a bomb shelter to wait out the fire. But there wasn't. The floor was solid concrete, including the drainage channels.

Roger blinked. The drainage channels?

What if …?

But that was absurd. It couldn't work. Or could it?

With no other option, Roger bolted into action as popping, crackling flames chewed their way across the roof. From the piles of rejected building materials, he grabbed three concrete blocks. These he stuffed into one of the floor channels, right at the point the channel exited under the brick wall. Using more bricks, he blocked the same channel about twelve feet in from the wall.

Now, he ran back to the pile, seized a concrete slab, and grunted and heaved until he succeeded in lugging it across the floor, where he deposited it over the drainage channel, butted against the brick wall.

Next, with strength born of adrenaline and terror, he dragged a second slab over the channel, where he butted it up against the first, effectively creating a long, narrow crawlspace of solid concrete.

Back and forth he shuttled, piling slab upon slab to cover cracks and construct as thick a heat shield as possible in the little time left.

Now an inferno raged overhead, fed by a constant rush of fresh autumn air being sucked inward through the broken windows.

With flaming splinters dropping around him, Roger knew the superstructure wouldn't last much longer. He unclipped the radio and tossed it. Then, lifting one side of the innermost slab—the only one with no others atop it—he crawled into the channel on all fours. Using his spine to support the slab, he eased it back into place.

Careful. Don't bust it, or you're toast.

Once the "lid" of his hiding place settled into position, Roger lay in complete, cramped darkness. Would he fry inside a tomb of his own making? Even if not, would he run out of air before the fire burned itself out?

In his haste, he'd forgotten both rifles. No matter. Right now, staying alive was the main goal.

Using fingers and toes, Roger managed to inch his way forward in the confined space. He wanted his head as close as possible to the barn's outer wall. Teenage experiments with campfires had taught him and his football buddies that, because heat rises, the ground directly under a campfire can remain relatively cooler for a surprisingly long time. Even longer with some sort of heat shield. His best odds were down here, beneath the spot where three layers of concrete separated him from the blaze overhead.

Roger willed his body to relax. He must rest, conserve oxygen. However, as he lay with the side of his head flat against the floor of the channel, a fetid odor assailed his nostrils.

Yuck. After all these years, he could still smell cow urine? Did God really need to humble him this much?

Instead of a reply from the Almighty, there sounded the muffled thuds of burning planks and timbers collapsing above him.

Please, dear Lord, keep me alive!

CHAPTER 45

Bill Baron halted at a point where the trees thinned, leaving them on the verge of another clearing. When Katherine and Melissa caught up, he pointed forward. "Smoke."

"And lots of it," Katherine added.

Enormous gray-tan billows rose in the distance, where the wind fanned them in a long, drawn-out trail that muddied the sky.

Melissa used the opportunity to unwrap a peanut butter protein bar, her third for the day. "The direction can't be coincidence. Somehow, the smoke must be connected to our mission."

Katherine regarded her, amazed her colleague could stand there, chewing with such calm detachment. "Agreed. But, what connection?"

Baron had switched programs on his phone and now used his thumb to peck out a message. "Doesn't seem logical anyone connected to a top-secret organization would light such a gigantic fire. Even weather satellites might detect it. I wonder if Roger is sending some sort of S.O.S.?"

Baron's suggestion of a distress signal both encouraged and alarmed Katherine. "You've decided he's on our side and calling for help?"

"The jury is still out. But it's one possibility."

Melissa swallowed a bite of her snack. "We won't learn anything by standing here. I suggest we get moving."

"You are not going anywhere," growled an unfamiliar voice with Slavic overtones. "Do not turn around. Drop your weapons, your bags, everything you are carrying. Do not try to be a hero. Or you will be a dead hero."

Baron emitted a grunt. They'd made it all this way, only to be caught when they were finally closing in. He lowered his phone and let it slip from his fingers into the tall grass. "Do what the man said."

Katherine tossed away Wainwright's rifle. Prudently using two slow fingers to avoid a bullet from behind, she withdrew her pistol and likewise pitched it away.

"Now turn around."

Katherine found herself staring into the muzzle of a rifle. She couldn't tell which kind due to the numerous strands of camouflage draped around it. The weapon's owner seemed to be a swarthy man, but she couldn't be sure. Instead of the expected shirt and pants printed with a camouflage pattern, he wore a shaggy ghillie suit of fake leaves and grass, which added bulk. With only his eyes visible, he looked like a creature woven from the terrain itself.

"Speak. Who are you?" the man said.

"We're visitors to Ukraine," Baron replied. "This is my wife, Melissa, and her niece, Katherine. For a long time, I've heard about the abundant bird life in Chernobyl's Exclusion Zone, so I applied for permission to come and study them."

Slick, Katherine thought.

Baron shrugged and played naïve. "If you're with the Ukrainian army or something, I'm sure we can get this straightened out."

To Katherine's surprise, Melissa spoke up. "Let's not waste time. We're not here to watch birds. You must be with the Heritage Organization. Am I correct?"

Katherine couldn't believe her ears. What was Melissa doing?

The man cocked his head. "What do you know of the Heritage Organization?"

Melissa plunged forward. "We're here because we're tracking an American who escaped from an H.O. laboratory in Germany a few years ago."

"Melissa!" Baron snapped.

Ignoring him, she said, "The American has a friend who is imprisoned in your underground facility. We have reason to believe this

American will try to sneak into your facility to rescue his friend, a scientist by the name of Dr. Sophie Gottschalk."

The veins on Baron's forehead bulged. "Melissa, shut up." He took a menacing step toward her, with his fist clenched. Only a quick jab of the H.O. man's rifle stopped him.

Clearly, her spiel wasn't part of any pre-rehearsed script.

"But who are the three of you?" demanded the man in the ghillie suit.

Melissa sidestepped away from Baron. "These two are officers with the American CIA. Well, technically, I'm in the CIA, too. My name is Melissa Hart. But I'm a longstanding member of the Heritage Organization, working covertly in the American intelligence community. H.O. number 422537. Go ahead; radio for confirmation, if you wish."

Mixed anger and astonishment filled Baron's expression. "Blindsided."

Melissa laughed. "Why, thank you, Baron. Coming from you, that's quite a compliment. You know, in my younger days, I considered a career in theater. As an H.O. mole in the CIA, I enjoy the best of two worlds—acting, plus adventure. Double the money, double the fun."

A dagger pierced Katherine's heart. "I can't believe it."

"Believe it, Miss Goody Goody. After all, who do you think tipped off the H.O. that it was time to exterminate Jaworski? He nearly figured out who I am." To the H.O. sniper, she added, "By the way, this naïve woman is definitely not my niece. Her name is Katherine Mueller, a blood relative of an H.O. elimination agent named Kurt Mueller. She went traitor a few years ago. I claim the bounty for capturing her."

Adrenaline surged into Katherine's system. Her hands trembled with outrage. Never had she wanted to kick someone in the gut so badly as she did now. But it wasn't worth a bullet to the head.

Behind the shaggy strands hanging from his hat, the gunman's eyes twinkled. In his Russian accent he replied, "Melissa Hart, you are—how do Americans call it?—quite a 'smooth operator.' Kurt Mueller is known to our security section. In fact, he is stationed here."

"Wonderful. I believe he will take personal satisfaction in being present when I turn this rogue *leutnant* over to the organization for interrogation."

The gunman laughed. "Only a *leutnant* when she rebelled? How much could she know?"

Melissa joined in the laughter. Two faithful organization comrades, hitting it off at Katherine's expense.

Her mind raced. Yet, try as she might, she couldn't make sense of Melissa's revelation. "But you didn't even want me on the op in Paris. And you shouted for me to shoot the Roger lookalike—even though you knew he was H.O."

Melissa regarded her with contempt. "Of course, I pretended not to trust you. Since I already knew I would be outvoted, what better way to disguise my interest in capturing you? As for the doppelänger, whatever he was, he had no clue I'm H.O. Another two seconds, and he would've slaughtered me as well as you. Yelling to shoot him was pure self-preservation."

"She killed one of the clones?" the gunman asked.

So, Katherine was right—the organization really was cloning humans.

Melissa nodded. "I'll submit a full report. Until then, do you have any intelligence on the escapee we've been tracking? His real name is Roger Greene. I'd hoped to deliver both Greene and Miss Mueller to the H.O. at the same time. You know, score a double bonus in one stroke?"

"Good plan, but no double bonus. The security section has been hunting your American troublemaker all day. According to radio messages, our security chief and rest of the section trapped him inside an old barn. This minute, they are burning the barn with your American inside it."

"What?" Katherine's knees lost strength and went wobbly. She literally grasped Baron's arm to steady herself.

Melissa didn't bat an eye. "That's a lot of smoke from one barn. Are you positive Greene is burning alive?"

"Long story. Not all the smoke comes from the barn. The forest is burning, too. But your spy never came out of the barn. He—"

In mid-thought, their captor stiffened. He clapped his left hand to his ear, where he must have an ear bud. "Radio message. Emergency. Big prisoner escape. No more time for talk. Walk that way."

This moment was the closest thing to a distraction Katherine could wish. Hoping their captor wore no body armor beneath the ghillie suit, she clicked into Isshinryu karate mode and struck a power kick to the man's groin.

"Unh!"

As he collapsed, she wrenched away his rifle by the barrel. Continuing the motion, she swung the weapon like a baseball bat to connect with the attack she instinctively knew must be coming from Melissa.

Whack!

Her instincts had been spot on. Just as Melissa had stepped forward with martial arts of her own, the rifle's hardwood stock had walloped Melissa's skull with bone-cracking force. Katherine had never heard such a sickening sound. Had she really broken Melissa's skull?

Her former supervisor dropped to the ground, where she lay groaning.

Katherine flipped the rifle and found the trigger. "Neither of you good-for-nothing H.O.'s move a muscle. Right now, I'm the angriest I've ever been. Don't give me a reason to pull this trigger."

The H.O. sniper might have raised his hands had they not been clutching his nether regions. Melissa just sprawled on the ground and clutched her face.

For the second time in a minute, astonishment washed over Baron's face. "Mueller, you are amazing. Fastest take-charge maneuver I've ever seen."

"Thanks, but let's dish out praise later. Grab your phone. Are you still receiving a signal from Roger?"

Baron plucked it from the grass. "Indeed I am. Either Roger escaped, or he's no longer wearing the ankle bracelet."

"We need to hustle. But what about these two?"

"I'd prefer to keep them alive for questioning." With his uninjured arm, Baron unzipped the backpack Melissa had carried and withdrew a gray roll. "Multi-purpose super-adhesive bonding material."

"Duct tape?"

"I never do an op without it. Cover me." Baron pulled Melissa's hands behind her. Once they were secured, he duct-taped her ankles. Then, in an impressive display of strength, with his uninjured arm he grasped her shirt collar and hauled her to her feet, where he pressed her spine against the trunk of a birch. "Stand there."

Melissa's eyes flashed. "You'll never get home alive. You bit off more than you can chew when you went after the Heritage Organization."

"Yeah, yeah." Baron stuck the end of the gray tape on the back of the birch, then proceeded to wrap it around her mouth, then her neck, and so on down to her knees.

"Nice job," Katherine said. "All she needs is a Christmas bow. Do the same to Swamp Thing, and we can get moving. "

But 'Swamp Thing' had no plans of submitting. All this time, he'd been hunched on his knees, as if in great pain. Without warning, he shot to his feet and lunged at Katherine.

Katherine, though, had realized one kick doesn't disable a male for long. With the grace of a bullfighter, she sidestepped the expected attack, then swept one booted foot at the proper instant to trip her attacker. He crash-landed face first into the ground.

She jammed the rifle's muzzle into his kidney. "Freeze, big boy, or I'll blast you so full of holes a screen door would be jealous. Understand?"

He hesitated, probably with mind racing to spring a counterattack.

She rammed the rifle muzzle hard enough to make permanent dent. "Surrender or die."

Defeated, he laced his fingers atop his head. "I surrender."

"Tape him up, Baron. But if this sucker so much as wiggles the wrong way, I'll blast him into Swiss cheese."

Before securing the H.O. man, Baron yanked off his hat and removed his ear bud and radio. With a knife, he sliced through the rear of the ghillie suit and pulled it off. The man inside turned out much leaner than the bulky camouflage suggested. After frisking him for weapons, Baron soon had him firmly secured to the tree beside Melissa's.

Still pointing the rifle at the H.O. sniper, Katherine picked up his radio ear bud. "There's a ton of radio traffic. Everybody sounds excited, but it's all in Russian. Or Ukrainian. Whatever."

"Only English and Arabic for me," Baron said as he put the finishing touches on the man's bindings. "Might as well smash the radio. It won't help us."

She dropped it. Three solid whacks of the rifle's stock destroyed it beyond repair.

Baron studied his satphone. "I'm still getting a strong signal. But if it's inside a burning barn, heat won't take long to consume it."

"*Contra spem spero,*" Katherine said. "Latin for 'I hope against hope!' Let's hurry."

CHAPTER 46

Overwhelming the few H.O. guards stationed outside the disguised entrance to T.R. III was coming as a surprise to Sophie. Instead of the costly battle she'd envisioned, her determined mob of scientists was overpowering the organization men. So far, the escapers had suffered only a couple fatalities and several wounded.

In contrast, the six H.O. guards stationed at the entrance were withering quickly. To their disadvantage, the architect of Talent Redemption III had included camouflaged concrete barriers on each side of the exit—but positioned to protect guards shooting outward. Evidently, no one had foreseen a need for shielding the guards from armed attackers exiting T.R. III. The onslaught had forced the H.O. men to abandon their post and dash for the nearest trees. In effect, the escapers held the best defensive position and blasted each glimpse of their former captors.

Now only one organization man remained alive, and he must've been low on ammunition. He turned and bolted into the forest.

Sophie was willing to let a fellow human live so long as victory was theirs. Her fellow escapers were less generous. They spewed a hail of lead at the fleeing guard. He collapsed in his tracks.

"Victory!" prisoners cheered in a medley of accents. They poured from the exit and exulted with grins, hugs, and much back clapping.

Without shooting muffs, Sophie's ears rang from the close proximity of countless gunshots. An acrid odor from the intense barrage filled her nostrils.

Still, she couldn't stop grinning. "We dared the impossible. And we achieved it."

"One moment!" It was Gavrilovic. He crouched beside one of the H.O. guards and brandished the ear bud of his radio. "Central Command radioed an alarm to Klimov. He's responding with full force!"

"We should've murdered everyone in the security office," someone griped.

Ignoring the bloodlust, Sophie glanced around. "Who knows about radios? Is there a quick way to shut down their communications?"

A brunette woman stepped forward. "Central Command will have an antenna. A high-gain, high endurance, bi-directional antenna is used to both transmit and receive signals. Usually, they're mounted on an elevation to steer clear of obstacles. If we destroy it, we cut off Klimov from anyone left in Central Command. All of their surveillance technology will be useless if Klimov can't talk to them."

All eyes turned to Sophie.

How much longer must she play the role of leader? "Everyone fan out. The antenna must be camouflaged, too. Find it."

Before long, someone up the slope shouted. "It's here. This dead tree isn't a tree at all."

Even before Sophie reached the spot, her colleagues were firing their weapons at the base of the "tree." Under their combined firepower, artificial bark and the sheathing beneath shredded. The cables inside disintegrated. The artificial tree tilted but didn't fall.

"Success." Gavrilovic threw down the ear bud. "Central Command was right in the middle of a message when it went dead."

The grin on the handsome Serb's face practically melted Sophie's heart. She could already picture the two of them alone, in a European café. But no time now for such premature thoughts. "Which way should we go?" Sophie wondered aloud.

Gavrilovic pointed to a column of smoke in the distance. "Klimov and his men are that way. I suggest go south—and quickly."

"South, then," Sophie agreed. "Stick together. Our strength is in numbers."

"Some of our people are wounded," Chakrala said.

Chakrala. It was the first time she'd noticed him since Natalia tried to kill him in the barracks. Sophie rejoiced her colleague was still alive—and even brandishing a pistol. Good for him.

She glanced around. "We leave no one behind. Take turns helping those who are injured, just as you yourself would want someone to help you."

So, they set out, with Sophie leading away from the forest road and straight into the woods.

Some leader. I could be leading them toward civilization—or into a bog.

She half-turned and surveyed her followers: A motley army of a couple hundred men and women dressed in yellow tunics and trousers. Most bore an assortment of modern weaponry. "Those in the rear, watch behind us. Shout an alarm at the first sign of pursuers. We'll turn and fight if we must."

As they plodded through woods, many of her followers talked, expressing gratitude and amazement for their good fortune. A few praised "our leader Sophie," but she pretended not to hear. Others were already discussing plans for new lives in freedom.

Sophie looked skyward. *Dear God, You don't speak, but You've answered my prayers in the most incredible way. Please help me to get these people to safety. And if Roger is still alive, protect him.*

CHAPTER 47

Flat on his stomach inside the impromptu fire shelter, Roger remained motionless. The muffled sound of an inferno roared above him. Never in his life had he expected to land in such a predicament. Suppressing the urge to panic was a challenge.

When the sound of a gunshot penetrated his hiding place, he jumped. Like a bundle of firecrackers in a campfire, dozens more rapid-fire shots followed.

It's only the AK-47 cartridges. Stay calm. Conserve air.

To distract himself, he searched his memory for facts he'd read decades ago, while still a prisoner in the underground bunker of the Methuselah Project. Old Doc Kossler had supplied a wealth of books to keep the prisoner occupied—which translated to "not pestering Kossler with questions." Among those volumes, an engineering textbook had caught his eye as challenging. Even now, Roger could picture the heading of Chapter 1: "Thermal Conductivity of Common Materials and Gases."

What was the R-value of normal-weight concrete when mixed with limestone aggregate?

The text had listed four types of concrete, ranging from lightweight to heavy stone. Most likely, this channel for cow urine landed in the middle range. So how long could concrete layers protect him from frying?

Let's see, the resistance of a material to conduct heat energy from one surface to another is its thermal resistivity ...

That's as far as his brain pursued the matter. During his years of captivity, engineering equations had served to distract him, to keep him sane. But focusing on such things brought back the feeling of being locked in the bunker beneath the Kossler estate.

Better to think about the blaze above than to relive even one minute in Kossler's dungeon. Bottom line—sure, concrete conducts heat, but not fast. It's a lousy conductor.

On a positive note, the longer his face rested on the drainage channel, the less he noticed the musty odor of cow urine.

If I live through this, it will make a great story for the grandkids.

He sobered. That is, assuming the Methuselah Project didn't wear off and leave him a doddering old codger. Given a choice, he'd rather die quickly, in a blaze of glory.

Except then, he'd never again see Katherine on this side of Heaven.

Images of her surfaced in his memory: Katherine strolling beside him in Paris, with her pert smile and dimples. Katherine delighted and pointing out landmarks when he took her flying in a rented Piper Archer. Katherine, looking stunning in her red-violet bikini against the white sand of Eglin Beach Park. Lastly, he recalled her expression the last time he'd seen her: Reserved. Straight-faced. Upset, but struggling not to show it. All because he hadn't been able to articulate that, yes, he'd once kissed Sophie, and yes, he felt a special allegiance for the German woman who risked her life for him, but no, he harbored zero romantic feelings for her. Why had he fumbled the explanation so badly?

If he ever saw her again, he had to set things straight ASAP.

From there, precious memories of Katherine rolled through his mind one after the other. The softness of her hand in his; the ecstasy of her kisses; her delightful giggles; the restaurants, beaches, and antique shops they'd experienced ... Why had it taken him so long to buy the ring?

Messed-up priorities.

After so many decades of being locked underground, he'd practically let flying become an idol. But right now, if he had to choose between flying and Katherine ...

No contest. He'd hang up his wings and never look back if that's what it took to make her his wife.

In this way, minutes ticked past. Memories of Katherine occupied his mind far more pleasantly than any engineering equation. Eventually, though, he realized the roar of flames had died down. Had the aged timbers expended their heat? Although the temperature in his hiding place hadn't risen to life-threatening level, the air had grown stale. In fact, he was panting, sucking in short breaths that didn't satisfy his body's yearning for oxygen.

To Roger's mind came a true-life drama he'd read about Colorado firefighters. When the wind shifted direction during a forest fire, they'd hurried to unpack portable fire shelters. As long as they stayed beneath the silica and aluminum-foil sheets, they remained safe. But one novice panicked. Not trusting the thin sheet to reflect heat, he cast it aside and attempted to run. Super-heated air seared his lungs, killing him instantly.

Roger reached for the bricks he'd packed into the drain's exit beneath the barn wall. Exercising caution, he wiggled the topmost brick to loosen it, then tugged it inward. He halfway expected red-hot embers piled outside his escape route. However, when the block slid free, instead of flames, pure sunshine flooded into the hole.

"Hallelujah."

Roger craned his neck to peer outside. No glowing coals. Just blue skies with scattered, fluffy clouds—a positive sign for any aviator. But what about Klimov and his boys?

He loosened another brick. Because his position in the drainage channel placed him below ground level, visibility remained limited. On the ground outside lay scattered gray ashes. A breeze swirled October air into his hiding place.

For a time, Roger contented himself simply to lie there, filling his lungs. After all, even if Klimov had counted him a crispy critter and left, the security chief might have left a few men behind.

How long have I been under here?

Not less than forty-five minutes. More likely longer. None of the organization men would expect him to crawl out unscathed. Yet, here he was—alive.

Nothing like faking your own death to make enemies stop hunting you.

But he was unarmed. If he crawled out and ran into organization goons, the fight would be bare fists against AK-47s. Not an attractive thought.

Better stay put a while longer.

Since death by gunfire or by flames wasn't an immediate threat, Roger yielded to the temptation weighing his eyelids. He slipped into blissful sleep.

*   *   *

Later, Roger jerked to full wakefulness, bumping his head against the slab above. He blinked.

How long had he been out? Impossible to say, but the ray of sunshine entering his hiding spot had shifted. He berated himself. What if an H.O. goon had walked past and heard him snoring?

On the other hand, he felt more energetic than he had all day. Fuzziness no longer clung to his thoughts.

Thanks, Lord, both for the sleep and for protecting me. What do You think? Time to wriggle out of my cocoon?

This time, instead of pulling bricks inward, he shoved them outward, beyond the brick wall. Extricating himself from his constricted hiding place proved easier thought than done. He literally inched forward using fingers and toes. At last, though, his upper body and hips cleared the outer wall. From there, pulling his legs free was simple.

No shouts. No alarms. He lifted his head from the channel. Nothing. Emboldened, Roger rose to his knees. Nobody in sight. At least, not on this side of the building.

He stood, stretched, and then padded leftward, to the corner of the brick wall for a peek around it. No H.O. guards. He reversed course and strode toward the corner on the opposite side of his hiding place. When he tilted his head for a look, he caught his breath. No guards, but on this side much of the brick wall had collapsed during the fire. If the wall above his hiding place had crumbled ...

Thank You, Jesus. No way I could've dug myself out.

A cautious reconnoiter of the area suggested what he'd barely dare to hope: He was alone.

So Klimov had written him off as fried to a crisp? Probably the security chief intended to return and locate Roger's charred bones after the ashes cooled down.

Meanwhile, I get a green light to waltz my way to civilization.

He had no Ukrainian cash, but that shouldn't be a problem. Surely the U.S. operated an embassy in Kiev? If he could hitchhike to the capital, he could contact Baron.

Of course, he'd contact Katherine, too. But Baron was the man who could arrange a raid on the underground prison, rescue Sophie, and supply a ticket home.

Which direction to walk? He set off eastward, away from the setting sun. As best he could guess, an easterly route should lead him away from the organization while staying inside Ukraine. This was no time to stumble into border guards for Poland, Belarus, or some other country. He didn't even have his passport.

No sooner had he passed a gnarled apple tree than a voice rang out. *"Stoi!"* For good measure, the order was repeated in English: "Halt."

Wincing at his misfortune, Roger raised his hands. "Out of the fire, into the frying pan."

CHAPTER 48

Hands up, Roger turned.

Sitting beneath the tree he'd just passed, a solitary man in camouflage clothing pointed his rifle at him, but surprise and a twinge of fear showed in the man's expression. Eyes locked on Roger, the man fumbled in the grass until his hand located a silver flask, which he recapped and tucked inside his shirt.

Clear enough: the lone guard had figured Roger was dead and had used this opportunity as a chance to relax. The man rose to his feet.

"You American," the man stated in a heavy Slavic accent.

"True."

"How you alive?"

Roger shrugged. "I like being alive. I've been doing it for nearly a hundred years."

His captor squinted. "But you were in fire."

"Yep, you're right. Didn't Klimov tell you? I have superpowers."

The man's eyes narrowed. Did he not understand the English words, or was he deciding whether to believe them?

Just for fun Roger added, "Want to see me fly?"

Looking fearful, the man gripped his rifle tighter. "You fly, I shoot. Walk." He jerked his head sideways toward the field Roger had crossed earlier.

"Great idea, pal. I'm not done with your buddy, Klimov." He lowered his hands and started in the indicated direction. There, to the south, the blaze he'd begun among the trees had burned itself out. Scattered wisps of smoke lingered over the charred mess.

Roger glanced over his shoulder. "Aren't you going to radio your base to report me?"

"Radio not working."

Roger chuckled. "See? I have superpowers."

"I no believe about superpower."

"Don't be too sure. After all, I walked through the fire, right? Maybe for my next trick, I'll help all your prisoners to escape."

"Ha. See? You not so smart. All prisoners already escaped."

The words plowed into Roger's mind. Even at the risk of being shot, he halted and stared. "They've escaped? How?"

Spooked, the gunman stopped but held his rifle at the ready. "I not know how. You not need to know how. Just walk. Our people catch them."

Roger obeyed, but questions flooded his mind. *How could all the prisoners escape? Had Baron traced his radio signal and pulled strings? Or maybe the prisoners had already been planning a breakout?*

However it happened, a mass exodus was the best possible news. Or was it? A big escape would explain why Klimov bugged out. But his well-armed force might mow down those yellow-clad intellectuals.

At best, they'll be recaptured in record time. Unless there's more to the story.

Roger lost interest in baiting his captor with smart-aleck remarks. More important worries crowded his mind. Like, what about Sophie? Did she escape with the others? Was she safe?

"Left," his captor ordered. "More left." This course veered away from the ashes and blackened tree trunks to an unburned area only sparsely dotted with trees.

"Tell me more about this escape."

"No more to say. Radio stopped working. Be walking."

"But you did say *all* the prisoners escaped, right? It's hard to believe."

"Not important. You prisoner, and you not escaping."

Before Roger could think of a retort, a familiar voice rang out: "Stop, or I'll shoot."

Miracle of miracles, from behind a lone pine tree out stepped Baron, training a sidearm on the H.O. man. From the opposite side of the pine stepped Katherine. In a glorious image of guts and beauty, she gripped a lethal-looking rifle of her own.

Instinctively, Roger guessed the H.O. man's reaction and dodged. As expected, the rifle behind him cracked, but the bullet missed Roger.

Two more reports split the air. His would-be executioner staggered, then toppled.

To be safe, Roger kicked the rifle away from the still fingers.

"Roger!" Katherine rushed forward and wrapped her arms around him, rifle and all. "We heard you were dead."

When her lips met his, the kiss forced from his mind all thoughts of fire, danger, underground prisons, and Sophie. For this moment, all he wanted was to soak up her presence, to relish the feel of her in his arms. In this moment, he didn't care if the whole world disappeared. The bliss of holding the most magnificent woman in the world belonged to him once again.

Baron cleared his throat. "Very touching reunion. But we're still on company business. I suggest we talk now, smooch later."

The boss's verbal intrusion pulled them apart. Still, Roger sensed in Katherine the same reluctance he felt. No hint of their earlier friction remained.

"Roger, about Paris ... I'm sorry. I just got so jealous."

"It's okay, Hon. We'll talk. But right now people are in danger."

To Baron, Roger said, "Let me skip the colorful details and jump to the bottom line. As you know from Sophie's message to the CIA, the Heritage Organization operates an underground prison. I was inside it. And get this: they're growing human clones. One of them looks exactly like me."

"He did look like you, but not anymore," Katherine said. "I shot him."

Her announcement jammed a wrench into the gears of Roger's brain. "You thought he was me, so you shot him?"

With a wry smile, she shook her head. "The clone tried to kill us. He took out a couple of our men. Turns out Melissa is H.O., too."

Roger digested the news. It explained the sling on Baron's right arm. "Listen, according to this guy, there's been a mass escape of prisoners.

The entire security department must be chasing them. They need protection."

Baron raced through a debriefing with Roger to clarify details, especially concerning the strength of the security department and whatever Roger knew of their weaponry. When he was satisfied with his grasp of the situation, he said, "All right, you two can go back to cuddling while I step away and coordinate the cavalry."

"Cavalry?" Katherine and Roger said in unison.

"You didn't expect me to plunge into the wilds of Ukraine without initiating a backup crew, did you?" Not waiting for an answer, Baron sauntered away while tapping his satellite phone.

Alone with Katherine, Roger took both her hands in his. "In Paris, something came between us. I've felt sick about it. I want you to know —I would never intentionally say anything, or do anything, to hurt you. You're the best thing that's ever happened to me."

"I know, Roger. Deep down, I understood. But I love you so much. Learning how you came to Paris only to find Sophie caught me off guard. I got jealous. I jumped to conclusions—"

Roger silenced her with a finger over her lips. "You don't need to explain. Misunderstandings happen."

Roger enveloped Katherine with his arms. When she raised her lips, he gladly met them with his own. In that instant of ecstasy, the world didn't blossom into a better place. But for now, Roger had done his duty. God had restored the love of his life, and he intended to enjoy her. They kissed again then simply stood, each relishing the tight embrace of the other.

Someone cleared his throat. Roger cracked one eye. Baron stood nearby, but not looking straight at them.

"You trying to get our attention?"

"Oh, only for the past minute. You two sure know how to tune out the world."

Still hugging Roger, Katherine simply turned her head. "With the world in its present condition, can you blame us?"

"Touché. But our ride is almost here. Time to go."

Roger cocked an eyebrow. "Our ride?"

As if on cue, the sound of mechanical rotors disrupted the silence of nature, growing louder each moment. A military helicopter swept into view, just a couple hundred feet up.

As the craft descended, Roger grinned. "A UH-60 Black Hawk. U.S. troops or Ukrainian?"

In a rare show of good humor, Baron returned the grin. "Both. Compliments of the U.S. – Ukrainian Training Center in Khmelnitsky. Intuition told me we might need boots on the ground. Our people have been busy administering polygraph tests to weed out possible organization infiltrators."

The Sikorsky Blackhawk touched down but left its rotors spinning, making further conversation difficult. Amid a sea of swirling grasses, Baron led them to the craft, whose door slid open. Inside, half the well-armed soldiers who greeted them displayed U.S. flags on their sleeves. The other half bore the yellow-and-blue patch of Ukraine.

A soldier pointed out two lightweight canvas seats in the rear for Roger and Katherine. Baron squeezed his way forward, where he took a position nearer the pilot. The helo lifted into the air.

Under other circumstances, Roger might've leaned toward the helo's open door to glimpse the results of his forest fire. He squelched the thought. With one arm around Katherine's shoulders, he drew her close for another kiss and didn't care who watched.

CHAPTER 49

Klimov wrenched open the passenger door of the service van and jumped inside. "Go, go, go!" he ordered Sokolov.

His lieutenant mashed the fuel pedal, jack-rabbiting the van into the fastest start of its mechanical career.

Clunks from the weapons compartment behind them indicated that the six men who had jumped in despite the lack of seating had toppled to the floor.

Sokolov shook his head while barreling down the road. "A mass escape. Unbelievable. How do you think it happened?"

If Sokolov had donned brass knuckles and punched Klimov in the face, he couldn't have sparked more irritation.

"No idea. We leave T.R. III for a few hours on a special mission; suddenly, everything unravels. Richter might be a biological genius, but as Facility Administrator, he stinks. I left behind plenty of men to maintain order. How could Richter foul up so fast?"

Sokolov simply shook his head.

Klimov was in no mood for conversation. He forced himself to suck in a deep breath and release it slowly. His blood pressure must be through the roof, but he needed to maintain composure, to think straight. He keyed his mic. "Glava-1 to Security Central. Come in Central."

No reply from Central Command.

"Glava-1 here. Security Central, respond!"

Still no reply. Klimov curled his fingers into a sledgehammer and slammed it down on the vehicle's dashboard. The glove box popped open, prompting a curse as he slammed it shut again. So much for composure.

"Sokolov, you're all right, but between you and me, I feel we're surrounded by incompetent fools. In just one day, everything is falling apart."

Sokolov kept his eyes on the rutted asphalt. At high speed, he rounded a curve, producing more clunks and a muffled exclamation from the rear.

If only there were a straight route from here to T.R. III. But of course, there wasn't. In its infinite wisdom, the organization had chosen obscurity over ease of access. Now the same obscurity served the escapers. And how long would it take his men to cut across country on foot? They were in excellent physical condition, but they'd gone all day without lunch or rest. Even jogging the whole way, they couldn't cover the distance quickly.

He talked aloud, formulating an emergency response on the fly. "We need to head off the prisoners. If they scatter in all directions, we'll never catch all of them. But if the prisoners bunch together—and I wager they will—then we have a chance. They're on foot. Untrained. Flabby. Plus, they don't know the terrain."

Sokolov's attention remained on the road, but he contributed his own thought. "If they stick together, we could take the roads to get in front of them. With the firepower in this van, even eight of us should be able to pin them down until the whole section arrives."

"Exactly. First, we perform a delaying tactic in front of them, then the classic pincer when the rest of our boys show up and circle them from behind."

Sokolov shot him a glance. "A sound plan. But we'll have to make sure we spread ourselves thin and wide. We can't let them outflank us."

Falling into his old, army-day mode of thinking, Klimov imagined the battlefield from a bird's eye view. "We will contain them. We're armed, trained, and we know the area. They made a bold move while we were distracted, but we're not distracted anymore. We can crush this escape."

Here, the ancient road disintegrated into asphalt rubble, forcing Sokolov to slow down as they went bumping and swaying over it. He spared another glance at the security chief. "You know, the situation could have been much worse. If they had invaded the security offices and killed our people, they could've adjusted the radio equipment to reach the outside world. Just imagine—the fools could have been broadcasting a description of our operations, even all of our names."

Sokolov was right. If that had happened, Klimov might as well commit suicide. The worldwide Heritage Organization would accept no excuse for high-profile failure.

"Fate has smiled on us, comrade Sokolov. Fate, plus the prisoners' lack of tactical experience. The day still belongs to us."

Day. The very word raised a fresh concern. This day was far spent. He must get this van full of men positioned in front of the escapers before the sun dipped below the horizon.

"Faster," he ordered.

*   *   *

The stop at T.R. III hadn't taken long. One glance at the carnage in Corridor A of Level 1 educated Klimov concerning the prisoners' firepower. Until this moment, he assumed they had somehow overpowered a couple guards and stolen some rifles. But they had raided the Armory?

As he'd hoped, his office staff hadn't been idle. Although the radio was nonfunctional, two security cams had picked up images of the escapers as they trekked southward. For Klimov, the big surprise hit when the surveillance tech handed him a video capture. The leader of this exodus was none other than Sophie Gottschalk.

Now, back in the van and speeding down bumpy dirt roads to head off the yellow horde, Klimov squinted again at the printout of Sophie. He wadded the printout into a ball.

The ungrateful *tyolka*. She had the best job, the best food, plus a private room. Now she was playing Moses?

She'll wish she'd never been born.

Sokolov braked at the spot Klimov had circled on their regional map. It was an excellent location, directly in the path of the escapers. Here, there was no more forest. Just wide grassland dotted by sporadic trees and bushes. A clear field of fire.

By the time he reached the van's rear, the men were hopping out.

"Each of you, take a spare mag of ammo. No, make it two spare mags. Central Command will ferry more of our men here, but until they arrive, we need to stall the rebels. You know what to do. Fan out right and left. Conceal yourselves in case of scouts. We'll halt the rabble in its tracks."

Klimov looked on with satisfaction as his half-dozen handpicked men deployed. This was more to his liking. No tramping through woods on the trail of a slippery devil. This situation required battlefield tactics: his small, hand-picked squad, preparing to engage a larger force of well-armed amateurs.

"Sokolov, hide the van, but not far. We might need more ammo. Just park it somewhere the rebels won't see it as they approach."

"*Tak tochno.*" Sokolov hopped in, revved the engine, and drove off.

Marusya over his shoulder and a bullhorn in his hands, Klimov strode forward, toward the center of the grassland. He would've preferred a secure position behind a stone wall, or even a large rock. In the absence of those, he made his way to a dead tree.

Good enough. He would see them long before they saw him. Now to wait.

After a check of his wristwatch, he eased down on his haunches. Not for long. In less than fifteen minutes, a yellow blob appeared in the distance.

We arrived just in time. If they had gotten past this point ...

But they hadn't. He—Nikita Klimov—had responded efficiently to prevent the possibility. This day had been the most frustrating of his life, but he'd bounced back and handled it like a professional. Who knows, maybe the High Council would reward him for averting disaster?

As he observed, the yellow mass became the distinct forms of men and women. A number wore makeshift bandages.

Outstanding. Assisting the wounded must have slowed them down. At least the guards at T.R. III didn't die in vain.

When the distance had closed enough for them to hear him, Klimov put the bullhorn to his mouth. "Stop where you are. Detainees of Talent Redemption III, this is Security Chief Klimov."

The escapers did, indeed, stop. Since he barely peeked around the dead tree, they probably wondered about the source of the disembodied voice.

"Detainees, your flight is over. You follow a foolish leader. If you persist, you face annihilation. If you wish to live, toss away your weapons, kneel, and place your hands atop your head."

A few of the more fainthearted obeyed.

"Gutless worms," Klimov muttered. Then, through the bullhorn, "That's a start. But you must all comply or pay the consequences."

From the mob, barely audible, a woman's voice floated across the field. "You're bluffing. You're one man. But even if there are more than one of you, we're leaving!"

"Bluffing? We'll see who's bluffing, Gottschalk. You're guiding your colleagues to their deaths." Addressing one of his own, Klimov called, "Pinkevich, pick a target and fire. Only not Gottschalk."

From his right flank, a shot rang out. A yellow-clad figure dropped like a marionette with cut strings.

"Antonov, your turn. Pick a target. Fire."

Another shot, and another yellow figure fell.

Several more detainees dropped their weapons and hit their knees with upraised hands.

However, Sophie Gottschalk's voice remained resolute: "You can't stop us now. Come on, everybody—forward!"

The mob surged toward him, flowing around the few on their knees.

"Fire," Klimov bellowed.

The rifles from his ambush came alive, but so did the weapons of Sophie's ragtag followers. They might not be crack shots, but the sheer amount of lead they were shooting was bound to hit his boys.

A barrage of bullets tore into Klimov's tree. He ducked, leaned around, and fired into the mass of bodies.

Fools. They're all bunched up. We don't even need to aim.

Then, over the din of gunfire came the last sound Klimov would've expected—the steady *thump-thump-thump* of helicopters in flight. From the north, four dark helicopters appeared. They swept around the field, as if visually sizing up the situation.

Klimov stared skyward. Who was this? Had Richter actually transmitted an emergency message to General Wolf? Did the H.O. maintain a fleet of helos for emergencies?

The helicopters broke formation, each taking position to form a square box around the organization men's positions.

Over the racket of rotors an amplified voice boomed from the nearest helicopter: "Nikita Klimov, and security department of the Heritage Organization—stand down. The armed forces of Ukraine are taking control. Do not resist."

Impossible! The organization had Ukraine's local generals in its pocket. And surely Ukraine didn't possess—. The realization struck him like a club: Americans! Greene must have sent his countrymen a message before dying. But only four helicopters? They weren't enough to stop Nikita Klimov.

Through his bullhorn Klimov bellowed to his men. "Shoot them down!"

The atmosphere crackled with gunfire. Klimov and his men blasted their weapons skyward. The helicopters, in turn, twisted left and right while raining minigun rounds from the sky.

Eager for revenge and liberty, the yellow horde advanced, still blasting their own weapons toward the organization men.

Although battle-wise, Klimov considered himself a realist. He didn't need years of military experience to see he'd been dealt a losing hand of cards. Sokolov was dead. Two more men down. Was he so loyal to the organization he was willing to let a Ukrainian kid with a fancy machine gun snuff him?

No way. Survive to fight another day.

Clutching his beloved Marusya, he bolted back the way he'd come. He'd reached the dirt road before the nearest helicopter began shooting at him. The line of bullets stitched a path toward him. Klimov twisted, changed direction, running not away from the chopper, but directly beneath it, where the gunner couldn't see or shoot him.

By the time his airborne enemy swung around for a clear shot, Klimov had reached the copse of trees. So many leaves had fallen, the trees offered little concealment from above, but it didn't matter. He yanked open the driver's door and threw himself behind the steering wheel.

Yes! Sokolov's keys dangled from the ignition.

Another second, and Klimov had fired the engine and was racing down the dirt lane, back to the protective cover of the overhanging forest. The outside mirror revealed the helicopter giving up the chase, veering back to rejoin their comrades.

Klimov's laugh filled the van. Once again, he'd beaten the odds. He—Klimov—had survived, when others hadn't.

But what now? After this debacle, nothing would restore him to the good graces of the High Council.

He pondered options aloud. "I could slip across the border into Belarus. From there, getting into Russia would be child's play. Plenty of army buddies owe me favors. I could get a new identification. Of course, leaving will mean missing my revenge on Gottschalk."

In his haste, Klimov roared past the turnoff to T.R. III. He braked, backed up, then turned onto the adjoining dirt road.

"No. Not skipping revenge. Merely postponing until a better time and place. First, one last stop."

Chapter 50

When Katherine pulled away from Roger's lips, every soldier in the helo was grinning. Despite the chill wind from the open door, heat crept into her ears and cheeks.

Roger winked and leaned close so she could hear him above the racket from the helo's rotors. "They're jealous of me."

Rather than raise her voice to compete with the noise, she simply nodded and rested her head on his shoulder. In one day, she'd believed Roger was dead twice. But now she had him back. The real one, not a laboratory-grown duplicate. The two of them would still need to talk. But she and Roger were together again. Now she could face anything.

The din from the rotors was loud, but peace filled her heart. Her world remained intact. For now, all she wanted to do was sit and enjoy the ride to whatever military base Baron and all these soldiers had in store for them.

Out one of the open doors, a dark shape hove into sight. Their chopper wasn't alone. They had joined a formation of identical helicopters, each one evidently packed with U.S. and Ukrainian military.

"What's happening?" she shouted to Roger.

"Beats me. Above my pay grade."

Baron wore a pair of headphones and had been engaged in conversation with someone. Now, though, he motioned for Roger to look at the ground. Katherine leaned over, too.

Below, in the fading light, a group of thirty or forty men in identical greenish clothing were jogging across country.

"Klimov's men," Roger shouted. He flashed Baron an excited thumb's up.

The helos fanned out, evidently in a pre-planned maneuver. Their own helicopter overran the troop on the ground, rotated one hundred eighty degrees, and settled for a somewhat bumpy touchdown. Instantly, the soldiers bailed out, leaving her and Roger alone in the helo's rear. Up front sat the pilot, copilot, Baron, and a soldier manning an impressive-looking weapon. The pilot lifted off again.

All around the H.O. men, other helos likewise disgorged their warriors, and then lifted back into the air.

Despite her bird's-eye view, Katherine didn't understand exactly what was happening. Clearly, though, their rescuers had no intention of zipping them straight to a safe haven. This joint force of U.S. and Ukrainian troops was encircling a well-armed H.O. security unit.

An exterior loudspeaker boomed a message to the organization men. Katherine caught only fragments: "United States and Ukraine," and "Illegal paramilitary operation," and "Surrender immediately."

Miraculously, the men on the ground complied. They were tossing down weapons, dropping to their knees, and placing hands atop their heads.

Roger's face lit with joy. "They're giving up without a shot! Klimov must not be with them. That guy would never surrender so easy."

As the helos hovered with guns ready, the U.S. and Ukrainian ground forces tightened the ring. Katherine halfway expected a last-minute trick. But the H.O. men yielded. Evidently, when faced with the choice of staying alive or having their brains blown out for the glory of the Heritage Organization, they chose life.

Roger motioned to catch Baron's eye. "What now?" he shouted.

"We find their underground complex. If we can capture their computers, we'll reap a goldmine of information!"

CHAPTER 51

Hands flying, Nikita Klimov snatched each firearm from the wall of his private quarters on Level 1 and stuffed them into the backpack on his bed.

"I might be running, but not empty handed."

His collection safe, he whipped open drawers and cabinets, rummaging through personal effects. He wouldn't need much. A pair of jeans. A couple of civilian shirts. And most important of all, the money.

He removed the bottom drawer from his wardrobe and extracted five bulging envelopes with a solitary word printed on each: "UKRAINE." "BELARUS." "POLAND." "RUSSIA." "EUROS."

"Can't forget the cash. With this, I can start a new life anywhere."

Congratulating himself for such foresight, he stuffed the envelopes into his backpack and zipped it shut.

"As the Americans would say, time to rock and roll."

He dashed into the corridor and race-walked to Security Central Command. When he entered, fear showed on the faces of Richter and Vladimir Pavlovich, the duty officer in charge of surveillance.

"What's happening out there?" Richter demanded.

Klimov ignored him. Instead, he approached Vladimir Pavlovich. "Status update."

"From bad to worse. We do not know the full picture, but those four helos you reported are not the only ones. A second contingent of helicopters bearing troops has encircled and contained the bulk of our security force."

"They're locked in a firefight?"

Vladimir Pavlovich shook his head. "It would appear our men have surrendered in the face of superior forces." He pointed to one of ten monitors mounted on the wall. "We have a drone providing a live feed."

The image on the screen was distant, and daylight was fading, but his men were definitely on their knees and surrounded by these cursed newcomers.

Richter stepped in front of Klimov, blocking his view. "I asked you what's happening out there."

With one hand, Richter shoved him aside. "Zoom in," he said to Vladimir Pavlovich.

"The camera is already on maximum zoom."

"Then maneuver the drone closer."

"But sir, if we advance the drone—"

"Do it."

The duty officer manipulated a control, resulting in a growing and clearer image. Klimov cursed. How disgusting. After the countless hours he'd spent training his men, they'd surrendered like sheep.

But wait. Who was that?

Because the camouflage gear worn by the men of T.R. III was darker than that of the American-Ukrainian force, it was easy to pick out each organization man. So, who was the figure garbed in T.R. III gear, but standing free, among the U.S.-Ukrainian soldiers? With a woman, no less! Had his earlier guess about a traitor been correct?

Klimov tapped the screen. "This man. I need to see his face. Fly it closer."

"Sir, if the drone gets closer, we compromise—"

Klimov slammed his mallet of a fist on the man's desk, making ink pens, paper clips, and every other object bounce. "Don't question orders. I'm willing to sacrifice one drone if it will reveal the man's face."

Vladimir Pavlovich paled and sat straighter. Without further argument, he manipulated the controls. The image magnified as the drone advanced. However, the whirring of its tiny rotors must have become audible to those on the ground. Faces turned toward the camera. Soldiers pointed.

When Klimov's person of interest likewise turned toward the drone, his heart lurched.

"Greene? Impossible. I burned him alive!"

But there onscreen was the face of Roger Greene, identical to the photo in the file Kurt Mueller had given him. And where was the sniveling Mueller, anyway?

A new possibility clicked into Klimov's mind. "Wait, maybe it's not Greene at all. The American is dead. This must be our clone, Number 49."

However, his mystery man joined in pointing toward the camera— and shouting. Number 49 was mute. Logically, this man couldn't be either Greene or the clone. Who was he?

Soldiers in the image fired their weapons at the camera. The picture suddenly spun out of control, and then went dark.

"Drone off-line," Vladimir Pavlovich reported.

The riddle of the man who dressed like the H.O. yet allied himself with the enemies fueled the tension headache raging inside Klimov's skull. It made no sense.

"Dr. Richter, is it possible the man with the Americans is another of your clones?"

"Absolutely not. He must be the original American, as Mueller suggested."

"Impossible. I killed the American." Klimov rubbed his temples. He needed out. Now, before a spineless traitor led the Americans here. He reached a decision. "Situation 'Critical.' Vladimir Pavlovich, announce General Destruct Sequence."

Vladimir Pavlovich blanched. "General Destruct Sequence?"

"Do I detect an echo in this office? Yes, General Destruct Sequence. Announce it. Then everyone run. Flee for your lives."

Richter grabbed Klimov's sleeve. "Are you insane? I'm Administrator of T.R. III, and I forbid it. Cancel that order, Pavlovich."

Klimov wrenched his arm from Richter's grasp. "Carry out the order, duty officer. Evidently, Dr. Richter has forgotten H.O. chain of command. I quote, 'In the potential event of Situation Critical, the authority of the senior security officer overrides all other levels of command.'"

"Tak tochno." The duty officer rolled his chair to the neighboring desk, where he flipped a procedural manual to the last of its vinyl-sleeved pages. He keyed the system-wide mic and read from the manual: "Attention all personnel of Talent Redemption III. The security of this facility has been irreparably compromised. Situation Critical. General Destruct Sequence countdown begins now. You have 15 minutes to evacuate. I repeat ..."

Richter paled. "But my years of research. My accomplishments ... The new crop incubating on Sublevel 5 ..."

"Doctor, it's my sworn duty to prevent T.R. III from falling into improper hands. If you choose to salvage anything, I suggest you run as fast as you can."

Richter gasped, then dashed from the office.

Klimov dropped into an empty chair and typed his authorization code into the computer. Clicking his way through the Security Protocols, he located the final section, titled "Situation Critical." A couple more clicks to start the self-destruct sequence resulted in a pop-up: "Authorization code?"

Klimov swore and typed his personal code a second time. As he did, Vladimir Pavlovich and the two secretaries rushed from the office. Klimov ignored them.

Another pop-up on the screen: "This command will result in complete annihilation of Talent Redemption III. Are you sure?"

"Of course, I'm sure." He jammed the Enter key.

A third pop-up: "Clicking Yes will initiate fifteen-minute auto-destruct. Proceed?"

Klimov hissed between clenched teeth. Even this technology questioned his orders. He mashed his fist on the Enter key. "Yes, you miserable piece of junk. Do it."

A blaring alarm erupted through overhead speakers. Simultaneously, Klimov's screen filled with digital numerals, starting at 15:00, but beeping as every second ticked by.

Done. Time to evacuate. Klimov stood and flung his backpack over one shoulder. As he crossed to the office exit, an odd thought materialized: If this were a Hollywood movie, he would magically know how to pilot an aircraft and could abscond with the jet in T.R. III's hangar. Unfortunately, the reality of his military career had never left time for aviation lessons. The security service van must suffice.

The office door slid open and, in his rush to exit, Klimov nearly collided with someone. In the corridor stood Kurt Mueller—his face pale, his thin hair disheveled, and his clothing rumpled and wet down the front. Traces of something disgusting clung to his unshaven whiskers. Worse, a foul stench emanated from Mueller. By all appearances, the man could've been wallowing in a pigsty. Over his shoulder was a rifle.

Klimov stepped backward to protect his nostrils. "Mueller? What happened to you? On second thought, never mind. I don't care."

Mueller's eyes burned like angry coals. "What have you done?"

"Me? I have done my duty. Out of my way."

Mueller stood rooted to the spot. "Incompetent idiot. Security chief? What a mockery. You have betrayed the organization. Now you are destroying an irreplaceable facility. Who paid your thirty pieces of silver, Klimov?"

Klimov's left hand shot out and caught Mueller by the throat. "Me? Incompetent? You miserable failure. You are the one who transported a spy straight into this facility. You wish to see a traitor? Then look in a mirror."

If Mueller had been younger or stronger, Klimov would've rearranged his face with a fist. But precious seconds were ticking.

"Bah. I have no time, old man." Klimov shoved Mueller by the neck, sending him sprawling to the floor. "I'm leaving."

Klimov strode for the main exit.

"Klimov."

He ignored the voice behind him. Let the explosion consume Mueller.

"Klimov, halt!"

Klimov kept walking. To him, the German had become as significant as a mosquito, about to be swatted. Already his thoughts raced ahead. How far could he drive with the amount of fuel in the service van? And which road out of the Exclusion Zone would be best for evading the American-Ukrainian troops?

"Klimov!" Mueller shrieked.

Enough. Klimov turned only to yell "Shut up!" The words lodged in his throat. Prone on the corridor floor, Kurt Mueller aimed a rifle straight at him.

"No!"

The rifle barked over the clamor of the alarm.

Pain erupted in Klimov's gut even as the impact sent him stumbling backward.

"Die, you traitor." Mueller fired again.

Agony. Shock. Klimov pictured himself whipping a handgun from his pack. Returning fire. Yet, he couldn't. His vision clouded as he dropped to his knees.

No. Not like this. Not at the hands of a geriatric maggot like Mueller? He struggled to rise but collapsed as darkness engulfed him.

CHAPTER 52

Outside the illuminated ring of American G.I.s and Ukrainian troops guarding the organization prisoners, Roger offered his right hand to U.S. Colonel David Boiko, commander of the California National Guard's 79th Infantry Brigade Combat Team and commander of Joint Multinational Training Group-Ukraine. "Colonel Boiko, I want you to know what a privilege it was to watch your men in action. Quite an impressive show."

"Ditto from me," Baron said.

Colonel Boiko shook Roger's hand, and then Baron's unwounded left hand, and lastly Katherine's. "Thank you. Of course, it was a team effort. Our American guys, plus the Ukraine Forces, plus the intel you all provided. None of us could've pulled off this coup without the others."

"What happens now?" Katherine asked.

"For one thing, I need to transport the prisoners to Kiev. Both of our governments will interrogate them. As a commander on a battlefield, my next step should be to seize control of an enemy's command post. According to what we've learned, this so-called 'Talent Redemption III' lies about two klicks in that direction. However ..."

"However what?" Baron asked.

"The prisoners claim the entire place is rigged with explosives. Ever since we shot down the drone, they declare their administration might blow the place up just to keep us from gaining access. Not a single one is willing to guide us there. Partly they're afraid of getting blown up, but partly they're scared of their own leaders. Vengeance seems to run deep in this outfit."

Roger weighed the information. "Their facility is huge. Five floors, all below ground. Massive amounts of concrete. Destroying it would require tons of explosives. I wonder if they're lying just to stall? You know, give their bosses time to shred documents and wipe comput—"

Before Roger finished the sentence, a rumble like a gargantuan avalanche shook the air. At the same time, the soles of his boots registered tremors like an earthquake. In the direction Colonel Boiko had pointed, massive billows of dust and smoke gushed into the darkening sky.

The prisoners broke into excited jabbering.

Katherine sighed. "Looks like the prisoners knew what they were talking about. The H.O. blew up my uncle's house in Atlanta to cover its tracks."

"Excuse me," Colonel Boiko said. "I need to coordinate a perimeter to hunt for organization people who may have escaped." He marched away.

"A shame," Roger said to Baron and Katherine. "I was looking forward to giving you a tour. The place really was impressive."

"I wonder if Uncle Kurt got caught in the explosion?" Katherine said.

"We may never know," Roger replied. "But as a guy who spent most of his life in the H.O., your uncle struck me as the type who take care of himself."

The chopping of an incoming helo grew louder, and the three turned to watch the craft descend. With the aid of its brilliant landing light, the helo's pilot selected a vacant patch of grass and eased down, tail gear first.

"Military brass coming to oversee the cleanup?" Roger asked.

Baron placed his good hand on Roger's back. "Not exactly. Someone requested special permission to speak with you face to face. Come on."

As the three approached the helo, Roger's first guess was Security Chief Klimov. Or maybe the head scientist, Richter? However, among the G.I.s jumping down, the sight of a solitary woman being assisted from the helo shot a thrill through him. The soldier assisting her pointed to Roger.

"Katherine, it's Sophie Gottschalk."

Not waiting for the spinning rotor blades to stop, Sophie jogged to the trio. She and Roger blurted the identical greeting: "You're alive!"

Sophie gave him an enthusiastic hug, but not a romantic one, for which Roger felt gratitude. Perhaps the sight of Katherine standing beside him encouraged Sophie not to overdo it.

Roger introduced Katherine and Baron.

"You're quite the actor, Captain Greene. Not until I read the note you left behind did I realize you were the real Roger, not the clone everyone claimed you were."

He laughed. "I'm glad my charade worked."

Baron shook her hand. "Miss Gottschalk, I want to congratulate you. Sending the CIA your covert message took brains and guts. If not for you, we wouldn't be here."

Sophie brightened. "You received it? I assumed, but never knew for sure."

Showing no jealousy, Katherine added, "I'm sure all of us would like to hear each other's side of the story. In fact, if this were written into a book, I bet it would become an international bestseller."

"For now, let's set aside all notions of book deals," Baron cautioned. "You were engaged in a CIA operation. Limited information will be released to the public, but there are proper channels. Besides, we've exposed only the tip of the iceberg. We don't want the Heritage Organization to learn how much we find out."

Sophie nodded. "Smart. There are two more talent redemption prisons, but I don't know where. I would enjoy trading stories, but right now, I'm exhausted. Maybe in the morning?"

"Morning would be good," Roger agreed. "I've had a long day, too."

The glow of Baron's satellite phone lit the officer's face against the deepening of dusk. Without explanation, he began patting Roger's pockets.

"What in the world are you doing?" Roger asked.

"There's one small matter I'm trying to understand. Back in Paris, I handed you an ankle bracelet with a radio-tracking device so we could follow your movements. We followed the signal all the way from France to here, and my app still registers the signal—but where's the bracelet? It's not on your ankle, and it's not in your pockets."

Roger laughed. "You might recall I have a strong aversion to any technology that gives away my location. Instead of locking the bracelet around my ankle, it was in my pocket all the way here."

Katherine took a turn patting his pockets. "So, where is it? I didn't feel it during our hug."

"When I found myself inside T.R. III, I realized their security people might capture me and take away the ankle bracelet. I couldn't let that happen. Instead of fearing technology, I had to embrace it to survive."

Understanding dawned on Katherine's face. "Same place as the original?"

"Yep." He touched his left bicep. "I used my pocketknife to cut the tracker from the ankle bracelet. Then I slit my arm enough to push it in. It hurt like the dickens, but I really needed that signal."

Sophie winced. "Thank goodness for the Methuselah Project and your fast-healing ability."

"Yeah. Thank goodness." Her comment touched a delicate topic. He hadn't yet told Baron and Katherine his wounds no longer healed quickly. This wasn't the time.

However, Katherine knew him too well. Her concerned eyes searched for the unspoken meaning behind the slight change in his voice.

"I can't stay," Sophie said. She jerked a thumb toward the helicopter she'd arrived in. "They're arranging temporary housing for all of us 'detainees.' I'm told they want to debrief us about the H.O. while beginning paperwork to bring us all back from the dead. But I need to warn you—Klimov got away. If I remember your pilot jargon, you will want to watch 'your six' very carefully."

"The old boy escaped, eh? I'm not surprised. Come on, we'll walk you back to your taxi."

Roger glanced toward the helo. Had a shadow hopped aboard the craft just as he turned? In the deepening gloom, he wasn't sure. Probably the pilot. After all, he was due to fly Sophie back to her colleagues.

As they strode across the grass, Sophie said, "Roger, I once told you my ideal husband would be a scientist—intelligent, but humble. Someone I could partner with inside and outside of the laboratory."

"I remember. You declared when you kissed him, there would be magic in the air. Have you found Dr. Wonderful?"

A shy smile grew on her face. "Perhaps. Among the prisoners there's a scientist named Gavrilovic. Handsome. Brave. I noticed him in the past. He has noticed me, too. But not until today have we truly talked heart to heart. We seem to ..." She gazed skyward, as if searching for the proper words. "We seem to click, like magnets."

"What about the kiss? Magic?"

Her shy smile showed more teeth. "I'm still waiting to find out. I believe it will come soon."

Roger held up Katherine's hand and kissed it. "Magic is how it feels with Katherine and me. God brought us together."

Katherine slipped an arm around his waist. "I love your analogy, Sophie—clicking together like magnets."

When the four had nearly reached the helo, a voice rang out. "Greene!" From the darkened interior leaned a figure gripping a pistol. The man looked haggard, unkempt. His eyes practically glowed with a maniacal effect.

Katherine gasped. "Uncle Kurt?"

"Greene, you destroyed my life. Now I will destroy yours." He raised his pistol.

"No!" Katherine jumped between Kurt Mueller and himself.

Roger, in turn, grabbed Katherine and pivoted, putting his back to Mueller.

The shot rang out. Pain exploded in Roger's back.

"Unh."

His back side radiating agony, Roger slid down Katherine's body and collapsed as two more shots fired.

The mingled scents of cold topsoil and grass filled Roger's nostrils. As if from a distance Baron's voice shouted, "We need a medic!"

Katherine's face appeared beside his own. "Roger, please tell me it will be okay. Your body—it will heal quickly, right? Just like Indianapolis?"

Gritting his teeth through the pain, he shook his head. "It's gone. After I came here, the Methuselah thing wore off. I love you!"

His vision clouded even as Katherine's desperate voice sounded above a tumult of pounding feet and voices. "We need a medic *and* a pilot!"

CHAPTER 53

When consciousness dawned, Roger became aware he was lying on his stomach. Gone from his nostrils were the earthy scent of untamed meadow. In its place was a fragrance like fresh-laundered linen.

Does Heaven have bedsheets?

But his backside still hurt. Surely pain doesn't exist in Paradise?

He cracked one eye. The sight filling his gaze wasn't Heaven, but it was the next best thing. Katherine—still dressed in camo gear and dozing in an armchair—prompted him to open both eyes. The white walls and Spartan surroundings suggested a hospital. A window provided a glimpse of overcast sky.

He lay there, content in the simple pleasure of gazing at the woman he loved. Rings beneath her closed eyes hinted she hadn't slept enough. Her perfect lips were slightly parted. Somehow, even her quiet breathing touched his heart. The military gear wasn't as becoming as a sundress or swimsuit, but clothing didn't matter. What did matter was her wonderful heart.

Eventually, she shifted, lifted her head.

"Hi, gorgeous. Does your boyfriend know where you are?"

A smile crept onto her lips. She slid off the chair and knelt beside him. "How do you feel?"

"It hurts. But it's a good hurt, you know? It means I'm alive."

"You almost didn't make it, Flyboy. You lost a lot of blood. If not for a medic and that empty helo, you'd be singing with angels."

"Where are we? Langley?"

Her soft fingers brushed back his hair. "A special hospital in Kiev. Baron stayed until the end of the surgery. Sophie, too. She's nice."

311

"I'm glad you two got acquainted. No problems?"

Katherine shook her head. "Now that I know her, I would've kicked you in the behind if you hadn't tried to rescue her."

"Your Uncle Kurt. What happened?"

"He gave me no choice. I had to shoot. He's alive, though. In another wing of this hospital. Turns out he's wanted in connection with quite a number of high-profile assassinations. Plus, the authorities want to press him for information on the H.O."

Roger began to rise up on elbows, but a fresh wave of pain emanated from his injury. He grimaced and lay down again.

"Accept that pain as a lesson. Rest. It seems you need to heal the old-fashioned way."

"Yeah. My last quick-healing trick was right after we landed, when I inserted the tracker in my arm. Later I noticed my body wasn't rejuvenating as fast as usual."

"Baron consulted with the Langley doctors who know your case. Some of their theories involve exposure to sunlight in freedom or the nuclear radiation zone you've been in. They're trying to figure it out."

Roger grunted. "Well, it was handy while it lasted."

With gentle fingers, she caressed his forehead, his cheeks.

"Katherine, do I look different?"

"Different how?"

He considered how to pose the question without sparking alarm. "Do I look, say, older?"

She leaned forward and kissed his cheek. "Not a bit, handsome. But the Langley docs have studied and discussed an analysis of your blood. They say it's normal. No more special characteristics. They can't guarantee, but their opinion is your body will now pick up where it left off in 1944."

"Same as you?"

She touched the tip of his nose. "Same as me. Oh, they believe there's a tiny chance your Methuselah metabolism could redevelop someday. If not, you should age one day at time, like everybody else."

That burden off his mind, Roger decided it was time. "Katherine, could you ask the nearest nurse for a Band-Aid? An ink pen, too."

"A Band-Aid? Are you bleeding?" She scanned him with concern.

"Just get them. You'll see."

She slipped from the room, giving him a moment to compose his thoughts.

A minute later, Katherine reappeared. "Here you go." Once more, she knelt at his bedside, where she placed a foreign-brand adhesive strip and ballpoint pen on the bed sheet.

Roger pushed aside the bedcover. Wincing from the ache in his back, he slid to the floor.

"Stop, what are you doing?"

On one knee, he said, "Katherine Elissa Mueller, I have an important question for you."

She gasped. Both hands flew to her mouth.

"Babe, God has granted me many blessings in my long life, but you are the most amazing treasure of them all. I don't want one more minute to pass without asking—will you marry me?"

Laughing through joyful tears, Katherine blurted, "Yes. A thousand times, yes!" She circled Roger with her arms.

The sudden pressure over his wound caused a shooting pain. Roger sucked in a breath.

"Oh, sorry! I got so excited." Katherine repositioned her arms around his shoulders and planted her lips on his in a deep, impassioned kiss that exhilarated him like none before.

After they parted, Roger said, "I bought an engagement ring. It's in my room at Eglin. But for now ..." He peeled the backing off the Ukrainian version of a Band-Aid. After wrapping the plastic strip around her ring finger, he took the pen and drew a large diamond on it. "Just a symbol, until I can get the real one on you."

Wiping her eyes, Katherine grinned and admired his handiwork. "So romantic." She leaned in for another kiss.

Roger closed his eyes and lost himself in a tidal wave of emotion. The girl of his dreams had agreed to be his bride. He almost wished the kiss could last forever.

When they eventually drew apart, he said, "Katherine, it doesn't matter where in this wide world we are. As long as I'm in your arms—I'm exactly where I belong."

She buried her head in his chest and snuggled close. After a contented sigh, she whispered, "Roger that."

A Note from the Author

Dear friend,

Out of all the books in the world, you chose to read one of mine. Roger, Katherine, and Sophie join me expressing a heartfelt "Thank you!" (Security Chief Klimov refused to comment. Sorry, but you know how he is.) I wrote most of this novel while serving as a caregiver, which required much time. Some days, only the hope you might someday enjoy it kept me going back to the computer to add a few more paragraphs.

If you did enjoy *Methuselah Project S.O.S.*, would you do me a favor? I'll be so grateful if you do any of the following ...

• **Leave a review online.** Reviews are incredibly helpful. Simply look up the title at an online book vendor, scroll down to Reviews, and click to write a review of your own. Don't spoil it for others by revealing what happens in the story. Simply jot a few sentences telling how the story made you feel, what you liked about it.

• **Stay in touch!** On my site, rickcbarry.com, you can sign up for my mailing list to learn about future books.

• **Tell friends about the book.** Enthusiastic word of mouth is the best advertising! Your personal recommendation (in person and on social media) is more powerful than you realize.

• At your library, **suggest that they add it to their collection.**

• **Share copies** as Christmas or birthday gifts.

Let me close by saying you are a vital link in this writer's life. Even if I wrote hundreds of books, they would be a waste of time if no one ever read them. Thank you again for joining me on this imaginative journey. I hope we can do it again.

Blessings,
Rick Barry

GROUP DISCUSSION GUIDE

1. Part of Roger's personality is a belief that he was "born to fly." Is there anything that you strongly feel you were born to do?

2. At first, Roger has no interest in assisting the CIA or traveling to Europe. However, after he learns that Sophie Gottschalk is alive and being held prisoner, he changes his mind out of a sense of duty. Is duty a good thing, a bad thing, or neither? Why do you think so?

3. When Katherine learns that Roger's main reason for helping the CIA in France is to find and help Sophie—and that Roger had kissed Sophie in the past—she wonders whether he's as dedicated to her as she'd assumed. What are some ways that dating (or married) couples can avoid doubts, suspicions, and jealousies about each other?

4. Roger is confident about his ability in a fighter jet. Yet, circumstances compel him to pursue his goal of helping Sophie without an airplane, even alone. In real life, do you think God ever puts people in situations where they must overcome adversity, but without their best skills?

5. Ben and Gerard are highly competent in areas of technology, but their interest in science fiction is what drives their friendship. When you and your best friends get together, what are the mutual interests that you appreciate most? Also, do you think it's possible to be close friends with a person whose interests are very different from yours?

6. When Roger needs courage or direction, he sometimes recalls words from "The Airman's Creed." Have you memorized specific things that encourage you in difficult times?

7. At one point, Gerard tells Roger, "I guess religion is all right for you. Me, I'm going to stay in charge of my own destiny."

What do you think—is it possible for a person to be in control of their own destiny?

8. Throughout the story, Roger often speaks to God in his thoughts. He prays, but not always with head bowed or eyes closed. What do you think—is a conversational way of praying too casual, or should a Christian always stop and pray formally? Why do you think so?

9. Early in the story, Roger is somewhat aware of how easily some things can make him angry. But not until he sees his duplicate's face full of rage does he realize how ugly anger can make him look. Has there ever been a circumstance or a friend who helped you to see and correct a flaw in yourself?

10. The ethics of cloning humans has been the subject of debate. What do you think—should human cloning be forbidden worldwide, or is it something worth trying? Why?

11. In the story, "Heritage Organization" is an innocent-sounding name for a group that has few, if any, morals. It has operated in secret for decades. In your opinion, if a person or organization had sufficient money, could they manipulate world events, yet remain secret? Or would the truth eventually come to light?

12. Circumstances compel Sophie to grow and change from a captive scientist into the leader of a mass escape. She doesn't enjoy the role and lacks confidence, but she forces herself anyway. Have you ever stepped into a role that you didn't feel confident about? Share about that!

13. When you realized that Roger had definitely lost the special metabolism that the Methuselah Project had given, how did that make you feel? Why?

14. If you could send the author one message about this book, what would you tell him? (Why not do it? See the Contact tab at www.rickcbarry.com.)

THE AIRMAN'S CREED

I am an American Airman.
I am a Warrior.
I have answered my Nation's call.

I am an American Airman.
My mission is to Fly, Fight, and Win.
I am faithful to a Proud Heritage,
A Tradition of Honor,
And a Legacy of Valor.

I am an American Airman.
Guardian of Freedom and Justice,
My Nation's Sword and Shield,
Its Sentry and Avenger.
I defend my Country with my Life.

I am an American Airman.
Wingman, Leader, Warrior.
I will never leave an Airman behind,
I will never falter,
And I will not fail.

OTHER NOVELS BY RICK BARRY

The Methuselah Project: A Novel
ISBN 978-0-8254-4387-9
312 pages

Shot down during World War II, Captain Roger
Greene becomes both a prisoner and a guinea pig
in a bizarre German experiment. The war ends, but
the Methuselah Project doesn't.

Gunner's Run
ISBN 978-1-59166-761-2
215 pages

During a bombing mission over Nazi Germany,
machine gunner Jim Yoder falls out the bomb bay of
his B-24. His chest parachute saves his life, but now
this gunner is alone, on foot, and on the run across
Hitler's Europe.

Kiriath's Quest
ISBN 978-1591669050
200 pages

When the barbarous Grishnaki capture Prince
Kiriath's father, the kingdom cannot give the
ransom they demand. Desperate to rescue his
father, Kiriath resolves to sneak into the
Grishnaki's valley—alone if need be. (Young adult,
fantasy)

Available wherever books are sold

CPSIA information can be obtained
at www.ICGtesting.com
Printed in the USA
BVHW041602221020
591502BV00024B/1769